T0072300

Other books by **Gary B. Boyd**

# Single Best Clue

GARY B. BOYD

authorHOUSE

*AuthorHouse*™
*1663 Liberty Drive*
*Bloomington, IN 47403*
*www.authorhouse.com*
*Phone: 833-262-8899*

*Published by AuthorHouse  02/21/2023*

*ISBN: 979-8-8230-0143-4 (sc)*
*ISBN: 979-8-8230-0144-1 (e)*

# CONTENTS

# DEDICATION

None of my work would be worthy of publication without the help of my wife **Shirley** and my daughter **Tina**. Their inputs to correct my mistakes and keep the story straight were invaluable.

# PREFACE

Subject matter is important.

If the speaker or the writer is not an expert on the matter, the words applied to it are of little consequence. But ... hear me out anyway.

I'll go on record as saying I'm not an expert on the subject of women. Though, to my accreditation, I have been married to the same woman for 56 years. Of course, that could mean my wife is an expert on me. Either way, my time on this earth has afforded me the ill-advised belief that I'm capable of saying a few words on the subject of women without too much damage to my reputation ... or body.

Specifically, my words will be directed toward my opinions of what makes a *strong* woman. As I see it, a strong woman is any woman who can not just survive but also can thrive in a world that does not favor women.

My mother was a strong woman. Widowed at the age of 26 with four children, the oldest being seven. That was in the "happy days" of the 1950s. The world was rosy and bright ... unless you were a woman raising children on her own. In a time when most women were housewives, my mother learned early that a strong woman had to work in a factory plus be a housewife. Her husband - my father - was not ... in the words of a former manager of mine ... real work-brickle. I'm not sure if he simply couldn't find the job that suited him, or if he preferred something different in life. Whatever the reason, my mother had to work outside the home to support her growing family during those eight years she was married to my father. When his life choices ended his life early, she had to work to survive.

But we thrived. It wasn't easy. Definitely not for her. My mother was a strong woman in a man's world, and I am the better for it.

But, this is not about me, or even my mother. Not exactly. As I write my books, I quite often write about strong women. Women who aren't subservient to anyone - man or woman. They overcome adversities and enjoy life on their journey. They leave a mark of some kind, even if the annuls don't venerate their works and deeds.

My most enjoyable character is Sarah James. Sarah is a strong woman. Sarah James came to life in the first book of what is now a five-book series dedicated to her. Initially, her conception was to be an actor in a larger story whose role was simply to move the tale forward. As it turned out, like an actress such as Marilyn Monroe or Hattie McDaniel, Sarah's personality was greater than the minor role assigned to her. She became the story.

Sarah James is not just a woman. She is every woman who ever pushed the envelope. She failed a time or two. Like Simone Biles, she didn't let failures impede her. She learned from every mistake and moved forward to become a force to be reckoned with within her chosen field of endeavor ... law enforcement. But, as her character developed, she encountered some of the same issues as any other successful person. Overwork. Over dedication. Sarah comes to realize there is more to life than her avocation.

Living ones life is important. Sarah has a life. A good life. As a strong woman, she succeeds ... thrives ... in her life. She doesn't charge headlong into obstacles. She meets them halfway, calculates her path forward, and moves around or over them. A strong woman does that with precision and focus. Success doesn't simply happen. It's earned. Sarah earns her successes. But one success has eluded her. Even a strong woman can miss an integral part of a successful life. She has failed to live her life. Does she stop living, or does she learn from her mistakes and reinvent herself?

Read on ...

# CHAPTER 1

## 1:45 A.M. Monday

The driver didn't say a word. The white pickup jarred when its right tire hit a pothole. The passenger grunted in response to the jolt. The pickup's headlights were on low beam. The dark asphalt didn't reveal its defects to the semi-circle of pale, yellow light. In the glow of the dashboard lights, the driver glanced at the passenger and smiled apologetically. The apology was wasted because the passenger's focus was straight ahead, lost in thought.

An unlit sign appeared ahead on the right. The driver knew it would be there. Fortunately. A sodium streetlight bulb bathed the sign in an orange glow. The light was too dim to properly illuminate the sign. It could have been easily missed at night. That part of the city was recently annexed, and the streetlights weren't upgraded to modern LED bulbs. The driver let off the gas pedal and turned off the headlights. No one was on the road at that hour, so the risk of being seen was minimal. The driver still wasn't taking any chance of accidental discovery. Slowly, the truck turned into the church parking lot. The driver knew where to go. A previous daylight drive through the lot helped set the plan. The driver cautiously guided the pickup across the barely lit lot toward the back of the church. Small security lamps under the corner eaves cast eerie shadows behind the building, barely pushing the darkness into the woods that bordered the back of a wide drive.

The truck tires crunched on gravel. The drive at the back of the church wasn't paved like the parking lot. SB2 gravel was compacted by seasons of rain, vehicles, and time. Even so, there was still some loose chat. The tires picked up small bits of rock and flung them against the inside of the fender well. The driver tensed; afraid someone would hear the sound of stones on sheet metal. A misplaced fear. The church was not near any businesses that were open after midnight. The nearest home was a hundred yards or more beyond an undeveloped, wooded hillock.

The security lights were high on each rear corner of the building and barely lit the entirety of the graveled area. They left dark shadows near a dumpster. The driver stopped the pickup in the least lit spot and exhaled quietly before speaking in a quivering voice. "This is it. Are you sure?"

The passenger's head nodded, barely noticed in the dark interior of the truck. "I'm tired of it. The bastard can't get away with it." The passenger fumbled with the door handle. The dome light came on, brighter than either of them thought possible.

"Hurry!" the driver said urgently. "Before someone sees us."

Fumbling to exit gracefully, the passenger banged the top of the cab with an object firmly grasped in a sweaty hand. "Damn!" seemed appropriate, though it didn't cover the sound that no one else in the world heard.

"Careful," the driver whispered hoarsely. "Call me when you're ready."

"Just be here," the passenger commanded, then closed the door … another noise too loud for comfort. The passenger quickly disappeared into the woods at the back of the church.

Gene yawned. He was tired. Night driving is tough. Even tougher when it's a long trip without adequate rest. He still had miles to go. Too many for someone with no sleep. Frequent stops to tend to nature calls, fuel, and energy drinks kept him from falling asleep at the wheel. Unfamiliar roads didn't make the sixteen-hour journey easy or enjoyable, no matter how good the roads were … or weren't. Without someone to engage in conversation, and help identify highway signs, he was forced to be cautious after the sun set. As he neared his destination, state highways replaced interstates. Good highways, but not easily navigated for someone unfamiliar with that part of the country. Too many small and large towns required slower travel and traffic lights at confusing intersections. Things that added to his stress.

Until his cell phone died, Gene could occasionally engage in conversation with someone and check his map app to make sure he was following the correct route. He forgot his charger. After the phone died, he was truly on his own. Fortunately, he had scribbled some general directions that covered the final stages of the trip to his destination. His nerves were rattled because he might have missed something necessary to reach the meeting place; something as simple as a left turn marked as a right or an unclear intersection sign. His phone's map app would have settled his worried mind.

Eugene Simpson worked at Walmart. He was an associate for the mega-corporation at a Panama City supercenter. His job was entitled Leader, an hourly position. Many of his duties were once handled by salaried associates, but corporate brains restructured store duties to accommodate increased hourly pay. With that came increased responsibilities. The restructuring reduced salaried roles, but it didn't reduce the tasks required to run the stores. In the long run, the raise in pay was a bargain for the company. He worked night shift, in charge of truck receiving and shelf stocking. The Home Office thought no more of him now than before the restructuring, but at least his store manager did. Gene, the nickname that had identified him since he was young, asked for a two-day emergency vacation to make the trip.

Sean Caster was a manager with a heart. The kind of manager who would have made Sam Walton proud. He valued his employees, his associates as they were called in the all-inclusive company. Besides, Gene had accumulated paid time off plus vacation time. The reduced number of employees meant the dedicated employees worked longer hours than their paychecks reflected. Giving Gene time off was the least the company could do for him. Gene had a future in Walmart … if corporate didn't restructure quality workers out of their jobs. Gene left work at 8 A.M. Sunday morning, loaded items necessary for the trip into his car, and set out on a journey that Sean only knew to be an emergency.

For more than fifteen hours, the reason for the journey replayed in Gene's mind. The rekindled anger the thoughts caused kept him awake. That was the only good thing about it, he supposed. The call for the sudden meeting was ridiculous. Something better could have been arranged. He knew it wasn't life or death, but he also knew it was something that he was required to do in one manner or another. He didn't like it, but the judge didn't care. The person who demanded the meeting cared even less. It was his choice to live in Florida. It was his duty to make the meeting on time. That meant driving all day and most of the night to a town in Kansas, a long and unfamiliar drive. He should have insisted that the meeting be at a halfway point. He didn't. It angered him that he was so easily manipulated. Fear of losing what he valued most controlled his otherwise logical mind.

His last gas stop was in Missouri. A Kum & Go store on Highway 60 near the intersection with Interstate 49. Once again, Gene had to spend money to use the station's air pump. It was money he could not afford to spend. He had two nearly bald tires. One of them had a slow leak that dogged his journey. He had ordered two new tires on-line. They were due for delivery and installation the same day the meeting in Kansas was scheduled. He argued against the sudden meeting, but he knew he would lose. He had no choice other than to make the trip and replace the tires when he returned. Worries about the tires plagued his mind as he raced through the darkness.

The trip across Missouri was almost boring, other than the obvious concerns about tires and directions. After he left Springfield, traffic thinned as he traveled west on highway 60. At least twice, his heart rate increased when he saw blue lights ahead in the darkness. A wasted response for two reasons. He wasn't traveling fast enough to be of interest to a police officer and if the lights were on, the police already had someone stopped. He shuddered, slowed, and glanced at his wallet which held his driver's license. It was in the passenger seat beside his dead cell phone. He nervously drove past the unlucky person. After passing through a small town called Neosho, the drive to the I-49 intersection was unusual in that east bound traffic was considerably heavier. If his phone worked, he would have checked his map app to see if there was a larger town west of the interchange. The area was close to Oklahoma. He didn't know much about Oklahoma, so he didn't have a clue what lay to the west in the darkness.

All of that was behind him and simply gave him something to think about, to keep his mind active. Gene made the journey north on I-49 without incident, other than the constant fear of a flat tire … or worse, a blowout. He was being a worry wart and he knew it. The leak was slow. It would be at least a couple of hours before the tire needed to be reinflated. At Joplin, he followed Highway 171. It took him into Kansas. From the Stateline, he moved as rapidly as he dared along the dark, unfamiliar road. Traffic became less and less as time passed and he progressed toward his destination. He hoped he was on the right course for his meeting. He cursed himself for the hundredth time for forgetting his charger. Everything from that point on was definitely dependent on memory and his scribbled notes ... notes he barely trusted.

A road sign indicated Gene was only twenty miles from the Kansas town where the meeting would take place. He sighed relief. His notes seemed to be good. He couldn't understand why Kansas was the chosen meeting place. As far as he could tell, the entire state of Kansas locked up and turned out the lights when the sun set. In truth, he was exasperated with the whole affair. He didn't try to understand. He simply complied. He lost the argument. His only option was to pack his car and drive north from Panama City. He was determined to meet his obligation. He was several hours early for the 7:00 o'clock morning meeting. He could use that time to get some rest. Recline the seat and sleep in the car. Not a great option, but the only one he had. He would need the rest for the return trip, a trip that would be just as long and just as exhausting. He was scheduled to go back to work at midnight Tuesday. He was close to his destination in the wee hours of Monday morning. If the meeting was on time, he had plenty of time to complete the round trip.

The directions he was given began to make sense as he reached each street and landmark on his scribbled list. Some of the knots in his stomach loosened as he drew closer. He felt better, knowing he would arrive at the preplanned destination with time to spare. Being late was never an option and he knew it. Finally, Gene saw the church sign ahead. The streetlight was dim. His eyes were bleary from straining through the night. His headlight lens covers were old and yellowed. Scratches, scars, and bugs dimmed them. He turned into the exit side of the parking lot. It was after 2:00 in the morning. It didn't matter. No one would be there until after daylight. That far from the center of the city, the police likely didn't even patrol the area. The entire circumstance made him nervous. A truck stop would have made a better meeting spot. The Kum & Go. Lights. Some sense of security. He saw the glow of a city ahead in the darkness, but he wasn't going into the lights of the city. That was another thing about the meeting that made no sense.

Gene slowly drove to the back of the church, the designated meeting place. He would have preferred the meeting to be out in the open. A public place. He knew that wasn't going to happen. He didn't even argue the matter after his suggestion was denied. Besides, at the time, he thought a church parking lot would be well lit. But, in the scheme of things, he knew who and what he was dealing with. It was easier to go with the flow. His headlights and small security lights high on the corners at the back of the church building revealed the back of the church didn't have asphalt paving. In truth, it was an odd structure for a church. REAL WORD CHURCH. It appeared to be a former business building that was converted into a church.

When Gene was younger, he heard about some of the upstart churches in Kansas. Non-denomination churches with a different take on Biblical teachings. Their beliefs were strong. From what little he recalled; he wondered if that was the reason this church building was chosen. It made him worry. Everything worried him. He was tired. He needed rest, but he had things to do before he could scoot his seat back and recline it. The only thing good he saw in the chosen spot was that while behind the church, he should be undisturbed until the meeting occurred.

The dome light came on when Gene opened the door. A gush of fresh air hit him. It was invigorating. Kansas in September is inherently cooler than Florida. He couldn't drive with his windows down. His AC barely worked. At night he hardly needed it. Besides, he was obligated to keep the inside of the car warm. He relied on outside air through his ventilation system … barely enough cool air on his face to keep him from dozing. He felt the gravel beneath his feet when he stepped from the car. He straightened and stretched his back. He didn't realize how tiring driving could be. He wondered how truck drivers could do it day in and day out. He inhaled deeply. The smell was different than the ocean air in Panama City. It was good. Just different. He sneezed. A reminder that the pollens were different too.

The sneeze also reminded Gene of what he had to do before he could get some sleep. He saw a trash dumpster at the edge of dark woods that bordered the gravel drive.

Gene made two trips to the dumpster. It's amazing how much trash can accumulate inside a car. Empty soda cans. Empty water bottles. Energy drink bottles. Snack wrappers. Some of the trash was poked inside Walmart bags, but not all of it. He grabbed all the loose trash his hands could hold for his first trip. For his second trip, he stuffed the rest of his loose trash inside always handy Walmart bags. The dumpster didn't smell too bad for a dumpster. The church didn't have garbage trash, at least not the kind that would generate obnoxious odors. He hoped trash pickup wasn't on Mondays. They would probably come about daylight and startle him awake with their clanging noises if they did. He needed rest and loud noises would prevent that.

His eyes couldn't accustom fully to the mix of lit and partially lit areas. Gene did notice the main parking lot was not lit. From the light cast by the streetlights, he could see there were light poles in the lot. He wondered if the lot lights were on a switch, only used when needed. His experience was with Walmart, a huge retailer with intense security protocols and photo-sensitive parking lot lights that revealed everything. He supposed a small church had fewer valuables to attract thieves and less money for wasted energy bills. Even in the low light, he noticed his front driver's side tire appeared low. He cursed under his breath. He was so frustrated he wanted to cry, but he knew better. He would worry about the tire later. He needed to sleep before the meeting.

At first, Gene thought the woods behind the church was comprised of tall trees. He stared into them, allowing his eyes to acclimate to the dim lighting. Some parts of Florida had tall pines. Most of Georgia and Alabama had tall trees, mostly pine. Tennessee and Missouri had decidedly different trees, mostly deciduous and generally tall. The darkness kept him from seeing what kinds of trees were in the Kansas woods. He walked close to the woods, to hide from no one in particular while he emptied his bladder. From that vantage point, facing away from the security lights, he realized the wooded area was actually a hillock with short trees and tall brush. He shivered. He didn't like the dark, especially dark that he didn't know.

Gene walked to the corner of the church. He had the urge to see if there was any traffic on the road that ran past the church. The woods and the church building blocked sounds. There was no traffic. He was alone … in the dark. The darkness of the woods made him nervous. He would definitely sleep with his windows up and doors locked. He didn't know anything about Kansas or the people who lived there. Just because the church trusted people by not having security lights didn't mean he would. He was sure they locked the church doors at night. He surveyed the area he could see from the corner of the building. Not much. A few small businesses were nearby, mostly little shops and fast-food restaurants. They were lit with night security lighting, something the church didn't seem to care much about. He walked to the car and briefly leaned to look at his low tire one more time before resting.

Sparks flashed inside Gene's head. Briefly.

Gene's head was pushed forward forcefully. It happened so rapidly that he didn't sense it. His forehead hit the car fender, then his head whipped backward when it bounced off the fender with an angry thud. His body twisted as it crumpled. His face hit the gravel. He didn't feel the gravel cut into his shattered face. Blood pooled on the hardpacked surface near the front tire. Packed SB2 doesn't absorb liquid rapidly. That's what makes it good for roads and parking lots.

<hr />

The driver of the white pickup jerked. The intense vibration of the cell phone was startling. With a thick voice, the driver answered, "Hello."

"Come get me. Hurry!" The familiar voice didn't sound familiar. Hoarse and chillingly urgent.

The truck was less than a mile from the church. The driver chose a closed bar parking lot. It was Sunday night. Even though the bar wasn't open on Sunday, there were always a few vehicles left behind at a bar. Patrons too drunk to drive. Female patrons who chose to leave with someone else, for safety … or something else. Most of the vehicles left Saturday night were retrieved on Sunday, but a few remained. The driver anticipated that. The pickup would not be noticed by passersby, if any passed during those wee hours. Hidden in plain sight. A stolen license plate kept the truck from standing out among the other Kansas tagged vehicles.

The driver's hands were shaking, barely controllable. The starter made an angry sound when the key was held too long in the start position.

Careful not to speed, the driver approached the church. As before, the headlights were turned off near the church. The truck carefully made its way to the rear of the church. A dark-colored car was parked behind the church. The driver's throat clinched in a failed attempt to swallow saliva that wasn't there. A form exited the woods when the truck cautiously crunched close to the car. A wave of recognition did nothing to ease the driver's anxiety.

The form - the passenger who was left behind - walked to the driver's lowered window. The darkness hid the urgency in the passenger's face, but not the tension in the voice. "Hurry! Let's get everything. I'll drive the car to the drop."

The two quickly transferred everything they could find from the car to the extended-cab back seat, carefully avoiding Gene's body as they hurried back and forth in the glow of vehicle interior lights which was brighter than the security lights' glow. The driver removed the Florida license plate from the car and replaced it with a stolen Kansas plate. The driver opened the pickup tailgate as soon as everything was moved.

The driver struggled to maintain composure while the two of them tried to lift the body into the back of the truck. The body was heavier than expected. The head was drooped and caught on the tailgate. The unexpected resistance caused them to lose their grip. The body fell to the gravel. The driver fought against vomiting. Blood smeared the tailgate. The driver almost puked. Close enough to feel and taste the acrid stomach juices that wanted to erupt.

"Stop it!" the passenger whispered sharply. "It's 3:00. We need to hurry. It's no different than loading a deer. Grab his legs. I'll grab him under the arms."

As soon as the driver's squeamishness was under control, the two of them lifted in unison. They correctly calculated the weight that time and the body slid across the tailgate into the truck bed. The driver closed the tailgate, almost vomiting again when the tailgate bumped against Gene's lifeless head.

"Damn it!" the passenger exclaimed. "He got blood all over my jacket." With eyes acclimated to the darkness, it was easy to see the heavy smears on the jacket sleeves. The passenger removed the jacket, looked inside the car, and retrieved an empty Walmart bag. "Good thing he works at Walmart." The passenger stuffed the jacket inside a Walmart bag and double tied the top. "Here. Get rid of this. We'll take the body where we planned, then we can dump the car. Follow me."

The driver held the Walmart bag with the bloodied jacket at arm's length and stared helplessly for a moment. The passenger approached the driver's door of the car, stopped, and kicked the front tire. "That stupid bastard! This tire is almost flat! That useless son-of-a-bitch could never do anything right. I need to put some air in this tire."

"No," cautioned the driver. "Stations have security cameras. We can't be seen with the car. We need to stick to the plan. Hide the body then get rid of the car."

"Fine. Follow me. I know the perfect place."

"Are you sure it's a good place? We can't make any mistakes." The driver's voice quivered. Being seen meant getting caught. That single thing was the greatest fear they faced.

"I checked it out last week when I was here scouting for the right place to shoot him. No security cameras and his body won't be found for days. All we need is one full day."

"Let's go then. I want to be out of Kansas before daylight."

As the passenger angrily got into the car and adjusted the driver's seat, the pickup driver considered what to do with the Walmart bag. When the car began moving, the pickup driver panicked. In a decisive moment, the driver ran to the dumpster and tossed the bag into it. Even in a hurry, something on the white gravel caught the driver's eye. The Florida plate was left on the ground while the stolen tag was attached. Quickly, the driver retrieved the plate, tossed it into the back of the pickup, jumped into the driver's seat, and caught up with the car.

Gene's car rolled from the church parking lot with the white truck close behind.

<hr />

After disposing of the body, the two vehicles made their way out of town, retracing the route taken by Gene until they reached I-49 in

Missouri. It was still dark, but dawn was fast approaching. At the interstate, the vehicles turned north toward Kansas City.

The driver of the pickup rode close to the back bumper of Gene's car, impatient because the car was moving too slow. They needed to be as far away as possible when Gene's body was discovered. If something went wrong, if the body was discovered sooner than the passenger thought, if they were caught with Gene's car ... those thoughts and more swarmed the driver's fear-filled mind. Repulsion for the deed done was not among the thoughts. Only fear of getting caught. Distance from the scene was their friend. Disassociation from the event was their salvation. The driver wanted both as soon as possible ... and the gas needle was too close to empty. The driver wasn't sure if they could dispose of the car before the pickup's tank ran dry.

Angry and disturbed by the headlights that reflected from the rear-view mirror, the driver of Gene's car cursed the pickup's driver every mile of the journey. As if the bright lights weren't distracting enough, the low front tire was becoming a major issue. The car was pulling to the left. The car's driver knew the tire would eventually fail. Failing catastrophically was not an option. A blowout could easily cause the car to wreck. A wreck would not be something they could easily put behind them. As daylight approached, there were more drivers on the highway, bound for jobs in Kansas City. A wreck would attract attention quickly. Their faces would be seen. The pickup would be associated with the car. Gene's stupidity for having bad tires for such a long trip could easily be the cause of their discovery. The driver gripped the steering wheel tightly and weighed the available options.

The driver chose an option. Not a good one, but the best of the few that came to mind. The car's driver guided the car to the right shoulder and parked with the right tires completely in the grass. Far enough off the road to not be hazard. Hopefully, far enough to not attract attention too soon. The pickup stopped behind the car.

The driver of the car looked at the flat front tire and wondered how it had made it that far. After locking the car, an intentional move to make anyone investigating believe that the car was not simply abandoned, the car's driver walked to the passenger side of the pickup and opened the door.

"What are you doing?" the pickup driver asked angrily in a voice tinged with fear.

"The tire's flat. If I keep going, I'll have a wreck. Just drive. Let's get out of here," the passenger snapped. "Go!"

"We need gas."

"Then let's go get gas. Just go before someone stops to help."

The pickup moved north. The driver drove silently for a few miles before asking, "Can you check your phone? See where the closest station is."

The passenger studied an I-phone screen. "There's a Love's at Harrisonville. Not very far. Do you have enough gas?"

"Yeah."

Love's signs are beacons to interstate drivers. Tall and visible. The driver pulled off the Interstate and drove the access road to Love's Travel Stop. Most of the pumps were occupied. The driver found one that was available and stopped beside it. The driver filled the tank while the passenger hurried to the restroom. Fighting nerves, the driver paced toward the back of the truck while the tank was filling and froze, face pale. The driver anxiously looked to see if anyone noticed the streak of blood that ran down the center of the tailgate, across the logo, and onto the stolen Kansas plate. Fortunately, the other patrons were occupied with their own activities. Hurriedly, the driver grabbed a sponged squeegee from the windshield washer station and washed away the evidence, at least enough to not be easily noticed. A car with a Missouri front license plate pulled behind the pickup and waited for the use of the pump.

The vehicle's presence worried the driver. The person was watching, waiting. Paranoia set in. *Was the person suspicious? Did the person see the blood being washed away? Was there more blood dripping from the truck bed? Were they about to be discovered?* The driver heard the pump shut off. The tank was full. Without hesitation, with head down to avoid being seen clearly by the person in the waiting car, the driver got into the pickup and drove it to a parking spot at the edge of the Love's building. Several men wearing work boots and dirty jackets were standing, smoking, and gossiping while they drank coffee and waited for whatever kept them from driving to their jobs. The driver watched anxiously for the passenger to exit the building.

When the passenger came out, the first thing the driver saw was the shocked expression at not seeing the pickup at the pump. The driver was afraid to honk or roll down the window to call for the passenger. Afraid the men would be alerted and remember the two killers' faces. The passenger's head swiveled to check the parking lot and registered relief upon spotting the white truck.

Inside the truck, the passenger asked scoldingly, "Why did you move?"

The driver put the truck in reverse and replied in a hoarse whisper while backing from the parking spot, "Someone pulled up behind me. There was blood on the tailgate. Let's go."

"Blood?" The passenger looked backward in a futile attempt to see the tailgate. "Did you clean it off?"

"As much as I could. No one saw me."

"Good." The passenger looked toward the back of the truck. "Aren't you going to the restroom?"

"I want to get as far away from here as possible. I can pee later."

"Okay. Is everything good in here?"

"No problems. Anything coming from the right?"

"Clear. Go."

# CHAPTER 2

## 7:00 A.M. Monday

Chief Sarah James parked her car in her reserved parking spot outside the police station. Because her car was electric, she could have opted to drive into the fenced compound at the rear of the building for a recharge. She didn't need a charge. She hadn't driven it anywhere except to her apartment and back three times since it was last charged. It was still good for two hundred fifty miles or so. Hers was one of five EVs in the Devaney Police Department fleet. A concession she made to former Mayor Jordon Kamen's progressive policies.

Sarah stepped from the driver's seat and adjusted her gray jacket. She liked the pale gray color that was identified on the color chart as Cloud Gray. It was her latest wardrobe addition. She straightened the gray scarf that accented her Sunflower yellow satin blouse. She had a lunch meeting with the President of the Chamber of Commerce. She tried to dress well for those public meetings, not that she wasn't normally well dressed. As Police Chief, she was often called upon for unplanned public meetings. She always wore gray slacks and jackets with colored blouses or Oxford style shirts. All freshly pressed unless the fabric demanded different. The varied gray tones of her slacks and jackets were selected to complement each blouse. The blouse colors seemed to change her eye color. The perception of topaz eyes is easily manipulated by surrounding colors … and mood. Each weekday was represented by a different blouse color. She established that pattern of dress when she became a detective. She only wore her official Navy Blue uniform for formal events, such as funerals.

Regular visits to the gym kept Sarah's body toned. Even though she was seldom involved in field work, she kept her hand-to-hand skills tuned. Sometimes a pistol was not the quickest or best way to arrest an unruly suspect. A final glance in the mirror before exiting the car revealed a face that didn't look to be in its early forties. From her mother, she was blessed with supple skin that didn't wrinkle early. From her father, she inherited teeth that were not perfectly straight. For her, only one tooth was skewed slightly. A dentist in her early years suggested braces to set it right. Her mother convinced her that the skewed tooth added a distinctive quality to her model-like features. Sarah was attractive and uniquely beautiful because of it. She was never self-conscious about it. In the real world, that single flaw added to her approachability. She picked up a paper sack that held her drive-thru breakfast order – egg white and Canadian bacon on a whole wheat English muffin.

Inside the station, Sarah walked to the Shift Commander's desk. Seven o'clock was shift change. The night sergeant was still on duty while the day sergeant held her pre-shift briefing in the squad room. She was exactly on time. "Good morning, Pete. I assume everything was quiet?" she said as a question.

"Scary quiet, Chief. But we like it. Here's a quick recap of calls and traffic stops." The Shift Commanders were diligent in providing Sarah with a printed executive summary of all notable incidents. She needed to know.

Sarah smiled and took the offered list. The entries began with dayshift Sunday when she last received a similar list for Saturday. She held her head back slightly and perused the bullet points. One caught her attention. "What can you tell me about this missing person call?"

"Overprotective mom. Her daughter missed curfew by a few hours. The girl showed up around the time the unit arrived." Sergeant Pete Blanchard grinned.

"No such thing as an overprotective mom," she replied. Sarah sometimes thought about her life choices. Being a peace officer, primarily a detective, was her life's ambition. Becoming a mother was never in her plans, though she sometimes wondered what it would be like to have children. "I'd rather we respond to false alarms than lose a child. Did the officers make an impression?" She smiled. Her subordinates were her children … though some were decidedly older.

"The lead was Micha. What do you think?"

"Micha? Is she on nights now?"

"Just for one night. Traded with Corporal Jennings."

Sarah nodded understandingly. "Good." She finished her scan. "Maybe we won't have to deal with that young lady again."

"I hope you're right. Micha said the girl was pissy."

"What teenager isn't? I'll call the mother later as a follow up. Let her know we take these things seriously and are willing to help." Sarah shivered lightly as the memory of her first solo case as a detective flashed through her mind. A missing girl who was a serial killer's first victim. "Maybe it would help if …" Sarah glanced at the list to read the girl's name, "Bianca rode with Micha. See a little bit of what's out there. Maybe she'll gain some understanding of her mother's concerns. It's not a pretty world."

"Maybe, Ma'am." Pete grinned and nodded. Pete was like the majority of Devaney police department personnel. He liked Sarah's compassionate, no-nonsense style of leadership. She found solutions to repetitive problems that most officers accepted as part of the job. "I'm sure Micha would welcome the opportunity. Here, let me add the mom's name and phone number." He scribbled a name and number on the bottom of the page.

Sarah glanced at the name. Beverly Campbell. "Thank you. How are your officers? Does anyone have issues that need attention?"

"One of the rookies is struggling with working nights. Wife issues," Pete said knowingly. He raised his eyebrows for emphasis.

"Who is it? Maybe I can visit with him. Maybe even stop by his house and talk with his wife, let her know how important he is to us. Connect her with some of the other wives who struggle with the same issues."

Pete visibly squirmed before he replied, "She. They're both *shes*."

"Oops! Wrong pronouns."

Pete grinned, "Not like that. They don't care. *She* works for both of them."

"I'll go talk to her. I assume she's here in the station?"

"Yes. She's filling out her shift reports. Do you want me to call her?"

"No. Let's not make it seem unnatural. I'll stroll back that way as I do my walk around." Sarah left and went to the patrol officers' report room, a small area with several computers aligned on a countertop attached to the wall. The Devaney police station was old. Fifty years old. It was retrofitted to current technology, but it was too small and too crowded for the growing city. She approached Officer Teri Caudle at one of the computers. They talked quietly for several serious minutes before Teri finally smiled and nodded agreement.

Officer Caudle said, "Thank you, Chief. I'm sure Seelie will appreciate your concern. She works days. That makes it tough ... being a police officer on nights."

Sarah smiled, "It's tough for marriages when one or the other spouse works the off-hours, regardless of the job. Sometimes it doesn't work out, but most of the time it does. It just takes extra effort, understanding, and moral support. Does tomorrow evening work for you?"

"I'll talk to Seelie. I think so, but I need to make sure."

Sarah left the office. Here she was offering marital advice even though she had never been married. She didn't really have any plans to marry. She shook her head at the irony. She met Sergeant Maria Honeycutt in a hallway. Maria had never been married either.

Maria's gray hair bounced as she heartily chuckled when she saw Sarah. Overweight ... some would say stocky ... and always cheery, Sergeant Honeycutt took Sarah under her wing as a rookie patrol officer. "I thought maybe you were going to ignore me. You know you can't do that." She wriggled her heavy eyebrows suggestively.

Sarah smiled. The veteran police sergeant always had something marginally inappropriate to say or do. Sarah probably should have stopped the comments, but the exchanges were innocuous. The woman was an unabashed lesbian who began teasing Sarah when Sarah was a rookie patrol officer on her shift. At first, Sarah thought the older woman was hitting on her, but quickly realized it was good natured banter, less threatening than comments from male counterparts. "I try, Maria. Believe me, I try."

"It's because I'm too much woman for you," Maria said with a teasing laugh.

"I will admit I'm not sure what it will be like around here after you retire." Maria had voluntarily worked weekend nightshift as Shift Commander for several years. She did it to allow the married shift commanders to enjoy weekends with their families. She was unattached and married to the department. She was finishing her final month of service on dayshift. That afforded the accounting and human resources departments opportunities to process her paperwork properly. Maria had been with the department longer than anyone else. More than forty years. She had earned her retirement … and a certain amount of leeway on her comments. "What's on your agenda today?" Sarah asked.

"Guard the banks," Maria chuckled. "That's what we always do."

Sarah knew the comment was in reference to a statement made by a former Devaney Police Chief who told his officers to never focus entirely on one single incident in town because *"someone needs to guard the bank."* She laughed. "One of these days, I'm going to drive by the banks and see if any officers are actually guarding them. Do any of your people need to talk with me?"

"I think everyone is okay … unless they want to complain about me." Maria smiled. "Some of these rookies are too sensitive and thin skinned."

"Don't make me have to punish you this close to retirement."

Maria's eyes sparkled mischievously. "You know I've always wanted you to punish me."

Sarah shook her head. "I need to check my choice of words. I think I'll go check on Taylor and Boston … if they're here."

Maria laughed. "You know Taylor is. Boston?" She shrugged. "Boston's clock doesn't work the same as ours."

Sarah walked up the stairs to the office area. Her first destination was the coffee maker. A cup of hot coffee to go with her breakfast sandwich that was probably already cold. She could smell the freshly brewed coffee. The bullpen lights were on, as she expected. Lieutenant Taylor McCuskey was an early bird, just like Sarah. The Lieutenant commanded the patrol units. In essence, she supervised the majority of Devaney PD personnel. Aside from the Police Chief, Lieutenant McCuskey was the face of the police department. In her late forties – maybe early fifties, Taylor had enough years to retire, but she liked her job. Sarah called out, "Good morning, Taylor," even though she didn't see Taylor's perfectly set dyed blonde hair above the bullpen partitions. Her desire to see those small cubicles turned into offices for the Lieutenants would not become reality until a new police station was built. There was simply not enough room for offices. A new building was not coming anytime soon. Former Police Chief Bill Keck talked about the need for years but was never able to get the Mayor or City Council to consider the expenditure.

A disconnected voice replied, "Good morning, Chief. Coffee's ready."

"And it smells good." Sarah walked to the coffee pot. The path took her past Lieutenant McCuskey's desk on one side and the Situation Room on the other. The lights were on in the Situation Room. Senior Detective Boston Mankowitz was sitting in the room staring at several documents and photographs strewn across a table, undistracted by the world around him. "Good morning, Boston." She didn't see a coffee cup on the table. The Situation Room, or Sit Room as it was called, held a whiteboard and a corkboard. It was the room where the details of hard cases were laid out for study, where crime solvers tried to make sense of the disjointed details that make up a criminal case. Where they searched for the elusive single best clue that could solve the case. "Do you need a coffee?"

Boston glanced up. Without smiling he replied, "Good morning, Boss. Sure. It wasn't ready when I came in."

Taylor approached the doorway and grinned, her face radiant with perfectly applied make-up. She always appeared to be a decade younger than she really was. Her eyes sparkled excitedly whenever she engaged with Boston. She was happily married, but something about Boston's bad boy persona commanded her attention. "If the men in this office would start the coffee maker rather than wait for us women to do it, …" She laughed rather than finish the sentence. Boston made coffee too strong for everyone else. They preferred he didn't make the coffee. "I'll get you a cup, so the Chief doesn't have to do it for you."

"Women!" Boston replied with mock disgust. "I'll get my own. Too much danger of contaminating it with sugar or creamer." He rose from the table and followed the two women to the coffee maker.

Sarah knew the two would wait for her to fill her cup first, a gray cup with pink lettering. The cup was a gift from a detective she met while working on her first solo case. That case provided a major life lesson to novice detective Sarah James. She had to scramble to undo a mistake in her investigation. Detective Daniel Sanders, who worked for a police department several hundred miles from Devaney, had a motto that he shared with Sarah on the gifted cup. The motto was attributed to Davy Crockett. *"Make sure you're right then go ahead."* It was fitting that she saw that motto at the beginning of each day. There was no room for mistakes in law enforcement. Aside from the physical dangers, there was the danger of convicting the wrong person.

A half-spoon of sugar at the bottom of the cup was roiled by the addition of coffee. If the filling process worked properly, the last sip would be the sweetest. Sarah liked it that way. Her cup full, she asked, "What brings you in early, Boston? You seemed intense in the Sit Room."

The dark-eyed Detective scowled and shook his head in disgust. "Idiots." He took a sip from his coffee. He didn't say anything, but his reaction indicated the coffee was too hot. He needed a shave; an indication that he had gotten out of bed and hurried to work. Abruptly awakened by an emergency of some sort.

Sarah didn't take her eyes off Boston, though she wanted to glance questioningly at Taylor. Sergeant Blanchard reported to Taylor. "I didn't see anything on the recap list. What happened?"

"Drugs," Boston replied forcefully. "These damn fool kids can't seem to get the message. I got a call straight from the ER."

The hospital emergency room staff knew Detective Mankowitz was the primary contact for drug overdoses. Sarah felt her heart flutter. Boston took drug use personally. His career was defined by his fight against drug dealers and traffickers, by his own personal demons associated with pain-killer addiction. He usually won when pitted against drugs dealers, but it never seemed to be enough. There was always someone else waiting in the wings. "Did we lose someone?"

Boston shook his head. "No. Apparently, she had Narcan. She puked her guts out at the ER, but she'll live … if she learned anything."

"What is her name?" Sarah asked. Attaching a name made the girl a person and not a statistic. Boston needed to see that.

Boston grumbled as he checked his notes. "Sasha. Sasha Pierce."

"Did her parents call the ambulance?" Boston didn't give up information automatically.

"No. Someone called from a quick stop store."

"Who called?"

"The clerk. He went out to smoke and saw her at the side of the building. Didn't know how long she'd been there. She was out. The EMTs said a Narcan box was next to her."

"Apparently, she had ID on her?"

"Driver's license. Seventeen. Devaney high school ID. The hospital called the parents."

"Did they offer any information?"

"Not really. Concerned but not talking. I think they wanted to hear the girl's story before they said anything to the authorities. I was able to talk to the girl … Sasha … a little bit before they arrived."

"Do we need to send uniforms to talk to them?"

"No. I'll try to talk to them after the girl is released. They were hurt. Hurt, angry, and grateful she was alive."

"All the emotions one would expect."

"Did the store have surveillance cameras?"

"She was left out of camera range. I did get a picture of two cars approaching and leaving that side of the building. No license plates visible on the video." Boston toward Taylor. "I'll put something together for a BOLO."

By the time the short update finished, Boston and Sarah were inside the Situation Room. Sarah held her paper sack out to Boston, an offer that he dismissed with a wave and a half-smile. Taylor stood at the doorway and listened. Her lips twitched. Sarah could tell the Lieutenant was upset that her people weren't made aware of the incident. Sarah said, "I suppose we can be happy that our efforts to make Narcan available saved another life."

Boston snorted. "I sometimes think we're encouraging drug use by providing Narcan. The risk takers think it makes them bullet proof."

"I'm sure there is something to that," Sarah replied. She didn't entirely believe it, but she wanted to encourage generally taciturn Boston to talk. "What have you learned?"

"Aside from the fact that we're surrounded by idiots?" Boston tapped a stack of papers on the worktable. "The girl was like a fountain. She not only spewed her stomach contents, but she gave me all kinds of names. I'm sure those cars and the names are connected. Scared to death … or away from it."

Sarah glanced at the papers. She could see Boston's scribbled handwriting. Dark bullet points and stars indicated things he deemed important … or doodling while waiting for answers. Upside down, she couldn't read them well. As bad as his writing was, she doubted she could read them right side up. "Who?"

"Other kids who were with her but didn't get sick. The name of their dealer." Boston shook his head. "A stranger. It's just a street name. I'll never find him, but I'll plaster that name all over the city and tell Blake to snoop around. I'm betting he's an opportunist, nothing more."

"How so?"

"The word is out. We won't tolerate drugs here in Devaney. The bigger dealers know better than to set up shop here. But the void of an established dealer allows transient dealers to hit and run. Come in. Make quick sales and get out of town."

"That doesn't sound good. I would think it would be harder to stop."

"It is." Boston exhaled. The act seemed to calm his anger. The anger was replaced with concern. He was on his drug soapbox. "And more dangerous. These kids are going to get themselves killed if we don't do something to stop it. Education. They need to know these quickie dealers sell contaminated junk. Stuff that gives a quick high without concern for how it does it. No quality control to protect their customers. Someone's going to get a hard hit of fentanyl by accident. It's the cheap high for unscrupulous drug cutters. Maybe one of our schmoozers could do some outreach in junior high and high school. Maybe Glasgow."

Sarah contained her wince reaction. Boston still harbored ill feelings toward Lieutenant Melvin Glasgow after former Mayor Kamen promoted him to act as her liaison with Devaney PD. Most of the Department recognized the role for what it was. Spy and snitch for the anti-police mayor. Melvin redeemed himself in Sarah's eyes, but some of the employees in Devaney PD hadn't forgiven him. Mostly Boston. To best utilize Lieutenant Glasgow's rank and communication skills, Sarah had sent him to Negotiator training. He had proven himself by using his skills and knowledge to defuse a couple of tense hostage situations and three potential suicides. He saved lives. "I think he would be a good choice, if he's up to it."

"You're the boss. Put him up to it."

"I'll take that under advisement. Is there anything you need from me on this?" Sarah glanced at Taylor. "I'm sure Taylor's people will be glad to help. You're not in this alone."

"I think I've got it." Boston looked at Taylor. "I probably should have notified the Shift Commander." His unspoken apology was noted and accepted by Taylor with a smile and eye sparkles. His eyes lingered on the stack of papers. "An officer or two could have helped get all these statements. I need to follow up on the names of her friends she was with last night."

"I'll provide whatever help you need," Taylor replied. "All you have to do is ask."

Sarah was relieved to see Boston's tension subside. The man was stellar as an undercover cop. An undercover cop has to be suspicious of everything and everyone to stay alive. Currently the Senior Detective, his scruffy, undercover demeanor sometimes came out when he encountered behaviors he categorized as stupid. He couldn't absorb the fact that most people preferred to learn from their own mistakes rather than learn from the mistakes of others. "Anything else I need to know about? Either of you. It's been routine and quiet for so long that I'm getting used to it."

"Don't jinx it," Taylor said as she knocked on the door frame.

Sarah laughed. "I'm sorry. The Mayor may decide we don't need a police chief if there's nothing happening."

"How is Bill?" Boston asked, a segue presented and obliged.

Bill Keck was Police Chief prior to Sarah's appointment to the role. He was forced into early retirement by former Mayor Jordon Kamen. A polite way to say fired. An intensely political move. Mayor Kamen was anti-police, among other things. Her actions as mayor eventually led to her removal from office, but not before Sarah was appointed Interim Police Chief by the Council. Bill Keck was appointed Interim Mayor after Mayor Kamen was removed. He went on to win the office in the following election. Sarah became full-time Chief. As mayor, Bill Keck supported Devaney PD, but he kept the department at arm's length to avoid the appearance of favoritism.

"I have a budget meeting with him at 8:00."

Taylor glanced at a wall clock. "You need to prep then. I know you're a stickler for details and being prepared."

Sarah smiled. "I worked on it over the weekend. Liz came in for a couple of hours after church to put it in proper order. I'm sure it's in folders on my desk ready to go." Liz Sweeney was a longtime administrative assistant for the Devaney Police Chief. She was accustomed to Bill Keck's style but easily adapted to Sarah's … or Sarah adapted to hers. Liz knew how to prepare a presentation for Mayor Keck better than Sarah did. She had served him for years. Her finishing touches made Sarah comfortable, even though she hadn't seen the final product yet. She trusted Liz. She went to her office, to settle down to review Liz's work and to eat her cold egg white sandwich.

# CHAPTER 3

## 8:00 A.M. Monday

Sarah walked into City Hall. Her feelings and the atmosphere of the building were much different than when Jordon Kamen was Mayor. Even though Bill Keck was a police department supporter, he was still Mayor for *all* Devaney citizens. The Mayor was her immediate superior, her boss. She couldn't help but be nervous. But it was a confident nervousness. Bill Keck was professional in everything he did. She clung to the folders Liz prepared for her. One for her with talking point notations. A duplicate for the Mayor ... without the notations. The Mayor's office was easy to locate, not just because she had been in it several times during her career as Police Chief, but because City Hall was arranged so the Mayor's office was readily accessible. A few employees were moving toward their offices to begin their day. A few early-bird citizens were there to conduct business of one kind or another. They all greeted Sarah.

"Good morning, Chief James."

Even after three years, the title seemed unreal. Becoming Police Chief was not in Sarah's original goals when she became a police officer. Her goal was to become a detective. Police Chief Bill Keck promoted women within the ranks with an eye on performance rather than seniority when practical. She mistakenly assumed the Police Chief would always be male. Maybe former Mayor Kamen did offer some improvements. In spite of the woman's failings as a mayor, she did open the door for Sarah ... even though the Mayor intended to shove Sarah out the same door on the way to achieving *her* objectives.

Sarah acknowledged each greeting with a sincere response. She liked her job, and she liked the citizens of Devaney. They trusted her to protect them. She would never violate their trust. She reached for the knob on the door marked *Mayor Bill Keck*. He preferred the diminutive rather than William. She turned the knob and entered at 7:59 according to the clock in the lobby. Not early and not late.

Missy Jerrell was arranging documents on her desk in preparation for the day. A cup of iced coffee from a coffee shop was at one corner, out of the way to avoid spilling it. She looked up and smiled. Her pale blue eyes sparkled when she smiled. The twenty-five-year-old woman was former Mayor Kamen's assistant and sycophant. Bill Keck kept her as his assistant and helped her overcome the bad habits formed under the domineering control of Jordon Kamen. Fortunately, her period of servitude was short lived. He could have summarily dismissed her as part of the old regime, but that was not Bill's style. Missy was now married. She was pregnant, barely showing, but her face had the glow associated with pregnancy, or at least associated with *knowing* she was. "Good morning, Chief James. The Mayor is ready if you want to go in."

"Good morning, Missy. How are you this morning?"

Missy smiled. "No morning sickness yet. Maybe it won't hit me."

"That's good. Let's hope you don't have any issues with it. A woman should be able to enjoy her pregnancy. Is there anything I can do for you?"

"My mom and Jim's mom are doing everything that needs doing … which really isn't as much as they are doing." Missy laughed. "I think they are more excited than Jim and I."

"Grandmas." Sarah chuckled. "I guess I better go face the music." She walked toward the Mayor's door.

Missy laughed. Things were a lot different than when Jordon Kamen was Mayor. No double assistants to go through. No tension throughout City Hall.

Bill looked up when Sarah entered. "Music? Is that what you think of me?" He laughed and stood to reach for Sarah's hand. "How are you today?"

"Good. You? How's that retirement going for you?" The question was a standing joke between them.

"Better doing this than rocking on the porch and growing senile. Do you want some coffee?" Bill nodded to indicate a small coffee maker on a credenza as he gathered papers and walked around his desk.

"Sounds good." Sarah handed Bill one of the folders she carried and filled a cup.

Bill seated himself at a small, round conference table in one corner of his office. Sarah set her coffee cup on the table and adjusted a chair before she sat. She smiled bemusedly as an old memory flashed through her mind. A small door at the back of the large office was another of the changes Bill made after he took office. He reinstalled a restroom that Jordon had removed so she could add a separate exit door for her office. She didn't like people to exit back through her gauntlet of assistants. Mayor Kamen didn't want visitors to know who met with her before them. The less they knew, the more power it gave her.

"So, what have we got here?" Bill asked as he scanned the items in the folder Sarah gave him. He found the bottom-line number. "Hmmm. I see we have work to do."

"Budget cuts?"

Bill laughed, "If you mean no increases, you could be right. Inflation aside, we still have to operate within the money the taxpayers give us."

Sarah mock gasped, "What? We can't just tell them they need to give us more money because we want it?"

Bill looked over the top of his reading glasses. "That would be nice. Tell the boss how much money you need to maintain your chosen lifestyle." He lifted his eyebrows to indicate a topic change. "In reality, as our population grows, so does the tax base. The base increase offsets the increased costs of services … for the most part. We also get increased sales tax revenue created by inflation. Don't let the politicians tell you different."

"Giving away the trade secrets?"

"Just reality. But, before we get into the details, how are the EVs doing?"

"Performance is acceptable. I drive one. Boston and Taylor drive electric. We have two electric units for patrol."

Bill nodded. "I'm not really concerned about the three of you in electric cars. How are the two patrol units performing?" The subject was not a new one, but the fact that Sarah was seeking replacement vehicles in her budget proposal made it relevant to the subject at hand.

"They're only three years old. The field units experience the same suspension issues as all the rest. Normal wear and tear. We've not had mechanical issues with the motors. Not that there is much about them that is mechanical. The cost of repairs to the motors will be high … when something like that hits us. And battery replacement when it happens. *Very high.*" Sarah emphasized her words. "Obviously, there is a fuel savings … if we ignore the cost of charger infrastructure. With higher gas prices, that makes a difference. We definitely didn't budget for the inflation we're experiencing at the pump."

"Understood. What do the officers say?"

"Complaints about acceleration."

Bill grinned, "Yeah. Cops like to push it to the floor on take-off and hear the roar of internal combustion horsepower. Probably a few bumped chins before they figured out the difference between the interceptors and the EVs, though everything I'm reading indicates the new EVs have improved take-off. Any issues with charge capacity?"

"Of course. We don't allow the officers to house the EVs because they are placed on chargers at the end of shift. The cars are ready for alternating shifts. It's a scheduling nightmare."

"Are they assigned to the same officers?"

"To the same shift. We only use them on dayshift. We don't want a power issue on night patrol."

"Sounds like your being tentative. They need a stress test. You're asking for five replacement units. From what your telling me, if I only approved EVs as replacements, you'd being going into the future without much more understanding than you had three years ago."

Sarah squirmed. She didn't expect to address gasoline versus EV for patrol vehicles. She was planning gas for gas replacements. "Pursuit is questionable. Speed and endurance, especially near shift's end."

Bill raised his eyebrows. "Pursuit is always questionable. Too much danger of harm to innocents."

"You know it's the only viable option sometimes."

"Sometimes, but radios are much safer for everyone. Traffic cameras and GPS locators in vehicles are very good at tracking and they don't destroy property or risk lives."

"GPS locators require a court order."

"I would caution to remind us all, unless it's a serial killer on his way to his next victim ... or a kidnapping in progress, pursuit is not necessary to bring the perp to justice."

Sarah knew not to argue. Bill was prepared for that very argument. She wasn't. Police pursuits were emotional events. The public wants the criminals caught quickly until that quickness involves one of them in an accident caused by the pursuit. "We have pursuit policies in place. Authorization is required from the Shift Commander before the field units can engage in prolonged pursuit."

Bill smiled. "I know ... and we've ... *you've* done a good job enforcing it. I'm not keen on EVs for patrol. No more than you. But we need to prepare ourselves for the day when EVs are the standard option, maybe the only option. It ... or something like it ... is coming."

"I suppose," Sarah replied.

"Unless hydrogen becomes the new green thing, expect EVs to be legislated within the decade. In the meantime, federal grants are available to offset the difference in up-front cost ... plus some other incentives. I'll approve the five units if three of them are electric. How you disperse them is your decision ... but I would encourage you to get as much understanding as possible in patrol applications. And I understand the eight-hour stand down for charging requirement. That makes EVs unreliable for emergency use, but if that's the future, you need to be prepared." He grinned. "The next mayor may not be as easy as me."

Sarah leaned back. "I can do that. Will the extra cost impact my bottom line? I've actually pared this thing as much as I think I should to remain effective. I've had to add some patrol officers to help with the recent annexations. We're stretched thin on the streets. Plus, we need some building remodels to house technology and people. I put money in for both of those." She watched for Bill's reaction as she spoke.

Bill considered her words before speaking. "We'll add the grant numbers to get a wash on your bottom line. And we'll include the grant for additional charging stations. Just work out a rotation for charging because we can't support a dedicated station for each EV."

Sarah nodded and leaned forward. "We can do that." She was slightly concerned that he didn't respond to her building remodel money. That money made her budget request higher than previous years.

"Alright. Let's dig into this and throw out the coffee and donuts." Bill laughed. He knew the coffee was paid for by the office personnel, not the department. Snacks came from vending machines.

Sarah's cell phone vibrated against her breast. She kept her cell phone where the vibration would be easily noticed. Startled at first, she retrieved the phone and glanced at the lit screen. A Slack message from Liz. *"911."* A simple code befitting an emergency organization. "Mayor, I need to call Liz."

Bill Keck understood the duties of the Police Chief. "Go ahead. I'll study this."

"Hello, Liz. What do you have?"

"A body has been discovered on the bike trail near Overton Acres."

Overton Acres, named after the developer of a recently annexed area on the north side of Devaney, was still in the early stage of development. Only a few houses were completed and occupied. The city required bike and walking trails as part of the approval process for new residential developments. The trails were completed even though most of the proposed homes and apartments were a year or two from completion. "COD?" Sarah asked the anacronym for cause of death.

"Boston muttered something about a drug deal gone bad before he left."

Bill overheard enough to pique his curiosity. *"What's happening?"* he mouthed.

Sarah pulled the phone away from her ear. "Boston is enroute to investigate a body on a walking trail. No details yet."

Bill shook his head and nodded toward the budget folder. "You've got more important things to do then. I'll go over what you have here. If I have questions, I'll get back with you. Hopefully, it's a heart attack or something and not foul play. Go."

Sarah told Liz she was on her way and thanked Bill for understanding. She was no longer a detective, but murders were not something Devaney PD had to deal with regularly. This … if it was a murder … would be the first in almost three years. Her presence at the scene seemed appropriate.

# CHAPTER 4

## 8:45 A.M. Monday

Sarah parked her car at a trailhead accessed by Osage Road along the edge of the Overton Acres development. Osage Road was a paved county road, part of the annexation. There were no houses on the side of the road that included Overton Acres. The area was relatively isolated, but that would change when the development was completed. The parking area was asphalt covered, large enough for a dozen or so vehicles. She always thought it odd that people would drive their cars to a place to walk or ride bicycles. She dismissed the thought when she considered her routine trips to the gym. A black and white police car was parked with strobe lights flashing blue and white. Bright lights. It was one of the EV units. Monday morning was not a busy time for the trails. No other cars were parked at the trailhead. She wondered if Boston was on scene yet.

Sarah exited her vehicle and approached the officer milling around the area and monitoring yellow police tape across the trail. "Corporal Baldor, how are you today?"

The officer noticeably straightened when she saw the Chief approach. She smiled, appreciative of the seriousness of the situation. "I'm doing well, Chief. I've got this end cordoned off."

"Where's your partner? Patrick, isn't it?"

"He's controlling the scene."

Sarah glanced toward the trail in the direction Corporal Baldor indicated. "Has Detective Mankowitz arrived?"

"Yes, Ma'am. He arrived just ahead of the Coroner. Not long ago."

"Good. How far is it to the scene?" Sarah mulled the thought that the Coroner arrived so quickly. Usually, the Detective in charge called for the Coroner. Maria Honeycutt was an efficient Shift Commander. She wasn't afraid to anticipate field needs. It was likely that she called the Coroner.

"It's quite a way in there, Ma'am. Nearly a quarter mile. You probably want to drive. The trail is wide enough. Detective Mankowitz drove."

Sarah mulled the Corporal's suggestion. "I suppose the Coroner drove in too?"

"Yes, Ma'am. If his van can do it, these EVs can do it easy enough." The Corporal grinned.

"I'm sure they can. I think I'll walk. I don't want to risk blocking the Coroner. Besides, the exercise can't hurt me." Sarah knew Boston would opt to drive. So would Henry Mason, the Coroner. It made sense that they both drove to the scene. Boston had his evidence kit and other supplies in his car. Too much to carry in and out. The Coroner needed to load the body. It was necessary for them to be as close as possible. She had no reason to drive other than to appear important. She began to walk along the concrete trail.

Sarah studied the area surrounding the trail as she walked. The city's trails were typically built in floodplains, drainage areas, or along the edges of development. Areas with minimal development value. The Overton Acres trails were designed to complement the several tracts Overton Enterprises was developing. From upscale housing to starter homes to apartment complexes, Terrance Overton was providing housing for Devaney's growing population. When and where feasible, the trails were bordered by natural vegetation and shade. In other areas, young trees were planted to provide future scenery and shade as well as separation from the residents. Even the adamant trail supporters didn't want random strangers to invade their privacy. The trail Sarah walked was through a wide, swampy area covered with low shrubs and brush. A few taller trees shaded the entire area. It was scenic, if not beautiful. It offered the feeling of seclusion, if not actual seclusion. She was in the boonies to all extents and purposes.

The concrete trail was eight feet wide, plenty of width for Parks Department vehicles to traverse the trails for maintenance, though the real reason for the width was to meet minimum national trail standards. The grass along the sides was trimmed out to at least the width of a riding mower. That provided some degree of protection from assorted natural hazards – such as snakes, ticks, small creatures. A snake seen was a snake that could be avoided.

A yellow line demarcated two equal sides of the trail. Apparently, walkers and bicycle riders needed to be reminded to stay to one side to avoid opposing traffic. Sarah walked slowly, almost immediately aware of compressed grass at the sides of the trail in some spots. Black smudges on the edges of the concrete marked the point where vehicle tires had slipped off of and back onto the concrete. Most of the marks were on the left side of the trail. She knelt and studied the compressed grass. Some blades were smashed. The juice from the grass was relatively fresh, not yet exposed to harsh sunlight. The damage was recent. Either the Coroner or Boston had difficulty staying on the trail even though there was nearly a foot to spare on either side of their vehicle tires. As she walked and surveyed the area, Sarah concluded that the Coroner's van was the likely culprit. Boston's smaller EV should have been easy to control on the concrete surface.

Other than the lack of vehicle control by Coroner Henry Mason, Sarah saw nothing out of the ordinary as she strolled.

The distance was slightly more than a quarter mile, but it was a good guesstimate by Corporal Baldor. Yellow police tape cordoned the trail in two places. The nearest was several feet behind the Coroner's van. The farthest kept anyone from approaching from the front of Boston's vehicle. More importantly, the yellow tape stretched from the cordoned area into the surrounding vegetation on the right side of the trail. That particular part of the trail cut through a morass of tangled overgrowth and underbrush that clogged a wooded area.

Officer Patrick Bohannan saw Sarah approaching and moved to lift the yellow tape for her. "Good morning, Chief."

"Good morning, Patrick." A small group of people strained to see into the wooded area cordoned off by the tape near Boston's car. "Maybe the trail should be blocked at the other end."

"It is, Ma'am. Officer Banks has a unit at the next trailhead. These

33

folks apparently live somewhere near the trail between here and there."
Officer Bohannan shrugged. "It's hard to fully control rubberneckers,
especially if it's their neighborhood. They know how to access the trail."

Sarah nodded. She glanced toward the woods. Trampled grass and
bent brush limbs indicated recent passage. "I assume the scene is in there?"
she asked.

"Yes, Ma'am. About ten yards. Maybe less. This area makes you think
you're in the deep woods out in the boonies, doesn't it?" Officer Bohannan
thought a moment then added, "I wouldn't want my wife in here by
herself."

Sarah smiled reflectively. She understood the man's point of view.
From what little she knew about the discovered body; it wasn't just women
who should be concerned. She looked at the brushy area. There were signs
of two different points of entry. One was well marked with small branches
intentionally broken to make room to pass. She stared into the brush but
couldn't see anything. "Are the Detective and the Coroner in there?"

"Yes. Like I said, boonies."

"Which of the trails did they use?"

"The one on the right. Detective Mankowitz studied the area before
he began breaking a new trail. The other one looks like it was used by the
victim and whoever killed him ... and the woman who discovered the
body."

"Where is she?" Sarah glanced toward the sightseers at the tape. "One
of them?"

"Detective Mankowitz put her with Banks at the other trailhead. She's
pretty spooked about it ... finding a dead body while on her morning jog."

"I can imagine. I suppose I'll go see what we have. I appreciate your
help, Patrick."

Sarah slowly picked her way through the thick brush. The broken and
smashed brush made it easier to see, but it didn't make it easy to walk. Her
feet tangled more than once on vines and broken branches. She wondered
how the jogger saw the body from the trail. She had to hunker low to
avoid overhead vegetation. She heard muffled voices and worked her way
through the underbrush until she could see Boston taking photographs
and the Coroner bent over a body on the ground. "Good morning, Henry.
What do we have?"

"A dead man." Henry Mason was curt when in his role as County Coroner. A professional and compassionate mortician with his own funeral home business, he was elected to be Coroner because no one else wanted the job. He wasn't afraid to handle the dead. That was the first requirement of a coroner. He didn't proclaim himself to be a medical examiner. He wasn't trained for the task, though he made it a point to read and study the subject after he became County Coroner several years earlier. He could provide cursory rulings but offered nothing more.

Sarah didn't let Henry's response bother her. She knew the man and respected him. He respected her. "Do we have an ID?"

"No. I just got here," Henry straightened and replied. "But off hand … to your next question, I'd say someone shot him. Looks like a bullet hole in the back of his skull."

Sarah nodded understandingly. She grimaced as she studied the body. Male in appearance. The victim was belly down with the head turned slightly to the left. Only a portion of the left side of the face was visible. The bullet entry point was unmistakable. Short hair didn't hide the obvious wound. Slightly left-of-center on the back of the skull. The victim's clothes were twisted, as if the body had writhed after being shot. She spoke to Boston. "Liz said you thought it might be a drug deal gone bad."

Boston growled. "I need to watch what I say. People take everything too literally."

"Was that what you told her?"

"Not really. I made the comment that it was *probably* a drug deal gone bad. When the call said it was out in the woods, it did make me think they were doing something illegal … other than the obvious."

Sarah didn't let Boston's grumbling tone affect her. "I see. Liz just tried to pass along as much as she could."

Boston snorted. "Another reason I shouldn't be allowed to talk to the media. I say what's on my mind." He paused then moved the conversation to another path. "I thought the trails were closed at night."

"Not closed, though city PSAs remind people that the trails are not patrolled at night. They're not particularly safe for single walkers, especially in the secluded areas."

Boston glanced around to emphasize his words. "I'd take my chances in a homeless camp over a place like this after dark. No one out here at night is up to any good. Too many places to lie in wait."

"I can't say I disagree." Sarah pulled a small notepad from her jacket pocket. "I think I'll mention something to the Mayor about areas like this. Secluded and cool seems good for a pleasant walk during the daytime, but it attracts predators after dark."

Boston nodded as he surveyed the area next to the body. He was searching for clues.

The Coroner mumbled as he studied the body, "No apparent GSR."

"Does that mean it wasn't an execution?" Sarah asked.

The Coroner shook his head and scowled. "It means there's no apparent GSR. Maybe I shouldn't be allowed to talk to the media either." His lips turned up in a small smile. "I don't know what it means, Chief. We'll probably need to swab the area near the wound for gunshot residue, just to be sure." He watched Boston retrieve a test kit from his forensics case.

Sarah studied the area while Boston tested for residue around the entry wound. The body was in a small break in the thick brush. Not a big enough area for the three of them and the body to congregate comfortably. Too many small saplings and other flora. The ground appeared damp beneath the years of accumulated leaves and fallen limbs. The area did not lend itself to a gathering of people. The path the victim and his murderer used was only obvious because of the disturbed leaves on the ground. From a cursory look, only a few broken twigs were evident. It led her to believe they stumbled their way through the thick brush. The path she, Boston, and the Coroner used was more obvious. Broken limbs, shoved aside to make room for passage. Boston and the Coroner knew they would be carrying the body out when they finished the scene survey. Boston made the trail. It was his scene to control. "Did you look at the entry trail?"

Boston glanced up from his kit. "No GSR. The barrel of the gun was not close when it was fired. No. I haven't, other than to avoid trampling over it. I've concentrated on the immediate area." He shook his head as he looked around the constricted space. "Not much to see here. The body and thick brush. Henry, are you ready to turn him over? Let's look at his face. I've got all the pictures I need from this angle."

The Coroner nodded. "Maybe we can find some ID in his front pockets. Nothing in the rear."

Sarah watched as the two men carefully turned the body onto its side. That was all the room available for the turn. She suppressed a gasp. The exit wound was horrendous. The victim's lower right jaw was essentially gone. Bullets are meant to kill. The bullet used on the man was meant to inflict maximum damage. From her position a few feet away, she surveyed the ground beneath the head, looking for bits of flesh and bone. There was very little other than small globs of coagulated blood on the leaves. "Shouldn't there be more here?" she asked aloud, knowing the answer.

Henry Mason shook his head as he inserted a liver probe while Boston checked the victim's front pockets. "That's a question for you detectives to answer. I work with what I've got. Liver temp indicates time of death about six hours, plus or minus a half." He wiped the probe and stowed it in its case. "Did you find anything?" he asked Boston."

"No ID. No wallet." Boston looked perplexed. "Not even a cell phone."

The Coroner mulled the Detective's response. "Hard to imagine anyone without a cell phone. Robbery?"

"Maybe. Sometimes the victims of drug deals gone bad are stripped of ID." Boston glanced at Sarah and quickly added, "But I'm not saying it's a drug execution. All I can say for sure is that we have ourselves a John Doe." John Doe cases are tougher because identity helps connect the dots that lead to solving the crime. If the detective knows the identity, known associates are easier to locate. Questions can be asked and answered. Leads can be developed.

The Coroner generally ignored the speculative conversation. "I'm ready to bag him and get him out of here." He looked back at the path he would have to traverse to carry the body and sighed heavily. "I'm not sure the county pays me enough for this. No telling what kind of insects are already attaching themselves to our bodies." He rose and pushed aside brush to reach a black bundle on the ground, a folded body bag. He returned and laid the bag beside the victim's body. The brush and small saplings prevented a smooth transfer into the bag.

Boston and Henry grunted as they struggled to get the body into the bag. Sarah donned examination gloves and knelt to assist. The three of them were forced to reach around the small undergrowth that clogged the entire area. Nothing was easy about bagging the body. Finally, the Coroner was able to zip the bag closed.

"Now comes the hard part. Carrying him through this mess to the van," the Coroner said with disdain.

"You let us do this," Boston demanded of Sarah when she reached to help. "You're dressed for your job, not mine."

Sarah accepted Boston's strongly intoned suggestion. She was interfering. She was not a detective. She was the Police Chief. As Police Chief, she had other responsibilities, and one of those was to not interfere with subordinates' tasks. Besides, the trail out was too precarious for three people to walk in unison. "Okay. I'll go ahead to hold limbs out of your way."

The sightseer group quieted respectfully when the body bag emerged from the brush. Sarah opened the van's rear doors and watched Boston and the Coroner stow the body. She stepped aside to allow the Coroner to close the doors. "How much autopsy will you be doing?"

Henry shook his head and scowled as he removed his gloves and tossed them into a trash bag before he closed the doors. "We've had this discussion. I'm not an ME. I'll send the body to the State and request a full autopsy."

"I was hoping you could give us a preliminary analysis, something Boston can work with while he waits for the State. They're going to proceed at their own pace, not ours. Catching the killer may be time sensitive."

"I'll draw some blood, if there is any." The Coroner's eyes cut toward the van. "Head wounds can bleed out if the victim's heart doesn't stop immediately. I'll take some tissue. See if there are any bullet fragments inside the skull, though I doubt it. That exit didn't look like it stopped anything." He shuddered.

Sarah glanced toward Boston, who was preparing to revisit the scene. "Is there anything in particular you need from Henry?"

"I'd like Alicia to look at his clothes. There might be some clues there, and she can do it faster than the State."

Devaney PD Forensic Specialist Alicia Kettering had developed her small laboratory's reputation to the point that she was called upon by surrounding towns for forensics. Mayor Keck had supported the department's requests for lab equipment. A few pieces added every budget cycle created a regional presence for crime solvers. Small but enviable.

Henry nodded. "I doubt the State cares if our John Doe shows up clothed or naked. Less for them to do. I'll also inspect for anything out of the ordinary. Bruises. Scratches. Ligature marks. Fibers. Like I said, I'll also gather some tissue for Alicia. Toxins and drugs – though it doesn't look like he died of poison or drug overdose." He smiled ruefully.

"That sounds good," Boston replied. He exhaled and looked toward the brush. "I need to gather some more information from the scene. I'll take my shovel and a bucket. Dig up some soil. Maybe find the slug … and the rest of his face."

"Was he leaned forward when he was shot?" Sarah asked, unsure the search would yield anything.

"I don't know. I'll never know if I don't look." Boston shrugged.

Sarah looked toward the brush. The trail used by the three of them was apparent. Easy to see someone had entered the area. The indiscreet trail attributed to the murderer, victim, and the woman who discovered the body was barely discernible. It would have been even less obvious for the woman. She added some to the disturbance. "How did the citizen say she discovered the body?"

Boston shook his head. "I haven't talked to her." He glanced toward Officer Bohannan. "Scene control was already in effect when I arrived. I recommended the witness be isolated and detained with one of the responding units. They may have taken statements. I'll find out later."

"Okay. Do you mind if I talk to her? She's probably a wreck."

"If you're determined to act like a detective," Boston replied with a note of barely disguised disdain.

"I'll just calm her and assure her you will have questions for her," Sarah replied apologetically. "PR is important too."

"Speaking of PR," Officer Bohannan interrupted, "the press has arrived." He nodded toward the group of onlookers at the yellow tape.

"How did she get here?" Boston snarled. "That's yours," he said to Sarah with a dismissive wave of his hand. With a bucket and shovel in hand, he turned to walk into the brush.

Officer Bohannan looked at Sarah and answered Boston's question. "She came through the same way the neighbors got here; I suppose. Do you want me to send her away?"

Sarah grimaced. "I'd like to say yes, but that won't serve us well. I'll go talk to her. She's new. I don't recognize her. This is as good a time as any to establish boundaries."

# CHAPTER 5

## 9:30 A.M. Monday

Sarah knew Kyren Bailey, the seasoned local TV reporter, had finally nailed the big break she sought. Kyren grew up along with Sarah. The bottle-blonde reporter covered Sarah's first solo case and was there when Sarah became Police Chief. Sarah didn't recognize the new reporter, though she recognized the markings of a freshly minted journalism major. For some reason, the females in journalism thought their paths to success improved with blonde hair. Maybe they were right. Maybe journalism professors set the tone for reporters and for advancements. Maybe those stodgy old professors imprinted their predilections on the industry.

Sarah saw the reporter's camera crew had not yet arrived. She smiled to herself and approached the reporter who was holding a microphone with the station logo long used by Kyren Bailey. The microphone wasn't connected to anything. "Good morning. I'm surprised to see you here this quickly. I don't have any information to share. What's your name?"

The young woman's brown eyes cut in the direction of her scrambling camera crew. "Tammy Nunn. I recently started. What can you tell me about the murder?"

"What makes you think it's a murder?"

"That's the rumor I heard. A man was shot."

Sarah smirked. "Rumor? Are you going to report rumors or wait for the police to investigate? Facts make a better story." She was determined to set the tone by challenging the young reporter's approach to information gathering.

Tammy's blonde hair jerked as she kept turning to check the status of her delayed camera crew. "What are the facts? What's the victim's name? If they weren't shot, how did they die?"

Sarah hated the pronoun usage of the press. It made it sound like a group of people had died. An untrained listener might think it was the scene of a mass killing. "I have no details to give at this time. The investigation has only just begun. I can tell you that a member of the public reported a body in the woods. The Coroner and a Devaney PD Detective arrived on the scene a short time ago. I will also confirm the body is that of a white male."

"Were they murdered?"

"The Coroner will send the body to the State Medical Examiner for an autopsy to determine the cause of death. One constant in every case is to never get ahead of the evidence. We are searching for evidence at this time."

The young reporter's eyes widened with excitement. "Autopsy? Then you suspect foul play?"

Sarah scowled with derision, an emotion she would have guarded if the reporter's camera crew was on the scene. "Autopsies are performed anytime there is an unattended death. That is standard protocol."

"When can the public expect to know something?" Tammy pointed toward the trail through the brushy area. "A lot of people are concerned about the safety of the trails in areas like this."

"The public will know something as soon as we know something."

"What about the safety of the people who use the trails?"

"That's a subject I *can* address at this time." Sarah took advantage of the segue. She could divert attention toward something other than the body. "People should avoid the trails after dark, especially some of the less visible and unlit areas. And people should never walk alone. Most of the trails are in out of the way places. Floodplains. Land that is not suited to development. Trails are not supposed to be a nuisance to the homeowners and businesses they border, so natural barricades are left in places where high fencing isn't practical or preferred. By design, the trails are isolated to some degree."

"So, you're telling people to not use the trails because they're dangerous?"

"You didn't hear me say that. Common sense is required for using the trails, especially after dark. Last year, the fire department was called for a water rescue because some folks decided to walk during a rainstorm. A lot of the trail system is in floodplains. It can be dangerous."

"Dangerous because of potential for muggings and sexual assaults?" Tammy challenged. She believed she had the upper hand, apparently a tactic taught by a journalism professor who never actually worked as a reporter.

"We have had no reported rapes or muggings in this area since the trail was completed. They can be dangerous because low lying areas are susceptible to flash flooding. Dangerous because there is always danger being alone after dark … no matter where you are."

The reporter glanced to see where her camera crew was. Still scrambling toward the tape. She was visibly angry with them. "Are you investigating the case?"

"No." Sarah glanced toward Boston who apparently decided to linger at the edge of the trail to watch her with the reporter and to watch the Coroner's back and forth turn around on the narrow trail. Officer Bohannan provided directional support for the Coroner's labored turn around. "Senior Detective Mankowitz is the investigator."

Without cameras, Tammy didn't feel obligated to smile. "This seems like a critical case. Why aren't you investigating it? Weren't you once a detective?"

Sarah smiled and pointedly replied, "I was … about the same time you were cheerleading in high school. Roles change. We will make a statement when we have some facts. Thank you." She turned and saw Boston still standing at the edge of the brush. He was smiling mischievously.

Boston snickered and softly asked, "Changing your approach? That sounded like something I would say."

Sarah shook her head and withheld the urge to look back at the reporter. "That obvious, huh? I guess my patience with novice reporters is wearing thin. The experienced ones know what to ask and when. Did you already get the samples?"

Boston held up his empty bucket. "No. I wanted to make sure Henry got turned around. To see if I needed to move my car and let him drive forward to the next trailhead." He grinned. "And I wanted to see you in action. Maybe learn a few tricks in case I have to answer questions."

Sarah shook her head. "And you will. Believe me. You will."

Boston grinned harder. "Well. In the meantime, I'm going to get my samples. If you want to wait, you can ride back with me."

"No, thank you. I think I'll walk. It'll do me some good. I may walk to the other trailhead. Get some perspective of these trails. I don't use them. And, if it's still okay with you, maybe I'll talk to the witness. I can't understand how she found the body."

"Maybe she needed to pee," Boston said with a shrug.

"Oh, by the way. Did you have trouble keeping your car on the trail? I saw several places where there was freshly smashed grass along the edges and some fresh black marks, like maybe a tire slipped off the edge of the concrete."

"Not with that little car," Boston nodded toward his EV.

"Maybe the Coroner," Sarah suggested.

"I doubt it. Henry knows how to drive better than that."

"Maybe I'll stop by the funeral home and check the insides of his tires. See if they look freshly scraped."

"Probably should have looked before he turned it around. He was all over the place, back and forth. Probably got lots of sidewall scrapes."

Sarah felt remorse for not thinking of it sooner. "You're probably right." As soon as Boston made his way into the brush, she walked to the area where the Coroner maneuvered his turn around. She saw several places in the grass and on the concrete where he forcefully twisted his tires to make tight turns. A few spots indicated that his tires spun on the slick grass to regain the concrete surface. In all of it, she didn't see anything to indicate that his tires slipped off the edge. The tracks and marks she saw from his van were directly attributable to the short back and forth turns. He intentionally drove off the edges to make the turn. She wasn't sure she would find answers to her questions about the smashed grass on the van's tires. But she would look anyway.

"Chief James," Tammy yelled. "May I have another moment of your time?" The camera was recording at last. "Can you give me a formal statement for my viewers?"

Sarah inhaled deeply. She smiled and approached the young reporter. The woman had a job and a career. Devaney PD needed the media to be on good terms. She cleared her mind of contemptuous thoughts before Tammy jutted the microphone toward her face. "Earlier this morning, a citizen jogging on the trail discovered the body of a white male. Currently we have no details. No ID was found on the body. Coroner Henry Mason has taken the body and will request an autopsy be performed by the State Medical Examiner. That is protocol for an unattended death, regardless of circumstances. Senior Detective Mankowitz is the assigned investigator. We ask the public to come forward if you have any information regarding this incident. Thank you." She lifted the tape that separated her from the reporter and walked past the camera crew.

As an afterthought, Sarah turned to the group of onlookers. "How did you get here? Is there a side trail between here and the next trailhead?"

A few of the onlookers shied away, afraid they had violated a law. Tammy responded. "We came across a vacant lot about one hundred yards from here. There's a beaten path through the tall grass. No backyard fences on the undeveloped lots." She was pleased with herself.

"Thank you. Is it easy to see?"

Another neighbor felt safe. "We use it all the time to get to the trail. Our kids use it to go bike riding sometimes.

"Apparently, it doesn't look as forbidding as these woods," Sarah posed questioningly.

"Not at all. Tall grass and a few bushes. We started the path before spring, when the grass was dead, and the bushes had no leaves." The neighbor motioned to indicate the surrounding area. "Not like here. We don't let the kids come down this way unless an adult is with them. And they stay in a group." She added the last comment after she glanced at the camera. She wanted to assure everyone listening that she was a responsible parent.

"That's always a good idea," Sarah said with a reassuring smile. "I hope more people think that way. How often is this trail used? Do you see a lot of people?"

"Not a lot," the neighbor replied. She tilted her head toward the undeveloped area out of sight behind the heavy brush. "I'm sure that will change when the rest of the houses are built. It's a nice trail though. The city did a good job."

Sarah nodded. "Credit goes to Overton Enterprises. The city made it a condition for the annexation and development. Do you ever see cars on the trail?"

The woman looked puzzled. "Uh ... not until today." She glanced toward Boston's car. "I don't think they're supposed to ... unless it's emergency vehicles. And the lawn mowers. Sometimes we do see those small four-wheel drive vehicles with tools when they're mowing."

"Do you know if the trails are used after dark?"

"Oh! I hope not. I don't think I would feel comfortable doing that. No streetlights."

"You haven't seen the trails used at night?"

"No, but this part is completely obscured by the trees and bushes, so I couldn't see it anyway. Maybe the new houses will be able to see it. Or maybe Overton Enterprises will remove the brush and leave the bigger trees."

Sarah studied the faces. Everyone seemed curious, even the ones who moved away from her to avoid being singled out. She hoped to see someone with nervous eyes. She saw nothing to make her suspect anyone there at that moment. To everyone within hearing, she said, "I think it would be better if everyone moved away from the area until the investigation is completed. The detectives will need to study the entire area for clues. Congregating could disturb something important. We wouldn't want to lose that single best clue that could solve the case." She smiled and watched until the people slowly moved away from the area. The camera crew remained to shoot a few more angles and were still shooting when Sarah turned to go.

# CHAPTER 6

## 9:50 A.M. Monday

Sarah followed the small group of onlookers as they left. Most veered onto a grassy path and disappeared from view. A couple continued on the trail, apparently bound for the trailhead on the opposite end of the cordoned area. She lost sight of them quickly because she walked slowly, surveying the trail for any signs and clues. She saw more smashed grass along the trail. She used her cell phone to take additional pictures of the smashed grass and of the black marks at the edge of the concrete. The frequency of tire marks on the left side of the trail increased and became more pronounced. Drunks tend to guide left when they drive, but that was normally associated with their tendency to gravitate toward oncoming headlights. She wondered if the murderer was drunk. The case could be as simple as two drunks arguing and only one had a gun.

The fact that the smashed grass and black marks continued in the area not used by either Boston or the Coroner assured Sarah that neither of those vehicles was the source. The only conclusion she could reach was that someone had driven on the trail recently, maybe even as recent as the early morning. She was reasonably sure the tire marks were associated with the body, but that was purely conjecture.

The walk to the second trailhead was not much different than the walk to the body. In total, Sarah realized the walk back to her car would be at least half a mile. Yellow police tape and Officer Banks' vehicle strobes kept the trail closed from that end. She greeted Officer Banks. Crystal Banks normally worked jail duty. Apparently, there was slack in that area, so she was sent to help control the scene.

"Good morning, Crystal. Any issues on your end?"

The young officer smiled. "No, Ma'am. Fortunately, there are not many trail users this time of day. The few who I've turned back just grumble, ask questions I can't answer, and wander away."

"Is the witness still here?"

"Yes, Ma'am. She's in my unit. Her name is Sandy Tatum. She's kind of nervous. I think she's upset by what she found."

Sarah nodded. "I can imagine she is. I'm going to go talk with her. Do you mind if we sit in your car?" She knew the answer, but respect went both ways.

"Of course not. There's some bottled water in the back if you want some. I gave her a bottle."

Sarah walked to the police car. A young woman was talking on her cell phone and anxiously watching her approach. Sandy appeared to be in her mid-twenties. She was dressed in yoga pants and a loose top, ideal for running on the trail. Sarah politely waited until Sandy ended her phone call. "Hello. I'm Chief James."

Sandy smiled nervously and got out of the patrol car to stand facing Sarah. "I'm Sandy Tatum. How long am I going to be here?" She glanced at her cell phone. "That was my boss calling again. I should be on my way to work by now."

"I'm sorry for detaining you. If you don't mind, I need to take a statement."

"I told that first cop - uh, police officer - everything I know." Sandy was visibly agitated.

"I understand. The officer was trying to gain control of the scene to avoid contamination of evidence. The officer may not have asked about everything we need to know to help with the investigation. I'll make it quick. You say you've talked with your employer?"

"Yes. He's not happy, but he understands. I need my job."

"Understood. I'll write a note if it will help. If you don't mind, tell me what happened, what you saw."

"I jog a couple miles every morning before I go to work. I work at the mall. The store opens at ten. We bought a house not far from here. I run from my house back that way," Sandra talked fast as she pointed further back the trail, "to the next trailhead then run back home. It's about two miles all together."

"Seems like a nice place to run," Sarah said to encourage Sandy's conversation. She noticed a scratch on Sandy's arm when she pointed.

"I thought so too, until this morning. I thought the new trail would offer new scenery. I'll not run this way again, not unless there is police protection." Sandy's tone grew accusative.

"Scary," Sarah replied. She didn't want to engage in a discussion of police coverage. Nothing would come of it at that moment. She simply looked Sandy in the eyes and waited.

"I ran to the trailhead and came back. I thought something looked odd. A trail or something I hadn't seen before."

"How did it look?"

"Just like something big had pushed brush aside. I wish I hadn't been curious." Sandy shuddered and crossed her arms defensively. She winced when she touched the fresh scratch.

"How did you get scratched?"

"Some kind of sticker bush in the woods." Sandy loosened her arms and pointed at her yoga pants leg. "It snagged my pants." There were several snags on her pants legs. "I didn't even notice my arm. Too much happened too fast."

Sarah pointed to a couple of snagged spots on the legs of her slacks. "I think I got into the same thorns. It's a vine. I think they're called green briars by some of the locals. Do you need something for that scratch? The squad car has a first aid kit."

Sandy lightly touched the scratch. "No. I'll do something when I get home after I take a shower."

"What did you see?"

"The body. I didn't get too close. I saw a spot on his head, like a gunshot. I think it was a man."

"It was," Sarah said reassuringly. "What did you do then?"

"I think that's when I scratched my arm and tore my pants. I probably would have stopped if it happened going in there. I panicked and stumbled when I rushed through the briars to get out. As soon as I got out, I called my husband and told him what I saw. He was already at work. He told me to call 9-1-1. So, I did and waited like they told me. I was scared. What if the murderer was still there?" Sandy's eyes widened as the thought materialized. "I could have been killed too."

Sarah wrote notes in a small paper notebook she always carried in her jacket pocket. She preferred paper to electronics for investigative notes. She would address the instructions Sandy received. Leaving her there alone wasn't a good idea. "Did you see anything that stood out? Anything unusual?"

"Besides a faint trail into the woods? Not really. I'm not even sure why I thought I should investigate. It was just laid over weeds and disturbed leaves. Not much. Weird, huh? If I hadn't done it, the body would still not be found." Sandy shivered. "I wouldn't have this image of a dead man in my head. God! How stupid!"

Sarah put her hand on Sandy's shoulder. "Not stupid at all. We're all curious when we see something unusual, something different. As bad as it is, I'm personally glad you were curious. You may have given us the time we need to solve this case." She intentionally avoided calling it a murder. Never feed the rumor mill. She quickly redirected the conversation. "Do you think you made the path bigger when you went in there?"

"I don't know. Probably. It was just enough to catch my attention, though. Bent limbs. Bent bushes." Sandy shook her head. "You've probably seen a lot of dead bodies. How do you forget you saw them?"

Sarah's mind immediately focused on an image from years earlier. Her first solo case as a Detective. The putrefied body of a young, teenaged girl, Chelsea Weldon, was found inside a trashcan. The sight and smell came back to her in a wash of emotion and phantom odors. The killer eluded her to his very end. But he did meet his end. She wasn't sure which was more horrific, the Weldon girl's rotting body or the pulpy remainder of Bentley Overton's head on the carpet of his bedroom. That was another case that involved a child. She pulled her thoughts together. The current body, as destroyed as the face was, didn't compare to either of those. And it wasn't a child. But he didn't have a name yet. A name increases the significance of the memory. "You don't. You just have to compartmentalize. Do you have someone to talk to? Maybe an employee assistance program?"

"I work for a small store at the mall. They don't even offer insurance. I can talk to my husband … or my mom. What next?"

"For you, nothing unless you think of something. Detective Mankowitz might contact you if he finds a need for a descriptive comparison of the scene before and after we trampled it. Maybe you can help him explain some pieces of evidence he finds."

"Like what?"

Sarah motioned toward Sandy's scratched arm. "Maybe you left some blood evidence near the body. We will need to eliminate it from the evidence."

"I didn't touch the body," Sandy exclaimed defensively. "As soon as I saw it, that's when those green sticker things caught me. I wasn't paying attention because I was trying to get out of there."

"That's good that you didn't touch the body. How close do you suppose you were?" Sarah knew visibility was poor through the thick brush. "Two, three feet?"

"I don't know for sure. I saw it and panicked." A wave of shame washed across Sandy's face. Her shoulders slumped and she leaned back against the police car. Her eyes teared up. "I … I was so scared. I didn't even think to help. Just leave. Call Jason. Maybe he died because I didn't try to help."

"No. He was already dead. There was nothing you could have done other than call the police. You did the right thing."

Hope replaced shame. "Are you sure?"

"Positive. We know what time he died. It's been several hours."

Sandy sobbed and regained her composure. "Good. Not that he's dead, but that I didn't cause him to die."

Sarah pulled a business card from her jacket pocket and handed it to Sandy. "If you think of anything, please call me." She fumbled in her pocket until she found one of Boston's cards. "Or call Detective Mankowitz. We will appreciate anything you can add."

"Can I go now?"

"Sure. Thank you for staying. I know it's been trying for you. Do you need a note from me to settle things with your boss?"

Sandy glanced at the two business cards in her hand. She smiled appreciatively. "No. These should be enough."

Sarah spoke with Officer Banks for a few minutes, then walked the trail toward the scene. She moved slowly, scanning for anything she might have missed on her earlier trip. The hum of an EV caught her attention. She looked toward a large curve and watched Boston's car slowly move in her direction. She stepped onto the grassy edge and waited.

Boston opened his window. "Did you learn anything from our witness?"

"Not much. She was curious about the trail. It was something different. I saw the path you made. It's very obvious, but I didn't think the original trail was very obvious. She's got a good eye for changes in her environment. She investigated. She saw the body and panicked. Did you get what you needed?"

"I think the fact that I don't think I got anything is more telling than what I have in the evidence buckets." Boston shook his head.

"What did do you mean?"

"No fragments. I searched a wide area. Everything I found was immediately beneath the body … and it was nothing. Not enough blood to account for a head wound. No bone or flesh fragments. The missing parts are gone."

Sarah was surprised. She waited for Boston to continue. She loved detective work. She also knew it was Boston's job to investigate, not hers. At that moment, she was struggling with the differences between her passion and her job. A flash of former Senior Detective Carl Franken formed in her mind. He was her mentor from the beginning. He seldom told her what to do. He asked. Carl encouraged his young protégé by framing every suggestion in the form of a question, by making her find the correct answers … even if she had to stumble with the wrong answers on her way to finding the single best clue, that clue that tied the evidence together.

"If he was standing, the fragments would have sprayed out. They should have been within a few feet." Boston pointed toward the dirty knees of his pants. "I searched on my hands and knees. I found nothing. Maybe I'll find something in the dirt and leaves when I get it to the lab, but I'm not sure about this."

"Is it possible that carrion eaters were there? It was dark and I'm sure animals abound in this area."

Boston shook his head. "I doubt it. The area was disturbed, but not to the extent a scavenging animal would have disturbed it. I'll ask Henry to check for bite marks around the exit, though."

Sarah nodded thoughtfully then asked, "Do you have some gloves and evidence bags I can use?"

"What for?"

"Something the witness mentioned. I want to dig into the path she used."

Boston's face clouded. "I'll do it. That's my job."

Sarah shrugged. "I'm going that way. I'll just check it. I'd prefer to have sample bags in case I find something. Probably nothing. You need to check your evidence, see if what you're looking for is hidden in the dirt. If it's not …," she let her voice trail so he could finish the sentence in his mind.

Boston scowled. "Don't contaminate my scene. If I don't find anything, I'll probably be back. I told Bohannan to keep it secure until I released it. Don't override me."

"I wouldn't dare. If I find something, I'll bring it to you." Sarah waited until Boston exited his car and retrieved gloves and bags from the trunk for her. Almost as an afterthought, she asked, "Can you ask Taylor to have Corporal Canton investigate the tire marks on the edges of the trail? They get worse on this end, especially on this side." She pointed out a black mark and smashed grass near Boston's car.

Boston looked at the smudge and the grass at the edge of the trail. "What do you think he will find?"

"I don't know. It just doesn't make sense. Maybe it's nothing. Someone was on the trail with a vehicle and couldn't stay on the concrete. Most of the marks are on the left side coming in this direction. Drunk, maybe? Maybe Canton can make sense of it for us. I can't make sense of it. Can you?"

Boston studied the black mark and then looked at Sarah. "I'm not a traffic guy. I'll talk to Taylor."

"Thank you." Sarah motioned toward the back of Boston's car. "Hopefully, your single best clue is in those buckets."

Boston grimaced. "Yeah. Yeah. Single best clue. You don't know you have it until after the fact." He was accustomed to Sarah's use of that phrase, one coined by former Senior Detective Carl Franken.

Sarah arrived at the scene. Officer Bohannan was milling around, engaged in conversation with Corporal Baldor on his cell phone. He was passing time while he stood watch. It was boring duty at best. "Officer Bohannan, can you assist me?"

"Yes, Chief. Gladly." The young officer quickly responded and moved closer to Sarah. He smiled embarrassedly. "This is boring."

Sarah laughed. "I know what you mean. Maybe this will give you something to break the boredom until Boston releases the scene."

"When do you suppose that will be, Chief?"

"You're guess is as good as mine."

"I hope I get relieved pretty soon. Otherwise, I'll be in the woods getting rid of morning coffee."

"If you need a break, I've got the scene until you get back. There's a restroom at the trailhead back there." Sarah pointed in the direction she meant. "It's a shorter distance than where you're unit is parked."

Sarah slowly walked into the brush along the original path. She stopped and looked for details before taking each step. She used her phone's camera to take pictures each step of the way. She carefully pushed limbs and vines aside as she moved. She studied every leaf on the vegetation and on the ground. She noticed an area where the low vegetation and dead leaves were mashed as if something heavy had pressed them down. She wasn't sure if that was caused by the murderer and the victim. Maybe the victim knew what was coming and resisted. The two could have struggled. Maybe Sandy Tatum actually fell in her rush to escape what she saw. Anything that appeared out of order caught her attention. A single leaf near the spot was oddly colored. Mid-September was a difficult time to distinguish color oddities on vegetation because some leaves were already losing their vibrant green summer shades. Not many, but enough to confuse a search. Still, the leaf caught her attention.

Sarah used her cell phone to photograph the leaf, then she carefully removed it from the bush. It appeared to contain a spot of dried blood. A couple more leaves had similar spots. All of them were above knee level but below waist level. Without disturbing the area any more than necessary, she leaned forward to study the ground. A few flies erupted into the air. Her eyes immediately focused on the spot where the flies had been.

A small - almost unnoticeably small - piece of flesh was on top of a dead leaf. After taking several pictures to establish exactly where the evidence was located, Sarah put the fleshy piece into an evidence bag. She wished she had evidence markers. If the victim was facing toward the path when he was shot, she may have found Boston's missing evidence, the splatter from the exit wound. She backed out of the path and stared at the path Boston and the Coroner made to access the site where the body was found.

Sarah called Officer Bohannan, who had just arrived at the trailhead restroom. She asked him to bring evidence markers and sample bags from Officer Banks' unit. Every police car had a supply of them.

Standing near the entry point of the primary trail, Sarah noticed a larger limb that was broken and dangling from a sapling. She wondered why she hadn't noticed it earlier. It was obvious. The exposed wood was discolored. It had been exposed to sunlight and the sap was dried. She took pictures of it from several angles and from the trail. That dangling limb probably caught Sandy's attention initially and created her curiosity about the less obvious signs. Someone marked the entry point a few days earlier. She made a note in her book. That clue could prove useful.

Sarah waited for Officer Bohannan to return with a bag of numbered yellow evidence markers. She used her wait-time to talk with Liz, to get an update on other things in her schedule. Boston was right. This was his job. She had her job. Her schedule was full. Still, she couldn't resist helping. Connecting the dots on a murder case was exhilarating. Murders were not normal in Devaney.

When Officer Bohannan arrived, Sarah said, "Thank you. I have something that will take care of the boredom for you. I think I found something. Follow me."

Sarah led the way along the path Boston and the Coroner made parallel to the original path. Again, she was taken by how small the area was where the body was discovered. She saw where Boston had disturbed the ground gathering his samples. Other disturbances were created by Boston and the Coroner … and probably her … when they bagged and removed the body. She snagged her slacks repeatedly during the process. The underbrush was filled with green briars, more than she remembered. Every limb and twig wanted to grab at her slacks and jacket. She motioned for Officer Bohannan to stand at her side.

"This is what we're going to do, Patrick." Sarah showed the young officer the two evidence bags with leaves and the piece of flesh. "I found these on the ground on the original path. I stopped after I found them. Boston doesn't think he found all the exit wound splatter inside this little area. I think these indicate the shooter was standing over here and shot the victim this way." She pointed toward the path. "If I'm right, we should find some bloodied leaves and pieces of his face along that trajectory."

With Patrick close behind, Sarah carefully moved from the spot where the body was found toward the path. She studied the ground and the leaves. "Look for anything that doesn't belong." She expected to find bloodied leaves higher than the leaf she found near the beginning of the path. Approximately head high at the highest point, then dropping quickly as gravity pulled the blood spray and face fragments lower. She found a leaf that appeared to have a blood spot. "There. See it?" She looked to Officer Bohannan for confirmation.

"Yes. Man, that doesn't jump out at you, does it?"

"If you know what to look for, it will. It will be even better if you will use your flashlight." Sarah didn't have a flashlight, but all the officers carried flashlights in their equipment belts. "We want to put those in an evidence bag. Place an evidence marker on the limb and take a picture." Sarah motioned for Patrick to use his cell phone camera. "I need to leave for a meeting soon, but if you could gather evidence for Boston, it would be appreciated."

"I've had training," the young officer answered eagerly. Helping the Chief of Police was always good for one's career. "Is that what I think it is?" He pointed toward the ground.

Sarah looked. Patrick's eyes were keen, and the flashlight helped in the shadows. "Yes. It's a bloodied dead leaf. Several, in fact. Place a marker, photograph it, and bag them. ID the bag and seal it." She watched as Patrick nervously complied. "Perfect. Let's see what else we can find."

From a squatted position, the two of them carefully studied the ground and moved dead leaves and sticks as they searched. After finding a few more high leaves with blood spots and blood on dead leaves on the ground, Sarah was satisfied Patrick could perform the task satisfactorily. She was disappointed that they weren't seeing bits of flesh, the exit wound splatter she expected to find. Another area of flattened vegetation and the appearance of a struggle provided a few more bloodied dead leaves from the ground and spots on green leaves on bushes. One more piece of flesh was revealed by frightened flies.

Sarah turned back and allowed Officer Bohannan to continue the search. "I need to leave now. I will tell Boston, so he knows what you are doing. He may come to check on you."

"Yes, Chief. I can handle this." Patrick smiled. "As a matter of fact, I'm happy to do it. Better than standing guard."

Sarah chuckled. "Absolutely, but don't forget to keep an eye on the area. It's still a crime scene until Boston says otherwise."

"Yes, Chief."

Sarah called Boston and told him what she had found, and that Officer Bohannan was searching for more evidence.

# CHAPTER 7

Boston was in the Situation Room when Sarah arrived at the station. His back was to the door. He was pinning photos on the corkboard. He used the corkboard to link the photos of the crime scene to a suspect. He didn't have a suspect yet. Sarah preferred a fishbone diagram on the whiteboard. The fishbone flowchart allowed for the addition of information along a timeline. Photos linked by colored strings didn't fit her way of assimilating data. It worked for Boston. That's all that mattered.

"Making sense?" Sarah asked.

Boston turned his weary face toward Sarah. "Not really. I talked to Taylor. She said she would send Corporal Canton out to investigate the tire marks. Maybe he can tell us if they mean anything."

"Good."

"So, as I take it, you didn't get anything useful from the woman who found the body?" Boston posed the comment as a question.

"Nothing. She jogged past and thought there was an unusual trail into the brush." Sarah opened her phone's photo file and showed it to Boston. "I did find this. It looks like a trail marker. It's a few days old. No doubt that is what caught her eye. She probably saw it when she first passed but it took the second look for curiosity to get the better of her. I'm sure she added to the disturbed vegetation, but there was enough before that for her to notice the ground was disturbed. The victim and the murderer stumbled a couple of times on their way in. I have several photos. I'll send them to you."

Boston nodded and sorted through his stack of crime scene photos. "It was a mess in there. Maybe the victim was forced to go in there. Did you say you found something?"

Sarah handed several bags of evidence to Boston. "These are what I found. Bloodied leaves about waist high in these bags. These have leaves from the ground." She held two bags for Boston to see. "But these appear to be bits of flesh. I found them on the ground along the first trail."

Boston leaned forward to study the bagged bits of flesh. "Not much. I'm surprised you could even see it in that mess. Maybe there's more. There was nothing significant in my sample buckets. Alicia is going to comb through them a little better. I expected to find blood and bone. I didn't notice much except on the dead leaves under his head. Not a lot, even there."

"I'm thinking he was facing back toward the trail when he was shot. Maybe trying to leave the area. If so, the spatter is scattered in the brush in or along the path."

Boston pulled a photo of the body from his stack. "The body appears to be facing the wrong way. You think the killer moved the body?"

"I don't know. The ground shows a lot of disturbance."

"That could have been us. It was tight quarters. No place to stand."

"I saw you two. Both of you were cautious. Did you take photos before you went to the body?"

Boston nodded. "Yeah." He checked his collection of pictures and showed it to Sarah.

"The leaves were already disturbed. You didn't add to the mess until you bagged the body. Maybe the body fell into the path and the killer had to move it to get out without breaking a new trail."

Boston studied Sarah's photograph of the path from the site of the body. "I don't know. Did you see a heavy blood spot? That head wound would have soaked the ground. It should have been obvious to us."

Sarah shook her head dejectedly. "No. And there were very few flies. There would have been more if there was a lot of blood … and flesh. I guess I'm getting ahead of the evidence."

Boston smiled dismissively. "Easy enough to do, especially when there are no apparent clues. I suppose I need to go out and dig some more."

"Officer Bohannan is gathering evidence from the surrounding area and along the path."

Boston winced. "Does he know what to look for?"

"I showed him. He seemed quite comfortable and confident. They all get training in evidence gathering at the academy."

Boston nodded, unconvinced. "Maybe I'll send Keith out to help." Sergeant Keith Locke was Boston's Junior Detective. Even after three years, Boston still harbored ill feelings toward Sergeant Locke, enough so that he held up Keith's promotion to full-grade Detective, normally a Lieutenant position. Keith was in the same category as Lieutenant Melvin Glasgow as far as Boston was concerned because both men worked for Mayor Kamen in her Public Relations Division. "Are you going to take that to Alicia, or do I need to?"

"I will. I want to make sure she's aware of the evidence that will be coming from the Coroner."

"I told her when I took the bucket to her."

Sarah nodded. Boston's expression told her she was meddling. "Have you heard anything from Henry?"

Boston exhaled. "Not yet." He glanced at his wristwatch. "It's not been long. Just seems like it."

Sarah's phone vibrated in her jacket breast pocket. She checked it and glanced toward the bullpen. "Hmmm? Taylor?" She answered, "Hello, Taylor. How may I help you?" Sarah's face paled as she listened.

"Chief, I'm on the scene of a TA. Two fatalities and three serious injuries. Teenagers."

"Where?"

"On Porter Road at the Buffalo Creek curve where Mayor Clairmont died." Sirens provided intense background noise. Lieutenant McCuskey's voice was strained. "The car missed the curve completely."

Sarah knew the curve well. A long, straight stretch of paved, two-lane road that culminated in a tight 'S' curve that followed the terrain to avoid building a bridge over a bend in Buffalo Creek. The entire road lacked paved shoulders. It was a former county road that wasn't upgraded to comply with new standards. "Any identities yet?"

"Yes, but we're sitting on them as best we can. We've closed the area and rerouted traffic, but there are several on-lookers already."

"Clear them. I'll be there as soon as I can." Sarah ended the call and tucked the phone back in her jacket breast pocket. She grimaced as she turned and left the Situation Room for her office. She located Liz. "Liz. I'm going to the scene of a traffic accident with fatalities. Lieutenant McCuskey is already on scene." She realized she still held the bag of evidence for Alicia. "Can you take this to Alicia?"

Liz nodded. Her grayed hair barely moved. "Don't forget your luncheon with Doctor Castleman."

Sarah cringed. She glanced down at her slacks. "I did. What time?"

"It's almost eleven. Lunch is at twelve."

Sarah closed her eyes to think. "Okay. How do these slacks look? I snagged them. And my jacket. In the brush were the body was found."

Liz stood and said, "Turn around. Let me look." After a brief inspection, Liz replied, "I really don't notice. It's a sit-down lunch. As long as you don't mention anything, he won't notice either. Do I need to call him and warn him you might be a little late?"

"No. The President of the Chamber deserves better. I'll be there on time … if I have to run Code 3." Sarah smiled grimly. There was no way she could justify using lights and sirens to go to a lunch meeting. "Call me fifteen minutes before noon to remind me. The wreck is on Porter Road. I can make it to the restaurant from there."

"Okay," Liz nodded as she cautioned, "just don't poke around at the scene. Let Taylor and her people do the work."

"Chief," Junior Detective Keith Locke called to Sarah as she crossed the bullpen to the stairs. "Got a minute?"

"Hello, Detective. I really don't. I'm on my way to a TA. Can we walk and talk?"

"Sure." The Detective scrambled to walk beside Sarah. "Is this going to be a sprint?" he asked with a chuckle.

"Pretty much. I'm on a schedule. What do you have?"

"Copper theft."

Sarah shook her head. "Another one? That's the third one this year. Where?"

"That melt-blown factory that closed last year."

Sarah stopped. "Enviro Solutions. Didn't someone strip that one a few months ago?"

Keith replied, "Yeah. Same one. About six months ago. They just completely rewired it to prep it for sale. Should have had a guard. Didn't think they would get hit twice."

Sarah continued down the stairs and Keith stayed apace. "Sounds like they thought wrong. What do you have? I hoped the thieves you arrested would deter anyone else."

"Copper is valuable. And criminals are stupid. I have a lot … but I'm not sure I have anything. I gathered everything I could find at the scene. It's a big building and they got nearly everything copper, including some plumbing that was easy to reach."

"Really?" Sarah asked incredulously. "How long were they in there?"

"Over a weekend, probably Friday night and Saturday night. They took a lot. Too much exposure to do it during daylight. They knew where everything was."

Sarah pushed the exit door open and left the building. "Do you know which weekend?"

"Could have been either of the last two. The realtor was in there with a client two weeks ago. He brought the client in for a second tour this morning and couldn't get the lights to come on."

"Sounds interesting. What do you need from me?" Sarah suspected Keith needed a sounding board. Boston wasn't amenable to being a mentor for the man who was once a public relations police officer for disgraced Mayor Jordon Kamen. Some people don't forget the past easily.

"I've surveyed the scene. I'm going to gather every scrap of evidence I can find. I will need a place to analyze it and Boston appears to have a big case going in the Sit Room." Keith looked at Sarah expectantly as Sarah paused while opening her car door.

"Talk to Liz. See if she can make the secondary conference room available for a few weeks. If not, maybe there's something in the jail."

Keith grinned. "I suppose that would be secure for my evidence. Okay, thanks. I'll talk to Liz. Good luck with whatever you're chasing, Chief."

Sarah got in the driver's seat and watched Keith reenter the police station. She usually had an answer to personnel issues, but the unease between Boston and Keith defied reason. She knew Boston could have rejected Keith as his Junior Detective, but he felt obligated to give Keith a chance. However, he didn't feel obligated to recommend Keith's promotion.

Sarah and Keith had history. Boston generally knew about it. Everyone did. When Senior Detective Carl Franken was out on medical leave prior to his death, Officer Keith Locke was assigned to Detective James to assist with the case load. He proved to be a good investigator. The two had a personal relationship prior to that assignment. The relationship ended before Sarah ascended to become Police Chief. Keith became enamored with a consultant, Zoey Kopechne, hired by former Mayor Kamen. Zoey's loyalty to Mayor Kamen put her at odds with the entire Devaney Police Department. Zoey's youthful sensuality and Keith's lust brought them together even within the war zone between the Police Department and City Hall.

Sarah drove with lights to the Porter Road accident scene. Lights could be explained for that trip.

Sergeant Maria Honeycutt was the scene commander, even though her superior, Lieutenant McCuskey was on scene. It was difficult to find parking on the narrow, shoulder-less road, but Sergeant Honeycutt managed to direct Sarah to a safe spot. Her usually cheerful face was grim. She barely managed a weak, deferential smile. "Chief, it's not good."

"How bad is it, Maria?"

"One decapitation. Barely old enough to drive. Two dead. Three injured. All kids. The ambulance left with one."

A helicopter's rotors filled the air with a heavy staccato beat. The sound changed pitch as the rotor's speed increased. Sarah saw dust and debris fly into the air as the helicopter gained altitude. "Life flight?" she asked though it didn't require verbalization. Sometimes words were used to maintain a connection with another human being. She saw Taylor holding tightly to her hat and hair in the rotor wash. The leader of the Traffic Division always wore her uniform.

"Yes. Two." Maria pointed toward the sky. "The second one is inbound. Wichita."

Sarah saw the second helicopter approach as soon as the first one left. The second helicopter settled in the same spot vacated by the first. Sarah approached cautiously, careful not to venture into the full wash of the blades. She wasn't afraid to get dirty doing a job, but her job required that she not get dirty today. She watched as four first responders scrambled to carry a victim on a backboard to the helicopter as soon as the onboard medical personnel opened the bay doors. She observed the accident scene from afar. She saw the Coroner's van. Henry Mason was standing near a car that was crushed from its impact with a steel guard rail and a large tree. The top of the car was completely gone, cut away by the firefighters who were working to extricating someone from the crumbled vehicle.

An entire section of steel guard rail was wrapped around the front of the car, crushed between what was once the front end and the tree that stopped the car. Some smoke drifted from the wreckage, but there was no longer a fire danger. The first responders made sure of that. Sarah watched the helicopter rise above power line height before it bolted away toward Wichita. As the noise abated, she called out to Lieutenant McCuskey. "Taylor."

Taylor reacted to the call and walked to Sarah. "Chief."

"Life flight. Must be bad," Sarah said grimly.

"Very. I'm not sure either will make it." Angrily, Taylor glared in the direction of the wreck. "I don't know how fast they were going, but the car completely obliterated the guard rail system. It was going so fast that it negated the energy reduction capabilities of the rail." She pointed to the remnants of the guardrail still attached to the wood posts that secured it in place three feet from the pavement. "That section apparently caught one of the backseat passengers. Decapitated her." She shuddered and pointed toward a broad ditch. "The head was found in the ditch."

"What time did this happen?"

"We can't say for sure. The 9-1-1 call came in about forty-five minutes ago. First responders said several people were on the scene, blocking access, pretending to help with their cell phone cameras."

Sarah surveyed the scene from the road. "The car is barely visible from the road, especially if drivers are preoccupied with negotiating the curve."

Lieutenant McCuskey looked toward the crash. "Just the guardrail damage, but you're right. If drivers are paying attention to the road, they might not notice the car. Plus, they were looking into the morning sun."

"You said you had identification?" Sarah asked.

"Preliminary. Devaney high school girls. Not sure why they were driving in that direction. It's not toward school. Unless this happened earlier than we think, they were late anyway."

Sarah nodded toward the wreck. "What's going on now?" A wrecker was sitting on the roadway, making no obvious move to tow the car from its resting place at the edge of the dry creek bed, twenty yards from the roadway.

"They're cutting the dead from the wreckage. They focused on the survivors first."

"Understood. The driver?"

"Dead … thankfully. I wouldn't want to live if I was the cause of something like that."

Sarah nodded understandingly. "I see Channel 6's newshound is here."

Taylor grimaced. "The area is secured. Honeycutt won't let anyone in. Not until we clear the scene. We don't want any gory pictures out there."

They watched as Sergeant Honeycutt forcefully strode to police tape across the highway where an officer was confronting the TV reporter who was at the crime scene on the walking trail. They couldn't hear but Maria's body language made it obvious that Tammy Nunn wasn't wanting to be compliant.

"I imagine those cell phones have already posted pictures." Sarah sighed. "I suppose this is where my job starts. What do you think they need to know at this moment."

Taylor snorted. "They can wait until the investigation is completed as far as I'm concerned."

"If only. They will make up something if they don't hear anything." Sarah looked toward the car. It was reasonable obscured from where the cordon tape was set. "I'll disallow filming the wreck scene. Someone might identify the vehicle. We can't have that, not until notification of next of kin. I assume you're taking the lead on that?"

"Yes. The responding officers found driver's licenses and student ID cards scattered inside the car. That's how we know they are Devaney students."

Sarah walked to the tape barricade. Tammy Nunn motioned for her camera crew to film the Police Chief's approach. Sergeant Honeycutt glared at the reporter and positioned her body in front of the camera lens, much to Tammy's chagrin.

Other news reporters were gathered near the young TV reporter. Sarah knew most of them on a first name basis. Most were respectful and considerate of the situation when they came for the news. The experienced reporters knew victim privacy was paramount. Reporting a victim's name before the family was notified was a Cardinal Sin to professional reporters. She nodded for Sergeant Honeycutt to allow the camera to focus on her. Her eyes met those of veteran newspaper reporter, Bernie Stone. He would be her focal point so she could avoid Tammy's insistent aggressiveness.

"Ladies and gentlemen, I'm sure you are anxious to know details, but I have very little to share at this time. First responders are currently engaged in rescue operations, so very little is known. A single car accident has left several people injured. Some of those were taken by helicopter to Wichita trauma centers. There is nothing more I can tell you at this time." Sarah gently nodded to recognize Bernie.

Before Bernie could verbalize his question, Tammy pushed forward and shouted, "Chief, we heard there were deaths. Can you confirm?"

"I recognized Bernie," Sarah responded with a scowl without looking at Tammy. "Bernie, do you have a question?"

"Thank you, Chief James." Bernie cast a withering glance toward the novice reporter as he spoke. "We all recognize that this accident is still in the stages of being cleared and there is very little you can confirm, so we won't plague you with unanswerable questions at this time. We do see the Coroner's van. Does that mean there are fatalities?"

"There is at least one fatality. All those details will be made available as soon as we know them definitively. Privacy and confidentiality dictates we move slowly dispensing information. Even for the injured, notification of next of kin is paramount. They deserve to know before anyone else. Our concern is to make sure all of those in need of medical attention receive it in a timely manner." Sarah looked into Tammy's eyes. "No camera shots of the scene, especially not the vehicle."

Bernie responded, "That makes perfect sense. If someone recognizes the vehicle, rumors will start."

Sarah answered a few inconsequential questions before closing the press briefing. She walked toward the scene and arrived in time to see the firefighters and paramedics extricate the driver's body behind a tarp held to block the view from onlookers. A female with short hair dyed purple with black streaks. Young. The Coroner provided a body bag for the young woman. He and three others carried the body bag to his van. Sarah opened the door for them.

Henry Mason acknowledged Sarah's presence with a slight nod. He climbed into the back of the van to guide the body bag alongside another filled body bag. "Chief. It's been a busy day," he said after the body was secured.

"It has. I hate cars. They kill and cripple more people than guns."

"That's certainly true in our part of the world." The Coroner closed the back door. "I was going to call Boston with COD for our John Doe. I'll tell you so you can pass it on. Bullet to the head. It was through and through. No slug remnants. I suppose it's somewhere near the body, but that's for Boston to determine. I hope he finds all the pieces of the face."

"Thanks. I'll tell him. Have you found anything else? Was there evidence of scavengers?"

Henry glanced toward his van. "I didn't see scavenger evidence. There are too many other things happening to find anything else. Plus … I also have a business to run. I have a funeral this afternoon. The family expects the funeral director to be on hand," he added sarcastically.

"Understood. Whatever you can find before the body goes to the State ME will be appreciated. We appreciate everything you do."

"Thanks." The Coroner got in his van and slowly drove toward the tape that would be moved to allow his exit.

Corporal Canton was measuring and photographing the area, making copious notes regarding the impact point at the missing guardrail and the plowed trail to where the car was stopped by a tree. Sarah gravitated toward Lieutenant McCuskey who was watching as Sergeant Honeycutt guided the wrecker into position. The car was wrapped in a large tarp. The news cameras and the onlookers' cell phones wouldn't capture any more unwanted images.

"I need to leave for a meeting. Is there anything you need from me before I go?" Sarah asked Taylor.

Taylor shook her head, which caused her bottle-blonde hair to bounce predictably. "I think I'm good … as good as I can be with dead children."

Sarah patted Taylor's forearm. "There's so much we don't know about young minds. Why they do what they do."

"I have to wonder why they were driving this time of day rather than being in school."

"Playing hooky. It happens. Focus on finding the answers to the questions rather than letting the tragedy consume you," Sarah offered solemnly.

"Tragedy is an understatement. Five mothers and fathers are going to hear the worst words they will ever hear today." The experienced police lieutenant looked away and blinked rapidly.

"I'll be a phone call away, Taylor. Call me … anytime."

Taylor smiled through her pain and nodded. "Sadly, this is not the first time we've gone through this. It's just the first time with this many families about to have their lives ruined. I'll be fine. I've already contacted the Chaplain."

A local minister accepted the duties of Department Chaplain with minimal compensation. She ministered to officers with emotional crises and helped notify families in times of crisis. She would earn her stipend today.

Sarah knew the number of casualties would require additional clergy to help with notifications. The Chaplain would arrange that detail. She walked to her car. Maria guided her from her parking spot onto the highway. Traffic would be held off that section of Porter Road for another hour, or until Corporal Canton finished his measurements. He wouldn't be measuring much in the way of skid marks on the pavement. Sarah didn't see any leading toward the crash site.

As she drove to her meeting with the Chamber President, Sarah called Boston and told him what the Coroner said.

Boston's weary voice dolefully said, "I'll see if Taylor has any officers available to scour the brush. Bohannan told me he thinks he's found all there is to find. A few more bloodied leaves and two more small bits of the face. One tooth. Not enough bits to account for the missing part of the face."

"Okay. Taylor may be tied up for a while. We just lost some kids in a TA."

Boston's voice tightened. "If it's not drugs, it's cars. Damn! Okay,

I'll not push her. I've still got Bohannan and the two units blocking the trailheads. I don't need the trail blocked. I suppose Corporal Canton won't be available to check the tire marks on the trail." The last comment was questioning.

"Probably not. Have them keep the tape at the trailheads. At least slow the usage until Corporal Canton can look at it. Oh, by the way, I left the evidence bags I was going to take to Alicia with Liz."

"Yeah. She told me she took them to the lab."

Sarah ended the call and called Lab Tech Alicia. "Hello, Alicia. I know you're loaded, but I wanted to tell you that the Coroner will be sending the shooting victim's clothing to you. I don't know if you'll find anything useful, but if anyone can, it will be you."

"Hi, Chief. I was aware. Boston has brought me plenty. And Liz. I'm running DNA on the fleshy bits and on the blood. I can compare them to the victim's DNA when I get the blood and tissue from the Coroner." Alicia paused, "Taylor called and said the Coroner would have TA tox-samples too."

"Unfortunately. It's a busy Monday. I'll stop by and see how you're doing later this afternoon. I'm on my way to a meeting." There was no reason to share that with the Lab Technician, but it seemed to be an acceptable segue into ending the call.

# CHAPTER 8

## Noon Monday

The parking lot of Jeannie's Café was nearly full. With bare minutes to spare, Sarah parked her car and entered the upscale restaurant popular among the movers and shakers of Devaney. She wasn't a fan. The best part about their fare was that the portions were small. Ideally proportioned if the avant-garde culinary offerings weren't exactly to her liking.

Byron Castleman was waiting to be seated. His anxious face melted into a smile as soon as Sarah arrived. "Good morning, Chief. How are you today?"

Sarah became acquainted with Dr. Byron Castleman, a local ophthalmologist, through his wife, Sharon Castleman. Sharon was Vice President of Operations for a tire manufacturing company with a large factory in Devaney. She also served as President of the Chamber of Commerce's Large Business Council. The role was rotated among the major industry leaders but because of her organizational skills, the role fell to her every couple of years. She was that good. Sharon domiciled in the local facility because she preferred being close to the workforce rather than to the corporate gamesmanship. Byron and Sharon created a stir in the elite social circles when they moved to Devaney years earlier. Sharon is black and Byron is white. "Good morning, Doctor Castleman. I am doing well. How are you?"

"Hungry. Sharon said the chef has a new menu item. Thin sliced tofu as an open-faced sandwich smothered in a tarragon sauce."

Sarah barely disguised her reaction. "That sounds interesting."

A smiling hostess dressed in lavender led the pair to a table that was too small for a large meal. She handed each a single page menu and told them their server would be Jill. Sarah tried to read the menu before Jill arrived to take their orders. After a moment, and sensing impatience, Sarah complied with Byron's suggestion to try the tarragon enhanced tofu sandwich.

While they waited, Byron smiled caringly as he adjusted his glasses. "I think you and I need to meet in my office."

Sarah's topaz eyes flashed displeasure but she quickly regained her composure. She knew what the ophthalmologist was implying. "My eyes are just tired. It's been a tough day." She changed the subject with the only question that came to mind. "How is Chamber business?"

Byron raised his eyebrows and accepted the defensive shift as a required segue. "We have a big event planned. It will be a family theme more than just a business expo."

Sarah sipped her oddly flavored tea. "That sounds interesting. What is the venue?"

"Centennial Park," Byron replied effusively. "We've booked a small carnival with rides for the kids. Small rides. Nothing dangerous."

Sarah was puzzled. The Chamber had never done family events before, especially none with a carnival. She was surprised she hadn't heard anything about it before that moment. "Sounds like traffic could be an issue. There's not a lot of parking at the park. What are your dates?"

"It won't be until next May. Plenty of time to plan. I wanted to get ahead of the details. We're thinking they could park at the high school, and we could bus people to the park."

Sarah was relieved ... for the moment. "That's good. Are you not doing your usual fall event?"

"Oh, that? Sure, but it shouldn't be an issue. Past Presidents have laid the groundwork for that. It'll be at the bank's convention center like before. I want to do something different. Something to show the community that the Chamber is not just about staid businessmen and white collars. Families. That's what I want people to think when they think Devaney Chamber of Commerce."

Sarah couldn't help but smile. The Castleman family recently welcomed their second grandchild. Byron, if not also Sharon, became more focused on family issues as their family grew. "I think that's a wonderful idea." Even as she replied, Sarah couldn't help but think of the five families whose lives were changing on that day. "I will begin planning for the traffic. Are you using school buses?"

"Yes. I've talked to the district. We are making arrangements for that. Unless something unexpected happens, it should be an easy process. The high school stadium parking is designed to accommodate heavy traffic. It'll be great. Oh, here's our food. I can't wait."

Sarah wasn't sure if Byron was referencing the event or the open-faced sandwich. The food had eye appeal and an appetizing aroma. She resolved to eat it without reservations. Other than a glass of Merlot and a delivery pizza now and then, she maintained a healthy diet. Tofu was reputed to be healthy.

The first bite was different but not off-putting. The cauliflower bread was not unfamiliar to her palate. The small portion was a blessing.

Byron became serious. "I heard that you found a body on one of the trails this morning and that foul play is suspected. The first thing that comes to mind is drugs. As Chamber President and a family man, anything that could impact the business climate or family safety merits questioning and planning. Are we facing a new wave of drug dealing?"

Sarah expected questions about the body. "Byron, I wish I had more to tell you. We don't have enough information to determine the cause. Henry is tied up now with the victims of a traffic accident." She knew Byron was probably aware of the car wreck as well. The President of the Chamber of Commerce was obligated to stay in the know about everything.

Byron contemplated Sarah's response while he chewed a bite of his meal. "I understand. Nothing official yet, but I also heard we had an overdose last night. We almost lost Bob and Anna Pierce's daughter, Sasha. Drugs can tear families apart and they aren't good for business. Is there something we need to prepare to face? I'm a planner."

Sarah was amazed at how expertly Byron juxtaposed family and business. He and Sharon were more alike than she had imagined, able to straddle the demarcation between the two. "We don't think there's a pattern of drug use beyond the normal experimentation kids seem to do.

Our sources tell us there isn't a permanent dealer presence in Devaney. That said, we will be looking for any connections to the body we discovered." She looked Byron firmly in the eyes. "I'm a planner too. I don't like surprises."

Sarah's cell phone vibrated against her left breast. "Excuse me. I need to see what this is." She looked at her phone. A Slack message from Liz. Lieutenant McCuskey's people were definitely doing their jobs well. Based upon the IDs found scattered in the car, they were enroute to notify parents. The list of names was included in the message she received. Only the driver's identity was confirmed. They still weren't positive which survivor went to which hospital. Her stomach turned, not from the tofu; rather, from compassion for the families. They would hear the worst news of their lives with a huge dose of uncertainty. She returned to her sandwich.

Byron's phone buzzed. Without apology, he checked it. His eyes widened. He carefully read the message he received. He looked up at Sarah, his eyes wide. "A wreck? Were you aware of a car wreck with a group of high school girls?"

"Yes. I left the scene to meet you here." She didn't volunteer anything more than that.

"My secretary just sent me a text. Two dead. Tamara Yates was a close friend of Sasha Pierce."

Tamara Yates was the driver of the car. Sarah got that information at the scene. Tamara's driver's license helped identify her, though confirmation only came after some investigation by Taylor's people and the Coroner. The IDs of the passengers were shuffled in the wreck. Attaching them to a specific person was not as easy. Sarah only had those names on the message list. She sternly asked, "How did your secretary get the names? We aren't releasing them until the next of kin is notified. Every one of them." She almost glared at Chamber of Commerce President. If someone in her department leaked the information early, she wanted to know who it was.

"Tamara Yates is my secretary's niece. Her sister's oldest girl," Byron answered sharply. "There's no leak if that's your concern. Her sister called her. But you know the names will get out soon enough."

Sarah felt guilty relief. "I suppose you're right. As long as it's after the parents are notified." She realized Byron was completely distracted from the previous conversations. "Do you need to go? This has to be traumatic for your secretary and the other Chamber employees."

Byron looked anxiously around the café. A planner struggles with anything that doesn't fit the plan. "I suppose it is, though I think Tamara was destined to cause problems for her family."

"How so?"

"Mr. Yates is manager of North Park Mall. Mrs. Yates is a real estate broker. They're both Chamber members. They are workaholics. That means family life is second." Byron looked down sorrowfully for a moment. "I can identify with that to some extent. They struggle with Tamara's rebellious nature. My secretary has mentioned that her niece occasionally experimented with drugs."

Sarah shook her head. "That's tough. How bad was it?"

"I'm not sure. I do know Mr. and Mrs. Yates were concerned about how their daughter's actions would impact on the family's reputation. They worried they might be perceived as failed parents. Their jobs are in the public eye. They were especially concerned that Tamara's behaviors might influence their younger daughter who is a straight A student."

"This definitely won't help the sister."

"Why do you say that?" Byron asked.

"I've seen too many instances where the death of a child creates untenable strains on the family unit, especially one with preexisting strain. The surviving children suffer the most, generally through neglect or overindulgence."

Byron nodded. "I suppose you're right. My secretary used to share her sister's concerns … and anger … regarding Tamara's behavior. Now they will have to remember all the anger and try to reconcile those emotions with the loss of a child."

Sarah listened to Byron as she slowly ate her tofu sandwich. She was not a fan of the tarragon sauce, but it was a new flavor profile to experience. More important, the portion was small.

# CHAPTER 9

## 1:00 P.M. Monday

Sarah called Mayor Keck while enroute to the police station. "Bill, did you have any questions about my budget proposal?" Her morning began smoothly with the budget as her primary focus. She felt as if the discovered body was distracting her from her duties. A misplaced feeling. Her duties were encapsulated in the police department's motto "*To Protect and Serve.*" Budgets were a small component of her service to the citizens of Devaney.

The Mayor replied, "Nothing that will keep me from bringing it before the Council. It looks like a budget I would have prepared." He knew Liz played a part in its preparation. "Besides, from what I hear, you've got your hands full. Do you know the identities of the girls in the wreck?"

"We know names, but we can only positively identify the driver. Her license was in her shorts pocket. The others' IDs were in purses that were scattered by the impact. It is difficult to determine which goes with which girl because the survivors were rushed to trauma centers. The paramedics were focused on saving their lives, not establishing identities. The Coroner took the IDs so he can determine the ID of the other dead girl. Lieutenant McCuskey is using what we have to contact who we believe are the parents. Two girls were aired to Wichita. We don't know which."

"I hated wrecks like that. It's difficult enough to deal with parents and family but even worse when they have to confirm identity in the morgue or the hospital. Stay strong. I'm here if you need a shoulder or an ear." The Mayor paused before adding, "Or a shield."

"Thank you, Mayor. I can send you the names we believe are attached to the victims."

"That would be good ... but it is an ongoing investigation. You don't have to do that."

"I'm not worried about you using the information politically or releasing it early. Maybe if you know the names, you can be ready for the official release. In the meantime, I need to follow-up with the Coroner, Boston, Taylor, and Alicia. Plus, Keith's working another copper theft at the old Enviro Solutions factory."

"Again? You'd think those folks would hire a guard or a security service."

"One would think that. Welcome to Monday." Sarah ended the call as she parked her car in front of Mason's Mortuary and Funeral Home. Talking to the Coroner would be more effective face-to-face, largely because he would be busy and would let his wife take any phone calls. He likely wouldn't stop what he was doing even for the Police Chief. He would let her watch ... or look away ... as they talked.

A doorbell sounded when Sarah opened the door and entered. The lobby was decorated with live flowers rather than the normal fake ones. Soothing music played through unseen speakers. A young man in a dark suit was carefully arranging a registry book on a small podium near the entrance to the chapel. Sarah forgot that Henry had a funeral scheduled for 2:00. Almost instantly, Ellen Mason appeared from an office barely visible from the lobby. Her somber face quickly morphed into a smile when she recognized Sarah.

"Good afternoon, Sarah." Henry Mason's wife and business partner dabbed at the corners of her mouth with a paper napkin. Apparently, she had been eating a late lunch or a snack. "I suppose you are here to see Henry."

"Good afternoon, Ellen. Sad to say, you are correct. I figured it would be easier for him if I came in person rather than try to call him. I know he is busy."

"Yes. We have a funeral at 2:00. He will be leaving with the family limousine shortly. He's concerned that the families of the two deceased girls will be brought to the mortuary to confirm their identities during the funeral. He's dressing now. I will tell him you are here." Ellen turned and disappeared down a dim hallway.

Sarah was disappointed with herself for forgetting about Henry's funeral schedule. "As far as I know, there is no plan to bring the families for ID. We will definitely let you know and clear it with Henry." She wasn't sure if Ellen heard what she said, the woman seemed intent on finding her husband. She smiled at the young man and an older man who were both part of the funeral home staff. Both men softly exchanged greetings with her as they made last minute adjustments to put things in order for the funeral. She couldn't see into the chapel, but she knew the casket and flowers were ready for the service.

After a few minutes, the Coroner in his real-life job as Funeral Director appeared. He was carrying a cardboard box and scowling. "I didn't expect you to be here until after the funeral."

Sarah responded rapidly to Henry's agitation. "I'm sorry. I was in the neighborhood. I forgot about the funeral. I just told Ellen that we will forewarn you if the parents are brought to assure identification. No surprises. I also wanted to make sure you drew blood from the wreck victims."

Henry Mason's face reddened angrily. "I know how to do my job." He pushed the box toward Sarah. "Here are the clothes from our John Doe. Blood samples from the accident decedents are also in the box." He regained his composure. "And before you ask, I contacted both hospitals and requested blood samples from the injured. I don't know if Wichita will comply. That'll be between you and them. I also put all the IDs in the box. The second decedent is Yvonne Timmons."

Sarah replied apologetically, "Thank you. I was afraid you might have been overwhelmed considering how many cases you have."

Henry made a humph noise. "I've been at this long enough to know how to do the job. John Doe will be sent to the State ME in the morning. That's the best I could do under the circumstance."

"I understand. I'll call Doctor Kemper at the ME's office. See if she can expedite for us. She's done it for me before."

"That was before she became the Medical Examiner, but you can hope," Henry replied gruffly. "By the way, I noticed some pale colored soil and bits of white gravel on the shirt and around the exit wound."

"White gravel? How would white gravel get there? Was the body moved?"

"I don't know. If it was, he wasn't dead long enough for lividity to tell us for sure ... or he was placed exactly as he was when he was killed. I'm just telling you what I found. Maybe there was some gravel beneath the leaves. Left over from when they were building the base for the trail. Ask Boston. Maybe he can dig around. I put what I found in an evidence bag for Alicia."

Sarah instinctively glanced at the box she held when Henry talked about its contents. "Thank you. I'll tell Boston. I'm sorry I interrupted you."

Ellen, who was standing nearby, replied dismissively, "He has plenty of time. He always allows more time than necessary in case something unexpected happens. Families don't always respond well at funerals. They cause most of our schedule issues. Delays are inevitable. It's good to see you, Sarah. Come see us when it's not business." She touched Sarah's forearm, a substitute for a handshake that Sarah couldn't do with the box in her grasp.

Sarah smiled appreciatively. "It's good to see you too, Ellen." She suspected the wife of the mortician had a small circle of friends, a product of his profession and hers. "Maybe we can go out for dinner sometime." She glanced at Henry and smiled.

Henry nodded. "We'll see. I need to check on the arrangements before I go get the family." He squinted his eyes and shook his head. "I also expect to hear from the girls' parents very soon despite your best planning. Parents usually want to see the bodies, to make sure it really is their child. Denial is the first step." Henry Mason faced a lot of misery on a daily basis. "The Timmons child's remains are an issue. There are things a parent doesn't need to see."

Sarah wished she didn't always feel creeped-out by the visits to the mortuary, but it was a fact of life. Even as a police officer, she couldn't shake the feelings that arose when she entered the funeral home. The aura of death is cold.

At the police station, Sarah went straight to the lab with the box from the Coroner. Alicia was busy with various analyses. The lab was always busy for the Lab Technician. Other municipalities, and even the County, relied upon Alicia for tests results when they needed them quicker than the State Forensics Lab could provide.

"Hello, Chief," Alicia said cheerily when she noticed Sarah. "What do you have for me?" she asked as she reached for the box Sarah held.

"Evidence from the Coroner. I thought I'd save some time by picking it up on my way back from lunch."

"Lunch? Where did you go?"

"Jeannie's Café."

"I've heard about it. Is it any good?"

"Too pricey for me. And too avant-garde for my taste."

"I heard it was good."

"If you like tofu." Sarah made a face to emphasize her thoughts on the subject. She didn't eat a lot of meat, but when she did, she wanted it to be real. "The blood samples from the two TA fatalities are in the box. We need tox screens as quickly as possible. Apparently, the driver and another girl who ODed last night are friends. The driver has a history of drug use."

"Wow!" Alicia exclaimed. "Small world. I'll do them right away." She motioned around the lab. "I'm doing DNA on the samples Liz brought to me earlier. I should know something by tomorrow afternoon."

"Good. Has Boston brought anything more?"

Alicia rolled her eyes. "The two buckets earlier from where the body was found. He then brought a bucket with several sample bags. He said they were gathered by patrol officers. They contain some bloodied leaves and a couple with flesh and bone bits."

"Were there any bits of flesh from the exit wound in the first two buckets?"

"I found one small piece. About twice the size of the samples Liz brought me. Not very big. What else do you have in the box?"

"I'm not sure. Henry had a funeral scheduled at 2:00, so I was in and out. A bag with the clothes from our John Doe. He said he found some gravel in the shirt and in the wound. He put those in a separate bag. Was there any white gravel in Boston's buckets?"

"There was some gravel, but I really haven't studied the composition. I was sorting for organics ..." Alicia paused, "and prepping DNA tests. I'll compare the samples."

"That sounds good. Thank you, Alicia."

Alicia smiled. "Do you want me to tell you what I find?"

"I wish I could say yes, but Boston is the lead detective. He needs to know first."

"Then you. I got it."

Liz heard Sarah talking with other employees when she entered the office area from the jail stairs. "Chief, the Mayor called to set up a lunch meeting tomorrow. I told him your schedule was clear, but I wanted to check with you first."

"Hmm? I was on the phone with him earlier. Did he say what it was about? Budget?"

"He did say a couple of the Council members would join you. He wants to talk about citizen complaints regarding the trail system."

Sarah shook her head. "That doesn't surprise me. I heard a little of that at the scene this morning. What do I have this afternoon?"

"Just several requisitions to review and sign. Taylor has some employee reviews ready for you to see before she sits with them. No meetings." Liz walked with Sarah to her office and laid a stack of folders on Sarah's desk. Liz always put documents for each topic in a separate folder. That made it easier to focus on one topic at a time … and it helped avoid mixing pages. "These are the requisitions."

"Anything pressing?" Sarah asked as she sat in her comfortable desk chair.

"Gasoline."

"Of course, gasoline. It's killing our budget." Sarah opened the folders one at a time. She only signed to approve high-cost requisitions, unbudgeted items, and budget line items that were over budget. Any budgeted item under one thousand dollars was approved and signed by the department head. She merely initialed it to prove she reviewed the requisition. Liz would forward all of them to the city's purchasing department for execution after they were signed or initialed.

"Back to the reason for the Mayor's lunch meeting, have we received any complaint calls about the trails this morning?"

"A few." Liz presented another folder. "I compiled a recap for your review. I also put a raw copy of each complaint in the folder if you want to read them individually. Most are polite. A couple are habitual complainers without social skills. You'll recognize the names." She smiled.

Sarah quickly read each complaint. There were only six. She pursed her lips as she read and thought about each one. She generally agreed with the concerns. She smiled at the complaint from one man who was a perennial complainer about government spending. *"Tear the damn trails up and save taxpayer money!"* He made his opinion known on a variety of subjects on a regular basis and he was never anonymous. "I suppose I need to think about what we should do regarding safety on the trails. Is Lieutenant Glasgow in the building?"

"I can check. Do you want to see him?"

"I do. Also," Sarah pulled a note from her pocket and glanced at it before handing it to Liz, "Do you mind reaching out to Mrs. Campbell? See if she is available for a visit this afternoon. The sooner the better."

"I don't mind," Liz replied bemusedly. Her job was to make the Police Chief's job easier. Sarah generally phrased commands as questions.

"Thank you, Liz. I'm going to check with Boston while you locate Glasgow." Sarah rose and walked to the bullpen. She saw Lieutenant McCuskey bent over her desk. "Hi, Taylor. How is the TA investigation going?"

"Corporal Canton has all the measurements. He's not through with the calculations, but he estimates the car was traveling nearly one-hundred miles per hour when it hit the guard rail. He said he saw no evidence of braking. The car is in impound. He wants to see if there was a mechanical brake failure. He can't estimate the time of the accident."

"Maybe the Coroner can give a TOD … if it's not too late. The other option is to pull the EDR. That could answer a lot of questions."

"He's contacted that insurance investigator you know to download the data from the recorder. That will give us more detail than his measurements can provide."

"Good. Maybe we need to get our own software system to download EDR data."

Taylor smiled, "You're the boss. I think Brandon would go for that. He's good at accident reconstruction. Old school, but I think he trusts the EDR data enough to accept that as his source. The biggest issue is whether the vehicles involved support EDR."

Sarah nodded understandingly. "I suppose that is the real issue. We're lucky to have someone as proficient at accident reconstruction as Brandon Canton is. It's not too late to put that in our budget. Work up something and send it to me."

Taylor made a notation on her desk calendar. "I will do that by tomorrow."

"I don't know how important this is, but I heard that a couple of the girls in the car, in particular, the driver, were good friends with Sasha Pierce, the girl who ODed last night. Alicia is doing tox-screens on the two deceased. We're trying to get samples from the hospitals where the injured girls were sent."

"That's interesting. Do you think it's relative to the crash?"

"Never ignore a clue. It may be the single best clue that brings everything together. Have you seen Boston?"

"He came through right after lunch. He told me he will need Baldor, Bohannan, and Banks for the rest of the day. He didn't seem too happy about what he was finding … or not finding. He said they found a few things for Alicia. I think he needs some rest. He looked haggard."

"I suppose I'll call him. I wanted to talk face-to-face, but if he's busy …" Sarah let her comment fade. She stepped into the Situation Room. Boston hadn't updated his corkboard and he had written nothing on the whiteboard to establish a timeline. Sarah liked timelines, but she wasn't the detective in charge. She sat in a chair and called his cell phone.

"Hello, Boss," Boston snapped in answer to his phone, obviously bothered by it. "Checking in on me?"

"Updating you. The Coroner sent our John Doe's clothes to Alicia. He mentioned that he found white gravel in the wound and white dirt on the shirt. Are you seeing any white gravel? Maybe where the trail construction crew piled base gravel."

Boston snorted. "White gravel? I've been focusing on blood and lead bullet fragments. Something isn't right. I've got three uniforms crawling through brush and thorns on their hands and knees looking for bloody leaves, pieces of meat, and a bullet that isn't anywhere. We've studied every tree branch and leaf in the area trying to find where the bullet went after it tore the victim's face off."

Sarah thought about Boston's words. She could sense his frustration.

Sensing his emotional state didn't require a detective. He seldom spoke in complete sentences, let alone full paragraphs. He was venting. "You still haven't found evidence of pooled blood?"

"No. I even took your idea that the killer moved the body to get out of the woods. We haven't left a single dead leaf unturned. We've completely exposed the ground. No blood saturation. All we found was under his head and the few spots of blood that we found along the original path. And not enough flesh and bone to amount to anything. There should be splattered blood and flesh somewhere in the area. Nothing."

"Maybe you need to call it a day. Get some rest and hit it fresh tomorrow." Sarah knew Boston would be relentless in his pursuit, to the detriment of his health.

Boston snarled, "I can't stop. We've got several trash bags of leaves to sort through. And curious rubberneckers will be in here the minute we leave. Morbid. No consideration for the victim."

"Is the trail still cordoned?"

"No," Boston replied dejectedly. "No need. We're almost through here."

"I hate to ask, but have you had time to look at the black marks on the edges of the concrete?"

"Corporal Baldor spent some time training with Corporal Canton. She apparently knows enough to form some ideas. She thinks there were two separate vehicles that made the marks. One of them had a low front tire on the driver's side and made most of the marks on that side of the trail."

"Really? Two? What made her think it was two?"

"She said the smashed grass was different where the tires were completely off the trail. One tire was wider. The tire with the low pressure made a heavier black mark when it dropped off and climbed back on the trail."

"I wonder if the Parks Department can tell us if they had a vehicle in there with a low tire."

"I can ask … when I get time." Boston was exasperated.

"I can do it, if you want me to," Sarah offered.

"Sure. It's your idea." Boston was curt. He was ready to hang up the phone.

"Okay. I'll let you know what I learn. Boston," Sarah waited for a response.

"Yeah?"

"Get some rest. Our John Doe isn't going anywhere."

"But his killer is." Boston ended the call.

Sarah checked her phone contacts. She called Delbert Shipley, head of the city Department of Parks and Recreation. As soon as he answered, she spoke, "Delbert, this is Chief James. I have a situation that posed a question only you can answer."

"Hi, Chief. Sounds like you're putting me on the spot." Delbert chuckled, then turned serious. "Does it have to do with the body you found near the Overton Acres trail section?"

"It does. I found some evidence of a vehicle driving on the trail. It appears the driver was not doing a very good job of controlling it. Is that a problem around the trail system?"

"Occasionally we see where someone has driven on the trail at night. Usually, it's kids who think it's cute to leave black marks squalling their tires. Or cut donuts at the trailheads. What are you seeing?"

"No intentional tire marks. Not like that. It looks like they couldn't keep the vehicle, possibly two vehicles, on the trail very well. Several areas where it appears the tires slipped off the edges and left black rub marks. Smashed the grass where they drove on it until they got back on the concrete. Have you seen that?"

Delbert responded slowly. "I don't remember anything like that recently. We have seen it in the past though. We reckoned it was kids dare-deviling out there. Seeing if they could drive on the trail at night with their lights off so no one would see them."

Sarah thought about the explanation. "I don't recall the police being called." She knew it could have happened when she was still a detective. She wouldn't have heard about it. Lieutenant McCuskey would have handled it.

"We don't report it unless there is damage done. We just add some more signage and place a few barricades to narrow the trailhead entrances."

"I didn't see barricades at the trailheads on Osage Road."

Delbert stammered momentarily, "Ah … ah … that section of trail is new. It's on our work list. I'll move it up on the list."

Sarah chuckled to herself. "That won't be necessary. I was just wondering about the tire marks. You've helped a lot. Thank you, Delbert."

Sarah sat in the Situation Room and thought for a few minutes. She left the room and stopped at Taylor's cubicle. "Taylor, do you have a record of calls about the walking trails?"

"Sure. Do you want a copy?"

"For the last two years, if you don't mind. I'd like to see it tomorrow morning. No hurry."

"Does it have to do with the body?"

"It might, but I'm not sure." Sarah went to her office. She found the State Medical Examiner's phone number and called Stacy Kemper.

"Hello, Doctor Kemper. This is Chief Sarah James, Devaney PD."

"Hi, Chief. It's been a couple of years since we've talked. I understand your Coroner is sending a John Doe this way."

"Fortunately, it has been awhile. I only call when we have a murder we're trying to solve. I should stay in touch more. But we've got a real puzzler on our hands. No ID and, so far, no clues. We know he was shot in the back of the head and left in the woods. We are concerned his killer will be long gone if we don't get something soon."

"Sounds like a drug execution."

"We're not ruling out anything. We don't want to lose this one."

"How about I move it up the list? We have a few mysterious circumstance cases, but we don't have a defined murder."

"That sounds great. It will help us tremendously," Sarah replied enthusiastically.

Stacy chuckled, "Well, it will help if we find anything of value."

"Oh, I don't know if the Coroner mentioned it or not, but we are running the clothes through our local lab. We really do need clues."

"Ah. You took the hard part. I understand. We should have something within a day of arrival. Will that work?"

"Definitely. Thank you." Sarah ended the call after a few minutes of pleasantries when Liz stepped into her office.

"Mrs. Campbell said she will be available around 3:00. I told her that would work for you."

"Thank you, Liz." Sarah glanced at a small clock on the credenza. It was almost 2:30. The afternoon had rushed past. She needed more time to do everything she wanted to do. "I'll head that way."

"Lieutenant Glasgow is here as you requested," Liz said slowly.

"Of course. Send him in." Sarah forced a smile. She felt overwhelmed, but she didn't want to show it.

"You wanted to see me, Chief?" Lieutenant Melvin Glasgow asked expectantly.

"Hello, Melvin. I'm sorry I didn't get with you earlier today. I've been out more than I've been in."

"I understand. There seems to be a lot going on all at once. How can I help?"

"We need to hit the high school and junior high school hard with anti-drug messages. Can you set something up?"

"Of course. Are we seeing a resurgence?"

"I'm not sure, but we had an OD overnight. She survived, but only by good fortune. I don't want to look back six months from now and wish we had done something."

"I understand. I'll call the school Superintendent and set up a schedule. He's been asking for something on vehicle safety for the high schoolers. He must have seen today's wreck coming."

"Teen drivers. It's always coming," Sarah replied in exasperation. "If that's the case, he may try to push his agenda ahead of ours. Push back and offer traffic safety later."

Melvin smiled. "Easy enough to do."

"One more thing. Can you assist Boston with his case? He will need someone to prepare a rendering of the John Doe from the trail. Maybe you can use FACES to sketch a full face and post it to the law enforcement network. Maybe someone knows who he is. Alicia will be checking AFIS with fingerprints and trying to match DNA, but there's no guarantee."

Melvin's face twitched. "Is Boston okay with my interference?"

Sarah understood. "Ask. He has the photos of John Doe with half a face. He's busy with an OD case and with the body. He'll appreciate any help he can get ... if it's offered."

Melvin grinned nervously. "I'll try. I know he still doesn't trust me. Maybe an overture from me will improve that. I'll call him."

"Thank you, Melvin. If you need anything from me, let me know."

After Lieutenant Glasgow left her office, Sarah wrote Boston a quick synopsis of Delbert Shipley's comments regarding black marks on trails. She taped the note to the whiteboard in the Situation Room. Melvin returned and paused to smile at Sarah before she left the room to go to her car. With only a smile from Sarah as she exited, he sorted through Boston's photos. She assumed Glasgow's call to Boston went well enough.

# CHAPTER 10

## 3:00 P.M. Monday

Sarah located the Campbell house on a quiet suburban street. It was a mature neighborhood with two-story homes that were well kept. The homeowners kept their lawns green and trimmed. Sarah reckoned that most of them used a lawn service with plenty of added nutrients and frequent watering. The greens were faded into autumn tones, but the lawns were still neat. The Campbell property was no different. Solid middle class. The house was white with dark gray shingles and charcoal-gray faux shutters. Only the concrete on the driveway and sidewalk revealed the true age of the home. Sarah parked behind a mid-sized SUV.

Sarah imagined Beverly Campbell normally presented better than she did when she invited the Police Chief into her home.

Beverly's face was drawn and pained. "Your secretary said you wanted to talk to me. Is this about Tamara's accident?" Her eyes were red. There was no doubt she was emotionally stressed.

Sarah smiled reassuringly. "No, though I imagine your family is reeling from that loss. I understand Bianca and Tamara were friends."

Beverly's hand shook. "And the other girls, though Tamara was closest. Most of the girls have been friends since kindergarten. Slumber parties and dates." She expectantly looked toward the second-floor stairs.

"Is Bianca home?"

Beverly forced a smile. "Yes. She came home from school when word of the wreck reached the school. She's in her room. Crying." The mother's eyes blinked back tears. "I don't know what to do for her. We were angry with her for making us think something happened to her. She doesn't want to have anything to do with me now because I called the police. I just don't know what to do."

Sarah thought about her plan to have Bianca shadow Micha. Maybe it wasn't such a good idea. Bianca was obviously in a fragile place. Reaching out to her through grief could be difficult. Maybe impossible. "That's the reason I am here. I would like to offer something that might help Bianca cope."

Still standing in the small foyer, Beverly motioned Sarah toward the living room. A small spark of hope flashed in her eyes, begging for more. "Please. Sit. Would you like something to drink?"

"No. I'm fine, thank you." Sarah sat on the sofa. Comfortable and modern. The interior of the house was recently remodeled. Beige and gray. Wood floors. Studio portraits of the family members. Smiling. Happy. Beverly was a very attractive woman in the pictures, smiling and confident.

Beverly smiled hopefully. "You said you have something to help Bianca cope?" Her comment was a question.

"I know the timing of her friends' accident is bad, but the reason I'm here is to offer some help regarding the incident last night."

Beverly averted her teary eyes. "I suppose I overreacted. Made a mountain out of a mole hill."

"No. No you didn't. A good parent is concerned about her child. Bianca violated a trust by being gone at night. Nothing happened this time, but ..." Sarah paused, "but she could have been in trouble. Not only did her friends have a wreck, but another young girl experienced a near lethal overdose last night."

"What? I wasn't aware of that. My husband and I were only concerned about the fact she was out nearly all night without permission. On a school night ..." the distraught mother's voice trailed off. "Clarence went to work as usual this morning. He insisted Bianca go to school even though she didn't get much sleep. That was her punishment." The last comment was said softly, apologetically.

"I'm sure he considered that as reasonable punishment. Something to make her think about staying out late at night, to consider the consequences of her actions," Sarah offered.

"He didn't even talk to Bianca before she left for school. He ignored her." Beverly's words were bitter. "He told me to make sure she went to school on time."

Sarah sensed the pain and anger. Family crises often drive a wedge between married couples because each person processes the situation differently. Some people are open and reach out to embrace solace. Others withdraw into themselves and process the pain in their own way. Too many lash out at the ones they love. "Is Bianca talking to you?"

"No. The only reason I knew she was home was because of our door camera. It alerted me. I saw her, so I came home to see why she was here. The only thing she said to me when I asked what was wrong was that I wouldn't understand. I called the school to find out why she left. A lot of kids left after news of the wreck came out." Beverly struggled to maintain her composure. "I tried to talk to her, to console her, but she locked her door. It's like she blames us for her pain. We've been good parents. Provided everything for her and her sister." She buried her face in her hands and sobbed.

Sarah was not an emotional person by nature, not one who instantly empathized. Her chosen profession demanded she remain at arm's length. She had to remain detached when solving cases. Emotions interfered with logical thought processes. Bianca's incident was not a case. At least, not a criminal case. She rose from the sofa and moved to sit beside Beverly and embrace the woman. "Everyone processes grief differently. Maybe she wants alone time." She felt Beverly respond to the embrace. She patted her back. "She's not blaming you."

For a moment, Beverly absorbed the comfort, then she righted herself, sniffed away her tears, and inhaled deeply. "You're probably right, but I feel helpless. She won't talk."

"Do you mind if I talk with Bianca?" Sarah paused before explaining the reason she was there. "I don't know if the death of her friend will push her into a dark place or not, but before the wreck happened, my officers and I discussed offering Bianca a chance to see what could happen to a young girl who ignores parental guidelines." She waited for Beverly to process what she said and appear attentive. "I have an officer, Micha

Michalski-Jensen, who has offered to mentor Bianca for a day. Micha is the officer who was shot while on duty. She is a caring, loving person who has the ability to communicate with young people. She wants to help Bianca. If you're willing. If Bianca is willing."

Beverly thought for an uncomfortably long time. The Police Chief was sitting on the front edge of Beverly's chair, close enough that they were both breathing the same air. Sarah was inside the mother's personal space. The intrusion was made more awkward by Beverly's silence.

Finally, Beverly replied. "Do you think you can talk her into it? Tamara's wreck scares me. Bianca ran around with her all the time. What if she had been with her friends? And the girl who overdosed. What's her name? Is she a friend of Bianca's?"

Sarah replied, "I can't tell you the name of the girl. Medical privacy and a minor, but I can tell you that she was friends with Tamara."

"So, likely a friend with Bianca," Beverly said. She asked her initial question again, "Do you think you can talk Bianca into riding with your officer?

Sarah responded to the question by rising from her precarious seat. "It's worth a try. Where is her room?"

"Should I go with you?" Beverly got to her feet and glanced toward the stairs.

"Let me try alone. Maybe she will respond to a stranger. Funny how that works sometimes."

Beverly told her which room was Bianca's. Sarah walked up the stairs and gently knocked on the door. "Bianca? This is Police Chief Sarah James. May I come in?" She waited a moment with no response. She knocked again, a little harder. "Bianca. This is Police Chief Sarah James. Can we talk?"

Sarah waited. She didn't want to force the door open. She needed Bianca to open it, to at least be partially receptive. She thought she heard movements on the other side of the door. She heard the door lock release. The knob turned and the door opened inward slowly. Bianca's disheveled, red and black dyed hair frizzed around her questioning face.

Without speaking, eyes sullenly vacant, Bianca turned back to her bed and sat on the edge. She stared at her folded hands, waiting for whatever came next.

Sarah noted the girl's red eyes and tear-stained cheeks. "Bianca, do you feel like talking? I know something is bothering you. I would like to help," Sarah said soothingly.

Bianca twisted her mouth and bit her lower lip without looking up.

Sarah waited for the girl to respond in her own time.

Finally, sad eyes turned upward and blinked once. "How can the police help? My friends are dead."

Sarah responded, "Don't think of me as the police right now. Think of me as a friend who cares about you."

"Since when is the police a friend?" Bianca's voice was stronger. Her eyes showed a flicker of fire, of anger.

"Like I said, don't think of me as the police. I think I can help you manage the pain and sadness you feel right now. I can help you move past what hurts."

"How? What makes you special? Can you bring my friends back to life."

Bianca was engaged, but it could end as quickly as it happened. Sarah kept her focus on the young girl, resolved to help. "I cannot say that I am special. No, I cannot bring your friends back. What happened to them was the result of choices they made. I can help you understand the value of good choices. I have a friend who can help you sort through the events that have caused your pain and put them in perspective."

"A psychiatrist?"

"No. Someone who has experienced pain and survived. Someone who knows how to survive." Micha Michalski-Jensen's story was compelling, but if Bianca wanted to compare notes, the two of them had completely different experiences.

"Who?"

"Officer Micha Michalski-Jensen. She was the responding officer when your parents thought you were missing."

"Oh. Her. How's she going to help?" Bianca asked cynically.

"By listening and sharing. She would like you to ride with her. To see what she sees. To understand what she knows."

"Sounds stupid."

"Maybe, but she thinks it will help. I do too. Officer Michalski-Jensen has endured a lot in her life. She can share how she overcame her problems. Are you afraid to try?"

Bianca glowered at Sarah. "No. I just think it's stupid. My friends are dead."

"If Micha comes to visit, will you at least talk with her?"

"I don't want visitors." Bianca's shoulders slumped.

"So, you want to curl up in a ball and avoid reality?"

"Reality sucks."

"Yes, it does … if you let it. Micha will come see you within an hour … if you let her."

Bianca swelled up and glared at Sarah for a moment. "Sure. If that will get you and my mom off my back."

Sarah smiled and left the room. Downstairs, she nodded to Beverly. "She's willing to talk with Micha. I need to call Officer Michalski-Jensen. I'll have her come over here as soon as she can. I think Bianca will respond to her. She's young and determined … both of them."

"Do you think it will help?"

"It can't hurt. Bianca has a lot of anger. Maybe Officer Michalski-Jensen can help her channel it."

"What about Tamara's death?"

"I'm not sure it has fully hit her yet. She's in the denial stage."

"What will happen when it does fully hit her?"

"I suppose she will need you a lot. Be ready."

Sarah walked to her car and dialed Micha's number.

"Hello, Chief. What's up?"

"Hello, Micha. I was hoping you were awake after switching shifts."

Micha laughed. "Barely. I took a short nap this morning. I didn't want to mess up my pattern tonight since I have to work tomorrow dayshift. What's up?"

"I have a favor to ask. Something that's right up your alley."

"Anything for you, Chief. Girl power all the way." Micha laughed.

Sarah chuckled. "That's the spirit. This actually has to do with a girl. The young lady who was reported missing, but came home before you responded to the call, Bianca Campbell."

"Oh. The troubled girl. Hateful to her parents. The father was irate. What has happened?"

"Her friends were in a TA with fatalities. She's in a vulnerable state. Lost her best friend and is convinced her parents hate her. Maybe you can help her get her head on straight before she loses it."

"Sounds fun."

Sarah paused. "I know it's your time off, but there is another part to the favor."

"What's that?"

"Can you go visit with her in the next half-hour or so? I told her you would be there. Introduce yourself. Appraise her before you take her on patrol. If you think we have a chance, I'll talk to Sergeant Honeycutt and arrange a car for you and her without your partner."

"He's going to miss me," Micha laughed. "I'm his TO. Two shifts in a row and his training will be set back a month."

"Sounds about right." Sarah chuckled. "Here's the address. Her mother's name is Beverly." She read the address to Micha. "Good luck. If you need anything, call me. Oh, by the way, her friends were in the car wreck this morning."

"Wow! A wreck just happened? I wasn't aware of an accident this morning. It must have happened when I was asleep. I haven't checked the news today. How bad?"

"Two fatalities … so far. The driver was her best friend. It hasn't quite hit her yet."

"That makes this important. To save Bianca, I'll make it work."

"Thank you, Micha. I'm serious. Call me if you need anything. She's worth saving."

# CHAPTER 11

6:30 P.M Monday

Micha called Sarah shortly after 5:00 as Sarah was preparing to leave the station. "Chief, Bianca will ride with me tomorrow. We hit it off."

"Good. Were you in uniform?"

"No. I figured it would be better if she saw me in civvies first. She's a confused little girl. We talked about her friends in the wreck. The word is that they skipped school. I think she knows why, but she didn't say."

"There's no doubt they skipped. Have you told Lieutenant McCuskey?"

"I'll call her. I wanted to tell you how it went with Bianca."

Sarah replied, "Thank you, Micha." She knew how people's minds worked. Since she was at the top of PD hierarchy, she got first consideration. "Lieutenant McCuskey has arranged everything with Sergeant Honeycutt for you."

The drive to her apartment was uneventful. Sarah thought about Shawn. He usually called later in the day. He hadn't called. He probably knew what was happening in her world. She kicked off her shoes and removed her jacket as soon as she walked through the door. For the moment, the world seemed to be calm, but she knew it was just a momentary lull. A murder in her city meant every minute between the occurrence and the arrest would be tense and unpredictable for everyone in the city, especially for Devaney PD personnel. She poured a glass of Merlot and left it on the kitchen counter. She went to the bedroom and removed her slacks, blouse, and bra. A pair of loose shorts and a slip-over cotton shirt felt good on her body. She could relax.

Relaxing didn't mean Sarah vegetated in front of a television. It meant re-reading her budget, reading the recap of calls about incidents on the walking trails that Taylor prepared much sooner than promised, and transferring mental notes and questions onto the pages of her notepad in a quiet zone. She was always thinking and planning. The software required to download EDR information that Taylor found was not as expensive as imagined. She was certain she could work it into the budget. She could leverage the Mayor's decision to convert more of the fleet to EVs to get the addition. Or she could simply go over budget now and ask forgiveness later. She knew how the system worked. There were always contingency funds in the city coffers.

The trail calls were relegated to major and minor assaults, or attempted assaults. No rapes. That was a good thing. A few mugging attempts. People on the trails don't typically carry valuables other than cellphones, earphones, and identification. Mugging someone for a Fitbit wasn't very lucrative, even for a desperate druggie. Generally, the calls were for disturbances between walkers and bicyclists who had difficulty co-existing. The calls about motorized vehicles on the trails were relegated to mopeds, motorcycles, or four-wheelers. Generally, calls for auto traffic was found to be Parks employees performing maintenance on the trail.

Sarah could not free herself from the hold investigative work had on her. She loved mysteries. She had thoughts and ideas about the body. She jotted her thoughts on a piece of paper. She was convinced that the tire marks on the trail were connected to the John Doe. She just didn't know how yet. If the killer and the victim both drove a vehicle to the spot, who drove the victim's car away from the scene? Did that mean there were two killers? Did the killer live close enough to commit the crime, take his vehicle home, then walk back for the victim's car? Or ride a bicycle and haul it away in the victim's car? She wanted to call Boston, but he needed rest … if he would. She could wait. It was his case, after all.

Sarah popped a microwave meal in the oven. Nutritious if not stellar cuisine. It wasn't tofu. She sipped her wine and savored the grapey tang of it. Chocolate hints with a blackberry base. The wine was the better part of her meal.

Sarah's attention was drawn to her cellphone just as she poured her second glass of Merlot. The ringtone was Taylor's. She glanced at the time before she answered. It was after 6:00. "Hello, Taylor. You aren't still at the station, are you?"

"No. I was home. Sergeant Honeycutt called. We received a concerned citizen call. Something that looks like blood stains behind the New Word Church."

Sarah sat upright. "Blood? Another body?"

"No. But Maria was curious. She went to the scene to check it after a unit responded. She called me. She said it looks like a lot of blood in the driveway. I'm on my way."

Sarah stood up and moved toward the bedroom. "Did you call Boston?"

"Yes. I think he was asleep. He said he would go check it out."

"Okay. I'm on my way."

"I didn't mean to call you out," Taylor protested. "I was just letting you know. I'm going out there."

"Too much is happening right now to ignore it."

The New Word Church was on the far east side of Devaney. The area was generally undeveloped. A smattering of small businesses and fast-food places dotted the county highway. Many of the businesses were closed, failed when the pandemic forced customers to stay home. The chain fast-food restaurants survived and still welcomed people who traveled the road into and out of town. The sun was rapidly sinking. The photosensitive streetlights were still waiting for waning daylight to bring them to life. Two patrol units and two EVs were parked at the side of the metal building. She recognized the EVs as Boston's and Taylor's unmarked cars. She assumed one of the gasoline powered black and whites was Sergeant Honeycutt's. She parked near them.

Sarah saw two uniformed officers standing beside Sergeant Honeycutt who were watching Taylor and Boston attentively listening to an animated, casually dressed man. They were all standing near the center of a driveway at the back of the building. The driveway behind the church wasn't asphalt. It was gravel. White gravel. Her heart pumped a little faster. Blood and white gravel seemed like a clue.

Taylor saw Sarah and motioned for her. "Pastor Joseph, this is Chief

James. Chief, this is Pastor Joseph Cline. This is his church. He is retelling what he saw."

The pastor was in his late forties or early fifties, nearer Taylor's age than Sarah's. His light brown hair was heavily stained with gray at the temples. His face was lightly creased with concerned compassion. "Please call me Joe. Even my congregation calls me Joe. We don't stand on ceremony here. It is a pleasure to meet you, Chief James, though I suppose this is not a pleasurable circumstance."

Sarah smiled her best political smile and shook Joe's hand. His handshake conveyed his core compassion. His aura had a calming effect on her soul. "I'm pleased to meet you." She looked askance of the pastor and her Lieutenants. "What are the circumstances?" She saw Boston's look of chagrin. He didn't like interference or unnecessary delays. She was providing both. His evidence case was on the ground near him. He was ready to collect evidence.

Joe looked at Taylor and Boston, "I will restate what I've told the officers and the detectives."

"Thank you," Sarah said. There was a time when she would have relegated herself to secondary status and caught up as soon as she could. That time was not now.

"This is my church. It was once a dollar store, but pandemic restrictions killed their business. We find the building suitable for worship. Make something good out of something bad. We're not a big church. We don't need a big fancy building to worship and do the Lord's work. We are here to serve the people … much like your police motto. Protect them from the wolves of the secular world and serve their spiritual needs."

Taylor saw Boston's impatience. "That's excellent, Joe. What prompted you to call the police?" She heard the reason before Sarah arrived, but she wanted Sarah to hear a summarized version … if the pastor was capable.

"Yes. Of course." Joe smiled understanding. "As briefly as possible. I arrived before daylight this morning. Monday is our food pantry day. We provide food for those who suffer food insecurities. No one should go hungry in our land of bounty. Food banks in the area provide donated food and we disseminate it to the needy. The local Walmart, Aldi, Dillons, and many other businesses donate what they can." With compassion rather than pride, he stated, "We serve nearly one-hundred hungry families every week. That affects more than four-hundred souls, many of them children and senior citizens."

"Why did you arrive that early?" Sarah asked.

"I set up the sanctuary. We try to clean everything after Sunday evening service, but I want to make sure it is presentable for worship services throughout our day of giving." Joe smiled warmly. "We start our day with a service of thanks for our volunteers. They give their time and effort to serve the people less fortunate. Charitable people doing God's work. We are thankful that God provides us good fortune and good health so that we can minister to the needy."

"You said throughout the day?" Sarah posed questioningly.

"Yes," the pastor nodded vigorously. "Every hour, we hold a spirit-strengthening service for our volunteers and invite the people seeking assistance to join us. The soul needs nourishment as well as the body."

"Does everyone have to attend a service to get food?"

"No. That is not a condition for assistance. We care for sinners as we do for believers. God accepts all into His Spiritual Church. We can do no less in our earthly church. We are the New Word Church, new only because we teach the Word as it was intended. As sad as it may sound, hearing God's Word as intended is new to most people today. No trappings. No false prophets. No materialistic entanglements." Joe motioned toward the building and a vehicle parked near a pedestrian door. "As you can see, neither this building nor the car I drive reeks of wealth and substance. The car gets me where I want to go in this world and the church gets me where I want to go in eternity."

Sarah hoped the introduction was about at its end. "Where is the blood?" She hoped the question would redirect Joe.

"There." Joe pointed to a spot near the center of the gravel drive, midway between the corners of the building. Sergeant Honeycutt and the two patrol officers were standing near it, protecting it from further contamination.

Sarah looked toward the dark spot. "Why didn't you call sooner?"

"I didn't see it when I first arrived. It's still dark at six o'clock and the security lights barely cover the back of the building. Just enough light to see the door and avoid stumbling over something. We don't waste money that can be used to help those in need." Joe explained his rationale, though no explanation was necessary.

Sarah noticed Boston and Taylor both looked toward small, unlit lights near the top of the corners of the building. The shadows from the surrounding trees where long and the sun's light would be gone in less than an hour. The lights would come on when it was dark enough to activate the sensors. She asked Boston, "Am I caught up?"

Boston growled. "As much as me. I got the initial report from Sergeant Honeycutt when I arrived, but I haven't heard Pastor Joe's version in full." He looked at Joe to encourage him to continue.

"Of course," Joe said. "You probably need to investigate before it gets too dark. First, I'm the only one who parks back here. I park close to the keyed entrance." He pointed toward the pedestrian door with an awning. "The front doors and side doors don't have outside access when they are locked. They only unlock from the inside. It was dark. I simply went inside to do my work. The volunteers and the recipients park in the main lot and come through the front doors after I unlock them. We prepare the food gifts by placing enough for each family in boxes that are sized to suit the number of family members. They come inside … unless they are infirm, and we pray together while a volunteer fills their boxes and then helps them carry the boxes to their vehicles."

"So, you didn't see anything when you arrived?" Boston asked impatiently.

"Correct. I might not have noticed it when I prepared to leave an hour ago but there was a bunch of crows in the trees and on the ground." The corners of Joe's mouth lifted in a small smile. "Did you know they call a flock of crows a murder?" He stopped and his eyes widened. "You don't think …?"

"We don't think anything yet," Boston groused impatiently. "What next?"

"I came out with some bags of trash for the dumpster. When I opened the door, the raucous crows scattered in protest of my disturbing them. Some were standing on the dumpster. I immediately thought someone may have stolen use of our dumpster and left the lid open or they dropped garbage on the ground that attracted the crows." Joe's eye dropped. "I hate to admit it, but the thought upset me. I shouldn't feel that way. People need to dispose of trash properly. Our dumpster is provided by God, and I shouldn't begrudge them the use of it."

"So, you tossed your trash bags and came to look at what attracted the crows?"

"Yes. I was surprised to see nothing. Or I thought it was nothing at the time. I was in a hurry to finish. It was a busy day, and my mortal body was tired. My first thought was that a vehicle parked here and leaked oil or something. It could have been there a long time, maybe even from the trash truck. They leak stuff all the time. Later, I realized crows wouldn't be attracted to oil." Joe paused. "They wouldn't, would they?" By the time he asked the question, the four of them were near the dark spot, Boston with his evidence case.

"No. When did you decide it could be blood?" Boston studied the dark spot as he questioned Joe.

Sarah studied it also. It was blood. There was no mistaking that. Blood on white gravel. She wanted to perform a phenolphthalein test to see if it was human blood, but she knew that was Boston's job. And the test kits were inside his case. He would ask if he needed help.

"I went inside for more trash. It's sad to say, but many donations we receive from individuals are expired or unusable in other ways. We toss those items in the dumpster." Joe paused to consider the sadness of expired food in a world of hunger. "And, when I came out, the crows were back. They scattered when they saw me. I put the trash in the dumpster and came over to look." He paused again. His face contorted. He spoke softly, apologetically, as if ashamed of what he was saying, "I hunted deer when I was young. Blood-soaked soil is not completely unfamiliar to me." He paused again and glanced toward a white envelope Sergeant Honeycutt held in her hands. "I saw something that looked strange. Something I've seen when tracking a wounded deer. A bit of bone and flesh. I went inside and got a pair of the plastic gloves we use when we prepare meals for the hungry on Wednesdays. I picked it up and put it in that envelope. I thought it might be useful."

Boston scowled as he accepted the envelope from Sergeant Honeycutt. Sarah knew she was completely caught up on Joe's story when she saw the exchange.

Joe continued. "I know it's blood. I called because I thought maybe a poacher had killed a deer and dressed it here. There are lots of deer here near the edge of town, but it's not hunting season yet. I even looked inside the dumpster to see if the guts were in it."

"Are they?" Boston asked.

"No. Just trash. Some of it doesn't look like church trash. I suppose someone did need to dispose of some small amount of trash. Fast food packages mostly. Empty drink containers." Joe sighed. "Better there than in the parking lot."

Boston had his digital camera in his forensics case. He set an evidence marker near the spot and took several pictures. His actions caused everyone else to step away. Once he was satisfied with the pictures of the spot and the immediate area, he handed the camera to Sergeant Honeycutt. "Take some pictures around the area. If you see something interesting, drop a marker." He donned exam gloves and motioned for Taylor to do the same. "Lots of samples needed." He motioned to an ample supply of evidence bags. "Bucket and shovel in the back of my car."

The two officers didn't need to be told anything more. They immediately walked toward the side of the building where Boston's car was parked.

"What do you want me to do?" Sarah asked.

"Hand me a phenolphthalein test." Boston squatted over the dark spot and scraped a small sample from the spot. It was ready to be tested as soon as Sarah handed him the test material. He prepped the sample and waited a moment. "Human. Bags."

Sarah pulled several small evidence bags from Boston's case and handed him one. She watched as Boston used a bright, tightly focused LED flashlight to examine the blood spot. The light helped in two ways. It helped focus his search to a precise area and it provided intense light in the shadows of the low sun.

Boston grunted as he duck-walked during his search. He tucked anything that caught his attention into a bag. He sealed each bagged sample and exchanged it for an empty one with Sarah. He knew Sarah would mark each bag for testing. Within fifteen minutes, he had six bags. He grunted as he tried to rise to stand. He grimaced and accepted a lift under each arm from Taylor and Sarah.

"Getting old sucks," Boston said with a grimace.

"What do you think?" Sarah asked. She knew what her thoughts were, but she had to keep reminding herself that Boston was the Detective.

Boston smirked. "Probably the same thing you're thinking. Our John Doe was shot here, and his body dropped by the trail. DNA of the blood and a few bits of bone can confirm." He glanced toward the darkening woods behind the church. "If it is, I have to wonder why they didn't just drag the body into the woods here." He shined his flashlight toward the woods. Darkness was filling the spaces between the trees and low growth.

Taylor asked, "They? You think there was more than one?"

Boston shrugged and glanced toward Sarah. "It appears there were two vehicles on the trail where we found the body. Some areas indicated tires off the concrete on opposite sides at the same time. If our boy was shot here, his body definitely wasn't dragged there."

Taylor nodded enthusiastically. "Two people strong enough to carry a dead body."

Boston said to no one in particular, "Cordon this area." He looked toward Joe Cline's car parked near the rear pedestrian door. "Move the car. Back it out so nothing more is disturbed. The killer drove a vehicle on this gravel. He had to leave some signs." The shadows were deepening and the security lights on the corners of the church flickered on.

Joe fumbled in his pocket for his car keys. "Do you want me to turn on the parking lot lights?"

Boston looked around before answering. "I can't see the lights from here, so they aren't going to provide much help. Leave them off."

Sarah knew the use of the focused flashlight would reveal more than parking lot lights would. She smiled to herself. Boston was in his element. She missed that element. "What do you need from me?" she asked Boston.

Boston paused his area survey. "Understanding."

Sarah was puzzled. "Understanding of what?"

"Of why I'll probably be late in the morning." Boston looked at Taylor. "If the two unies can stay to assist, the rest of you can go home. This will take a while ... and it will go faster if we don't have any more contamination."

Taylor hesitantly replied, "Officers Cobb and Shrum's shift ended at seven. I'll have Sergeant Blanchard send replacements ... if that's okay."

"Fine. I just need someone to make sure no rubberneckers show up."

He paused then redirected his focus to Sarah. "And thanks for sending Glasgow to help get John Doe's picture out there."

"No problem." Sarah knew there was no need to say anything additional to the surly Detective. The acknowledgement was a big step for him.

Boston impatiently waited for everyone to leave the area behind the church.

Sarah saw the Detective begin a methodical sweep of the graveled area. She would have to wait until morning, or later, to find out what he found ... or didn't find. Her original mentor, Detective Carl Franken, taught her patience. She was naturally methodical, but patience was not in her personality.

# CHAPTER 12

## 7:00 A.M. Tuesday

Sarah didn't hear her alarm. She seldom did. Habit brought her out of sleep before her alarm sounded. She sat up on the side of the bed and turned off the alarm before it could awaken her. She often wondered if the alarm sound function still worked. She turned on the lights and made her way to the bathroom for her early morning rituals. She didn't shower because she was going to the gym for her morning workout. She would shower and dress for work in the locker room.

All through her workout, Sarah thought about Boston and the cases he was working on. The John Doe body and Sasha Pierce's overdose. She knew Boston assigned undercover cop Blake House to dig into the drug scene. Blake methodically plied the dark recesses of Devaney for information on drugs, or any other nefarious activities. She wondered if the cases were connected. A random body, shot in the head and dumped in the woods, reeked of drug deal gone bad. Even though there was no indication of organized drug activity in Devaney, that didn't make it so. She knew Blake would find any evidence that connected the two cases, if there was any. Whatever scenario played out, she had to worry. It was her city.

At the gym, Sarah finished her workout and showered. She dressed in a white blouse. It was satin textured with cream-colored floral embroidery across the front neckline. Charcoal-gray slacks and a matching jacket accompanied the blouse. Her blouses and shirts were the centerpiece of her attire. The color schemes drew out the raw topaz color of her eyes.

It was 7:05 A.M. when Sarah entered the station through the parking compound and garage entrance. She put her car on a charger vacated by the patrol unit moments earlier. She missed the roll call in the daily briefing room, but she could still touch base with some of the dayshift units before they all left the station on patrol.

Officer Micha Michalski-Jensen called out as Sarah approached the inside security door. "Chief! Gotta minute?"

Sarah turned and smiled. The trademark rattle of police officers' equipment belts as they walked toward the garage filled the hollow hallway. "Of course, Micha." She adjusted the folders she had carried home with her.

"I thought I'd let you know that I'm going to pick up Bianca today."

"Good. Isn't it a school day?"

Micha nodded. "Yeah, but her mother felt this would be more beneficial to Bianca than a day at school when the focus would be on the girls in the wreck."

"Probably true, though there could be some group grief counseling that she will miss. Embracing friends could be therapeutic."

"Possibly, but I think she needs one-on-one counseling. Like I said yesterday, there's something Bianca hasn't told us about her late-night Sunday night."

"If anyone can get her to open up, it will be you," Sarah said as encouragement.

"Will it be okay if I show her the lab? I think Alicia's work might have an impact on her, especially if Alicia is doing some tox screens."

"I don't see what harm it will do. Just remember confidentiality and evidence contamination are our primary concerns."

"Okay. Thanks, Chief."

Sergeant Honeycutt was at the Shift Commander's desk, issuing last minute instructions to a pair of patrol officers. She saw Sarah and interrupted herself to call out, "Good morning, Chief. Did you rest well last night?"

Sarah smiled and shook her head. The question seemed innocuously friendly to a casual observer, but it was nuanced in a manner that only

Maria Honeycutt could slant it. "I did. Thank you, Sergeant. I take it the night was peaceful."

Maria grinned. "If you mean no more dead bodies, yes." She handed Sarah the daily summary. A short list that included what Sarah already knew.

As she scanned the list, Sarah said, "That's good. Do you know what time Boston finished at the church?"

"Pete said his officers were released about ten with instructions to patrol it frequently, to make sure no one crossed the tape. Apparently, Boston wants to go into the woods in the daylight. See what he can find."

"Did Pete say what, if anything, Boston found?" Sarah was curious. If Boston was planning to search the woods, he probably wouldn't be at the station first thing. He wouldn't be available for an update.

"No. He said the officers weren't too happy that Boston assigned them dumpster duty." Sergeant Honeycutt grinned. "I guess their recruiter didn't tell them about dumpster diving."

"They never do." Sarah shuddered. She remembered digging through rotten garbage and trash in the search for clues and evidence. Criminals leave or dispose of evidence in some unsavory places. It is the nature of criminals to be unsavory. "Did they say whether they found anything of value?"

"Boston took some of it, but I don't know what."

"I'll check with Evidence. Hopefully, he brought it to the station." Sarah paused to move the list further from her eyes and reread one of the bullet points. "A vigil?"

"Yes. Some of the kids held a vigil for the girls on Porter Road, at the wreck site."

"Did it create problems?"

"Not really at that time of night. Pete set up units on both sides. People slow when they see the blues flashing. They left about midnight."

"I guess the kids needed it. No disturbances?"

"No. Peaceful. No one to direct anger toward, other than the driver."

"True." Sarah went up the stairs to the office area rather than to the evidence locker. Her egg sandwich was cooling. She was hungry and she needed coffee. She didn't eat or drink before a workout. The smell of fresh coffee greeted her nostrils as soon as she entered the bullpen. "Good morning, Taylor," she called out without seeing the Lieutenant.

"Good morning, Chief. Coffee is almost ready." Taylor McCuskey's blonde hair haloed her head when she poked it above the partition around her cubicle. "Did you hear from Boston after we left?"

"No. And it's driving me crazy." Sarah's gray cup with the pink lettering of her motto was on a designated cup rack on the counter that held the coffee maker. She knew Liz cleaned if for her every evening. That was not part of the Administrative Assistant's formal duties, but it was one she selflessly embraced. A half teaspoon of sugar Sarah put in the cup was roiled by hot, brown coffee when she poured it. Without stirring, she lightly sipped even though she knew it would be too hot to drink. Habit.

Sarah saw that the Situation Room lights were off as she slowly walked with Taylor toward the Lieutenant's cubicle. Detective Blake House came through the hall from the rear entrance. Blake's long hair was clean and pulled back in a ponytail. Even his beard was clean and combed. He seldom came to the station. He seldom appeared in clean clothes. "Good morning, Lieutenant House. What brings you to the station?"

Blake laughed. "You mean *what got you cleaned up* don't you?" As an undercover cop, he normally dressed like a homeless transient, a nameless person who most people went out of their way to avoid. A non-person who melted into the background of everyone's memory. "Boston said he needed some help on a drug case. A teenager ODed and spilled her gut. He thinks there's a story." He motioned toward himself. "I didn't want to risk being recognized by my street friends, so I cleaned up as much as I could. It'll take me a couple of weeks to regain my aura."

Blake's presence assuaged some of the misgivings Sarah had about Boston not being immediately available for updates. Blake had information. "What do you have on the drugs?" The undercover cops initially reported to Lieutenant Anthony Kendall, but when Tony was hired as Police Chief for a city in Missouri shortly after Sarah was promoted to Police Chief, Sarah reorganized all detectives and undercover cops to report to the Senior Detective, Lieutenant Boston Mankowitz.

"Nothing from my side. I was hoping he had something more than he gave me over the phone. He said his notes are in the Sit Room."

Sarah nodded and walked to the Situation Room, opened the door, and turned on the light. "He has a lot in here." She glanced around to see if there was something to differentiate the John Doe case from the drug case. "Probably that pile there. The other one is John Doe evidence." She saw the pictures that Lieutenant Glasgow borrowed to use with the FACES software. A copy of his rendering was in the middle of the table. She handed it to Blake. "Does he look familiar?"

Almost without looking, Blake replied, "No. Boston sent it to me late yesterday. I've not seen anyone like him, either." He smirked. "Too clean cut for my circle."

"Okay," Sarah said. A thought struck her. "You might want to talk with Officer Micha Michalski-Jensen. Not right away though. She has a teen shadow today, a girl who may know something about the OD case."

Blake looked at the cup of coffee in Sarah's hand. "Coffee." Without invitation, though none was needed, he walked toward the coffee maker. "What does Micha know?"

"Nothing, other than her shadow and the OD are friends. She'll try to get the girl to talk about it. The girl said a few things that made Micha suspicious. She's got her ears to the ground better than most."

"Maybe she needs to be a detective," Blake said as they walked to the coffee table.

"I suppose that's something for her future. She likes patrol."

"Even after being shot? Tough cop. I've never been shot. It would probably make me think about a career change. I've been punched. That was almost enough to think change. I'll give Boston's notes a look. How long should I wait for Micha?"

"Part of the shadowing will involve the lab. Maybe wander to the lab while they're in the station. Let it come naturally." Sarah motioned at Blake's appearance with her eyes and grinned. "You don't look like a cop. Don't mention it. That might help Bianca speak more freely."

"Bianca. She's not the druggie, right?"

"Right. She was out with friends most of the night Sunday night."

"Sneaking out with her boyfriend?"

"No. I don't think so. We think it was with the same girls in the TA yesterday morning."

"What's the connection to the OD?"

"They are all friends is the only connection." Sarah reckoned Blake was asking questions that he already had Boston's version of answers to. He was a good detective and a much better conversationalist than Boston. "Taylor may know more about the girls' travels prior to the wreck. Her people are investigating the accident. I don't think Boston spent any time on it. He was busy all day on our John Doe."

"Do you think there's a connection between the dead body and the OD? Maybe the same drug dealers?"

Sarah was surprised that Blake asked the question that was on her mind. "Did Boston say he thinks they are connected?"

"No. He told me he was working a DB, a possible drug deal gone bad, and he needed help with an OD case. I just thought there could be a connection. I'm not sure of the timing, but maybe the parents or friends of the OD cornered the dealer and popped a cap on him."

Sarah jerked with surprise. That was a connection that had not occurred to her. She didn't know what the OD timing was relative to the shooting. "Maybe you can sift through Boston's notes and the 9-1-1 call log on the OD. See if the timing fits."

"Will do," Blake replied as he stepped into the Situation room with his cup of coffee. He surveyed the entire room. "So, this is what it's like to work under a real roof." He sipped his coffee. "The coffee's better." He laughed and began searching through Boston's notes.

Sarah walked to her office. A neat stack of folders similar to the ones she carried home with her waited in the center of her desk. Liz was nothing if not efficient.

Sarah opened the top folder and read through it. Sheriff Ballard Berringer proposed county and city collaboration to create a regional crime lab, funded by the Sheriff's Office and Devaney PD based upon population distribution, which meant Devaney PD would bear the bulk of the costs. It also proposed that the superior law enforcement entity would be the controlling authority. Ballard Berringer replaced long-time Sheriff Cecil Herriman who retired after a long career in law enforcement.

Sheriff Berringer was older than the former Sheriff. He was in his mid-sixties. He retired from the State Police five years earlier but grew bored in retirement. He didn't like Cecil Herriman's good-ol'-boy style as Sheriff. He believed law enforcement was an extension of the military and should function the same. He took the constitutional authority of his position

Gary B. Boyd

seriously and made sure city police chiefs in the county understood he was the primary law enforcement officer in the county.

Sarah shook her head. Sheriff Berringer's proposal was a thinly disguised plan to gain control of the forensics lab that Devaney PD ... under Bill Keck's leadership ... established and funded. Sheriff Berringer added a forensics-trained deputy to his staff in preparation for his plan. She didn't like his plan for several reasons. Berringer's proposal would have Devaney providing the lion's share of the funding and the forensics-trained Sheriff's Deputy, under the Sheriff's thumb, would provide the leadership. In essence, Alicia Kettering would be relegated to a subservient role in the laboratory she built, and Devaney PD would have no control.

Mayor Keck was already aware of the effort and assured her that he would stand against it. He had the County Manager's ear. Sheriff Berringer's turn-the-world-upside-down attitude grated on nearly everyone around him. Some deputies even left the department, either by their own choice or the choice of the new Sheriff. Devaney PD did gain the advantage of trained law enforcement officers seeking employment. Sarah highlighted areas of the proposal that she would use to counter Sheriff Berringer's offer. She wasn't foolish enough to believe the fight would end with a simple refusal on her part. Politics was never black and white with a simple yes or no. She placed a Post-It-Note on the outside of the folder asking Liz to set up a meeting with the Sheriff. As much as she hated the idea, she still had to discuss it professionally.

Liz softly announced herself when she arrived at 7:30. "Chief, the press would like an update on the body and on the traffic accident."

Sarah exhaled heavily. "We didn't have anything scheduled, did we?"

"No. They've been calling and asking if you could update them."

"I don't really have anything definitive on the John Doe. As far as the accident is concerned, all I can do is confirm names."

"It would probably be a good gesture with the press," Liz replied.

Sarah knew Liz was right. "Okay. Set up something this morning. I have that lunch meeting with the Mayor. I don't want to rush that."

"I think I can set up something for 9:00. In the lobby?"

"The lobby sounds good. Thank you, Liz."

Sarah finished the review of Liz's folders then went for another cup of coffee. She walked downstairs to the evidence locker. She met Boston in the hallway. "Good morning, Boston. Blake is in house."

"Good morning, Boss. Yeah. He called me."

Sarah waited for something more, but nothing came. "Did you find anything after we left?"

"Most of it is in the evidence locker waiting for Alicia. I just carried some to Alicia for immediate analysis. The bits of flesh and bone that the crows didn't eat. She'll see if they match the DB." Boston's haggard face expressed disgust. "The preacher and the officers put a lot of foot traffic in the area before it was cordoned."

"What about the dumpster?" Sarah didn't want to wait for Boston to get around to mentioning it. She had a press conference in less than half an hour.

"Aside from the big, black trash bags from the church, and some unlabeled canned goods, we found some food wrappers and a couple of Walmart sacks stuffed with trash."

"Is all of it in evidence?" Sarah asked incredulously.

"No. Just loose trash, the bags from the top, and the Walmart sacks. The freshest stuff. I locked the dumpster so it can't be used. If we decide there might be something else there, we can go back."

"You didn't find anything in the gravel?"

"I didn't say that. The bits of flesh and bones, I mentioned. Between the preacher and us, everything is probably corrupted. I gathered up a half bucket of bloodied soil. Hard digging. It probably won't tell us any more than what we already know."

"What else did you find?"

"I took some photos and a couple of tire impressions. Probably won't lead us anywhere. The area is not completely unused. Could be anyone from any time recent. I got a decent picture of a bloody partial footprint. Somebody stepped in the blood. The photos are in the Sit Room in a folder. Maybe Alicia can match some of the prints and impressions to a brand. The bloody print might prove useful if we find a suspect."

Sarah nodded. She thought about asking if he had considered whether there might be a connection between the John Doe and Sasha's overdose. She pushed the thought away for the moment. "What next?"

"I've got on my hiking boots."

The comment made Sarah glance at Boston's shoes. His normal shoes. It was a rhetorical comment.

"I'm going to check the woods to see if I can see anything. Look for signs of the bullet. I checked the outside of the church building last night. No holes. Nothing."

"He wasn't on the ground when he was shot?"

"Not there, if he was. Maybe he was shot in the woods and carried to the gravel before the killers loaded him in a car. But there wasn't a blood trail across the gravel."

"Or pickup."

"Or pickup. Yeah. But I need to go. I overslept. If the shooting scene is in the woods, the crows could be already cleaning it."

The thought of carrion eaters consuming human flesh caused Sarah to shudder. She had seen a body after animals and birds picked away flesh. Bad enough to think about. Worse to see. Boston left and she walked to the lab.

"Good morning, Alicia."

Alicia withheld a groan. "Do you have something for me too?"

Sarah grinned. "No. I was hoping you had something for me."

Alicia smiled. "I do. For you or Lieutenant McCuskey. I have the tox screens on the driver and two of the passengers, one being the other deceased. Adderall."

"Adderall? Prescription drug. What about the OD earlier? Same thing?"

"No. She had meth, laced with fentanyl. The fentanyl is what hit her. She's lucky it wasn't overloaded with fentanyl."

Blake's thought about an angry parent made sense. Kill the dealer with the tainted supply to protect a child. Their John Doe could be a case of *good riddance*. "What about the blood samples from the other TA victims? Did the hospitals send them?"

"I got the local hospital sample late yesterday. That's why I know the two deceased and the one in Devaney hospital took Adderall. I'm going to speculate the two from Wichita will show the same when they get here."

"So, they are sending them?"

"Yes. They should be here within the hour."

"You haven't told Lieutenant McCuskey what you've found?"

"Not yet. Do you want me to call her?"

"If you have the paperwork, I can carry it to her. Save you some time. We have a press conference at nine. She'll be there." Sarah checked the wall clock to confirm the time. "Any other information yet?"

"Boston brought me some samples to compare DNA with the dead body. Those are all rush, of course. He said he had a bucket of bloody gravel in evidence." Alicia scowled. "He's big into digging up dirt lately. He did say he knows the blood is human and the samples he brought should match the John Doe. If the samples match, I don't need to rush the gravel … unless you think I should. Remember, it'll be at least 24 hours before I can confirm anything."

Sarah knew it would take time for DNA results. That didn't keep her from wishing they were faster. "No. Boston's running the case. I'm just staying informed so I can deal with the public. Speaking of public, has Officer Michalski-Jensen told you she will bring someone to the lab today?"

"No. A dignitary?"

"A troubled teen. Her name is Bianca. She stayed out late. Caused her parents a lot of concern. Enough to call the police. Also, the girls in the TA were close friends of hers. We need to keep confidentiality in mind."

"Understood. I'll keep anything from the wreck away from her."

"Also, Detective House might drop in while Micha and Bianca are in the lab."

"Blake? He's actually going to be here?"

"He plans to."

"Good deal!" Alicia grinned. "I've only seen him a few times."

"Don't mention who he is in Bianca's presence. He wants her to be at ease around him. Maybe she can tell him something worthwhile."

"Gotcha."

# CHAPTER 13

## 9:00 A.M. Tuesday

Liz and Sergeant Honeycutt were directing the activities of two station officers as they set up a small podium facing a semi-circle of fold-up chairs. Channel 6's crew was attaching the station's microphone to the podium with logo prominently displayed. The lobby was barely large enough to accommodate the local news outlets. Arrangement of everything required careful planning. Even so, there was enough standing room to accommodate any citizens who were in the building and wanted to observe.

Sarah smiled at Taylor, who was anxiously watching from the base of the second-floor stairs. Lieutenant McCuskey liked police work. She didn't care for press scrutiny. Sarah knew the senior peace officer could acquit herself professionally in front of the press, but, except on rare occasions, Taylor wasn't in the public eye. "Alicia has tox results on some of the wreck victims" she whispered as she handed an envelope to Taylor.

Taylor opened the envelope and studied the lab results. She shook her head and said softly, "Not surprised. If these are only residual readings, the driver was definitely under the influence, and the others probably weren't aware of much. It's a crying shame." Her eyes moistened slightly. "Are you going to mention this to the press?"

"I think it bears mentioning, but I need to clear it with legal. This has all the signs of a drawn-out civil suit ... several lawsuits. Plus, the onus will be on us to find the source." Sarah saw Liz approaching. "Are we about ready, Liz?"

Liz smiled reassuringly. If she harbored concerns, she wouldn't let them show. She believed it was her job to encourage the Police Chief in pressure situations. Meeting the press is always a pressure situation. A poorly chosen word could escalate into a political faux pas. "I think everyone is here. I don't like that new reporter much. She insisted that she be allowed to ask the first question because Channel 6 is the leading news station. Maybe she'll mature. Be wary." She glanced at her wristwatch. "It's nine o'clock." She handed Sarah a folder with notes and the FACES sketch of the John Doe.

The reporters who were murmuring and joking amongst themselves quietened when Sarah stepped to the podium. "Ladies and Gentlemen, I will make a statement regarding a couple of incidents that have occurred within the last thirty-two hours." She paused to make sure she had everyone's attention.

"Both incidents are on-going investigations, but I will provide as much information as is prudent. Monday morning, a citizen reported a body in a brushy area near the Overton Acres section of the city trail system. As of this moment, we do not have an identity for the body. The body is that of a young, white male. We have no local or general area reports of a missing person." She paused briefly and pulled the FACES sketch from Liz's folder.

"We have a sketch of the victim for immediate release to the public." Sarah nodded to Liz and waited for Liz and Sergeant Honeycutt to hand out copies. "This has been sent to law enforcement in the six-state area. Obviously, we hope someone recognizes him and provides information that will help with identification. Additionally, if anyone near the area where the body was found saw anything unusual between 2:00 A.M and 7:00 A.M. on Monday, please contact Devaney PD. I am relying on the press to get this picture and the message out to the public." She paused and smiled. "This is where the press can help solve a case." She saw every reporter busily writing notes, even those who were making either audio recording, video recording, or both. She knew most of the notes would be used to form questions. "The Coroner determined the cause of death to be a gunshot wound. At present, we have no clues to identify the killer, or the type of weapon used.

"I know that is not a lot of new information, but it is all we have to disclose at the moment. As I said, this is an ongoing investigation. On a side note, I know there are concerns regarding safety on our walking and bicycling trails. The city in general discourages use of the trails after dark. Most of the trails are in green spaces and low-lying areas that are left in their natural state to help control run-off during periods of rain. They also provide habitat for small wildlife and birds. We don't patrol the trails after dark."

Sarah took another page of notes from the folder. "On an entirely different subject, as everyone is probably aware, tragedy struck our community yesterday morning. Five Devaney High School students were involved in a single-car crash that resulted in two fatalities and three injuries. All the victims were female. Two of the survivors were air lifted to Wichita trauma centers. The third survivor was transported by ambulance to Devaney hospital. As of this morning, one of those patients is still critical. The other two are stable."

Bernie Stone raised his hand. Sarah recognized him. She was ready for questions and intentionally avoided Tammy's urgent request for attention.

"Chief James, can you release the names?"

Sarah inhaled deeply. "I can confirm that the two deaths were Tamara Yates and Yvonne Timmons. Both were seventeen and seniors at Devaney High School. We believe Miss Yates was driving the vehicle at the time of the accident."

"Chief James, do you know the cause of the accident?"

Sarah gathered her thoughts before responding. "Our traffic investigator, Corporal Brandon Canton, is still in the process of evaluating data from the vehicle's Event Data Recorder."

"I've heard that the vehicle was likely traveling at a high rate of speed," Bernie said non-accusatively.

"Based solely on the degree of damage, that is our initial assessment but making determinations based upon damage … even by an expert accident investigator … is somewhat subjective. With the EDR data, Corporal Canton will be able to see exactly what occurred in the moments prior to the crash and provide an objective determination of cause."

Tammy Nunn forcefully and loudly stated, "There have been many reports of speeding throughout the city. I think we can all rationally determine that speeding was the cause of that wreck. When is Devaney PD going to clamp down on speeders? If the police had been doing their job, those two girls wouldn't be dead."

Sarah's topaz eyes darkened. She couldn't see it, but she knew everyone watching her could. Her eyes did that when she was angry. She inhaled to calm her tone. "Tammy, as I said, until we have all the facts, we can't make an objective determination. Drivers control of the speeds of their vehicles, not a police officer with a radar gun."

"But if your officers were monitoring the drivers, they wouldn't go fast."

Casey Messerschmidt, the reporter from the other local TV station interrupted, "Were blood tests done on the driver?"

Sarah knew Casey to be levelheaded and focused on the story. She also knew the more experienced reporter was intentionally bringing the presser back on the topic at hand. "Yes. That is standard procedure for fatality accidents."

"What did you find?"

Sarah thought before she responded. "That information is private medical information." She knew her answer was not true for victims who were dead, but she hoped it would satisfy. It didn't.

Casey responded. "I believe that in cases where the victim is deceased, the death removes the medical privacy protection."

"Casey, you are generally correct on that. I received the information regarding tox screens shortly before I came out here. I must run this through legal before I comment on it publicly."

"Was the driver drunk?" Tammy shouted above anyone who might ask a question. She smelled a scoop.

Sarah scowled at the young reporter's rudeness. "No. Blood tests did not indicate the driver had been drinking, but as I told Casey, medical privacy prevents me from making a public statement on the matter at this time."

"What part do the police play in this accident?"

"Investigating it," Sarah replied flatly. The young reporter was trying to make a name for herself ... and establishing a reputation as an adversary of authority, something that might appeal to a certain segment of her audience.

"Don't you think a more active role by the police would have stopped the driver from speeding? And wouldn't a police presence on the walking trail have prevented the murder you found? From what I can see, the taxpayers of this city deserve better protection from the police."

Sarah heard Taylor clear her throat. She glanced toward the patrol Lieutenant and Sergeant Honeycutt. Both women were scowling angrily. Sarah used her eyes to ask Taylor if she wanted to come forward. Instead, Sergeant Honeycutt stepped forward far enough to separate herself from Lieutenant McCuskey. Sarah withheld a grin and let Maria speak.

Maria's eyes flashed angrily, and she glared straight at the young, blonde-haired reporter. "Miss Channel 6, I've been a police officer more years than you've been alive. I've written more tickets than you could haul in your little news van. All in this town. Yet people still speed. I've had drivers fly past me so close that they blew my hat off while I was writing a ticket for a speeder. The drivers are in control of their speed, not a police officer. Drivers get behind the wheels of their cars in every shape you can imagine. Drunk. Drugged. Angry. Or just plain stupid. Ev-er-y day. Normally sane people become invincible and selfish behind the wheel of a car. I've had officers shot for pulling over speeders and druggies. Have you ever been shot at for doing your job? I'll be glad to take you out on patrol so you can see what it's really like out there, if you really care."

Tammy blanched. She saw the danger in her challenge. She knew Casey's station would play that clip, and she would not be seen as the heroic, hard-hitting news hound she wanted to portray. She meekly replied, "I just want my viewers to see how important police are to our safety." That was a far cry from where she was headed, but it gave her an out.

Sarah let Tammy have her out. "Thank you, Sergeant Honeycutt. By the way, for those of you who have had the police beat for a few years, Sergeant Honeycutt will be hanging up her baton and badge at the end of the month after thirty-five years on the force." She applauded, which led to a round of applause for the veteran who smiled proudly. Maria was not bashful. She knew she deserved the recognition, and she appreciated it. When the applause died, Sarah asked, "Are there any more questions regarding the two cases we are working?" She hoped not, but she knew better.

"What are the names of the wreck survivors?" Bernie Stone asked.

"The word is around town, but I prefer my readers receive that information officially."

Sarah read Liz's notes. "The survivors of the automobile accident are Elizabeth Torrez, sixteen, Gena Stevens, seventeen, and Bella Stamps, seventeen."

"How do you spell Gena?"

Sarah checked. "I have G-E-N-A."

Bernie wrote the name then asked, "Are you investigating an incident at the New Word Church? One of my sources said the Pastor there called about an issue behind the church and several department vehicles were there last evening."

"We are investigating an unusual sighting reported by Pastor Joe Cline."

"Is it linked to the dead body?"

"Bernie, your guess is as good as mine. We gathered some evidence that is being processed in our forensics lab today. If it is linked to the body, we will let you know. In the meantime, if anyone saw or heard anything unusual … vehicles or people … near the New Word Church Sunday night after their evening services, please notify Devaney PD."

# CHAPTER 14

## 10:00 A.M. Tuesday

Sarah left the press conference and walked to Booking. Lieutenant Robert Jarrett saw her and rose from his desk. He was the first lieutenant grade promotion for Sarah. She believed Booking and the jail required a lieutenant for adequate representation. She had a meeting scheduled with the Lieutenant.

"Hello, Chief. I didn't expect you this soon. I thought you were in a presser."

"Hello, Bob. It went better than I expected. We don't have much, so it was short and sweet ... mostly." Sarah sneered and rolled her eyes when she added the last word. "I suppose we need to look at the upgrade concerns you mentioned last week."

"This way," Lieutenant Jarret said as he swiped a security badge at the door that separated the jail entrance from Booking.

Sarah knew the area between Booking and the jail cells held two small conference rooms that were used for lawyer and client meetings. Both rooms had a small table and two uncomfortable chairs. The table was equipped with a security bar to secure handcuffed prisoners. Another security door separated that area from the cells. The cells were concrete block rooms. Most had bunk beds and could house eight prisoners without overcrowding. Those cells had wide iron bar doors that provided visibility

120

for the jailers. They were called pods. A few cells were single or double occupancy rooms with solid doors that had a single, barred window.

Sarah's phone buzzed. A message from Liz. *"Micha's here."* She didn't need to react to it. It was informational to let her know that Micha's shadow, Bianca Campbell, was touring the police department. She input *"Thanks. Notify Blake"* as acknowledgement. "Did Keith get all of his evidence in a room?" she asked the Lieutenant.

Bob grinned. "He's in Room Two. Tight fit. He carried a lot of stuff in. Must be one heck of a case."

"One that shouldn't have been. I'll look in on him after we see what you've got."

Lieutenant Jarret pointed out damage inside one of the empty single cells. "I think we need to upgrade the cots in the single rooms … and I don't mean make them more comfortable. I suggest solid concrete with a decent mat." He lifted the bare mattress from the steel cot. Several of the springs were missing. "They removed some of the springs."

"Shivs?"

"Possibly, but probably to use as a tool to remove nuts and bolts." Robert pointed toward one of the cot legs. "The flat iron brace is missing. It's a six-inch long piece of metal that could easily make a mean shiv."

"Have you found any shivs?"

"No. I have a feeling this was done some time ago and we just now noticed it. We did a complete shake down of existing prisoners. Nothing. Besides, everyone we have is on a short-term sentence for traffic or DUI violation. Not dangerous, and they are in a pod. A couple are from County awaiting trial, but none are considered dangerous or suicidal."

"Should we punish all future prisoners because of someone we don't know?" Sarah asked.

The Lieutenant shrugged. "I'd rather be proactive than face a State Police investigation. I think we need to do something in a couple of these secure cells. Especially for anyone with a history of violence or in for a capital offense."

Sarah thought a moment. She remembered some of the fights inside the pods. Tempers flared. Fists and feet. Maybe a few bites. Generally, wounds that could be treated with bandages by the jailers. She could only recall one incident that resulted in EMTs being called. She had no doubt that if that particular assailant had had the opportunity to fashion a weapon, the Coroner would have been called. "Okay. Put together some numbers. We have a repair budget. There's some room if you can make it fit."

Bob smiled. "Thank you, Chief."

Sarah stopped at Room Two before she left the jail. Sergeant Keith Locke was startled when she opened the door. She grinned. "Guilty?"

Keith smiled sheepishly, "Probably, but not about this." He waved despondently at an array of trash scattered across the floor, in the two chairs, and on the table. There was barely room to move.

Sarah initially thought Keith had simply tossed everything he gathered from the theft scene into the room. On second look, the trash seemed to be organized by type. Shreds of electrical wire insulation, large and small pieces. Small pieces of snipped copper wire, not big enough to steal. A pile of fasteners, such as nuts, bolts, screws, and wire clips. Anything and everything normally used to connect and support electrical wires was in that pile. An assortment of used D and C flashlight batteries were neatly stacked on one corner of the table. Big and small pieces of plastic, which ranged from snipped pieces smaller than a coin to empty water bottles including a gallon jug were in one corner of the room. Metal cabinet doors, probably removed to access the wire inside electrical cabinets, were leaned against a wall. Metal shavings and electrical box knockouts made up a pile on the table. Also on the table was a pile of paper trash that included full pages of installation instructions for packaged parts and torn bits of paper of all sizes. Nearly all the paper was darkened with footprints or factory dirt, tossed on the floor by the electricians to be cleaned by someone less skilled after the installation was completed. Two five-gallon buckets filled with dark and greasy floor sweepings were in a corner awaiting attention. Sarah imagined the sweepings contained smaller bits of everything in the piles. And there was a pile of assorted hand tools, wire cutters, pliers, screwdrivers, and a single open-end wrench.

"They left tools?"

"Most of them are broken or worn-out. I found the wrench inside a cabinet behind some big fuses. I guess the thieves didn't need the fuses. The wrench was probably left by an installer. I dusted all of them."

"Have you had time to make sense of any of it?" Sarah asked.

Keith shook his head. "Not really. I dusted everything for fingerprints, especially the batteries, but Alicia has her hands full with the John Doe and the TA. In the meantime, I've talked to the electrical contractor. I asked him for fingerprints from all of his electricians and helpers." He smirked. "If this was California, every electrician and contract employee would have fingerprints on file. But …" he continued dejectedly, "we'll play it out the old-fashioned way."

Sarah nodded. "Did he say how soon he'll get them? I can get Alicia some help if necessary." She reckoned she could borrow Sheriff Berringer's forensics-trained deputy. The downside was that it might make him think he had a chance to put his plan into play. It might give him the perception of the upper hand when they had their meeting to discuss his proposal.

"No. Mostly, he complained about Big Brother. I finally told him that if he didn't comply, I'd pull his contractor's license."

Sarah smiled and shook her head. "I hope he doesn't call you on it."

Keith grinned. "Me too. But I think I got the bluff in on him."

"What about the building owner? Does he have any ideas? Maybe former employees who know their way around the site?" Sarah continued to study the piles of evidence while she talked.

"He's confident it's not any of the employees who were skilled enough to strip the copper. Like the ETs and maintenance people." Keith picked up a piece of wire insulation. Though it was slit open, he held it to demonstrate its original size and shape. "Some of the mains were over an inch diameter. Heavy wire. The thieves knew enough to know the factory had heavy wire and a general idea of where the main power room was located, where the bulk of the copper would be."

"So, a former employee could be involved?"

"Yes, but the owner is confident in his old skilled craftspeople. They have too much to lose in their current careers to be involved in criminal activity."

"Maybe they just told the thieves but didn't physically participate. I'm sure some of them are disgruntled."

"Possible. If so, their fingerprints likely won't be on anything. It's been more than a year since the factory closed. Because the copper was stolen six months ago, everything inside the control cabinets was installed by contractors after those employees left."

"Let's hope it wasn't a contractor's employee," Sarah said with a shrug. She looked at the paper trash. "Anything of interest in this pile?"

"Trash that has been trampled. Installation instructions that experienced electricians didn't need, so they tossed them on the floor. Most are dirty but intact. Some of them were torn when they were stepped on."

"Some of the paper looks different," Sarah said as she poked into the pile of trash. "Have you given every scrap a close look?" She pointed toward another pile of trash. "What about the small water bottles and the gallon water bottle?"

"I dusted them. No viable prints. Greasy. They were probably wearing gloves."

"Do electricians normally wear gloves? A lot of what they do requires fine dexterity. Gloves would be clumsy." Sarah looked at a stack of photographs in a chair. "Are these the photos of the scene?"

Keith nodded. "Electricians might wear gloves when pulling wire, or latex gloves to keep their hands clean. I don't know. I'll ask the contractor. The thieves didn't need the same dexterity. Loosen. Cut. Yank. Gloves equal no prints." He paused before touching the stack of photos. "The pictures? I took a ton of pictures. It's a big building with three electrical rooms and a substation. The only thing they didn't touch was the substation, other than to power it down. They knew enough to isolate the power before they began stripping the copper."

"They were working in the dark?"

"Had to be." Keith nodded toward the pile of batteries. "They had to use flashlights to see. It's like a cave in the rooms. No windows."

Sarah looked through the pictures. Her eyes didn't linger too long on most of them. She saw one that interested her. "This one. I assume it's indicative of the floor scenes near the cabinets?" She posed her comment as a question.

"The primary electrical room." Keith craned to look over Sarah's shoulder. "What do you see?" He knew her well enough to know she had a reason for selecting that particular photograph.

"The gallon water jug. It's upright."

"Where they set it down. Makes sense, doesn't it?" Keith said querulously.

"You tell me. The fact it's not on its side could indicate it wasn't there long enough to be kicked around in the dark."

"I don't get it," Keith said confusedly.

"Maybe it's nothing." Sarah shrugged. "Do you think our thieves made all this mess? No doubt they did make some of it. Probably the batteries … or some of them, for sure. Most of the fasteners were probably tossed aside as they hurried to loosen the wires. The gallon jug might be theirs, set down when it was emptied near the end of the job." Her comments were querulously inflected to create thoughts.

Keith defensively responded, "I dusted it. No prints. Greasy smudges like from gloves."

"Where was it bought?"

"What?"

"They had to buy it. Maybe you can trace it. Everything has a barcode."

Keith scowled. It was apparent that he didn't believe the idea had merit … or was upset he didn't think of it. "I can try, but there's a lot of evidence to go through … and there's the fingerprint delay."

"I have confidence in you. When you come upon that single best clue, it'll all make sense. You'll figure out how it all fits together. Maybe even where they bought that brand of water," Sarah said with a smile. "Let me know when you do. This one is a puzzler."

Sarah's phone buzzed with a message. She expected to see another update from Liz. Instead, the ID caused her to flush lightly. Shawn Preminger. *"I think you need a break. Lunch?"*

Shawn was a lawyer. He relocated from St. Louis two years earlier. He wanted out of "big city law" and the stresses that came with it. He opened a law office in Devaney and started anew with a small practice. Starting anew wasn't new to Shawn. At age thirty, he divorced his wife of seven years and focused entirely on the duties of a junior partner in a large law firm. For a decade, the stresses and tensions gnawed at him. His status never increased during his tenure at the firm.

Shawn finally came to terms with his past. He wasn't proud of it. He wanted to get away from it. His ex-wife was a senior partner in the law firm, a status achieved when she gave herself to one of the founding partners while still married to Shawn. Initially, he thought losing the remaining part of his dream life, his standing in the legal community, would be more than he could bear. He drudged along, taking the cases that his ex-wife assigned him, nothing glorious but the job paid well. A single, soul-wrenching divorce case opened his eyes. He walked away from the money … and the pain.

In his newfound life, Shawn found time to smile. He found time to live. He found time to love. His dark hair was touched with gray, and his brown eyes laughed when he spoke. Sarah wasn't sure how the two of them got together, but he began pursuing her six months earlier. And she didn't run from him.

Sarah texted back, *"Lunch meeting with Mayor and Council."*

Shawn responded before Sarah passed through the security door for the return to her office. *"Do you need a lawyer to avoid violating Sunshine laws?"* He followed it with a smiling emoji and a GIF of a woman in handcuffs.

Sarah responded, *"Probably. Dinner?"*

*"Julio's? He prepares a mean steak."*

Sarah smiled as she confirmed the time and place. She briefly thought about their last date. Saturday night at her apartment and a lazy Sunday morning before she made her routine visit to the station. That seemed like a lifetime ago. It *was* a lifetime ago for John Doe, Tamara Yates, and Yvonne Timmons.

Another message rattled Sarah's phone as she ascended the stairs to the office area on the second floor. She shook her head and smiled. The day must be slow for Shawn. Not for her. The message was from Liz. Rather than respond, she went directly to Liz's office. "You messaged that Micha has something for me?"

"She does. She left the young lady with Alicia and Blake while she *"went to the bathroom,"* but she came to see you. The young lady told her about Sunday night."

"Did Micha tell you?"

Liz smiled. "She did. According to Bianca, she was with the five girls in the wreck along with another friend, Sasha Pierce."

"The OD?"

"Yes."

"They were all in that one car? That would have been a tight fit."

126

Liz shook her head. "No. Bianca was driving her car with the Timmons girl and Bella Stamps. Apparently, the Timmons girl was supposed to be driving her car, but she was too wasted. Sasha was in the car with Tamara Yates and the other two. They were all high, except Bianca. Tamara had scored some Adderall, but Sasha didn't want to take it. She preferred meth and was apparently proud of her new dealer's product. Said it gave her a bigger high than usual."

Sarah shook her head. "I can imagine. Laced with fentanyl. Bianca said she wasn't high? Is that her version or does Micha think it's the truth?"

"Bianca told Micha she isn't into drugs. She was drinking alcohol. Hard seltzers. Said she only had a buzz."

"Okay. Probably true. Were they all together when Sasha ODed?"

"They had left the Timmons' girl's house earlier and were heading to a boy's house. His parents were supposedly out of town. A *Risky Business* party."

"Kids!" Sarah said derisively.

Liz replied, "We were all kids once."

"I suppose you're right. I guess I was too focused on other things."

"Most of us were, but one bad choice could have changed all that."

"True. Did she say what happened with Sasha?"

"At some point, Tamara stopped and the riders in her car jumped out, panicked because Sasha had passed out. Bianca said one of the girls carried Narcan in her purse. They scrambled to spray the Narcan up her nose. When she didn't respond like they thought she should ... or would, they made a snap decision to seek medical help."

"At a convenience store?" Sarah asked incredulously.

"Now, you can say *kids*! They were afraid their own drug use would get them in trouble, so they decided to drop her off at the store so someone would find her and call an ambulance."

"If the attendant hadn't gone outside to smoke, she could have died there."

"That's a possibility. That's why Micha thought you needed to know about it sooner rather than later."

"None of them thought to call 9-1-1 anonymously?"

"Apparently, they were too frightened. Bianca decided to go home, too upset to continue with her friends. Until you visited her house, she was unsure if Sasha lived or died. Her friends didn't answer her texts."

"And the rest of them piled into Tamara Yates' car and drove around all night?"

"It would seem so. Probably afraid their friend was dead, and they were responsible."

Sarah's mouth twisted in thought. She finally shook her head in disgust. "This will require some consideration. I'll talk with the DA's office. There might be cause for criminal charges against the girls for abandoning Sasha. Can you reach out to Marcie? See if she has time later?"

Sarah knew Assistant District Attorney Marcie Ignack would be able to sort through the details of the case and determine if there was any legal reason to pursue the matter with the girls. She also knew Marcie would keep the discussion low key until a decision was made. Marcie was about the same age as Sarah. She had been an Assistant DA longer than Sarah had been a detective and police chief. A bottle-blonde with a harried persona, Marcie had a reputation as a tough prosecutor with a heart. Marcie was a newlywed, evidence that a career woman can find true love in her thirties ... late thirties fudged to appear younger. She had no desire to run for DA. She just wanted to win cases as a prosecutor and she used her feminine guile when necessary to influence jurors ... or distract them, as the case may be.

"I'll call her." Liz made a quick note on a pad. "Chief, don't forget you have a luncheon meeting with the Mayor and some Councilmembers."

"I haven't forgotten. Do you have any notes for me?"

"I do." Liz handed Sarah a single page with bullet points. "The Mayor said it would be an informal discussion of citizen comments and complaints. These are the calls we've received within the last week."

Sarah studied the short list and sighed. "I hope we don't expose ourselves to FOI laws."

"I can't speak to that."

# CHAPTER 15

## Noon, Tuesday

The list Liz handed Sarah was easy to read and easy to remember. It was easy to read because Liz used larger than normal font. Easy to remember because there were two repeated complaints, which Liz headlined prominently. Security on the *walking trails* and *speeding* on the streets. Citizen complaints tended to track recent events. If Sasha Pierce's OD was made public, there would undoubtedly be a third category.

Mayor Keck chose a small bistro near City Hall for the lunch meeting. The location was well known as a lunch place for city employees. A table with Councilmembers and the Mayor would not seem out of the ordinary. Still, Sarah worried there would be questions about a large group of city leaders at a lunch meeting. When she entered the bistro, she immediately tensed. Sheriff Berringer was talking with Mayor Keck. The first thought in her mind was that the lunch meeting was not just about citizen complaints. It was about the Sheriff pushing his forensic lab proposal to the Council. He was taking away her decision input.

Bill Keck smiled when he saw Sarah. "Chief, I was afraid your duties would keep you away. I know how busy you are right now." He stepped forward and gave her a gentle hug. "They're putting a couple of tables together for us. Sheriff Berringer has agreed to join us."

Sarah's anxiety was lessened by Bill's smile and tone. She extended her hand to the Sheriff, whose face seemed to be frozen in a permanent scowl.

"I didn't know we had a lunch date," she said with a teasing smile. She knew how to appear gracious.

Sheriff Berringer's eyes broke the scowl on his face before his lips followed with a small smile. "Last minute. The Mayor said you folks have issues here in Devaney. Thought my years of highway patrol might come in handy."

"That's good." Sarah turned to the three Councilmembers who were standing nearby and shook each one's hand. "Cary, Jim, Chase."

Councilwoman Cary Beecher was a Realtor. She and her husband owned Beecher Realty. A ready smile disguised the aggressive businesswoman she truly was. Councilwoman Beecher was the head of the Personnel Committee for the Council. Though the committee didn't make human resources decisions, they ensured the city followed employment laws. She was not afraid to make decisions on principle.

Councilman Jim Sloan was a strong advocate for the police. More than once during his time on the Council, he had kept past mayors in check regarding budget cuts for the Devaney Police Department. He knew the game and how to play it. He and Bill Keck were long-time friends.

Councilman Chase Mendelson was a CPA in real life. He was newer to the Council than either of the other two members present, but that didn't lessen his ability to maneuver the details of Council business. As one would expect, he was numbers and data driven when making decisions. He didn't think politically. His constituents probably didn't realize he was less concerned about his ward and more concerned about the city budget.

Sarah knew the three Councilmembers were probably the correct choices for an informal discussion of citizen complaints. Cary would measure the human side. Jim would cover the enforcement side. Chase would keep costs in mind. She still wasn't certain about Sheriff Berringer's role. When he was around, she felt as though a confrontation was in the offing. She likened their interactions to the turf protecting conflicts between Old West sheriffs and town marshals. And she knew as a duly elected Constitutional officer, the Sheriff was the highest law enforcement authority in the county.

The hostess came to seat them. Mayor Keck checked his watch. "We have one more. I hope he didn't get tied up." He nervously glanced through the sidewalk window. A relieved smile broke across his face. "There he is."

Sarah watched Bernie Stone enter the bistro. The reporter smiled at the six sets of eyes watching him. "Sorry. I got tied up at the West Wood light. Chic-Fil-A drags them in at lunchtime with their drive through lanes."

Bill extended his hand. "Glad you could make it. How bad was it?"

Bernie shrugged and chuckled, "No worse than usual. I should have known better than to come that way. There are always a few cars backed up on the street this time of day."

Sheriff Berringer growled, "Maybe a few patrolmen could stop that." His eyes were on Bill, purposely avoiding Sarah.

Bill laughed away the Sheriff's comment as he nodded to the hostess. "We're all here."

At the table, while waiting for their orders to be filled, Mayor Keck started the real conversation, "I think everyone here knows Bernie Stone. As a reporter for the local paper, he has agreed to represent the press, so we don't violate the sunshine laws with our discussions about citizen complaints."

Bernie sipped from a water glass and smilingly responded, "Anything for a free lunch."

The server took their orders and bantered with the Mayor. Bill obviously used the bistro regularly.

When the Server left, Bill looked at Sarah. "Chief, I suspect the police department has received a few complaints stemming from the discovered body. Would you care to share those to get started?" He pulled a folded sheet of paper from his jacket and put on his reading glasses.

Sarah responded without looking at Liz's notes. "We have. Not all were about the body, but that certainly precipitated some of the recent complaints. We received calls regarding security on the walking trails."

"Don't you have a patrol presence?" Sheriff Berringer asked accusatively.

"During peak usage. Summer and weekends. And only during daylight hours."

"Sound like night patrol is needed."

Sarah matched the Sheriff's intense look. "The trails were not intended for night usage. They are not lit."

"Doesn't ..." the Sheriff began but was cut off by Councilman Sloan.

Jim Sloan's eyes narrowed toward the Sheriff when he spoke. "We aren't here to resolve the complaints or assign blame. We're here to see what complaints we have. As I recall, it was made clear from the beginning that the trails are for daytime use and would not be patrolled. Devaney PD added patrols for peak hours because of disturbances." He glanced at Sarah and smiled, "Chief, how are the complaints poised? Angry? Helpful?"

"Thank you, Jim. Most of the complaints about the trails come with suggested solutions ranging from night lights to police presence. A few suggest tearing out the trails because they are *"an invitation to muggings, rapes, and murders."*

"Are they?" Councilman Mendelson asked.

Sarah deliberately paused before answering. "Data does not support that." The list Lieutenant McCuskey provided was in her pocket. She retrieved it and held it at arm's length to read. Typical bistro lighting made the print hard to see clearly, even if it was large font. She leaned her head back.

Bill Keck reached across the table. "Mind if I see that?"

Sarah flushed lightly and handed the sheet of paper to the Mayor.

Bill winked at Sarah and adjusted his reading glasses. He studied the list before stating, "Looks like there have been no reported rapes since the trail system began a decade ago. Much like I remember it. Hmmm. No murders to date, with the exception of John Doe."

Sarah interjected, "And the jury is still out on that one."

"Of course. Most calls are domestic disturbances. Looks like squabbles between bike riders and walkers. Surprisingly few muggings." Bill handed the list back to Sarah. "What other complaints do you have?"

"Speeding complaints began yesterday afternoon."

"More officers on the streets writing tickets will stop the speeding," Sheriff Berringer averred.

Councilwoman Beecher replied, "Not true, Sheriff. It's a known fact that towns with speed trap reputations still have speeders. Police presence has limited effect on overall speeding." She glanced supportively at Sarah, "We know the recent traffic tragedy that took the lives of two Devaney High School girls stemmed from substance abuse which led to the speeding."

Sarah cringed. She had not made any official comments regarding the state of the driver or of the other girls in the vehicle accident. "We've not released anything to indicate driver impairment," she protested with a sideways glance toward Bernie.

Cary nodded deferentially. "I apologize for making that comment." She then looked at Bernie, "Please don't make that public ahead of confirmation from the Chief."

"Was the driver under the influence?" asked Sheriff Berringer. "Why wasn't I informed?"

Mayor Keck waved his hand. "Cary is a friend of the Yates family. She and Stella Yates are Realtors. I wasn't aware of impairments ... if it is true." He glanced toward Sarah and furrowed his brow lightly.

Sarah knew Bill Keck well enough to understand his expression. He didn't want the conversation to continue in that vein. "As is usual with traffic accidents, especially accidents with fatalities, the driver's blood is tested. But when people hear there were blood tests, they assume it's because alcohol or drugs are suspected. It's routine. As it is, the results are not public ... nor should they be at this time."

"I'm not public," the Sheriff growled. "I'm the ranking law enforcement officer in this county."

"And the case is Devaney PDs," Sarah stated strongly. "No one else needs to be involved."

"If the lab was under County control, ..."

Sarah stopped the Sheriff. "But it's not. The Devaney PD Forensics Lab is under Devaney PD's control." She knew her response was sharper than necessary, but it felt good. "Now, back to the speeding complaints. Because of the accident, speeding is paramount on the minds of the public. This happens every time we have a fatality accident." She half-smiled at the Sheriff. "If there is anything positive that comes from a fatality accident, the number of speeders decreases for a week or so."

"Ten days." Chase Mendelson replied factually. Everyone looked askance. He continued, "The American public remains focused on a subject for about ten days. It makes sense that they are mindful of speeding for that length of time after a bad accident."

"I doubt it's that long," the Sheriff replied.

"Maybe not," Chase said without further comment. He wasn't there to argue statistics.

"Any other complaints?" Mayor Keck asked.

"The usual. Too much police enforcement. Gangs of kids on bicycles in the neighborhood. Noisy neighbors."

The Mayor nodded then added, "Calls to City Hall have picked up regarding the trails. We didn't get many on speed enforcement." He grinned. "When we hear about speed enforcement in the Mayor's Office, it's never a demand for *more* of it. Is anyone else getting calls?"

None of the Councilmembers offered anything more than what had already been mentioned. Sheriff Berringer shook his head to indicate he had nothing new. Since he was County Sheriff, the only calls he would have received would have been County related.

The Mayor continued. "Okay, let's talk about the trails. Speeding is an ongoing issue. In the eyes of the public, our police department is either too tough or not tough enough when it comes to speeding. I think Devaney PD is addressing the issue properly. Speeders gonna speed. Cops are gonna catch 'em sooner or later. Are the trails an issue?"

"Having them?" Councilman Sloan asked.

Bill replied, "We've got them. What do we do about them? Do we need to spend money for security twenty-four seven?"

"No!" Chase replied without hesitation.

"Let's not dismiss the idea without discussion," Cary said.

"I agree with Councilman Sloan. I think they're a waste of resources," the Sheriff said.

Cary stiffened. "They add value to our city. People expect the city to provide parks and recreation venues. They won't move here or stay here if we can't offer those amenities."

"They're just that ... amenities. They're not necessities. More patrol officers, better patrol cars, bigger crime labs, better cooperation between law enforcement agencies. Those are necessities."

"The citizens of Devaney ... even the county ... perceive the trails as value adding," Cary retorted. "That means we, as elected officials, should do the same."

The Sheriff's face reddened angrily. "As elected officials, we are charged with the public's trust. They trust us to use tax money wisely." He quickly glanced toward Sarah. "No redundant spending." He returned his eyes to Cary. "Sounds like the trails are a Chamber of Commerce thing."

Bill raised his hand and avoided direct eye contact with Sheriff

Berringer. "We have the trails," he stated flatly. "Generally speaking, the people like the trails. They even voted for a one mil trail and parks tax to finance them. And now, they have some suggestions to improve the trail system. I think we should listen to them."

Sheriff Berringer wasn't going to give up easily. "Are they willing to pay for the improvements?"

"That's something we can and will address once we understand the issues," Bill smiled. "That's why we're having this informal meeting. To see if we need to pursue it further, or if what we're hearing is simply a normal reaction to the discovery of a dead body near the trail."

The defiant anger in Cary's eyes subsided. She purposely avoided eye contact with the Sheriff. She addressed Sarah. "Is there a connection between the trail and the body, or are the two unrelated?"

Sarah smiled. She understood the Councilwoman's reasoning. "We don't have any evidence that indicates the trail is causally connected to the death. The isolation of the area is the only likely connection."

"But the trail made the isolated area easy to access," the Sheriff stated.

"So would a deserted county road," Bill said with a firm glare at the Sheriff. "I think all we can assume is that the person who committed the murder ... if it was a homicide ... knew the area is secluded and the body would go undetected for a few days. Time to cover his tracks." He looked toward Sarah for affirmation.

Sarah nodded. "We can assume that."

"What do we do?" Jim asked. "Discuss increased security on the trails?"

"I'm not sure our budget can support that," Chase replied.

Bill nodded. "We definitely need to dig into the need for changes. Bear in mind, if the city does something, it will cost money we don't currently have."

The Sheriff grunted, "Or the citizens can take care of it themselves."

Cary cocked her head sideways, "You mean like a neighborhood watch?"

The Sheriff half-smiled. "That wasn't what I meant, but I suppose that might work."

"What did you mean?" Cary asked.

"They can stay off the trail at night. I think I've seen PSAs from Devaney PD to that effect." The Sheriff glanced at Sarah.

Sarah nodded. "That is true." She knew more about the John Doe than the others. "But at this point, we can't make the assumption that John Doe was killed where we found him."

"Do you think he wasn't?" Cary asked.

"We don't know enough to assume anything. He was shot sometime during the night. We found him in the brush beside the trail after daylight. Other than that, we would be speculating without evidence."

"Isn't that what detectives do? Make assumptions?"

"Not as a matter of proof of crime or identity of a criminal. Assumptions can lead an investigation away from the evidence and cause the single best clue that will solve the case to be missed." Sarah shuddered internally. Her first case floundered in assumptions to the detriment of an innocent person. She saw Bernie was watching her intently, hoping for something he could make into a scoop.

Bill recognized the direction the table conversation was going. He grinned at Sarah. "Single best clue. That's what Carl always said. Crimes are solved by that single best clue. And nothing comes of it until you discover … or recognize it. Right?"

"That's it in a nutshell," Sarah replied, happy for the intervention.

The Mayor directed his attention to the group. "All that being said, can one of you prepare to lead a discussion regarding the trails at our next council meeting? Currently, because of the recent incident, we have an increased level of concern among trail users. Those concerns aren't new, just highlighted because of the incident. If we don't address the concerns, we risk someone going vigilante on us."

Councilman Sloan spoke first. "I can do that." He looked at Sarah. "I may need some data from PD. Who do I contact? You?"

"You can. Or Liz, the Administrative Assistant. We'll provide whatever we have."

Cary cautioned, "We need to make sure the trails are safe. To protect our environment, a good trail system supports the use of bicycles for our growing population. If people can access businesses via a safe trail system, they will make that choice." In a more upbeat tone, she added, "Plus, the more people use the trails for errands and shopping, the fewer traffic accidents there will be."

No one responded verbally, but a variety of facial expressions indicated reservations about the Councilwoman's commentary. The group engaged in banter for the rest of the meal. They all knew further discussion would create a risk of FOI violations.

Sarah's phone rang. She pressed the Bluetooth connection on her steering wheel. It was Alicia Kettering. "Hello, Alicia. What do you have?" Alicia never called to visit.

Alicia's bubbly voice came through too loud. "That girl has potential."

"Which girl?"

"The one with Micha. Bianca. She's a sad girl."

"Sad?"

"Sad. You know. Not happy."

"Her friends were in the accident yesterday."

"I know. I feel sorry for her."

"What did she do?" Sarah knew Alicia wouldn't have called if she didn't have something of value, but the conversation was off topic.

"Of course. Just so you know, I knew not to show any of the evidence from her friends' wreck when I showed her what we do in the lab. And I didn't want to show her the blood items from any cases, so I pulled out the bag the Coroner sent me. The bag with John Doe's clothes."

"Didn't they have blood on them?"

"Yes, but they were folded so it didn't immediately show. That wasn't what Bianca noticed. The second I took the clothes out of the bag, she sniffed and said they smelled like baby powder."

"Baby powder?"

"Yes. And she was right. They do. I collected some residue and am running it through the spectrometer. I think he might be married. At the very least, he's been in close contact with a baby."

"Or has jock itch," Sarah cautioned. She didn't notice a wedding ring on the John Doe. Alicia didn't normally get ahead of the evidence, but the excitement of Bianca's insight made her giddy.

"Oh. I didn't think of that. I'll call the Coroner to see if he noticed a rash."

"Good idea. Be sure to let Boston know what you find."

"For sure. I thought you might like to know Bianca was fully engaged with Micha. I might not have noticed the smell." Alicia sniffed. "Allergies bothering me."

Sarah knew the sniff was faked. Alicia probably detected her perturbation. The call should have been directed to Boston. "I do. Thank you for calling me. When you call Henry, if he didn't notice anything, ask him to contact the State ME to check the body for talcum powder or rashes."

"Will do, Chief. He'll probably say it was the white dirt he found, but it's different. I'm glad Micha brought Bianca to see the lab."

"Me too. Did Blake get to talk with her?"

"I think they did when they walked out of the lab. I'm not sure. But they did hit it off, even though she asked him if he was a cop as soon as she met him. I think meeting a cop who didn't fit the mold helped her."

"Good. I'll check with Blake later. I'm on my way to the station if you need anything else." Sarah disconnected the call. Her mind was working, sorting evidence from the John Doe, from the church, from the traffic accident, and from the copper theft. The budget, trail safety, and citizen complaints simmered with everything else. And there was the overdose to consider.

Sarah's cell phone rang as she entered the station through the side door near the stairs. She waved at Sergeant Honeycutt as she held the phone at a distance to read the Caller ID. Teri Caudle. "Hello, Teri."

"Chief, I hope I'm not catching you at a bad time."

"Not at all, Teri. What can I do for you?" Sarah slowly climbed the stairs.

"I talked to Seelie. She's willing to visit with you, but it will have to be in the evening … after she gets off work."

"What day is best for her?"

After a short pause, Teri replied, "Today or tomorrow. I'm on days off. I think we both need to be there."

Sarah reached the top of the stairs and pushed the bullpen door open. "Where do you want to meet?"

"Oh, at our house … if that's okay. Seelie said five or five-thirty would be best for her."

# CHAPTER 16

## 1:45 P.M. Tuesday

Sarah was in her office when Alicia called to follow up on the earlier call. "Chief. The Coroner said he didn't notice any powder on the body. Just the white gravel bits. He didn't notice a rash either. He said he would contact the State ME to double check for us."

"Interesting," Sarah mused aloud. "Does Boston have any ideas on what you've found?"

"I haven't really talked with him much. He's investigating something at the church. He brought a ton of evidence from there for me to sort through. That's in addition to the evidence from the John Doe scene. Plus, Keith has a load for me."

Sarah knew all about Alicia's workload. Alicia knew she knew. They had discussed it earlier. She recognized a call for help. "I know. It's a lot all at once. Maybe Lieutenant McCuskey can send some help."

"If they aren't Tech trained, my findings won't be admissible," Alicia stated.

Sarah mentally gritted her teeth. Nothing was ever simple. "I think the County has a forensics-trained deputy." She offered the comment even though it grated on her to do so. Pride and turf wars had no place in police work … but they were there.

"If they're certified, maybe I could use a little help for a day or two."

"I'll call Sheriff Berringer." Sarah immediately wished she was a

Detective again. In that role, she only had the pursuit of evidence to plague her mind.

The Sheriff answered after a few rings. He believed the phone should ring at least three times before it was answered. To do otherwise indicated he wasn't busy.

"Sheriff, is your forensics-trained deputy available?"

"For what?"

"My Forensics Tech is inundated. If your man is available, I would appreciate the loan of a trained Tech."

The Sheriff let silence consume almost a minute. "He's kind of busy, but I can probably send him over by three o'clock."

Sarah saw the time. She suspected the man wasn't truly busy. The Sheriff simply didn't want to rush to comply with her request. But his response would be good enough. "That's even better than I hoped. Tell him to check in with Shift Commander Honeycutt. She'll show him to the lab and introduce him to Alicia.

After a momentary pause, the Sheriff replied, "Sure. He'll be there. Of course, if we had a combined lab, this wouldn't be an issue. Maybe now would be a good time to discuss my proposal."

"I think Liz is setting up a meeting for that discussion. Thank you for your help, Sheriff." Sarah felt dirty, as though she had betrayed Alicia sacred trust by seeking help from the man who wanted to wrest control of the Forensics Lab from Devaney PD. She called Alicia and Sergeant Honeycutt so they would be prepared. Alicia was hesitantly appreciative. The Sheriff had made no secret of his desires. All of Devaney PD would be watching Sarah on this one.

Sarah called Liz. "Have you set the meeting with Sheriff Berringer?"

"10:00 tomorrow," Liz responded. "I'm working on your notes now. Do you need them right away?"

"No. Tomorrow morning will be fine. Something's come up. I just wanted to have that meeting sooner rather than later." Sarah exhaled heavily.

"He's really pushing this, isn't he?" Liz asked sympathetically.

"He is, but he doesn't have any support for it. I just have to face him and bring it to a close."

"You can do it. I have faith in you."

"Thanks, Liz."

Sarah heard the rattle of police gear outside her office. Sergeant Honeycutt peered through the open door.

"Chief, I dispatched a unit to Mason's Funeral Home. Thought you might like to know. Some kind of disturbance between parents of the kids in the wreck."

Sarah shuddered. "Did they say what?"

"Just that it was ugly."

Sarah rose from her desk. She holstered her service weapon. "Liz, I'm going to Mason's Funeral Home. Call me, if you need me."

Sarah ran with her lights, but not the siren. She didn't want to speed, but she also didn't want to be held up by traffic. She tried to anticipate what was happening at the funeral home. A disturbance between parents of the girls in the accident could be for a variety of reasons. The patrol unit was parked near the front entrance of the funeral home when she arrived.

Inside the lobby, Henry Mason was standing in front of an obviously distraught couple. Corporal Jennie Baldor was between the three and an angry man with an anxious woman a half step behind him. Officer Patrick Bohannan was nearby, poised and observing. Corporal Baldor was engaged with the angry man. She didn't notice Sarah's arrival, though Officer Bohannan did.

"Sir, I'm asking you to leave. One last time. Do you understand?"

"They killed my baby!" the man shouted. "They're going to be punished if I have to do it myself."

Corporal Baldor's expression changed from calmly coaxing to sternly commanding. "Sir. I'm no longer asking. Leave now or Officer Bohannan and I will place you under arrest."

"Arrest? For what? They need to be the ones arrested. They let their doped-up daughter drive a car. They killed my daughter."

"Disturbing the peace. Terroristic threatening. Sir, leave now!" Corporal Baldor noticed Sarah. Her eyes pleaded for help.

Sarah stepped forward. "Sir, I'm Police Chief James. Is there something we can help you with?"

"Good! Someone who understands the penalty for murder. Arrest those people ... those people who allowed their daughter to murder my baby."

"Sir, are you Mister Timmons?" Sarah fixed her eyes on the angry man's crazed eyes.

"Yes, and that's Jerald Yates and his wife, Stella. They are responsible for my daughter's death."

"Mister Timmons, are you aware of what occurred Sunday night and Monday morning?"

Paul Timmons blinked, momentarily stunned by the question. "Of course, I'm aware." He jabbed his finger toward the Yates. "Their daughter killed my daughter. It's all their fault. They are going to be punished."

Sarah knew Timmons needed a dose of reality to clear his thinking processes. He needed information so he could sort through the situation logically. His emotions were out of control. "Was your daughter home Sunday night?"

Paul glared. "What is that supposed to mean?"

"Just what I asked. Was Yvonne home Sunday night ... at any time?"

"What difference does it make?"

"If Yvonne had been home, she would not have been out doing drugs with the other girls."

Paul was stunned. "My daughter doesn't do drugs."

"Mr. Timmons, did you give your daughter permission to be away from home all night?"

"What difference does that make?" Paul's face reddened further, as impossible as that seemed. "And I said, my daughter doesn't do drugs!"

Sarah ignored the sound of her heart throbbing in her chest. Paul Timmons was on rage's edge. "The blood tests indicate otherwise. All the girls, including Yvonne, were under the influence of Adderall. So much under the influence that they left one of their friends at a convenience store to die of a drug overdose."

"No way. That's a lie!" Paul angrily pointed toward the Yates. "And if it's true, their slutty daughter was the ringleader ... just like she was the driver that killed my baby."

Sarah heard a light commotion behind her. She knew it was one or both of the Yates reacting to Paul's words. She also heard Officer Bohannan calmly caution them to stay quiet. "Mister Timmons, are you aware that Yvonne was supposed to be driving everyone in her car, but she was too wasted to drive? The decision for Tamara Yates to drive was made because

Yvonne couldn't. There's enough blame to go around for every one of those girls, but no amount of blame will bring back Yvonne or Tamara. Corporal Baldor told you to leave. I'm repeating that order." She held his angry eyes in a stare down.

Carol Timmons plaintively pleaded, "We need to make arrangements for Yvonne's funeral."

Sarah kept her eyes on Paul's eyes. His anger was deep. She knew his eyes would telegraph any physical action he might take. She responded to Carol, "I understand that. You can come back after the Yates family leaves."

"Paul," Carol said, touching her husband's bicep, "let's go. We can come back later. This isn't helping."

Paul was slow to lower his eyes, but only after he glared one more time at the Yates. "This isn't over." His words were more a threat than a statement of fact.

Sarah watched the couple exit the lobby. Officer Bohannan followed them out the door and watched them get in their car. Sarah turned to Henry and the Yates couple. Only then did she notice Ellen Mason standing outside her office, nervously watching events unfold. There was no doubt that Ellen placed the 9-1-1 call. "Mr. and Mrs. Yates, I am sorry for your loss. I'm sorry you had to endure something like this at this time."

Stella Yates sobbed deeply. "Is what you said true? Was Tamara on drugs."

Sarah cringed. "They all were, Mrs. Yates. I'm sorry I had to reveal that in this manner, but I think it was the only way Mr. Timmons was going to see the reality of the situation. It didn't matter which of those girls was driving, something bad was going to happen."

"And the girl they left to die? What of her?"

"She survived. Someone found her and called for help."

Stella leaned against Jerald, who pulled her to his side. "That's good, I suppose. We should have been better parents. Paid more attention. Listened."

Sarah felt for Stella, and all the parents involved. Recriminations would come for all of them. Gossip and rumors would abound, fueling self-doubts and self-flagellation. Some of them might go into an emotional downward spiral that ruined the remainder of their lives. Life would never be the same for any of them. "Don't do that to yourself. The girls made choices that brought them to this point. Don't blame yourself for the choices your daughter made. I suggest you talk with a professional counselor." She glanced at Henry. "I'm sure Mr. Mason has some contacts that will be helpful."

Henry made a head motion toward Ellen, who immediately went into her office. "We do have the names of some very good people. Loss of a loved one is difficult, especially when that loved one is a child."

Ellen returned with some business cards. She gingerly placed them in Stella's hand, squeezed lightly, and smiled caringly. "Any one of these can help."

"Thank you," Stella sobbed.

Sarah walked toward the hallway that led to Henry's office. Henry took the hint and followed. As soon as they were where Sarah felt comfortable whispering, she asked, "Is everything okay now?"

Henry shook his head. "This is not the first time I've had to deal with angry victims. It is the first time I've not been able to control it."

"Mr. Timmons *is* angry. Deep in his soul."

"Yes. He needs professional help for sure. They were scheduled to be here tomorrow. I didn't want to risk the two families crossing paths. But they just showed up. I'm sure it was him. Mrs. Timmons just tagged along."

"I'm sure he knew the Yates family was here."

Henry nodded. "Yeah. This wasn't an accidental meeting." He paused before he slowly said, "I'm worried they might overreact when they come tomorrow. I had to reattach the decedent's head. It was severed across the chin. Damage that is hard to conceal. I will recommend they not look at the remains. That never goes over well."

"We didn't release those details," Sarah responded hesitantly.

"You didn't have to. Even first responders talk. Word gets out. I'm sure that contributed to Mr. Timmons' anger, knowing his daughter was decapitated. I doubt he knows the extent of the damage. It's hard enough to lose a child. Harder if the death circumstances make the body unviewable."

Sarah nodded. "Corporal Baldor and Officer Bohannan will hang around for a while just in case Timmons returns. Tell Corporal Baldor what time Timmons will be here tomorrow, and she will be on hand … just in case."

"Thank you. I need to finish with Mr. and Mrs. Yates."

Sarah had a meeting with Assistant DA Marcie Ignak, officially Marcie Stapleton, at 2:30. She kept her maiden name on her door and business cards for professional continuity. Sarah drove from the funeral home to the County Courthouse. She was cutting the time close. Of course, she also suspected Marcie would be running late.

Marcie was late. She rushed into the office area clutching a bundle of folders tightly to her torso, which forced her breasts higher, precipitously close to exposure. Her face was flushed, and a stray strand of blonde hair drooped across one eye. She blew at the strand, but it wasn't going anywhere. It was styled to dangle there, an indication of how busy she was. Too busy to keep her hair out of her eyes. She might have changed her marital status, but she had not changed her harried persona. She smiled at Sarah who had barely taken a seat in the waiting area. "Sorry I'm late, Sarah. You know how it is at the DA's office. Too much work and not enough staff."

Sarah laughed. "Welcome to public service." She stood and opened Marcie's office door for her.

Marcie exhaled heavily after she dropped the folders onto her desk. Her breasts didn't change their danger-of-exposure position. An effectively designed position meant to attract ... or distract when legal arguments were being made. "So, you have a question about the law?"

"I do," Sarah said as she repositioned a chair before she sat. "The girls who were involved in the wreck yesterday ..."

Marci interrupted, "Tragic stuff. I can't imagine how those parents are coping."

"Yes," Sarah went with the change in conversation. "I don't think any of them have come to terms with it yet. In denial for the moment."

"I can imagine. It's hard to believe. So, what is the question? All I got from Liz is something about accountability for abandoning a drunk person ... or something like that."

"Essentially correct, only it's drugs rather than alcohol. A friend of the girls overdosed. They administered Narcan but were afraid to go to the hospital. They were all under the influence themselves. Instead, they dropped their friend off outside a convenience store in the middle of the night in hopes someone would find her."

Marcie sat forward in her chair and leaned on her elbows, a posture that forced her breasts together. "Hmm? So, you want to know if they are liable for their actions?"

"Exactly. I'm not keen on arresting anyone, but I also don't want to be derelict in my duty. If they violated the law, I need to do something … or, should I suggest, the DA needs to do something by pressing charges."

Marcie leaned back. Her brow furrowed in thought. After a long pause, she said, "Off hand, it does look bad. By administering Narcan, their actions admit they knew their friend was in medical distress." She paused to think.

Sarah tried not to fidget while she waited for Marcie to process the information.

Marcie leaned forward, "But, they are not by definition *caregivers*. They don't have a compulsory obligation to do more than they did. The reputation of Narcan among the general population is that it is a cure-all."

"But they left her unattended," Sarah argued.

"Yes. Yes, they did. But it was in a public place. They did so under the assumption that their friend would receive professional help quickly."

"That's a poor assumption. She could have died there if the store clerk hadn't gone outside to smoke."

"Could have. Maybe. Maybe not. They administered Narcan. What would a medical professional have done?"

Sarah thought a moment. The conversation was helping assuage her concerns. "Administer Narcan, or something similar, but maintained observation."

Marcie leaned back. "It would seem that they did the prudent thing to save the girl's life. Their biggest sin was abandoning a friend when she needed their emotional support. They did it out of fear their own drug use would be discovered. Their decision was faulty, affected by their own state of inebriation, but not necessarily criminal."

"You're saying you would not prosecute?"

"Under the circumstances, no. In fact, a good defense lawyer could argue that they saved her life by taking her out of the car. I don't think anyone can accuse Devaney PD of dereliction of duty … especially not since you brought it to my attention. I'd say focus on what is important, and this is not."

Sarah smiled. "Okay. I'm going to assume the DA won't send out a writ or something demanding the girls be arrested."

"I'll confirm with him, but I can't see that happening."

# CHAPTER 17

## 3:00 P.M. Tuesday

Sarah drove to the station after her meeting with Marcie. She wasn't sure the girls were completely out of the woods legally, but she was confident that her department was not derelict in handling the aftermath of the girls' behaviors. It was after 3:00 o'clock. Deputy Steger would be in the lab ... unless the Sheriff decided to play games. On the way to the lab, she encountered Sergeant Honeycutt. "Good afternoon, Maria. Is Deputy Steger in the lab?"

Maria smiled. "I hope Alicia can get some work done."

Sarah nodded. "As do I. We dumped a lot on her all at once. A trained technician will be a big help."

Maria laughed. "Not what I meant. If I was straight and a few years younger, I'd be chasing that man. I might anyway. I just hope Alicia isn't too distracted."

Sarah shook her head and smiled. Maria could always make her smile. "Me too. I'll go introduce myself to him."

Maria walked away chuckling, "Sure. You and the rest of the women in the department."

Maria was right. Deputy Waylon Steger was an attractive man. Young. Clean cut with a disarming smile. He missed his calling to be a model. Sarah introduced herself. "I'm Chief James. I'm glad the Sheriff allowed you to come to help. Alicia is inundated with evidence."

Deputy Steger smiled. His teeth seemed to sparkle as much as his eyes did. "Thank you." He glanced toward Alicia. "Tech Alicia has been showing me all the evidence. This is just like when I worked in a lab. Standard flow was feast or famine. She has a lot of evidence for just one case."

"Actually, she's working three cases and four scenes."

"Understood. I'll do all I can to help." Steger indicated the surroundings with his hand. "This is a nice lab. As good as the one in Wichita."

"It's all Alicia's doing. So, you worked in a lab?"

"Yes, Ma'am. Forensics lab in Wichita."

"Private?"

"No. PD. They have their own lab."

"How long?" Sarah didn't know anything about the Deputy.

"I went to work there right out of college." Steger glanced at Alicia. "Not saying I didn't enjoy my job, but it was too routine for me. Not the glamour of *CSI*." He chuckled. "I saw the exciting stuff the officers were doing and decided on a career change. After graduating from the Academy, the best offer I got was from Sheriff Berringer. He has several openings."

Sarah knew why the Sheriff had openings. "How long have you been a deputy?"

"About nine months. It's been different …" Steger paused and lowered his voice, "but I'm not sure what the Sheriff had in mind when he hired me. I thought his interest in my background was to develop me as a detective."

Sarah nodded. "Your background would definitely enhance your investigative skills. I wish you luck with that. I'll get out of your way. I know Alicia has work that's time sensitive." As she left, she felt sorry for the Deputy. The Sheriff should have been open with him. She made a mental note to mention Steger's name to HR. If the Sheriff's plan drove the young man away, he would be a good addition to Devaney PD. Maybe even have a shot at detective in time.

Keith called before Sarah reached her office. "Chief, got a minute?"

"What do you have?"

"I'm getting fingerprints from the contractor's people. He's sending them over here a couple at a time. Lieutenant Jarrett's people are handling it for me. I'm not sure how soon Alicia can compare the prints for me."

"She's got some help now. Get them to her. She can prioritize them. It shouldn't take very long. Anything else?" Sarah tried not to sound abrupt. Keith seemed needy, and she had work to do.

"Can you come look at some of this stuff? I think I've reached an impasse until I get those fingerprints … and there's no guarantee they will tell us anything."

"I'll be there."

Sarah checked with Liz before she walked down the back stairs toward the jail. Two of the contractor's employees were in Booking, waiting to be fingerprinted. She nodded politely as she walked past them. She heard them whispering as she walked to the security door and swiped her ID to open it. She paused, debating whether to confront them for their sophomoric remarks. She turned and scowled, "You gentlemen need to keep those thoughts to yourself." She went through the door, leaving two red faces behind her. She imagined their eyes were staring at the tile, afraid to look at her backside.

Keith was leaning against the doorframe of Room Two. He sheepishly grinned when he saw her. "Sorry to bother you, Chief. This one has me baffled. I need a fresh set of eyes. The last time the place was burgled, the idiots left a business card from a scrap dealer. All I had to do was check with the dealer and he remembered them. I've checked with every dealer in the area. No one has come in with a large volume of copper wire recently."

Sarah controlled a grimace. Keith was searching for an easy answer. He knew better. He *was* better. "What's bothering you, Keith?"

"What? This case bothers me. There's all this evidence, but nothing is evident."

She glanced at the piles of evidence from the theft scene. "I don't mean the case. Something has you distracted. What is it?"

Keith swayed from foot to foot. His mouth twisted nervously. "Nothing."

"No, Keith. It's something. You're not focusing on this case. You're missing the obvious. What is it?" Sarah knew Keith's thought processes. She learned that and more during their time together when he was a patrol officer, and she was a detective. He achieved detective status because of his innate curiosity and ability to see details, not because of their relationship … though their relationship probably contributed because they worked well together.

Keith struggled internally while Sarah waited for a response. Sarah wasn't going to allow him to escape the question. He finally said, "Zoey."

"Is she ill?" Sarah learned to like Mayor Kamen's hired consultant, Zoey Kopechne, after the young woman woke up to the Mayor's illegal activities and came to Sarah with clues and evidence. The fact that Keith married Zoey helped remove the tensions that would have existed between the two peace officers after Sarah became Police Chief.

"No. She got a job offer in Nebraska. In Omaha. It's too good an offer to turn it down. It's a good company with a promising future. She'll make almost twice what I make."

"And you're wondering what to do? I don't want to lose you, but there's only one option."

Keith's eyes stared at the floor. He responded softly. "Probably true."

"No probably to it. Follow your wife. I can contact Omaha PD. Police departments are always hiring, especially large departments like Omaha. It might not be a detective job, but it'll be a job. You're smart enough to make the grade soon enough." Sarah watched Keith's eyes dance as he processed what she had said. He knew she was right. He knew what he had to do. He just needed her approval.

Keith smiled appreciatively and nodded. "Yeah. It's hard to leave a career that I worked hard to develop."

"It's for your wife. It's for your life outside of the job. Now, what do you see in this room?"

Keith was relieved to change subjects. He pointed at the pile of paper evidence. "I was hoping I could find something worthwhile in the paper pieces. I did find a partial receipt. All it had was the store barcode at the bottom. I hoped it was for the gallon water jug."

"I take it that it wasn't?"

"No. It was an electrical supply company receipt for a box of fasteners. The contractor bought it for the job." Keith shook his head. "Nothing in that pile that remotely connects to an individual. Probably wouldn't matter anyway. Odds are that any personal receipts would be by the contractor's people. Snacks or something."

Sarah stepped inside the room, cluttered as it was with piles of evidence from the factory. "The gallon jug. What about its barcode? That should be traceable without a receipt."

"The product barcode is on the labels of water jugs. Part of the label is gone. The part with the barcode. They must have torn it off."

"It wasn't in the paper trash?"

"No. I even went back to check trash cans around the building. No labels."

"Will it be okay if I pick it up?" Sarah waited for Keith's approval.

"Sure. I've already dusted everything for prints. The jug had nothing useful. Smudges without clear prints … full or partial."

Sarah studied the plastic jug. "Every food product in America has a tracking number. Sometimes it's as simple as a *packaged date* for traceability. It will be on the container, not the label." She handed the jug to Keith. "It's usually positioned close to the *best used by* date."

"Do you think that can be traced to the manufacturer?"

"No doubt. That's why it's there."

"But I don't know where it was bought to start tracking it."

"Go to a store that sells gallon jugs of water. They can check their records to see if they have had bottles with that traceability code. If they have, they can search sales. Maybe the sale was with a credit or debit card."

"Can every store do that?"

"Nearly all of them can research traceability records. It's the law. The big stores like Walmart, Aldi's, and Dillions will have good records. Easy to access. Their existence depends on complying with traceability laws. I'd start with those before I went to the convenience stores."

Keith studied the water jug. The inked *packaged date* was clear, immediately above the *best used by* date. He smiled. "Thanks, Chief. Fresh eyes work every time. Maybe this will be my single best clue."

"You won't know until you check it out."

Sarah returned to her office. She saw the two electricians in the process of fingerprinting. Both looked in her direction when she approached but averted their eyes quickly. After she passed, she heard one ask the officer taking their prints, *"Who's she?"* She didn't see their faces, but she was sure they blanched when they received the answer.

Liz had a stack of folders in the center of Sarah's desk. Some held documents in need of a signature. Others were informational. One was a memo from Human Resources indicating a sexual harassment complaint against one of her officers. Sarah exhaled heavily. The memo contained no additional information. She decided to call the HR Manager, Paula Heston. Boston knocked on her doorframe before she could pick up the phone.

"Got time for an update?" Boston asked.

Sarah perked up. Boston didn't easily volunteer updates. "Certainly. What do you have? A suspect?"

Boston found a comfortable position leaning against the doorframe. "Nothing close to that."

"Was John Doe shot in the woods?"

"I couldn't find any evidence of that. I did find a sniper's nest."

"Really?" Sarah's eyes widened as she imagined a well camouflaged hiding place.

"That's about what it amounts to. I found a spot in the bushes with a clear view of the blood spot. The dead leaves were scraped clean, either to avoid making noise while standing there, or from nervous waiting. Someone was there for a while. And the shooter left a couple of partial shoe imprints. Alicia will check to see if there's enough to match the bloody footprint on the gravel."

Sarah listened intently. Boston was unusually verbose, spewing more words than she normally heard from him. She wanted him to continue.

"I found GSR on a forked tree branch. The shooter propped a gun … probably a rifle … on the limb."

"That seems pretty clear that he shot our John Doe from the woods. Did he smoke?" Sarah knew cigarette butts were a good source of DNA.

Boston scowled lightly. "Not that I could tell." He knew what Sarah was suggesting. "Nothing was left behind. Not even the shell casing."

"Do you think it was a professional hit? Policed the brass?" Sarah tried to imagine what the John Doe knew that would attract a professional killer.

"I can't say. I spent a lot of time trying to find the bullet. I looked at the side of the building earlier. Nothing. I checked for ricochet marks in the gravel. It was a long shot at best. Nothing. The bullet seems to have disappeared. If I had it, I could at least identify what type of gun was used. Maybe find a clue that leads to a suspect."

"So, we know the killer lay in wait from a distance."

"Not a great distance. Maybe ten yards."

"Really? That sounds risky. Being detected by the victim."

"It was dark. At night with no lighting. The killer had cat eyes or a good scope capable of capturing the minimal light from the security lights. Apparently, our John Doe had no reason to suspect someone was out to kill him, though we still don't know why he would have been behind that church at night."

"Maybe he was lured there."

Boston thought about Sarah's suggestion. "Possibly. Something drew him there and the killer knew he would be there."

"That's something," Sarah mused. She had hoped Boston had a lead, a clue to the killer, to the motive.

"Alicia called. Her helper began sorting through the dumpster trash. Most of the trash was in trash bags. Some broken boxes and bags of food. A handful of drink bottles and food wrappers were scattered near the top. A couple of Walmart bags stuffed with trash. The usual stuff you'd find in a dumpster."

"You think they might be connected to the killing ... or the killer?"

"One of the Walmart bags might. It held a bloodied jacket."

"A bloodied jacket? Was it our John Doe's blood?" Sarah asked hopefully.

"Alicia will hurry a DNA test."

"Do you think John Doe was wearing a jacket when he was killed?"

"I doubt it. Doesn't make sense to remove it after he's dead. Search for a wallet. Leave the clothes. I'm thinking the killer got blood on his clothes while loading the body."

"Kind of stupid to throw it in the dumpster." Sarah's face twisted in disbelief. "A killer who would plan an ambush like that has to be smarter than to throw away evidence that can be linked back to him. Epithelials are excellent clues. You said there was another Walmart bag. Did it have anything that might connect to the killer?"

"I doubt it. Alicia said it had a couple of dirty diapers and used wet wipes. Nothing unusual. People use old Walmart bags for trash all the time. Convenience. Probably from someone who came to get food on Monday."

"Probably ... but have her check it anyway."

Boston grinned. "I'm sure her helper will get that task. By the way, I've released the scene. I left some tape around the sniper's nest. It might keep the sightseers from going in the woods ... not that they'll hurt anything."

"Stay close to Alicia. If the blood matches, those epithelials could be your single best clue."

Boston pushed away from the doorframe. His conversation ended. He grunted as he turned away. "That's my hope."

Boston had an idea. Sarah could tell that much from his effusion, but all of his verbiage didn't reveal his thoughts. Whatever his thoughts were, they were apparently unsubstantiated at that point, therefore he said nothing. She thought about the church and the woods behind it. The idea of a secret hiding place in the brushy woods gave her the shivers. She remembered all the secret hiding places used by criminals in some of her past cases. Not all were in wooded areas. Some were in dark alleys. Some were in plain sight. All were a testament to the evil that lurks everywhere, evil that can swoop down upon unsuspecting victims at any time.

# CHAPTER 18

## 5:15 P.M. Tuesday

As Sarah drove, her mind was filled with a jumble of thoughts. She was accustomed to juggling tangled problems, rolling them around in her mind as she slowly unraveled them in a search for solutions. Her skills as a detective were built upon her ability to process several things at once. As Police Chief, she found that the problems were inherently more complex, defying clear solutions. The Sheriff's push to take over the crime lab. The need to justify a budget. Crimes that needed to be solved quickly, even though the resolution was the purview of the Detectives, not the Police Chief. Human issues, such as citizen complaints about officers and the department. And other human issues, such as the family problems of her officers. No room left for her personal needs.

Sarah parked her car in the driveway of a neat, ranch-style house in a mature neighborhood. Lower middle class. The favored "designer" trees were dressed in their fall colors. Some leaves had already dropped, and a steady breeze blew them helter-skelter along the curbed street and sidewalk. She watched the leaves dance while she prepared her mind for her next task. She inhaled deeply as she opened the car door, not to enjoy the fresh air, rather to brace herself for the conversation yet to come. As with most people, she was accustomed to discussing personal issues with friends, offering advice when it was needed. Advice that could easily be ignored without repercussions, or fear of repercussions. Nothing formal. As Police

Chief, her advice was often construed as an order. She didn't want that, but it came with the territory. Because of that, she had to measure every word. She followed the sidewalk to a small porch and pressed the doorbell button.

Officer Teri Caudle was among the first officers hired after Sarah became Police Chief. She was an Army veteran. She served as an MP. She was military crisp in dress and behavior. She took her job duties seriously. If anything, she needed to loosen up. But Sarah knew she was not one to talk. Being a police officer required a no-nonsense attitude most of the time, mixed with the proper blend of compassion. That proper blend was difficult to manage.

Teri answered the door with a nervous smile. "Come in, Chief. Thank you for coming by."

Sarah stepped inside and shook Teri's offered hand. "Thank you. I love your house."

Teri's house was different than Sarah's apartment. First and foremost, it was bigger. It also had more furniture. The décor was best described as modern lived-in with a feminine aura. Sarah instantly felt the warmth and comfort of the living room. It was also precisely neat. She imagined Teri's military background accounted for that characteristic. Either that or one or both of the inhabitants had OCD. Her own apartment had a professional appearance. Always visitor ready. It didn't have as much character as Teri's home, but its stark sophistication suited her and was easy to maintain.

"Thank you. We try to make it comfortable, our escape from the daily grind." Teri smiled. Her collarless black T-shirt exposed her neck more than her collared police uniform. The paleness of her generally covered skin contrasted with her short-cropped, dark hair. "Seelie," she called out. "Chief James is here to visit with us." Her eyes flitted nervously as she said, "She worked a little later than usual. She'll be here in a moment."

"No problem."

Almost before Sarah completed the two-word response, Seelie came down a short hallway straightening a bulky, pink sweatshirt over the top of matching sweatpants. Her voice was softer than Sarah imagined it would be. Seelie spoke hurriedly. "Sorry. I'm hurrying. Worked late." Her hair was vibrant green, long on the top but almost shaved on the sides. The short side hairs appeared more blonde than green. A gold nose ring pierced her septum and hung onto her philtrum but stopped short of her lip. She moved into Sarah's personal space and extended her hand. "Thank you for caring enough to come see us. You have beautiful eyes." Her own blue eyes were coy and her voice demure.

Sarah was momentarily taken aback by the closeness, the tone, and the compliment. She shook Seelie's hand and smiled. "I'm glad to be here. Thank you. You have beautiful eyes as well."

Seelie guided Sarah to the couch. She then curled one leg beneath her as she sat on the couch. Her position consumed the remainder of the couch. Teri confusedly selected a chair and took a seat. Seelie said, "You are much prettier than you appear on TV. And so trim." Her eyes danced playfully as she spoke.

Sarah nervously smiled. "Thank you." Seelie was flirty. Sarah quickly moved to the subject of the meeting. "How are things going for you?"

Seelie glanced toward Teri, whose dark eyes were fixed on her. She teasingly smiled at Teri's stoic expression. "Things are going well ..." she paused briefly, "though I'm sure Teri has told you I'm not comfortable with her work schedule."

Sarah nodded. The ice was broken. "Police work is different than most jobs. There is a lot of stress that comes with it."

"I understand the stress. Believe me. I do. But it's the hours. The away time. We miss so much of our lives together." Seelie smiled at Teri. "I don't want to miss life."

"It's not easy on married couples when one or the other works off-hour shifts. Only the couples who truly love one another, who truly care for one another, can cope. I wish I could give you an easy answer to your concerns."

"I know there are no easy answers. It's hard to get Teri to open up about her job."

Sarah looked at Teri, who quickly hid a scowl. "That's understandable. The nature of police work is in transition in America. We used to go about our job of enforcing the law without a lot of thought about how we were perceived by the public. The police were the law and that was it. Now, everything has changed. That adds to the stress ... and makes our jobs more dangerous."

Seelie half-smiled. "You're not helping."

Sarah winced. "I suppose not, but it's the truth. The dangers aren't so much from the people we encounter or have to arrest. The dangers are from emotional stress. Restraint has always been the hallmark of a good police officer. Now restraint is a requirement, one not easily met when the public is constantly scrutinizing our every move."

"What do you mean ... restraint?"

"Police officers today have to watch every move they make and every word they say. Body cameras are required not just to satisfy the suspicious public, but to protect the officer from false accusations."

"I suppose," Seelie slowly responded, her eyes fixed on Sarah.

Sarah felt nervous under Seelie's gaze. Seelie's eyes were naturally coy. The young woman lacked maturity. She lacked boundaries when it came to personal space. "You would be surprised how many times per week we review body cam videos to determine if a citizen complaint is legitimate or a smoke screen to distract from their wrongdoing. If they can prove the officer was not polite, the judge is apt to forgive them of their offense." Sarah felt like she was on a soapbox, and maybe she was. She knew the public only saw one side of police work ... the tickets, the arrests, the occasional over-aggressive response. Unfortunately, reporters like Tammy Nunn accented the actions of bad cops and painted the entire profession into that picture. She continued, "In essence, the new level of restraint creates additional stresses every day for police officers. We're only human but we must constantly appraise our actions. Am I right? Am I wrong? Will this person lie about me? Will anyone believe me when I testify in court? Is it even worth it?"

"If it's a lie, you said the body cams would prove they lied."

"The stress of going through an internal investigation is high. Even if found innocent, the officer has that mark on their record for life. It might not hurt them today, but if they do make a mistake in the future, the unfounded accusations can come back to haunt them. That's why so many officers are leaving the profession."

Seelie leaned back slightly. "How does that help me to know that? I still don't like our lives being put on hold so Teri can be a cop."

"Are your lives on hold because of her work hours?"

"I work days. She works nights. What do you think?" Seelie's eyes lost their coyness. Resentment took its place. "We sometimes go a whole week without seeing each other. I'd say our lives are on hold."

Sarah glanced around the room. "From what I see, you two are building a nice home. Seeing you two in the same room, I have to believe you're goals are aligned. I have to believe you want to be together for life, not just for today."

"We are. We do. Are you married, Chief?"

Sarah shook her head. "No, though I've never had the desire to marry."

"Why? Are you a lesbian too?"

"No. I'm not lesbian." Sarah had to force herself not to react defensively. "I have always put my career ahead of everything personal in my life. One could say I'm married to my job."

"Kind of lonely, isn't it?" Seelie's eyes bored into Sarah.

Sarah smiled dismissively to cover the discomfort of the question. "I always have my work associates. My family supports me. I believe I'm doing good work for the people. That's what I want from my life. What do you want out of life, Seelie?"

"My wife with me every day."

"Is that a requirement for a relationship? Constant togetherness."

Seelie thought a moment before answering. "Not really. Love is."

"Exactly. My sister lives a couple hundred miles from here. I see her once a month. Our love has never waned just because we are separated. Like I said, my family supports me even though they seldom physically see me. Your interactions ... the two of you ... are closer and more frequent than mine. Don't you see Teri on a weekly basis?"

"Yes, but ... maybe I've always thought marriage meant more time together."

"Was Teri a police officer when you two married?"

"Yes, but she was in training."

"On nights?"

"Yes, but I thought that would change once she was trained."

"It will ... in time. All of us worked nights at some point in our careers. It goes with the territory." Sarah looked at Teri. "I hazard to guess that Teri worked night duty while in the military."

"Yes," Teri responded without additions.

"I have to ask ... though you don't have to answer, does Teri bring her job stresses home? Do you feel like Teri is somehow holding you responsible for her stress?"

"No. I don't think so. Why?"

"Police stress is real. I don't like to belabor the point, but our jobs are dangerous. We interact with the not-so-good actors in society. We see people at their worst and under the worst circumstances. From drunk drivers to accident victims. The victims of crime to the criminals who commit the crimes. And we see abused children, which is the worst of it all. Before we go home to our families, we have to release those stresses. Too often, there's nowhere to unload. Sometimes the officer's family takes the brunt of those stresses."

Seelie looked lovingly at Teri. "No. Teri's never lashed out at me, if that's what you're asking."

"Sort of. The key is that her job stresses … or your job stresses … shouldn't become an issue for your marriage. Every couple has problems ranging from money to simple differences of opinion, but couples who love one another, who want to stay together, resolve those problems. They stick together as a unit." Sarah knew she was being preachy. She didn't mean to be, but Seelie seemed to draw it from her. Seelie was almost childlike. Seelie wanted to hear someone's voice reassuring her that everything would be okay. Seelie was insecure.

"We're going to stick together. I promise you that," Seelie said as she moved her leg from beneath her. She got up and walked to Teri's chair, sat on the plush arm, and leaned her head on Teri's shoulder. "We're soul mates. I just worry about Teri when she's not with me, about her safety."

Teri wrapped one arm around Seelie. "My safety isn't an issue."

Sarah replied, "Teri's safety is less of an issue if her mind is clear and on her job. Her training will keep her safe if she's not distracted."

Seelie winced. "You mean like wondering if your wife is upset with you?"

Sarah nodded. "Those kinds of things create distractions. A distracted police officer is in immediate danger, even if it's as simple as a driving error while on patrol."

"How long do you think Teri will be on night patrol?"

"I honestly don't have an answer for that. It's a matter of seniority. Most senior officers prefer day shift, but some don't. If an opening on day shift arises, Teri will be considered along with any others in line for it. And there are other opportunities in the department that are not patrol. They come open every now and then."

"Maybe I'll find a job with flexible hours," Seelie said as she hugged Teri.

"I would warn against changing your own career goals to accommodate Teri's. Each of you has to have individual goals as well as having family goals. Make sure they are compatible. Like I said, I'm not married, but if I was, I would never ask my spouse to change jobs nor would I change mine. It's not a good relationship if you can't exist as individuals."

"All that said, is there anything I can do to keep Teri safe? Keep me from worrying about her?"

Sarah smiled thoughtfully. "First of all, there is nothing I can suggest that will keep you from worrying about Teri. I worry every hour of the day and night about my officers on patrol and my detectives on cases." She briefly thought about Micha's and Boston's injuries. Micha was shot while on patrol and Boston was stabbed while investigating a case. And then there was Officer John Wyatt. He was off duty when he was shot to death by a burglar at his neighbor's house. There were plenty of reasons to worry, but none that should consume her life. And none that she needed to mention to Seelie. "All I can suggest is that you try to understand, as Teri should do for you. Talk when you are together. Discuss what bothers you and work to resolve any difference. If you are going to last as a couple, all of that will get easier and maybe become second nature in time. Understanding and acceptance."

The conversation evolved. Teri offered to fix coffee. They all settled on tea. Sarah had other things scheduled for the evening, but she allowed the couple to take more of her time. They talked for another half hour. Conversation. Friend to friend questions that helped Seelie understand the stresses of police work and how to assist Teri in alleviating those stresses. And Teri learned how to open up to Seelie about her stessors. They discussed what life routines would help. Good diet. Rest. Exercise. Entertainment. All those things that could be used as anchors for a "normal" life as a civilian when not on duty.

Sarah found herself under stress because of time constraints and the desire to know if any breakthroughs had occurred in the John Doe case. Alicia would be home. Boston should be home. She suppressed her curiosity and focused on getting to her apartment so she could change clothes before Shawn arrived.

# CHAPTER 19

## 7:00 P.M. Tuesday

Shawn was prompt. At seven o'clock, he was smiling at the door with a single white rose clutched in his hand. When Sarah opened the door, he said, "Love and peace," as he handed her the rose. "It's Tuesday. White is the color for the day."

Sarah laughed as she took the rose. "Thank you. And here I am in a blue dress." She tilted her head and kissed his lips lightly. "Maybe I'm not as predictable as you thought. Come in so I can put this in water."

"We can stay here," Shawn suggested with a wry smile.

"Not if Julio really does have a mean steak," Sarah laughed.

"Maybe it's not that mean."

"Sorry," Sarah reached for her matching jacket, "you said steak and I'm hungry. I'm not going to disappoint Julio, and you're not going to disappoint me."

Shawn helped Sarah don the jacket and kissed the back of her neck. "If you insist. Steak it is. We can't disappoint Julio."

Dinner was enjoyable. More than enjoyable. For the better part of two decades, Sarah's personal life was sparce and private. Her brief moments outside her public persona were generally not sharable. Her affair with Keith Locke was secretive. Though most of her associates knew they were seeing each other, the threat their fraternization posed to her career forced them to keep the entire episode generally private. Dinner dates were always surrounded by the fear someone who shouldn't see them together would appear. They restricted their time together to her apartment. With Shawn, it was totally different. Sarah didn't care if someone saw them together. Without flaunting it, she hoped they would be seen. He made her feel at ease … except for an underlying sensual anticipation that permeated her being when she was near him. Shawn exuded sensuality.

Shawn was witty. His smile was sincere. His eyes were attentive. His words were soothing and reassuring. Shawn was the sculptor and Sarah was the clay. She was convinced she was the only other person in the restaurant. Sarah watched, listened, and immersed herself in Shawn's presence … and shivered as her anticipation grew stronger. The feelings associated with Shawn were new to her. Marriage was never in the forefront of her mind when in past relationships … if it was in her mind at all. Shawn's personality provided the reassurance for her mind to consider more than an occasional night together.

Sarah's sister, Valarie, had a good marriage and three children. Valarie's husband was an engineer for a major corporation. He made more than enough money for Valarie to be a stay-home-mom. Not until Shawn did Sarah allow herself to wonder how her life would be different if she had chosen a person rather than a career to be her life-partner. It saddened her to process the possible outcomes of an early marriage. No fulfilling career; not for a woman in a traditionally man's field. If she was still in law enforcement, she would either be a lifelong patrol officer or maybe a jailer so her work schedule would conform to her husband's needs. She thought of Teri and Seelie Caudle. She couldn't imagine going through their marital problems. The fears. The suspicions. The doubts. And, frighteningly, Sarah knew their problems were not resolved yet. Only two years of marriage was not enough to ensure the outcome.

If Sarah had chosen marriage, she would have children … hopefully. Raising children is not a part-time job, and in her era, it was traditionally the woman's job to be the full-time mother, even if she didn't stay home. Bosses like Carl Franken and Bill Keck – men who supported women in the workplace, would find it difficult to provide support for an officer who couldn't be one hundred percent dedicated. Taylor McCuskey succeeded, but she had more years, more time to raise her children to the age where she could rededicate herself to the job. Taylor made time for her career with the support of a good marriage partner, a bank VP with enough flexibility to support their children's teen years. The Lieutenant and Sergeant Honeycutt paved the way for Sarah. They were as much responsible for her success as were Carl and Bill. The thought caused Sarah to gulp. She reached for her wine glass but drew her hand back when she noticed it was shaking.

Sarah's mind returned to the table. To Shawn. He was staring at her, a worried look on his face.

"I can see you are deep in thought. Tough case?"

Sarah blurted, "No. No. It's not … well, yes. It is tough, but Boston's got it under control. As much as it can be in the early stages."

"You seemed distracted. Do I bore you with my sweet talk?" Shawn's eyes regained their humor. "I can talk shop if you want me to. Lots of estate planning and divorce proceedings I could explain ad nauseum." He grinned and sipped from his wine glass.

Sarah laughed lightly. Her hand was back in her control. She sipped her Merlot and thought about how many glasses of Merlot she had consumed alone in her life. "Not into estate planning. Definitely not divorces. Continue with the sweet talk. I'm just assessing what you have to offer."

Shawn burst out laughing, which drew momentary attention from other patrons. "Anything you want. Money. Jewelry. Name it and I'll get it for you."

Sarah smiled demurely. "I have money and jewelry enough. You're going to have to do better."

"All I have beyond that is myself. A simple lawyer with simple desires." Shawn's eyes twinkled mischievously.

"Where are you going with that?" Sarah asked coyly.

"Back to my place, I hope."

"Can't."

"Why not?"

"My work clothes are at my place and I'm an early riser … unlike you lawyers who think nine o'clock is the break of dawn." Sarah sipped the last of her wine and watched his reaction down the stem of her glass.

Shawn winced in mock pain. "Ouch! Okay. Your place it is. Check." He motioned to the Server.

"What? No dessert?"

The Server approached. "Are you ready to leave?"

Shawn smiled, "Only after a piece of that chocolate caramel cheesecake and two glasses of tawny port."

"Two pieces of cheesecake," the Server said as she reached for her electronic order pad.

"One piece. Two forks," Shawn replied.

"But two glasses of port," Sarah said. "I don't share wine."

With dessert and the port came more conversation from Sarah. She didn't verbalize her thoughts about Shawn's brush with marriage. He had relayed the basics, but not the details. She knew his first wife was unfaithful. That made her wonder if he had given up on the idea of marriage forever. She didn't ask, but to broach the subject, she mentioned her conversation with Teri and Seelie Caudle … without naming names.

Shawn listened attentively. He was a good listener. After Sarah finished, he commented, "Sounds like you know a lot about how to keep a marriage together. Are you sure you haven't been married before?"

Sarah blushed lightly. "Only to Devaney PD. It's a demanding relationship."

"It's good to know you can handle demanding relationships." Shawn finished his port and set the glass aside. "Maybe we can discuss demands at your place."

Sarah smiled, finished her port, and replied, "I suppose … if talk is what you want."

# CHAPTER 20

## 11:00 P.M. Tuesday

Sounds that didn't fit rattled through Sarah's brain. Consciousness eluded her for an eternity ... or a few scrambled seconds. Her phone. Her department cell phone rattled on the nightstand. The combination of ringtone and vibration on wood reverberated through her brain until it yanked her from sleep. As she sat up on the bed and checked the caller ID, she painfully noticed the time was eleven o'clock. She had been asleep less than an hour.

"Hello," Sarah answered with a thick, sleepy voice. She cleared her throat and answered again, unsure if her vocal cords had worked well enough to be heard the first time. "Hello. This is Chief James."

"Chief, I'm sorry to disturb you. This is Sergeant Laney Patterson."

Sarah's foggy mind cleared enough to recognize the Night Shift Commander's voice. "Yes, Sergeant. How can I help you?"

"We have a hostage situation. It involves the parents of the two girls killed in yesterday's traffic accident."

In the soft, blue glow of her alarm clock's LED numerals, Sarah noticed the lump in her bed. Shawn. He was softly breathing, deep asleep. She had also been deep asleep only a moment before, with him spooned against her back. She lowered her voice as she swung her legs over the side of the bed. "Is it Paul Timmons?"

"Yes, Ma'am. Apparently, he wants revenge against the car driver's parents. The Yates. Mr. Yates was able to prevent him from entering the house, but when the unit responded to the 9-1-1 call, Mr. Timmons ran inside a neighbor's house. We think he has taken hostages."

"We don't know for sure?"

"Not yet."

"Whose on the scene?"

"I have two units there now. I called Lieutenant Glasgow. He's on his way."

"Good." Sarah didn't know what was good about the situation, but the word seemed to be the right one to say. "Slack me the address ... and if you can, Slack Timmons' cell number. I'll be there as soon as I can." She hung up and shook Shawn to let him know she would be gone. He didn't respond. She shook him again. He was a deep sleeper. He softly groaned and adjusted his legs without waking.

Sarah smiled and shook her head. Without turning on the bedroom light, she groggily fumbled her way to the bathroom. Her walk-in closet was accessible from her bedroom. She selected a pair of denim jeans and a denim Oxford shirt. She put her vest over her shirt. The weight of it wasn't a surprise, but she wasn't used to wearing it in her role as Police Chief. With only a moment's hesitation, she decided to wear a Devaney PD baseball cap. Her hair was short and easy to manage, but it was disheveled, and her brush didn't seem to have much effect. The cap would hide that fact. She left a note on the bathroom sink in case Shawn awakened while she was gone.

With her coat emblazoned "POLICE" pulled tightly around her, Sarah fastened her seatbelt and started her PD vehicle. The night wasn't cold, but it was cool, and she had just left a warm bed. She thought she recalled a weather forecast of snow. She wasn't sure. She input the address provided by Sergeant Patterson into her GPS. The drive was across town, but at least not through the heart of the city. She turned on her grill and back bumper strobes. As she approached the Yates' neighborhood, flashing blue lights marked the area of crisis. Two police units blocked the street from two houses on either side of the house where Mr. Timmons held hostages. She stopped her car near one of the units. The night breeze caused her to zip her coat higher.

"What's the situation?" Sarah asked Corporal Zeiger who was holding a bullhorn.

"Hello, Chief," replied the Corporal. "Standoff. He responded when we first arrived but hasn't responded since. He told us to leave, or he'd kill his hostages."

"So, he does have hostages?" Sarah's mind was clear, though Sergeant Patterson's initial response of being unsure about the hostages confused her.

"Yes. We think it's the older couple who live in the house. He said he doesn't want to kill them, but he said he will if we interfere with his mission."

"Did he say what his mission is?"

"To kill the Yates family. Something about the Yates killed his daughter. Those are the families from the wreck, right?"

"Yes. He threatened them at the funeral home this afternoon. I hoped it was settled. Apparently not. What did you tell him? It's obvious that you didn't leave."

"I told him I had to discuss it with my superiors. I didn't know what else to tell him other than to tell him he didn't want to do that. He didn't answer back."

Sarah saw the other officers, including Siegler's partner, hovering behind cover, eyes fixed on the house. "Did you use the bullhorn, or did you call him on the phone?"

"I didn't have his phone number until a minute ago. I haven't tried it yet."

Sarah nodded understandingly. "Do we have units dispatched to the back of the house?"

"One unit is in position to block traffic on the other street. Sergeant Patterson has called for SWAT."

Sarah knew their SWAT team was nothing more than tactically trained officers, generally volunteers. Devaney wasn't big enough to support a dedicated SWAT team. It would take a few minutes for them to gear up and arrive. "Have you heard from Lieutenant Glasgow?"

"He's enroute. He should be here shortly."

"Good. I'm going to try to contact Timmons. You haven't heard any gun shots or commotion since your last contact?"

"No. It's quiet. That's not good, is it?"

"No. It's not. We need him talking." Sarah checked Patterson's message and dialed the number.

The phone rang several times before it was answered with an angry, "What?"

"Paul, this is Chief James. I'd like to talk with you."

"Talking's over. Yates owes me. Both of them. You know that. What you said about drugs doesn't change anything."

"Paul, the only person who can change anything is you. You are in control. That's why I want to talk with you. Hear what you have to say."

"You had your chance and all you did was try to make it look like Yvonne was to blame. You know and I know, Yates is to blame. And he has to pay. Her too."

"Paul, let's talk about that."

"Talk's done. You've made yourself clear about what you're going to do. Nothing. Now, get your people out of here so I can get justice for Yvonne."

"Paul …" Sarah began.

"No! Get them out or you'll have the death of this old man and woman on your hands too. Go!" Timmons ended the call.

Sarah stared at the house where Timmons was reported to be. Only one window showed light. It appeared to be a small bathroom window. "Are Mr. and Mrs. Yates still in their house?" she asked Officer Siegler.

"No. We got them out before we pulled back. When we got here, Timmons fired a shot at us then rushed into the neighbor's house. Yates and his wife ran out the front while Timmons was running away."

Sarah scowled. No one had mentioned gunshots. Firing on the police indicated Timmons' state of mind was further gone than she hoped. "Did we return fire?"

"No. He dashed into the house. We didn't have a clear background."

A police unit arrived with lights flashing. Sarah saw Melvin Glasgow get out of the car. She started to walk toward him but stopped as an EV unit arrived. It was Taylor McCuskey. She waited for both Lieutenants to come to her.

Taylor's hair was neat beneath her PD ball cap. Sarah was sure the older woman wouldn't be seen without neat hair. In the flashing lights, it was apparent that Taylor had dabbed on some make-up. And her uniform was freshly pressed. Sarah expected nothing less from the proper Lieutenant.

"Taylor. Melvin," she said in greeting. "This may be a lost cause. Patterson has dispatched SWAT."

Lieutenant McCuskey replied, "He cleared it with me. I figured better have them even if we don't use them."

"Good call," Sarah said. "I'm not sure we can control this one and we have innocents at risk."

Lieutenant Glasgow grimaced. "Sounds like they're at risk either way we go. It's at least worth a try to negotiate. Does he have a phone or do I need to use a bullhorn." He nodded toward Corporal Zeiger's bullhorn.

"I have his number. I talked to him a few minutes ago. We had a run-in this afternoon at the funeral home. I'm not on his favorite person list. He's bent on making Yates pay for his daughter's death."

"Tough one," Glasgow said empathetically. He dialed the number Sarah gave him and waited for an answer. He shook his head when the call didn't connect. He redialed. He repeated the process three times before contact was made. "Hello, Mr. Timmons. This is Lieutenant Glasgow. I'm here to talk with you, maybe work something out for you."

Sarah watched intently, only able to hear Melvin's side of the conversation. The SWAT team members arrived in an armored van. She allowed Taylor to go update them and plan their move … if it came to a move. She waited to see if Melvin could make an impact.

"There's only so much I can do for you, Mr. Timmons. You are in control, but no one has absolute control. You're smart enough to know there are limits." Melvin listened intently to a voice that sometimes grew loud enough to be indistinctly heard by Sarah a few feet away.

"Mr. Timmons, I can assure you that no one will come in if you will allow the couple you are holding to exit the house. I want this to be resolved peacefully. Mr. and Mrs. Glenn are not involved. You have the power to keep it that way." Melvin listened. "Okay. I'll let you think about it for a few minutes. I'll call you back in five minutes."

"Did you promise him we won't come after him?" Sarah asked. "Is that wise?"

"If he'll release his hostages, he's no longer a danger to the public. We will have plenty of time to talk then. No need to escalate if there is no danger to the public."

"I suppose that makes sense. Do you think he will do it?"

"No. You're probably right. This may be a lost cause, but we can't turn our backs on the Glenns." Lieutenant Glasgow spoke evenly with no histrionics. Negotiator style.

"Is that their name? Glenn?" Sarah asked. She hadn't heard anyone say that.

"Yes. Before I left home, I did a city records search to see who lived in the house. He needs to know them by name … as human beings."

The breeze increased and became colder. Sarah pulled her coat around her and wished it was her heavy coat. She noticed both Melvin and Taylor were wearing heavy coats. The original weather forecast was for September snow to drop down from Nebraska, but that had changed. The cold that was supposed to accompany the snow didn't change. It did drop into Kansas. It was turning colder by the minute. Sarah wished she had paid more attention to the forecast. The cold made the five-minute wait seem longer. She told Melvin, "I'm going to have Patterson pick up Mrs. Timmons. She seemed to be more levelheaded than Timmons."

Melvin nodded. "Good idea. Maybe she can at least convince him to allow the Glenns to leave the house." After a few minutes, he dialed his phone. He dialed three times before he got an answer. "Hello, Mr. Timmons. I told you I would call back. Have you given any thoughts to the idea of releasing Mr. and Mrs. Glenn?"

Melvin's face contorted as he listened to Paul Timmons' response. After a moment, he said, "We can't do that, Mr. Timmons. Mr. and Mrs. Yates are not home now. They left their house after you started shooting at the police officer. No. I'm not lying. You scared them away. They are gone."

Sarah anxiously watched Melvin's face, as if by watching she would know what Timmons' was saying. Her negotiator was trying to reason with the angry man.

"As I said earlier, Mr. Timmons, you are in control. That control is limited to what exists here and now. I can't send Mr. Yates out onto the lawn." Melvin strained to remain calm when Timmons responded. "I don't know where they are, Mr. Timmons. Yes. I'm sure someone does. But I personally won't send someone out for you to kill them." He held the phone away from his ear and looked at it. He turned to Sarah. "He hung up. I'm not making any progress." He glanced toward the SWAT van. "It may be a lost cause. If he really does have the Glenns at his mercy, he might kill them anyway."

"I'm going to call Dr. Hyatt. Maybe he can get through to him." Sarah checked her contact list on her phone and selected a number. "If we rush in, he'll start shooting for sure." The phone call didn't connect right away. She imagined the Psychiatrist used by Devaney PD was in the early stages of sleep just as she was an hour earlier. "Hello, Dr. Hyatt. This is Chief James. We have a crisis and could really use your assistance."

Kyle Hyatt's sleepy voice was barely discernible, "What's wrong? An officer shooting?"

"No. We have a hostage situation. Our negotiator is concerned that the risk to the hostages has escalated beyond our ability to save them. I'm hoping your expertise might sway the hostage taker. I've also sent for his wife. Can you come assist?"

"Let me get dressed. Where are you and who is the hostage taker?"

Sarah quickly recapped the situation and gave Dr. Hyatt the address. She looked at Melvin and Taylor. "It can't hurt to try. Keep talking to Timmons if he'll answer."

Melvin nodded as he dialed his phone. "Yeah. I need to maintain contact. Keep his hope of success alive. Keep the Glenns alive." Relief washed across his face when the phone was answered after three attempts. He talked for almost five minutes, repeatedly hearing Timmons' demands, and responding as positively as he could. He asked if he could talk to the Glenns but was refused with assurances that they were safe for the moment. That conversation consumed more time than the previous conversation. But as with the others, Timmons grew inpatient and hung up.

Dr. Hyatt understood the urgency. He arrived within a few minutes after Lieutenant Glasgow's contact. He sought an update from Melvin and Sarah, glancing at Taylor to see if she had anything to add.

Taylor shook her head, and grimly smiled, "I'm the last resort." She nodded toward the SWAT van."

Dr. Hyatt understood Taylor. "Let's hope it doesn't come to that." He addressed Sarah. "You said his wife is on the way?"

"Yes. It will be a few minutes more."

"Okay. Let me try to contact Mr. Timmons." He used Melvin's phone. "I don't want to throw another unknown into the mix by using my phone," he explained while he dialed. Timmons didn't answer the first attempt. He finally answered on the third.

"Hello, Mr. Timmons. I'm Dr. Hyatt. I help the police department with difficult issues."

"Like hostage situations?" Timmons snarled.

"Not usually. Mostly when a police officer experiences an emotional trauma."

"Like hostage situations?"

"Ah … I would define that as traumatic. Wouldn't you?"

"It'll be traumatic for Jerald Yates and his wife. No need for it to be traumatic for anyone else."

"I understand your sentiments, Paul. May I call you Paul?"

"Maybe. What's your name?"

"Kyle. You can call me Kyle. It's a good name, like Paul. Paul, are Mr. and Mrs. Glenn okay?"

"They're in a closet so they don't get in the way." Paul paused before adding, "But if your people come in shooting, they will be in the line of fire. Yours or mine."

"No one plans to come in shooting. I understand Lieutenant Glasgow agreed not to come in at all if you released Mr. and Mrs. Glenn. That offer still stands. We don't want anyone to get hurt. We can talk without the specter of threats. We can resolve this without violence."

Paul responded, beginning with calm anger, and rising to a hate-filled rant. "What do you know about it, Kyle? Has someone murdered your daughter? The violence was started by Jerald Yates and his wife when they allowed their dopehead daughter to drive a car. They gave her a loaded weapon and turned her loose on my daughter."

Dr. Hyatt remained calm. "No. I have not experienced what you are experiencing. How will harming the Glenns help how you feel?"

"They are just as guilty," Timmons screamed.

Dr. Hyatt was puzzled. "How are the Glenns guilty, Paul?"

"They knew Tamara Yates was driving a car."

"A lot of people drive cars. Are they responsible because someone they know drives a car and has a wreck? I need you to explain that to me, Paul, so I can understand."

"All you need to understand is that Tamara Yates killed my daughter and her parents let her do it. They could have stopped her. The Glenns should have stopped her. My daughter is dead, and they killed her!" Timmons hung up.

Dr. Hyatt closed his eyes in thought before he said anything. "Chief, I'm not sure where this is going. He is beyond reason. Not rational. He blames the Glenns for not stopping Tamara."

"Stopping her from what?"

"Driving the car. In his mind, the Glenns should have stopped Tamara from driving the car."

"Where to from here?"

"I'll give him a few more minutes and reach out again. Hopefully, his wife will be here by then. What's her name?"

"Carol," Sarah answered.

Dr. Hyatt looked from the phone to Melvin. "I'll tell him I'll be calling from my phone after that. Your battery is low."

Melvin replied apologetically, "It didn't have time to recharge before I got the call."

Dr. Hyatt told Sarah and the others everything he learned from his conversations with Timmons. Sarah heard one key piece of information that might be useful to the SWAT team. The closet.

Sarah directed Taylor to prepare the SWAT team. The two of them walked to the SWAT van and the team gathered for a briefing.

Sergeant Bosko was the leader of the team. "Chief. Lieutenant." He acknowledged the two with a nod. "We've sized up the area." He pointed to a tablet with a satellite view of the neighborhood focused on the Glenn house. "Patrol units have evacuated houses on either side and behind the two houses. They've also asked everyone with dogs to keep them inside. We don't want a barking dog to alert the subject when we move. A quick recon indicates the subject is on the west side with a window view of the Yates house. For some reason, there is no privacy fence between the two houses."

"Does that help?" Sarah asked.

"It doesn't hurt." Sergeant Bosko traced his finger on the screen as he talked. "We don't have to worry about a squeaky fence gate when we slip close to the house."

"Do you have eyes on the Glenns? Timmons says they're in a closet that would be in the line of fire. A shield or a bluff." Sarah hoped he knew more than she did.

"Recon hasn't been able to pinpoint them."

"So … we put them at risk when we go in?"

"I operate under the impression that they are already at risk, Chief. If we go in, it's a Hail Mary to save them."

Sarah knew Sergeant Clyde Bosko as a calm yet intense police officer. He didn't panic. He had the unique ability to defuse tense situations in the field. At the same time, he could appear heartless. He didn't allow emotion to interfere with his duties. He did what had to be done. That characteristic was the primary reason Bosko was suggested by all of Sarah's lieutenants as the right person to lead SWAT. That characteristic was highlighted by Dr. Hyatt during his evaluation of the chosen leader. SWAT teams act with measured violence. They need a leader who is calm and unaffected by the violence as it occurs. "You're right, of course. I hope Dr. Hyatt can talk him down."

"We're on stand-by, Chief. Say the word and we go. If they are in a closet like the subject says, I think I know where they are. I pulled floor plans of the Glenn house from records. If they haven't remodeled without a permit, the subject is correct about the danger they're in. If nothing else, the Glenns could be caught in background fire."

Sarah watched as Bosko used floor plans from the Glenn house to describe what he believed was the best approach to reduce the risk to the Glenns. Even that was not a sure thing. Timmons could react by killing them without regard for his own safety. An act of vengeful desperation.

# CHAPTER 21

## 1:30 A.M. Wednesday

A squad car arrived. An officer opened the back door and Carol Timmons hurried out of the backseat. She almost ran to Sarah, her eyes wide when she saw the body armored SWAT team. "Where's Paul? What have you done to him?"

Sarah reached out and touched Carol's upper arm. "Paul's fine. He's inside the Glenn house. He's holding them hostage. He's threatening to kill them if we don't send Mr. and Mrs. Yates out so he can kill them." She focused on Carol's eyes. The woman was terrified and confused, as would be expected. "Are you willing to talk to him? To convince him to release the Glenns?"

"Are you going to kill him?" Carol demanded.

"If he releases the Glenns, we will simply wait him out. No one will get hurt."

"But you'll arrest him?"

"Yes. Terroristic threatening with a firearm is a crime. He also shot at police officers when they arrived. This is serious, Carol. We ... Paul needs your help." Sarah saw Dr. Hyatt on the phone again. She led Carol to the psychiatrist. Dr. Hyatt was listening more than talking. A few pacifying comments accented his attentive silence. Sarah could hear the sound of Timmons' angry voice, but she couldn't make out the words. The conversation lasted longer than previous conversations. The standoff passed the two-and-a-half-hour mark during that conversation.

Dr. Hyatt pulled the phone away from his ear and stared at it for a moment. He shook his head. He was perplexed. "He hung up again." With a somber smile, he looked at Carol and asked, "Is this Mrs. Timmons?"

Sarah shivered against the falling temperatures and increasing wind speed. It felt like snow whether the weatherman thought so or not. "Yes. Dr. Hyatt, this is Carol Timmons. She wants to help reason with Paul."

Dr. Hyatt extended his hand. "Thank you for coming, Carol. I'm Dr. Hyatt, psychiatrist for Devaney PD. I could sure use your help."

"Are they going to hurt him?"

Dr. Hyatt maintained eye contact with Carol. "No. We don't want him to hurt any more than he already is. I can only imagine the pain he's going through. How are you feeling?"

Carol sobbed and sarcastically responded, "My daughter just died, and my husband is about to die. How do you think I feel?"

"At a loss and seeking solace. Tragedies such as you've experienced are difficult to bear. Even harder to understand. Are you up to helping me?"

"Yes. I think so."

"Let me call him again. See if he will talk with you." Dr. Hyatt used his phone to call. On the third attempt, he said, "Paul, Carol is with me. She wants to talk to you." He handed the phone to Carol.

"Honey, please let the Glenns go. They haven't done anything to us."

Sarah couldn't hear Paul's responses. Carol held the phone too tightly against her ear. She moved closer to no avail.

"Paul," Carol pleaded, "you have to listen to them. They don't want to hurt you. You need help. This Dr. Hyatt seems like a nice man, someone who ..." She moved the phone away from her ear. Her face registered confusion and pain. "He hung up."

Dr. Hyatt took the phone. "We'll call back in a few minutes. Give him time to consider what you said. He's in a great deal of emotional pain. He's processing more slowly than normal." He patted Carol's shoulder. "We'll try again. We're not giving up."

Sarah glanced at Carol to allow Dr. Hyatt an excuse to not answer her if he felt the need to avoid talking in front of the wife of the subject. "What are you thinking?"

"His anger is bone deep. I don't know how else to describe it. He's reached the point where he needs the pain that caused his anger to go away. He's bargaining."

"Sounds like he's coming around if he's bargaining with you."

"He's not bargaining with me. He's bargaining with his pain. Killing the source of his pain is the bargain he's making. It's all internal. That's why he shut off Carol so quickly. He believes killing Mr. and Mrs. Yates … especially Mr. Yates … is the only thing that will make his pain go away."

Sarah exhaled heavily. "What about the Glenns? Are they part of his bargain?"

"I'm not sure. He has enough anger in him to lay blame on as many people as he can imagine. He blames the police, just so you know."

"Why the police? Because we didn't stop Tamara from speeding? Because we haven't been able to eliminate drugs?"

"Because the police stopped him from satisfying his bargain. Because the police are protecting Yates."

"Are you saying the negotiations have ended?" Sarah hated to ask the question. She didn't want to hear the answer. If Dr. Hyatt was ready to give up, then she had to make the decision that could cost the Glenns their lives if the SWAT team failed to execute perfectly.

"No. He's still engaged, but he's faltering."

"What does that mean?"

"He knows he's lost control of the situation. Right now, he's evaluating other bargaining options. Carol's presence should help." Dr. Hyatt's eyes conveyed something different than what he said.

Sarah made eye contact with Lieutenant Glasgow. "Melvin, can you bring Carol up to speed on how this process will work? Explain how she can help us help Paul."

Melvin understood. He touched Carol's upper arm and subtly guided her away from Sarah and Dr. Hyatt.

As soon as Melvin and Carol were out of earshot, Sarah whispered, "What other bargaining options?"

"Suicide."

Sarah thought for a moment, then grimly replied, "That's what I was afraid you meant. I suppose that would end it. Not the ending I want, but if it spares the Glenns …"

"That's the bargain option he's evaluating. Whether to commit suicide or murder-suicide. Kill the Glenns before he kills himself. His grief-stricken mind still wants someone to pay for the pain he feels. In his mind, he has already established that the Glenns played a part by not calling the police on Tamara. Killing Tamara's neighbors would be an alternative since we have stopped him from killing Tamara's parents."

"If you are saying we are at an impasse, my only option is to send in SWAT and hope we can save the Glenns."

"I'm not through yet. Discouraged, but not ready to give up. This is where I earn my keep. If I'm good enough at distant psychoanalysis, maybe … with Carol's help … I can convince him that his best bargaining option is to come out and allow me to help him alleviate the pain."

"Okay, but if you sense he's about to act, let me know. My priority at this moment is to save the Glenns, even if we can't save Timmons."

"Understood." Dr. Hyatt motioned for Carol, then dialed his phone. Again, three attempts were required before Timmons answered.

Sarah shivered and listened to the one-sided conversation. Melvin did not leave Dr. Hyatt's side except to distract Carol. He was attentive, listening, and trying to learn. Dr. Hyatt would say something, and Carol would take the phone to repeat his words if Paul seemed reticent to listen. The tactic kept the conversation going longer.

Taylor approached, her eyes watering because of the cold wind. "Where are we, Chief?"

Sarah spoke softly, "Because of Carol, Timmons is still talking. All we can do is try to keep warm until … well, until it goes one way or the other."

Another hour passed. Three separate connections with Timmons left Sarah frustrated. She knew negotiations with hostage takers didn't end quickly. She also knew they didn't always end well. Someone handed her a cup of hot coffee. It was Taylor. Sergeant Patterson arrived with the mobile command center. It was a motor home remodeled into a communication center with a few amenities. Warmth and hot coffee was available. And a bathroom. Sarah accepted the coffee but stayed near Dr. Hyatt.

"You need to get out of the cold," Taylor said as she handed the coffee cup to Sarah.

"Thank you. I'm going to stay here with Dr. Hyatt."

"There's no reason all of you can't be inside the command center,"

Taylor said with a glance toward Dr. Hyatt and Carol. She handed him a cup also.

Dr. Hyatt, not on the phone at the moment, responded, "Does the command center have cameras on the house?"

"Yes," Taylor replied.

"Then show me the way. My toes are past frozen." Dr. Hyatt guided Carol along with him.

Inside the mobile command center, Sarah located the screen with the best camera angle, sipped her coffee, and began absorbing the warmth. Like Dr. Hyatt, she had ignored the cold in favor of focusing on Timmons.

After Dr. Hyatt finished his first cup of coffee, he rubbed his hands together to increase circulation before dialing his phone. In keeping with past contacts, Timmons didn't answer until the third attempt. "Paul, it's Dr. Hyatt and Carol again. Have you considered what we discussed earlier?"

Inside the mobile center, Sarah could reasonably hear Timmons' responses as long as no one else was engaged in a side conversation.

"You sound different," was Paul Timmons' comment.

"I'm inside a warm place. It's cold outside."

"I wouldn't know."

"I understand. Paul, have you considered coming out and talking with me face-to-face? Carol can be with us. I assure you that I am unarmed. I would like to get to know you better. To understand how you feel. The promise still holds that no one will harm you."

"Carol needs to go home. No need for her to be involved. I'm doing this for both of us. I'm not coming out until Yates is brought to me."

Carol grimaced, tears in her eyes that could no longer be attributed to the cold wind.

Dr. Hyatt put his hand on Carol's shoulder. "Paul, you know we can't do that. We can assure you that you won't be harmed. We can promise that we will do all we can to help you."

"You can't help me. The only thing that will help me is justice for Yvonne. The only thing that will help me is if Yates pays for what he has done. For what his wife has done."

Dr. Hyatt looked at Sarah and grimaced. "I understand your heart. What has happened to you seems unbearable, but I promise we can work on the pain together. We can release the pain without anyone else having to suffer. Carol has the same pain, but she's not trying to kill someone to make it go away. Paul, were you and Carol friends with Jerald and Stella Yates?"

Carol nodded.

"What's that got to do with anything? Any friendship we had was destroyed when Yates let his daughter kill Yvonne."

Carol sobbed.

"If you were once friends, you know Jerald and Stella would never do anything to hurt Yvonne. Paul, you told me earlier that the girls visited back and forth in the Yates house, in your house. Isn't that right?"

"That doesn't change anything. He killed Yvonne. Give me Yates."

"I can't do that. What I can do is come to the house. I can come to you. I'll even bring Carol with me if that helps. It will be good for me to meet you. Can you do that for me, Paul?"

"Carol, go home! I don't want you involved. No one comes in here. If anyone does, I'll kill the old couple. In fact," Timmons' voice grew louder, "I may just settle for that. Kill them. It'll be on Yates because he's afraid to come face me. Let him live with their deaths too."

Dr. Hyatt looked at Sarah and shook his head. Carol sobbed louder; her face creased with dejection. Sarah understood the meaning of Dr. Hyatt's expression. She looked at Taylor, started to speak, but saw Carol, changed her mind, and walked out of the command center. She knew there could be no middle person. Even simply carrying her command to Sergeant Bosko would include Taylor in the investigation that was sure to follow. The loss of Mr. and Mrs. Glenn had to be entirely on her shoulders.

Sarah saw Sergeant Bosko standing near the SWAT van with two other team members. "Sergeant."

"Yes, Chief. What's the word?"

"We need to get into position. It's not going well. Dr. Hyatt thinks Timmons is near the end of his patience. He's going to act soon."

"Roger that." Sergeant Bosko spoke into the mouthpiece of his radio headset. "Move to position one. Wait for my command." The Sergeant grimly stated, "Chief, say the word."

"I want to save the Glenns. Timmons if we can."

The Sergeant nodded. "That's what we want as well. Glenns first."

Handed Sarah a handset. "TAC two. I'll be on scene." He left the glow of streetlights and melted into the shadows of ornamental trees near the Glenn house.

Sarah occasionally engaged in SWAT-like assaults on buildings during her career, but nothing similar to what was about to take place at the Glenn house. Her mouth was dry. She returned to the command center.

Dr. Hyatt's face was intense as he focused on his cell phone pressed against his ear. "Paul, you know we must agree on something. Let me come to you. I'm a doctor. You know I'll be unarmed. I can exchange myself for the Glenns. How about that? Can we do that?"

Carol was slumped in a chair nearby. She knew time was running out for Paul to surrender.

"You've not done anything to me. I want Yates or the Glenns to die. It's that simple. Someone has to pay. Which will it be, Doctor? Yates or the Glenns?"

"Paul, is it really that simple? Will the death of someone else bring Yvonne back? Will more deaths take away your pain? As I see it, your actions would only cause you more pain. Think of Carol."

Paul didn't reply.

After a period of silence, Dr. Hyatt looked at the phone to see if he still had a connection. He looked puzzled. "Paul, are you there?"

A loud pop caused Dr. Hyatt to yank the phone away from his ear. His eyes were wide and terrified when he looked at Sarah.

Carol gasped and turned pale.

"Go! Go! Shot's fired," Sarah almost shouted into the tactical radio. She didn't need to mention gunfire. The SWAT team was close enough to hear it firsthand. For a moment, it crossed her mind that a SWAT team member might have acquired a shot on Timmons and took it. She definitely didn't want that to be the case. She waited and watched the screen for any signs of activity. She listened intently to the comments of the SWAT team members on the radio Sergeant Bosko gave her. She wanted to ask for an update, but she knew they didn't need the distraction. She heard no gunfire. That was reassuring.

Within a few minutes, lights came on inside the house. Sergeant Bosko's calm, commanding voice took control of the radio transmission. "We need an ambulance."

Carol screamed. "Paul!"

Taylor took a non-verbal cue from Sarah and went to Carol. She gently led the woman into another area of the command center that offered some privacy and isolation from the communications that were to follow.

As soon as Carol was clear, Sarah tersely commanded over the radio, "Sit update."

Sergeant Bosko's unemotional voice responded against a background of a frantic female voice shouting unintelligibly, "Subject has GSW to the head. Elderly male in cardiac arrest. Elderly female inconsolable. Ambulance requested."

"GSW origination?" Sarah's heart was in her throat. A SWAT bullet would create a public relations nightmare, regardless of the circumstances.

"Self-inflicted," was Bosko's simple response.

Sarah was ashamed that the answer relieved her. A distraught man was dead. She asked the communications officer inside the command center, "Is the ambulance enroute?"

"Yes, Ma'am. ETA three minutes."

"Thank you." In the radio, Sarah asked of Sergeant Bosko, "Is it clear for me to enter?"

"All clear, Chief. Come through the front door."

Sarah grimaced toward Dr. Hyatt. "I'm going to the scene, but first I think Mrs. Timmons needs to know."

"I think she already knows," Dr. Hyatt said softly. "Go to the scene and confirm it's him. You know him. I'll sit with her until you call me with positive ID."

Sarah entered the Glenn house after the ambulance arrived. Two paramedics were working over Mr. Glenn who was flat on his back on the hardwood floor. A radio crackled with instructions from the ER team at the hospital. One paramedic was inserting an IV while the other was attaching leads for an EKG. By the time the ambulance reached the hospital, the ER doctor would have a treatment plan in place. The EKG was weak and erratic. Mrs. Glenn was held back by a SWAT officer.

Paul Timmons' body was sprawled near the center of a nearby bedroom. A large pool of blood soaked the carpet around his head. The ceiling had red organic matter splattered around a hole in the sheetrock. Some of the splatter had dripped back onto the carpet. Bits of what was once a hair covered skull had rained down immediately after the gunshot. A few small pieces dangled, ready to drop without provocation. A rifle was on the floor near the body. The first SWAT team member in the room had kicked it away from the body as a precaution. Though necessary for the safety of the team, Sarah's detective instincts didn't like it.

"Sergeant Bosko, other than the rifle, has anything else been moved?"

"A chair that kept the closet door closed from the outside," Sergeant Bosko pointed toward a wooden chair that was on its side near Mr. Glenn. "The lead officer kicked it aside after the room was cleared. We heard Mrs. Glenn's screams. It doesn't look good for him. Mrs. Glenn said he has a bad heart and went unconscious as soon as they were shoved into the closet."

Sarah didn't have exam gloves with her. She saw some in the paramedics' kit. Without asking, she took a pair and put them on. She began taking photographs of the body and the area between the room and the hall closet where the Glenns had been imprisoned. She studied the body, the blood pool, the ceiling splatter, the rifle, and Mr. Glenn. There was no case to solve. She would find the bullet, hopefully lodged in a two-by-four or in the roof. She had to be able to prove it was a bullet from Timmons' rifle that killed him and not a SWAT bullet. Public opinion would demand that much.

Sarah knelt beside the body, careful to avoid the blood-soaked carpet. The top of Paul Timmons' head was gone. A gaping red hole that exposed what was left of his brain. She glanced up to assess the chances of more brain matter rain while she was there. Satisfied that nothing more would fall, she studied Paul's face. It was surprisingly intact. Only the eyes bulged to indicate the tremendous force of the bullet that passed behind them. She took pictures with her cellphone. A lot of pictures. There was no need to gather evidence. The pictures told the story.

"Sergeant, do you have a tactical light I can borrow?"

Sergeant Bosko stepped away from his position overseeing the paramedics and handed Sarah a flashlight. "Sure, Chief. Do you see something?"

"I want to look inside his mouth."

"GSR?"

"Yes. Questions will be asked. I want to have answers."

"I understand. Do you need swabs?"

"Yes. I do. Can you contact Lieutenant McCuskey? Ask her to bring her kit. I'm also going to need to get into the ceiling. Hopefully, find that bullet. And someone needs to contact the Coroner. How's Mr. Glenn?"

Sergeant Bosko shook his head. "The Paramedics didn't say anything, but I doubt he's going to make it."

"That's a shame. The Butterfly Effect. A teenager's bad decisions led to all this."

"I'll have my guys locate a ladder. I think there's a room above this one. I'll go see if the bullet went through the floor."

"Let me do that. You've got an operation to command." Sarah saw the entry hole in the roof of Paul's mouth. A swab would confirm GSR, and a swab of the end of the rifle barrel would confirm Paul's DNA.

The upper floor was carpet covered, hard to see if the bullet penetrated the downstairs ceiling and upstairs subfloor. Sarah shined the flashlight's bright beam across the second-floor ceiling. She searched for holes that might indicate the bullet's travel. She saw nothing. The bullet stopped somewhere within the structure of the floor. She needed the ladder to find it. The ambulance siren blared and quietened as it raced away to the hospital.

Lieutenant Glasgow arrived with a forensics kit. "Taylor is still with Mrs. Timmons, so I brought my kit. Wow! That's gory. Shoved it in his mouth?"

"That's what it looks like. I'll swab inside his mouth and around the end of the rifle barrel. I'll also dust the rifle for fingerprints and swab his hands."

One of the SWAT members arrived with a tall step ladder.

Sarah asked Melvin, "Do you have something I can use to cut away the ceiling? I'm going to need access to the space above the entry hole."

"I think there's a box knife in the kit. I'll do that, Chief." Melvin donned gloves as he spoke. "Tell me when you're ready." The ladder would have to span across Timmons' body.

"While I finish this, see if there are some linens in the closet that we can spread over the body. I don't want to contaminate anything with sheetrock chalk."

Melvin returned with a bed sheet. They spread the sheet before setting the ladder in place. Sarah watched as he carefully preserved the ceiling entry hole by cutting a chunk of the sheetrock. He handed it to her. The hole was large enough to shine a light into the dark gap between ceiling and floor.

"We got lucky," Melvin grunted. "It hit a two-by-six beam."

"Take a picture before you dig it out. We have to show where it was lodged."

Within a few minutes, Sarah sealed an evidence bag that contained the flattened bullet. Even after passing through the sheetrock and into the wood beam, it was largely intact and there was blood evidence on it. She had several evidence bags by the time Coroner Mason arrived.

The Coroner was startled when he lifted the bed sheet. "I didn't expect something like this," he exclaimed. "I saw the SWAT team presence, but still didn't expect to see him shot in the head."

"Self-inflicted," Sarah replied.

"What brought it on? Any idea?"

"It's Paul Timmons."

"He doesn't live here, does he?"

"No. The Yates live next door. He came to kill them but ran into this house when we arrived. He had hostages until he decided to end it."

The Coroner shook his head. "You been here the whole time?"

"No. I got called after he took his hostages. I've been here since a little after eleven." Curious, Sarah checked her phone's clock. A few minutes after 3 o'clock. In the scheme of things, a very short stand-off.

Henry glanced around. "I take it the hostages are okay?"

"The man may not survive a heart attack. The woman is traumatized."

"Is the scene clear for me to bag the remains?"

"He's all yours."

Sarah and Melvin helped the Coroner bag the body, place it on a gurney, and load it into the Coroner's van. As soon as the Coroner drove away, Sarah dismissed the SWAT team. Some of them were like her. Their regular shifts started at seven o'clock in the morning.

# CHAPTER 22

## 3:30 A.M. Wednesday

Exhausted, Sarah walked to the command center with Lieutenant Glasgow at her side. A chill ran through her when she saw Sheriff Berringer's stern face inside the mobile unit. "Good morning, Sheriff." She didn't wait for a response. She asked the officer at the communications console, "Is Lieutenant McCuskey still with Mrs. Timmons?"

"Yes, Ma'am. They are in the private room."

When Sarah entered the small room, Carol angrily asked, "Why did you kill him? You didn't have to kill him. You promised."

Sarah was momentarily stunned. "We did not kill Paul. He took his own life before we entered the house."

"LIAR! You're a liar!" In a cracked, sobbing voice, Carol screamed, "You're all liars! Let me go!" She shook Taylor away from her and pushed past Sarah as she exited the room. Before she stormed from the mobile center, she screamed, "I'll sue all of you, you murderers!"

With only one word, Dr. Hyatt helped alleviate Sarah's doubts. "Denial."

Sarah nodded sorrowfully. "I suppose. Still, she's been through a lot."

"She has a lot more to go through."

Sarah nodded. She directed her attention to Taylor. "We can stand down. Have your night team maintain a cordon of the Glenn house.

Sergeant Bosko will debrief his team before he dismisses them. Melvin will sit in on that."

"Is Mrs. Glenn okay?" Taylor asked.

Sheriff Berringer stoically watched and listened.

Sarah ignored the Sheriff as much as she could in the small command center. "Distraught. In shock. I'm not sure Mr. Glenn is going to make it. He went a long time without medical intervention after his heart attack."

Taylor's eyes moistened. "They are the only ones I feel sympathy for."

Dr. Hyatt looked at Taylor compassionately. "Are you okay?"

"Me? Yes. Or I will be. This one is rougher than most, but we've been through situations similar to this one." To Sarah, Taylor said, "I'll get everything set. I may be a few hours late this morning. It's way past my bedtime."

Sarah looked at Taylor and Melvin, "I'll see both of you after you've had some rest … and me too."

A patrol officer entered the command center, "Chief, the press has been outside the tape for an hour or so. I don't think they're going to leave until they know something."

Sarah felt her shoulders slump. "I'll go talk to them. Cameras?"

"Yes, Ma'am. Two camera crews."

Sarah knew she looked a mess. She wondered if she had blood on her clothes. She had been careful, but violent death scenes were not neat and clean.

Tammy Nunn was bundled against the cold wind. She saw Sarah approaching the tape. She motioned to her camera man to get ready. "Chief. Chief James can you tell us what has happened?" Tammy wasn't about to allow the rival reporter to ask the first question, even if it meant shouting from a distance.

In Sarah's exhausted state, the new reporter's voice grated on her nerves more than usual. She forced a smile. The camera's light was bright, even in the presence of police car strobes and streetlights. "Good morning to all of you. I will give you what I can." Sarah positioned herself so both TV crews had equal access. "A hostage situation developed shortly before eleven o'clock. Devaney PD cordoned off the area to protect the public. We evacuated nearby homes for the safety of the residents. Police negotiators spoke with the subject in an effort to defuse the situation and save the hostages. The situation was resolved when the subject committed suicide rather than surrender. One hostage suffered a heart attack and has been taken to the hospital. We will secure the scene and bring in the State Police to review our operation."

Tammy asked, "Why are you bringing in the State Police?"

"Protocol. It is prudent to have an outside review of these situations so we can learn how to improve."

"Were mistakes made by Devaney PD?"

"Not to my knowledge. We have established protocols for hostage situations. Negotiation is always the preferred approach."

Tammy motioned toward the SWAT van that was loaded and leaving the scene. "We saw SWAT team members return from the house. Was the SWAT team required?"

"Only to assure the safety of the hostages. They went into the house after we heard a gunshot. They found the subject dead from a self-inflicted gunshot to the head."

"Could you have prevented the suicide if you had acted sooner?"

Sarah scowled at Tammy. "We'll let the State Police decide after their review."

"We saw a woman leave the scene a few minutes ago. She was crying and angry. She said you were a liar, that you killed her husband. Was it her husband?"

"The subject was her husband. She was here to help with the negotiations. It ended badly. She's upset."

"Why did she call you a liar?"

Sarah exhaled and internally debated whether to answer. "She's upset. Her husband killed himself. Our negotiators promised that if he would release the hostages, we would not force him out of the house. That we would not harm him. He was deeply troubled over recent events in his life and decided the only way out was to take his own life. She blames us for not stopping him."

"What is the victim's name?"

"I will release his name later today pending notification of next of kin."

"His wife already knows."

"He has other family. We will allow her to tell them. I'll make the names available later today. Now, it's been a long day and night. I'm going to bed."

Sarah took a quick shower when she returned to her apartment. Shawn was still asleep, apparently undisturbed by her absence ... though he wasn't accustomed to a bedmate anyway. She turned the alarm off, slipped under the covers, and crashed into sleep within a few minutes.

A man's voice scratched across Sarah's brain. She wasn't sure if it was a good man or a bad man. A bad man was chasing her before the voice took her mind off the chase. It could have been a distraction, something to delay her escape from Sheriff Berringer. His face was dark and angry. He wanted something she held close to her breasts. She couldn't let him have it, but the voice kept scratching until she forgot the reason she was running.

"Sleepy head. I thought you were an early riser." Shawn's voice was tinged with humor, not laughing but definitely chuckling. "It's after seven. You're going to be late for work. Did I cause this?"

"What?" Sarah pulled herself from the darkness. Her eyes fought to stay closed. She forced them open and was met with a warm kiss on her lips. Morning breath. Hers or his. She didn't know, but the smell helped her brain focus on the moment. She thought about the events of the night. She shook her head to clear the vision of Paul Timmons' face with its bulging eyes. She turned her head to see her bedside clock. Seven fifteen. "Oh," she moaned. "Three whole hours." She tried to raise from her pillow, but Shawn's body was across her torso and his head was leaned on his elbow.

"What excuse are you going to give for being late?" This time Shawn laughed. A soft, loving laugh that made Sarah smile.

"They know. Apparently, everyone knows but you." Sarah grinned. Her head throbbed lightly from lack of sleep. "I was called to a hostage scene about eleven."

Shawn jerked back. "What? And you didn't wake me?"

Sarah laughed. "I tried, but I guess I wore you out."

"What happened? Everything okay?" Shawn leaned away so Sarah could sit up.

"Not really. The subject killed himself and one of the hostages had a heart attack. An elderly man with a heart condition." Sarah looked at the clock again. "I suppose I need to get up. I have several meetings and I need to see what else has occurred since four this morning."

"Four? You didn't get back in bed until four?" Shawn sat up. "They can make it without you for a little longer. Go back to bed. Get some rest."

"I need to call Liz. She's probably wondering where Taylor and I are. And Melvin. He's our negotiator." Sarah reached for her phone and dialed. When Liz answered, she explained what had happened.

"I saw you on the news while I was getting ready for work. When I saw it, I checked your schedule for today. I'm on my way in now. Is there something you need me to do?"

"The only thing I remember is my meeting with the Sheriff at ten. Reschedule anything prior to that. I don't want to delay the meeting with Berringer." Sarah grimaced as she thought about Sheriff Berringer in the communication center. He never said a word, but he wasn't there for anything that would be good for her. "I'll be there within an hour or so." She wondered if Berringer would be in his office to honor the meeting.

Shawn got out of bed while Sarah was talking to Liz and went into the bathroom. She sat on the edge of the bed a moment before realizing she was naked. She saw her bathrobe on the back of her dresser chair. She got out of bed and pulled the robe around her. She then went to the kitchen and started a pot of coffee. Her morning routine was totally disrupted. She would drink coffee before she drove to work.

# CHAPTER 23

Sarah entered through the lobby side door. Her car didn't need to be charged. Sergeant Honeycutt saw her and waited at the Shift Commander desk with the daily summary.

"Good morning, Chief. You probably know most of what's in the summary, but here it is. Tough night." Maria didn't tease. She knew when to be serious.

"Thank you, Maria. I probably know the biggest bullet, for sure." Sarah held the page at arm's length and studied it. "What's this call? A citizen reported activity caught on a doorbell camera."

"Patterson said a woman called just before shift change to say she had something interesting from Sunday night on her porch camera. I sent a unit to her house. She lives on Osage Road. Osage runs near the Overton Acres bike trail. It gives access to the trailheads near where the body was found. I called Boston just in case it means anything."

"What does she have?"

"She said she's been out of town since Friday afternoon. She watched the news this morning. She heard the story about the hostage situation, then they mentioned the body on the trail. When the reporter said Devaney PD wanted citizens in that area to report anything unusual, she decided to check her camera recordings. Apparently, she's still not happy about the Overton development."

Sarah cocked her head attentively. "I hope this has value, and not some perennial complainer. Have you heard from your officers?"

"Yes. That's why I called Boston. They said it shows pictures of a car and pickup passing her house a little after three o'clock Monday morning. They're following up with other neighbors to see if anyone else has video or pictures from that time frame."

Cars on city streets, even at night, were not unusual or particularly notable, but any clue was worth investigating. "Is Boston out there?"

"I'm not sure. He uses the garage entrance ... charging his EV most of the time." Maria grinned. "I think he just likes parking out of the weather."

Sarah changed subjects. "Have there been any new developments with the Timmons situation since four this morning?"

"Mr. Glenn died at the hospital. The Glenns names are in the public as the hostages. I'm sure the newshounds were all over the hospital until someone talked. And, of course, they are calling, asking for more information. They have already reported Paul Timmons' name and want to know if we are classifying the incident as a murder/suicide."

Sarah shook her head. "Sensationalism sells ads." She left with the summary and went to HR. Too many distractions. She had not yet talked with Paula Heston about the sexual harassment complaint against an officer.

Paula was at her desk sorting through a stack of documents. She smiled when Sarah knocked on her door frame. "Good morning, Chief. I hear you had a rough night."

"Yes. It was rough. I intended to talk with you yesterday about our sexual harassment complaint. What can you tell me?" Sarah walked into the HR Manager's office and closed the door. She didn't sit.

Paula motioned toward the document pile on her desk. "That's what I'm working on now. I talked to our lawyer. He told me to send a copy of the complaint to the District Attorney. I hope you don't mind that I did it before we talked."

"Not at all. Time spent waiting on me is time wasted. I trust your abilities over mine in these matters. What next?"

"Today, I'll put together our investigation plan. That's what our lawyer said the DA would want to see first."

"Makes sense. Sexual harassment against a patrol officer is a first for me. As a woman, it concerns me. What is the complaint?"

"It's against Officer Teri Caudle. A drunk driver complained that Officer Caudle was "too familiar" when frisking her."

Sarah thought a moment. Hearing Teri Caudle's name was unexpected. "I assume the driver was being arrested?"

"Yes. She blew point one-one. I reviewed the car camera video. Sergeant Honeycutt and I.T. are arranging access to Officer Caudle's body cam footage from the same time. The car camera indicates the driver seemed more drunk than she blew. We didn't do blood, but I would bet she had something else in her system that exacerbated the alcohol."

"Illicit drugs?"

"I wouldn't swear to that."

"Why didn't we do blood, considering she was filing a complaint."

"Apparently, she wasn't unruly or upset until after she was bailed out. There was no reason to do blood work at the time of arrest and booking. A simple DUI."

"No one suspected illegal drugs?"

"Like I said, it was a routine DUI stop. It could have been prescription drugs, I suppose. People don't read those product warnings about not drinking alcohol with prescribed meds."

Sarah thought about what Paula told her. "I assume you've talked to Officer Caudle."

"She's back tonight. There's no particular rush. I'll talk with her in the morning and fill in some blanks."

"Did the driver contact a lawyer?"

"Not that I know. She filed the complaint on her way out the door. From what I understand, a friend came to bail her out. As she was getting her personal effects, she became incensed and began claiming the arresting officer was "too familiar" during the pat down."

"Pat downs *are* familiar. Weapons can be anywhere."

"True. According to notes logged by the jailer who signed her out, her friend overheard her and told her to file a complaint. He gave her a form and she filled it out on the spot."

"Just like that?" Sarah shook her head dejectedly.

"That's just the surface of it." Paula grinned. "The official complaint reads *the male officer was too familiar and copped a feel of my crotch and breasts*. With exclamation points."

"I understand what you're thinking, but it can cause issues for Officer Caudle, regardless of mis-identified gender. Any investigation can. Our people are under enough stress without false complaints. What is your next step?"

"Get Officer Caudle's side of the story. And her companion officer's story. If her body camera substantiates the car camera, I think she will be fine. The car camera indicates Officer Caudle was apparently talking with her companion as she conducted the pat down. I saw no unusual movements or touching. Definitely no groping."

"Caudle is a Training Officer. She was likely explaining the process to her trainee as she performed the pat down."

Paula nodded. "That explains a lot. I'll keep you updated on the investigation. I know you have bigger issues."

"Officer stress and distractions are big issues. Keep on top of it. I don't want Caudle's career harmed by an unfounded claim."

"If it is," Paula said as a cautionary reminder.

Sarah stopped outside Liz's office door. "Good morning, Liz. I made it."

"Good morning, Chief. You always look fresh. I don't know how you do it."

Sarah laughed. "Trust me. It's a façade. I'm exhausted. I suppose my notes for the meeting with Sheriff Berringer are on my desk?"

"They are. Mayor Keck also wants an update on last night's events when you get time. I think he already talked to Sergeant Patterson earlier, so he's not completely unknowledgeable of the matter."

Sarah checked her phone for the time. Nine-fifteen. "I'll call him before I go meet with the Sheriff. I want to check his stand on the lab."

"You know his stand," Liz replied quizzically.

Sarah nodded. "Just reassuring myself." She went to her office and reviewed the folder with notes for the meeting with the Sheriff. Liz had made a list of Sarah's margin notes on the Sheriff's proposal. Large font. Sarah blinked to clear her eyes. They were tired. Age and not enough rest did that. She thought about Byron Castleman's comment regarding the need for them to meet in his office. Maybe she should take him up on that.

That aside, Liz's bullet points were fully legible even without cheaters to read them. She tried to calm herself. She believed that if she failed to stop the Sheriff's quest, her leadership abilities would be questioned … by her if not by the entire department.

After reviewing the other folders on her desk, Sarah walked into the bullpen on her way to the coffee pot. She walked past Lieutenant McCuskey's empty cubicle. She knew Taylor stayed with the scene later than she did. The mobile command center was generally under Taylor's control. She would have followed it back to the garage and made sure it was stowed and ready for immediate use. The Situation Room light was on. She saw Boston looking at photos on his phone. He was wearing drugstore reading glasses. "Good morning, Boston."

"Good morning, Boss." Boston looked up over the top of his cheaters. "I heard about last night. Tough deal."

"Sergeant Honeycutt said you might have some new evidence on John Doe."

"I think so." Boston paused. He looked at Sarah's empty hands. "Go get some coffee, then I'll show you what I think I have."

Sarah took Boston's suggestion and returned with her gray cup filled with steaming coffee and the last donut from a box probably provided by Boston. She didn't stop for her drive-thru breakfast sandwich. "What do you have?"

Boston grinned at the donut in Sarah's hand as he handed Sarah his phone. "Some preliminary photos sent to me by Corporal Baldor. She and Bohannan talked to a few people along Osage Road." As an afterthought, he added, "That's the street that borders Overton Acres. The walking trail is about a hundred yards in the woods off Osage. Both the trailheads are on Osage."

Sarah set her coffee cup on the table and took the offered phone. She knew the area, but she let Boston explain. He was talking in complete sentences. There were several homes along Osage Road opposite Overton Acres. The development plan called for apartment buildings along the road. That was the reason the trail was setback. It was also one of the major obstacles to approval of the development. The people who lived along Osage Road didn't like the idea of apartment buildings across the street from them. Some of the homeowners proactively added security cameras in anticipation of "transient" neighbors. She squinted and held Boston's phone at full arm's length.

Boston chuckled as he handed his reading glasses to Sarah. "Here. Try these. They help."

Sarah didn't hesitate. She put the glasses on and blinked to refocus her eyes. They helped. The small screen became clearer even at normal distance. "Looks like a dark car and a light pickup truck."

"Yes. It's fuzzy because Baldor snapped a shot from a video. They'll bring the video and some decent pictures when they finish."

"Okay. We have video of a pair of vehicles on the road … apparently, Osage Road. I don't see a time stamp." Sarah squinted and held the phone further from her eyes.

"It's there but it's too blurry. Baldor said the video shows three-twenty-seven and some seconds. It's a good camera system. She said the pictures are reasonably clear. Maybe Alicia can enhance them enough to see the drivers or a license plate number."

Sarah swiped the screen and saw more pictures of the vehicles. "Are these from other cameras? Looks like they are traveling Osage."

"No. All from the same video. Baldor took several. Hoped to get more clarity. Keep going."

"All I see is a dog … or coyote. And a couple of deer. I still can't make out the time stamps."

"Too small. Baldor said after three. A few minutes earlier than the vehicle pictures. Notice anything about the deer?"

Sarah studied the pictures for a moment. "They are both does."

Boston chuckled. "Well, probably. I don't know much about deer sexes. They are staring back across the road. They noticed something. Maybe something that chased them and the coyote out of the woods."

"Where are the pictures of the car and truck? If those cameras picked up animals, they should have picked up vehicles."

"Exactly." Boston stood up and walked to the whiteboard and drew a horizontal line. "This is Osage," he said. He made a few Xes at intervals beneath the line. He drew another line above and parallel to the first. "This is the walking trail. He scrawled a circle that connected the lines at one end. "This is the first trailhead." He moved to the other end and drew a connecting circle a few inches from one of the Xes. "This is the second trailhead." He pointed to the X nearest that trailhead. "This is the house with the video camera."

Sarah understood what Boston was illustrating. She was elated. "The vehicles didn't travel along Osage Road. They drove the trail. They scared the wildlife."

"That's my thinking. We now have a break. Maybe our single best clue."

Sarah handed the phone back to Boston. "I hope video enhancement gives you enough for a BOLO."

"Me too. I hope Alicia has time to do it."

"Melvin can use the enhancement tools," Sarah suggested.

Boston scowled. "Is he here today? I haven't seen him."

"He was our hostage negotiator. He may be sleeping in. He also observed the SWAT team debrief."

"I'll see when I get the videos."

"Did anyone near the first trailhead have cameras?"

"No. That would have been nice, but we have enough for a start."

# CHAPTER 24

## 10:00 A.M. Wednesday

Sarah walked up the County Courthouse steps. The Sheriff's office was near the back of the building at ground level, but access was through a series of chain link security gates that guarded the Sheriff Department's equipment and impound lots. A small holding jail for prisoners due in court was also accessible from the back. A new, large jailhouse was located across town. The back entrance required more security checkpoints than from the front of the building. For Sarah, it was simpler to go through the front. As she approached, she remembered that she didn't talk with the Mayor to update him and to get his reassurance ahead of her meeting with the Sheriff. That made her nervous. She knew how far she was willing to go to prevent the Sheriff from getting his way. She believed she knew how far Mayor Keck was willing to go. She hoped she and Bill were in alignment.

Sheriff Berringer's office area was not as crowded as it was before the new jail was built. The jailhouse staff's relocation opened space. A civilian administrative assistant greeted Sarah as soon as she entered. "Good morning, Chief James. Can I get you something to drink? Sheriff Berringer will be with you in a moment. He was out late on a case."

"Good morning, Karrie. A bottle of water would be nice." Sarah didn't bother to mention the Sheriff didn't need to be out at all as far as she was concerned.

Sheriff Berringer stepped from his office after a short wait. "Sorry for the delay, Chief. I'm running a bit behind this morning. Come on in. Would you rather have coffee?"

"Good morning, Sheriff. No. Water is fine. I've had enough coffee. I think that cold wind dehydrated me."

Without smiling, the Sheriff replied, "That's why I stayed inside the command center." Inside his office, he walked around the desk and motioned toward a pair of comfortable guest chairs across the desk from his chair. "Please, be seated."

Sarah immediately noticed the difference between former Sheriff Herriman's décor and Sheriff Berringer's. For one, the old chair that leaned to one side because of a broken spring was replaced by a new, modern chair. The new one was undoubtably more comfortable for sitting. Sheriff Herriman tended to lean back and to one side, likely the reason for the broken spring. Sheriff Berringer sat upright.

Years of mementos that decorated … or cluttered … the Sheriff's office were gone. They were personal items collected by the old Sheriff. Sheriff Berringer's walls were adorned with photographs and certifications from his years with the State Police. A bookcase and credenza were the pieces of furniture beyond the desk and chairs. The tops of each were clean and polished. Even the Sheriff's desk was uncluttered with anything other than a folder similar to what Sarah carried. He didn't even have pictures of his wife, children, or grandchildren. Stoic and professional. Sarah adjusted one of the chairs and sat.

"Too bad your negotiator wasn't able to talk the man down," Sheriff Berringer stated flatly.

"Yes. Timmons was an angry man without hope." Sarah didn't want to delve too deeply into the situation.

"There's always hope."

"His daughter died in the traffic accident. He was emotionally lost." Sarah thought a moment before adding. "We had to separate him from the Yates family at the funeral home earlier in the day."

The Sheriff nodded in thought for a moment, "Why did the wife call you a liar? Was something promised?"

"We promised Timmons that if he released the hostages, we would not come in after him. We'd keep talking."

"Was that wise?"

"The psychiatrist thought so. It gave him an option. He was bargaining. He wanted something in trade for his pain."

"You didn't anticipate suicide?"

"We did, but Dr. Hyatt tried to keep hope alive and to save our hostages."

"Glenn died."

"Heart attack. Timmons' fault, but not by Timmons' hand."

"Oh." The subject was closed. Sheriff Berringer noticeably shifted focus. "How is Steger working out?"

"Alicia seems to appreciate his help. That's about all I can tell you. He arrived yesterday afternoon and I haven't been to the lab today."

"He has a strong forensics background. Probably stronger than your Tech. He worked in a major lab. And he's proven leader."

Sarah didn't take the bait. She knew Deputy Steger's background. He never mentioned leadership as part of his experience. "I appreciate the loan of Deputy Steger. It's always good when there is interagency cooperation. It makes us all stronger."

Sheriff Berringer nodded thoughtfully. "We can be even stronger if we bond our resources into a cohesive unit. A regional forensics laboratory will improve our criminal investigative capabilities. A single lab can provide value savings by reducing redundancies. Spend one dollar instead of two."

Sarah met Berringer's intense gaze. The man was a trained police officer, accustomed to staring down contacts he encountered in highway stops. She wasn't as experienced as he was, but she knew what he was trying to do. Intimate her with his presence. She had the same skills. Probably the same training. "So far, Devaney PD is the only entity that has spent the dollar. Alicia and Devaney PD have invested time and money to create a regional forensics lab. Alicia services smaller law enforcement departments with minimal financial recompense for the service."

"The County can provide finances."

Sarah kept her wits about her. At least the Sheriff didn't have the advantage of more sleep than her. His late-night involvement was for show, to flex his "constitutional office" muscle by being on the scene. She opened her folder, "As I read your proposal, Devaney will provide more financing than the County."

"Based upon population. Pro-rated according to tax base."

"But led by the County. Sheriff, no one in Devaney will support yielding control of the forensics lab Devaney built. If you amend your proposal to a contributory role for the County, maybe we can find common ground."

Sheriff Berringer's face remained stoic and his eyes fixed. He wasn't ready to blink. "Are you proposing that the Sheriff's office provide funds without input into management of a lab?"

"I'm proposing nothing. I'm perfectly happy with the current situation."

"By asking for help, you've admitted the lab is more than you can manage."

Sarah bristled. She leaned toward the desk. She knew her topaz eyes darkened. She could almost feel the darkness in them. "Managing effectively is knowing when to ask for help … and to appreciate the help when you get it. The help is to speed the process, not to achieve the outcome. The outcome will be the same, regardless. Only the timing changes."

Sheriff Berringer's face relaxed. "Chief, I know what's going on. Devaney rules this county. The Commissioner has already made it clear that he won't support a County takeover of Devaney's lab. The only exception to that would be if you agreed to it."

Sarah wasn't sure if the change in the Sheriff's body language was a shift of strategy or if it indicated he was standing down from his original proposal. "What are you saying?"

"Just what I said. There is no support for a County run forensics laboratory. I think it's a mistake, but it's not my call. The Good Ol' Boys are still in charge." The Sheriff leaned back. "But I think I hear you suggest we could come to an arrangement to create a Devaney PD run regional lab, one where a Sheriff's Deputy could become part of the staffing."

Sarah softened, but she remained poised. Berringer was a man with an agenda, and he had far more experience than she did. "I can support something like that, but there is one thing you need to consider. If part of your plan was to instate Deputy Steger as leader of the forensics lab, that isn't going to happen."

Sheriff Berringer blinked. "I admit, that was part of my original proposal. Steger has a lot of experience in a large lab. He knows the ropes. And I believe he has leadership skills."

"So does Alicia. She began here with our little lab that performed simple tests and prepared samples for external lab testing. She slowly grew our lab into what it is today. Not a full-blown lab like Wichita's, but she can evaluate a lot of evidence. Her only drawback is funding. We are a small city with limited resources, and frankly, limited need. Still, she has made a name for herself and our lab as a resource for solving crime in our region."

"I think I can bring funding to the lab, but I want Steger in it as an equal partner."

"Steger won't stay."

"What? Why wouldn't he?"

"He left lab work to move into law enforcement. If you stick him back in a laboratory, he'll leave. He'll find a job elsewhere. He wants to be a detective ... and I think his background will support that desire."

"Where did you hear that?"

"From Steger. He didn't leave a big lab in Wichita to work in a small lab in Devaney. He wants to be a police officer ... or deputy. Don't run him off." Sarah leaned back. "If you do, I'll snap him up in a heartbeat."

Sheriff Berringer thought about Sarah's comments. "Are you sure?"

"Positive."

"Do you have a detective opening?"

Sarah thought about Keith's dilemma. "I might ... soon enough." She knew she had internal candidates with more detective exposure than Deputy Steger, but the Sheriff didn't know that.

"Well, I do have an opening right now. Maybe I'll consider him."

"Either way, his passion is not in a lab."

Sheriff Berringer pushed himself to his feet. He smiled and extended his hand, "It's been a good discussion, Chief James. I'll talk to the Commissioner about funding support for Devaney's forensics lab. Come see me anytime."

Sarah called Mayor Keck as she drove to the station. "Good morning, Mayor. I'm sorry I didn't call sooner. I had my meeting with Sheriff Berringer."

"That's okay, Sarah. I think I got enough information from Sergeants Patterson and Honeycutt. At least, I know as much as the media. How did your meeting go with the Sheriff?"

"Quite well. I have a feeling you softened him up for me."

Bill laughed. "Actually, I didn't. I think Commissioner Dawdy might have, though. Berringer grates on too many nerves at the Courthouse. He's like a bull in a China closet politically. He hasn't learned that civilians don't like police officers acting like immutable authorities. How did it turn out?"

"He's dropped his proposal. He's offered to ask the Commissioner for lab funding to help us service the area more effectively. He still wants one of his people in there, but I think that's more of a hope than a requirement."

"Good. I knew you could handle it. How long were you out last night?"

"You mean this morning? I left the scene a little before four. It was a tough one. A no-win situation. I called in Dr. Hyatt. Even he couldn't make any progress."

"From what I've heard through the grapevine, the outcome was inevitable. Not much you or anyone else could do."

"That doesn't make it any better."

Sarah walked up the back stairs to her office. She thought about checking on Keith's case, but she wanted to check with Liz before she did anything else. She wanted to let Liz know she appreciated her help with the Sheriff's meeting.

# CHAPTER 25

## 11:20 A.M. Wednesday

Small victories keep one's spirits up. Sarah embraced the meeting with Sheriff Berringer as a small victory. Her preparations gave her confidence when addressing his proposal, but Bill Keck's behind the scenes work with Commissioner Dawdy turned the tide. Liz knew that her efforts were instrumental in the victory for Devaney PD.

As Sarah was relating the meeting to Liz, she heard Taylor's voice in the bullpen. She went to see Taylor and saw Melvin working at his computer with Boston hovering nearby. "Good morning, Taylor. Melvin. How are you two today?"

Taylor's eyes twinkled and crinkled when she smiled. "Not too much worse for the wear. What time did you come in?"

"A little after eight. I had a meeting with Sheriff Berringer.

Melvin looked up at the call of his name. He waited until Sarah mentioned the Sheriff before he spoke. "Good morning, Chief. How did the meeting go? And why was he there last night?"

"The meeting went perfectly for Devaney PD. His presence was a last-ditch effort to unnerve me before the meeting. He knew his proposal would be dead on arrival unless I offered to accept it."

Taylor said, "Good. Alicia will be glad to hear that. She's been worried, especially with the Deputy assigned to the lab."

Sarah nodded. "Good point. I should probably go tell her in person.

206

But before I go, what are you two working on?" She looked at Boston when she asked the question.

"Lieutenant Glasgow is enhancing the doorbell videos for me." Boston's disdain for the Lieutenant, though improving, still didn't allow him to be familiar with Melvin by using his first name.

"Interesting. Do you have anything yet?"

Melvin answered, "There aren't any rear images. No license plates to trace. The resolution is poor in that lighting, but I can see that the car is a mid-range hue, probably a gray color. The pickup is definitely white. The truck is a Ford F-150 extended cab four-by-four, maybe four years old. The car is an older model Toyota Corolla."

"Can you make out the drivers?"

"No. The lighting is poor, and it's reflecting off the windows. All I have is a glare. I can't cut through it." Melvin returned his attention to the screen. "Something odd about the car. Bad suspension or something. Let me see if I can determine what it is."

Sarah and Boston moved closer, almost crowding Melvin inside his cubicle. Taylor watched from a distance. All three anxiously waited for something that would identify the killers and solve the case.

After a few minutes of enhancements and magnification, Melvin sat back. "I think that's it." He smiled with relief.

Sarah leaned closer, but not too close. "What?"

"The front tire is low."

Boston asked, "What does that mean?"

Melvin replied smugly. "Depending on why it's low, that tire won't last too long."

"Unless he stopped and aired the tire," Sarah replied. The thought that local gas stations might have the driver airing the tire on camera elated her. Another small victory.

Boston stepped away from the cubicle and turned toward his own area. "I'll hit all potential stops with air along and near Osage Road. This may be our single best clue."

"Are you going to put out a BOLO on the vehicles?" Sarah asked rather than tell.

Melvin answered, "I can do that while Boston is checking gas stations. Boston, do you need me to help?"

Boston stopped in his tracks. He turned, "That might speed the process. Yeah. Thanks. I'll make a list and give you half."

"Do you need anything from me?" Taylor asked.

"Just have your people keep their eyes open out on the streets," Boston answered.

Sarah said to Taylor, "I have a presser this afternoon. Liz is compiling all the information we have about the Timmons situation. I can hand out photos of the vehicles to the press if you can get some good pictures ready."

Taylor hustled to Melvin's cubicle. "Just send me the file, Melvin. I'll do the BOLOs. You help Boston."

Sarah smiled as she left the office area to go to the lab.

Alicia saw Sarah enter the lab and smiled anxiously. Her face lit when Sarah gave her a thumbs-up. She looked to see Deputy Steger's location and level of attention to his task. She whispered to Sarah when Sarah was close enough, "What happened? Do we get to keep our lab?"

"In a word, yes. Nothing changes for now. Maybe down the road, the County will provide money and a technician for you to lead." Sarah patted Alicia's shoulder reassuringly. "I think we had behind the scenes help, but it happened." She looked toward Deputy Steger. "What have you found so far? Anything positive?"

"Slowly moving forward with DNA evidence. Also, the Wichita hospital blood samples prove the other two accident victims were under the influence of Adderall. Chief, I heard about the hostage situation with the Timmons girl's father. That is so sad."

"It is sad. The loss of a child is beyond doubt the most traumatic thing that can happen in a person's life. Mr. Timmons couldn't accept two things. One, that Yvonne could have made bad choices that led to her own death, and the second was that bad choices by him wouldn't change the results of his daughter's choices. Now, he's left his wife with even more grief to manage. What about the DNA?"

Alicia nodded toward Steger. "We're using CODIS to compare John Doe's DNA with the National DNA Indexing System. So far, nothing. All we can safely say is that he didn't have a criminal record and he didn't work in any job that required DNA testing."

Deputy Steger's focus was broken by the conversation that was no longer whispered. "I'm also setting up a comparison to some of the ancestry sites' DNA data bases."

"Do you think he might have sent his DNA sample to one of them?"

Deputy Steger's eyes sparkled when he smiled. "We might find a familial match if a relative submitted a sample."

"Really?" Sarah responded incredulously.

"It's possible. It's estimated that nearly ninety percent of Americans' DNA data is known because of close family members who submitted samples to ancestry sites. Father, brother, mother, sister. Your DNA can be accurately estimated based upon family members' DNA. We might get lucky."

Sarah liked what she was hearing, though she was impatient for results. "Is it that easy to access their data bases?"

"All that's needed is a court order to do it legally," Steger replied. He turned back to his work, apparently unwilling to add more.

Sarah considered Steger's comment. She knew he had connections from his time in Wichita. Getting legal approval to search for the identity of a dead person was not difficult. A good forensics technician knew the channels to use. "Where are we on the jacket epithelials? Did you find some?" The question was directed toward Alicia.

"A lot. I would say the jacket was worn frequently by whoever owned it. I say that because the colors were faded from frequent washings and probably sun exposure."

"A favorite jacket. When will you know something about the person?"

"We'll know tomorrow if the person wearing the jacket was involved with John Doe's death. Late tomorrow, we can compare the epithelials against CODIS. I think we should find something quickly." Alicia sounded confident.

"What are you holding back that makes you think that?" Sarah asked.

Alicia shrugged. "Someone who would commit murder has to be in the system. They have to be involved in criminal activity with an arrest record."

"I hope it's that simple ..." Sarah let the sentence end itself. She knew Alicia was being hopeful rather than scientific. "Was there anything else in the dumpster that might help?"

"Not really. Waylon opened the bags Boston brought in. Nothing you wouldn't expect to find in a dumpster. The patrol officers also took pictures of the stuff they left in the dumpster. The only things odd were boxes of cereal and what looked like food cans without labels. I thought about going to see it for myself, but I don't have time." Alicia waved her hands to indicate the evidence in process or waiting to be processed.

"If the church ran a food bank, they might have dumped outdated or damaged items. People donate what they can't use. As a matter of fact, I think Pastor Cline mentioned that. I'll call him to confirm." Sarah made a note in her notebook. "In the meantime, assume it's not abnormal for that particular dumpster."

"Don't forget the bag with dirty diapers and wet wipes," Deputy Steger interjected.

"Ew! There is that. Some people are so rude. Stuffing soiled diapers in a leaky grocery bag. They should have tossed the bag into a regular trash bag."

Sarah almost laughed at the look on Alicia's face. "Did it leak?"

"On my evidence prep table. Yes, it leaked. I had to clean the whole thing. I'd rather smell a DB than a dirty diaper."

"Maybe that's why they tossed it in the dumpster. It smelled too bad to leave inside in a trash can. Where is it?"

"We didn't find anything in the bag other than two dirty diapers. One with poo. The other with pee."

"Where are they? Did you toss them?"

"I never toss evidence," Alicia stated. "That's what Waylon is working on. He took some samples for DNA testing. Now, he's bagging them in a leak proof evidence bag for retention."

Sarah walked to where Deputy Steger was working. "Did you give that much attention to the other bags?"

"That much attention? Yes. This much detail. No. We're taking extra care with retaining the items that can be linked to a person … even if it is a baby." With a note of pride in her work, Alicia explained further, "Unlike regular trash, a diaper can tell you something about the people who were near the dumpster. We might need them later, but there's not much more we can do with them now."

Without touching anything in Steger's workspace, Sarah studied the diapers and wipes. "These aren't baby diapers."

"What are they?" Alicia asked with an offended expression. "They're too small for adult diapers."

"They're not baby diapers, but observation does tell us something about the person wearing them. They're pull-up diapers for toddlers."

Deputy Steger looked up at Sarah. "I should have noticed that. I have nieces and nephews. I've never changed a diaper, but when they graduated to pull-ups, it was a big deal for them."

"Whatever else you find, these pull-ups means the user is old enough to start potty training. Pull-ups are easy to pull down so they can sit on the potty."

"That means we can ask which church members have toddlers," Alicia suggested.

"That's a starting point. I'll ask Pastor Cline." Sarah made another note, then added. "Pull-ups are expensive. More expensive than diapers. Parents don't use them unless they have high confidence that the toddler will either go to the potty or tell them they need to go."

"That makes sense," Alicia exclaimed. "But why would there be two dirty pull-ups in a bag? The toddler didn't pee, get changed, then poo and pee. Maybe the two pull-ups were soiled at different times, and the parent delayed tossing them."

Deputy Steger offered, "Maybe someone who came for food and the toddler did both while waiting for the food."

"If you can't afford food, …" Sarah paused her comment to allow the two Lab Technicians to consider how the sentence should end.

"You're not going to spend money on pull-ups when diapers work," Waylon finished Sarah's sentence. "Do you think there's a connection to the murder?"

"There could be," Sarah answered. "The pull-ups can tell us something about the people who used the dumpster."

"We can run DNA on the poo to see who it belongs to," Alicia volunteered.

Deputy Steger shook his head. "I doubt we can find toddler DNA using CODIS."

"Maybe not the baby, but a relative," Sarah said. She smiled at the Deputy. "Your familial DNA idea might give us the answer. Have you found anything else?"

Alicia pointed to a small stack of papers. "These are the results of tests and analyses we've completed. For one, Boston's bloody shoe print and the shoe prints from the woods are a match. I don't know if that proves anything other than the same person was in both places."

"It substantiates his idea that the murderer hid in the woods then handled the body after shooting our victim," Sarah replied. "Keep up the good work. Both of you." She left the lab.

Sarah returned to her office. Lieutenant McCuskey called out to her as she walked through the bullpen.

"Chief, I sent the BOLO with special attention to Kansas and the surrounding states. Or did you want me to go national?"

"Regional is okay for now. Hopefully, Boston will find something at the gas stations around town and we can determine which direction they went."

Liz told Sarah that the press was expecting updates on the hostage situation and on John Doe. Sarah sighed and tried to relax in her chair before talking to them. "Can we set up in the lobby?"

"I've already asked Sergeant Honeycutt to assign someone. Taylor has vehicle pictures for the BOLO."

Sarah smiled tiredly, "They do love handouts."

# CHAPTER 26

## 1:00 P.M. Wednesday

During the press conference, Sarah received a text from Shawn. She didn't acknowledge it until the presser ended. She smiled as she read it. *"I know you're busy. I just wanted to tell you I love you."* Her hand shook slightly as she responded. Shawn was getting serious. She didn't know what his expectations were. She wasn't sure if she had any.

"Something wrong, Chief?" Liz whispered in a voice tight with concern.

Sarah's eyes were moist when she replied. "No. Everything's right." She watched the reporters leave the lobby before she headed up the stairs to her office. Sergeant Keith Locke, clutching a large manila envelope, met her inside the bullpen.

"Afternoon, Chief. Gotta minute?"

"Sure. Let's go to my office so we're not blocking the aisle." Sarah led Keith to her office. "Do you have something new on the copper theft?"

"I think so. Turns out that the trace code was for water sold at a Neighborhood Market. They still had a few bottles on the shelf and a pallet full in the storeroom."

"How many?"

"They sold one-hundred-thirty-eight gallons."

Sarah winced. "That's a lot of suspects."

"Not really … if we can make some assumptions."

213

"Such as?"

"That the gallon jug we found was sold Friday, Saturday, or Sunday and was purchased in a small order."

"Small order?"

"Yeah. Bought by itself or with a couple of other items." Keith pulled receipts from his manila envelope. "They provided me with six single gallon purchases during that time frame. Two of them were bought alone. The other four were purchased along with other items." He beamed as he held one receipt for Sarah to see. "This one included a package of batteries."

"That sounds promising. If they paid with credit card, you have a name … unless it was a stolen card."

Keith seemed crestfallen. "No. That one paid cash. I've asked for security videos for these four purchases, in case the batteries were a coincidence. All four purchases were made on the self-scan registers."

"When will you have them?"

Keith shook his head dejectedly. "It'll be tomorrow. The manager wants to get approval from the Home Office before she releases them. Something about customer privacy."

Sarah thought a moment. "Did you also ask for parking lot video before and after the times of the purchases?"

"Yes. She said she can provide those without approval but pulling out specific times will take a while. She will try to have those later today. She didn't sound too convinced that they would show much detail, like faces and such. The cameras are on poles looking down."

"Understood. Maybe their cameras will catch a license plate. Sounds like you have something that could move you closer."

"Single best clue?" Keith asked jokingly.

Sarah smiled. "Maybe. It all depends on whether any of those four buyers have the skills and background to remove large, industrial wiring."

Keith's face fell. "I suppose you're right. If they are all little old ladies, we won't have our thief. I'll let you know as soon as I know."

"Good luck … and keep you're focus on the case until the cuffs click." Sarah still saw the need to support Keith's behavior. His focus was split. The decision to follow Zoey was a tough one for him. Men don't handle the role of trailing spouse well. Egos.

Sarah was hungry. All she had eaten since dinner with Shawn the evening before was a donut. She had been on the go since arriving at the station. She heard Boston grunt *hello* in the hallway before he spoke.

"How is that copper case going?" Boston asked Keith.

Keith answered, "I think I'm close to solving it. I'm waiting on some video from Walmart to provide a face."

"Good. Let me know if you need help."

Sarah stepped into the hall, bound for Liz's office to let her know she was going out for something to eat.

Boston saw her. "There you are. I didn't expect you to still be here after an all-nighter."

Sarah froze. "Still here for now. How is your case going?"

Boston smirked. "Which one? I have an update on the OD."

"The OD? What is there to update?" Sarah's interest was piqued. Her early suspicion that the drug incident and the dumped body might be connected regained footing with Boston's comment.

"I visited Sasha Pierce to get some information for Blake. Blake's contacts gave him some descriptions of minor league drug dealers. Sasha confirmed which one sold her the tainted meth. Blake is going after her."

"Her? A female?"

Boston smirked. "Imagine that."

Sarah was still hungry. "Have you eaten lunch yet?"

"I grabbed a burger while I was out." Boston looked down at this shirt and tie. "Why? Did I drop mustard on my tie? I ate it while I was driving."

Sarah grinned. "No. No mustard. I haven't eaten yet. I'm starving. I thought we might get lunch together if you hadn't. I was going to tell Liz I'll be out for lunch. Did you find where the Corolla stopped for air?"

"Blake called and asked for help with Sasha. Distracted me for a bit. Glasgow is still out looking at stations. I left my list of stations in the Sit Room. Headed back out."

"Has Melvin reported anything promising?"

"Not so far. It's a long shot anyway."

"Probably. I'm going to get some lunch before I drop." Sarah walked in the opposite direction as Boston to exit the building. She kept her head down to avoid attracting anyone's attention.

Devaney had a variety of eating places. A lot of them were fast food eateries. None of them were known to be healthy. She wasn't obsessed with eating healthily, but she tried to be sensible. She opted for a Subway sandwich. It offered fresh vegetables and cheese along with cold cuts. The option allowed her to believe it was a healthy choice. She bought the sandwich and returned to her office to eat it.

The crispness of the vegetables provided proprioceptive feedback that satisfied more than hunger. The sensation of chewing fresh food were almost as fulfilling as the food itself. Sarah finished two bites before her desk phone rang. She saw the caller ID and answered, "Hi, Taylor."

"Chief, I didn't know if you were in your office or not. I have a call from Missouri Highway Patrol. I'm going to transfer the call to your phone, and I'll be right there."

Before Sarah could protest, a male voice came on the line, "Hello? Hello, is this Chief James?"

"It is. How may I be of service?"

The man paused before continuing. "I didn't realize the Devaney Chief was female. This is Sergeant Piedmont with Missouri State Highway Patrol. How are you, Ma'am."

Sarah suppressed the desire to confront the man for being presumptive. Instead, she replied, "I'm doing well. And you?"

"Great. Chief, I may have something of interest to you. One of our patrol officers encountered a vehicle that matches your BOLO regarding a murder suspect. A Magnetic Grey Toyota Corolla. 2012 model year."

Sarah's eyes widened in response to the caller's message. Taylor hurried into the room, placed both hands on Sarah's desk, and leaned across it. Sarah put the phone on speaker so Taylor could hear. "That's fast! Where did the officer encounter the vehicle?"

"Let me patch Officer Wilson on with us. He can answer your questions. Better firsthand than secondhand." After a few seconds of clicks and buzzes, Sergeant Piedmont asked, "Officer Wilson, are you there?"

"I am. Yes, Sir."

"Officer Wilson, I have Devaney PD Chief James on the line. She has some questions about the gray Toyota you reported."

"Hello, Chief James. What questions do you have?"

"Hello, Officer Wilson. I suppose my first question is where did you encounter the vehicle?"

"On Interstate 49 south of Harrisonville."

"I'm not sure where that is, Officer Wilson."

"It is a few miles south of Kansas City."

"When was the encounter?"

"The most recent was less than half hour ago. I did a wellness check and green tagged the car on Monday shortly before noon. It has a flat front tire. I assumed the owner would return in a day or so. It's safely off the highway, so I didn't suspect anything unusual. When I received the BOLO, I went to check it again, to confirm it fit the description on the BOLO."

"So, it's been there since Monday?"

"Yes, Ma'am, Chief. I was going to red tag it today if it was still there, and have it towed tomorrow."

"Are you going to tow it?"

Sergeant Piedmont interjected, "Do you want it towed to your location, Chief?"

"Yes. Of course. It's been a couple of days, but hopefully there's evidence that will help us find the murderers."

"There's more than one?"

"At least an accomplice. One of them was driving a white Ford pickup. It was on the same BOLO. Officer Wilson, did you notice anything unusual about the vehicle?" Sarah asked the question then paused. "I suppose we can have our forensics tech check it when it arrives."

"Yes, Ma'am. I noticed a couple of things I didn't notice when I green tagged it Monday." Officer Wilson continued apologetically, "I was only concerned that someone was in the vehicle. I saw the flat and assumed it wasn't abandoned, just a normal breakdown. That happens a lot on the interstate. There appears to be a blood smear on the front fender near the tire that's flat."

Sarah leaned forward expectantly, "Anything else?"

"I ran the tag. It's fictitious. Kansas tag. It came back for a white Terrain in Devaney. That's in your town, isn't it?"

Sarah jerked her head in surprise. "Yes. Yes, it is. Do you have that tag information handy? I have Lieutenant McCuskey with me. She's commander of our patrol units. She will contact the Terrain owner ASAP. There may be a connection other than the license plate."

"Or the plate was stolen," Taylor said softly.

"Do I need to arrange for pick up, or can you set up a tow from your end? We'll pay, of course," Sarah said. She was barely able to contain her excitement. A break in the case was needed and the car might be it.

Sergeant Piedmont answered, "I can have it put on a hauler this afternoon. They should be able to deliver it this evening or in the morning. Whichever suits you better. It's not that far."

"If they can have it here this evening, I'd like that," Sarah said. "Thank you. Both of you."

"You're welcome, Ma'am." Both men responded in near unison.

Officer Wilson continued. "I wish I had reacted differently."

Taylor cut in, "I don't know how you could have done anything different … or would have under the circumstances. Like you said, breakdowns are common. Even if you had seen the blood on the fender Monday, the logical assumption would have been that the driver ran over a deer and caused a flat tire. We see deer collision all the time around Devaney."

Officer Wilson seemed pleased with the excuse offered. "That's for sure. I see plenty of them on my beat. Especially in the fall during rut season. I'll see to it the car is loaded quickly. Good luck finding your murderers."

After the call ended, Taylor took her hands off Sarah's desk. "What do you think?"

"I think I need to call Boston and Alicia to let them know about the car. I also think the car BOLO can be dropped and the BOLO for the pickup truck needs to be expanded."

"I can do all those things." Taylor nodded toward Sarah's sandwich. "And you can finish your lunch. What did you get?"

Sarah grinned. Taylor's motherly tone gave her permission to relax for a moment and eat her lunch. "A vegetable sandwich with what looks like a sliver of roasted turkey. Tell Alicia I don't expect her to wait for the car this evening. I just want it in our possession and under our control. Tomorrow will be soon enough to start."

"You know Boston will be waiting for it."

Sarah lifted her sandwich to take a bite. "As will I."

Taylor shook her head. "Let Boston do it alone. You have other things to do … and you need some rest after last night."

Sarah blushed before she realized Taylor was referencing the hostage situation, not Shawn.

# CHAPTER 27

6:30 P.M. Wednesday

Shawn called. "How was your day?"

Sarah hadn't even been home long enough to kick off her shoes or to remove her bra. She had driven to the New Word Church to talk face-to-face with Joe Cline. She knew the church had Wednesday night services and that the Pastor would be there. The visit was disappointing in that it didn't offer anything new or substantial. Two of the parishioners had toddlers, but he couldn't say whether they used the dumpster on Sunday. He had plenty to say about the boxes and cans of food in the dumpster. She almost regretted asking before he was through with the subject. Apparently, some donors make themselves feel good by giving food to the needy even if the food is no longer fit to be used. He talked nearly a half an hour on the matter, a sore subject for him. Now, she wanted nothing more than to relax, physically if not mentally. "Busy."

"When is your day not busy?" Shawn laughed lightly. "I saw your presser. You looked tired."

"You sure know how to make a girl feel good." Sarah knew he meant it in the best way possible, but it still made her cringe.

"I didn't mean it that way. You looked like you need a break from the rat race."

Sarah knew where his conversation was going. "I just need some sleep."

"Are you hungry?"

"Not as hungry as I am tired."

"We can run get something to eat. We can be back before eight. I can tuck you in." Shawn's voice was filled with hope.

"I need to get some sleep. I wouldn't be very good company this evening." Sarah knew better than to allow him into her apartment. She wouldn't get any rest. She wouldn't want to rest. She hated the fact she had to put her job before her personal desires. That dilemma had never been part of her life before Shawn. "Maybe tomorrow night will be better."

"Are you sure? I can cook something or bring carry-out. We don't need to go out. A quick bite to eat and I will tuck you in. I'll even sleep on the couch."

Sarah closed her eyes and shook her head. She giggled. "You know better than that. Be here in half an hour." She ended the call. Her heart fluttered as she anticipated Shawn's arrival. If they were married, it would be simpler. She went to the bedroom to change into something comfortable. She removed her socks, wiggled her toes, and remained barefoot. She checked the bathroom mirror to see if her hair and face were presentable. A few brush strokes and she was ready.

Shawn brought Chinese. Orange chicken, fried rice, and egg rolls. Easy to eat. The food appealed to her stomach, but Shawn's presence caused butterflies. Sarah didn't eat all of her food even though she was hungry. Shawn watched her every move. His brown eyes expressed genuine concern for her well-being. She was torn between self-consciousness and desire. "Thank you. I would have probably gone to bed without eating anything."

"I know. I won't have it. If you won't take care of yourself, I'll take care of you." Shawn smiled warmly, the concern in his eyes turned to love. "I have hopes."

Sarah blushed. She wasn't sure what he meant. Short-term hopes or long-term hopes. Her phone rang. Shawn's eyes glared toward the device. She nervously looked at her phone on the kitchen counter where she left it.

"Go ahead," Shawn said dejectedly. He understood the role her obligations played in her life.

"Sorry," Sarah apologized as she rose to get her phone. The ID was Boston's. "Hello, Boston." She looked toward Shawn and winced apologetically. Her job might be more than Shawn could bear.

"Boss, the Corolla is here. I swabbed the blood on the fender for Alicia.

We'll see if it matches our John Doe. There were some blood stains on the driver's side carpet. Whoever stepped in the blood pool drove the car. Also, I ran the VIN. The car is registered in Florida to Eugene Simpson."

"Do you think he's our John Doe?"

"Possible. I'll run his name through Florida DMV tomorrow. Maybe his driver's license photo will match John Doe. Or we may find the car is stolen and we're no closer to an identity than we were. I figured you would want to know before tomorrow. This could be our break."

"I appreciate that, Boston. Are you leaving the rest for Alicia?"

"Mostly. I'll dust the insides and have the prints ready for her. Maybe she can give those to the Deputy."

"Sounds good. You need to go home. The car will be there tomorrow."

"And the murderers will have ten more hours to add to their head start."

"True, but I doubt they're running now. They're confidently going about their lives." Sarah paused then added ruefully. "Must be nice."

"Yeah. Taylor was working on something about the case, but I haven't heard back from her. And I assigned Glasgow the task of checking fuel stops along I-49 to where the car was found. Maybe they stopped between here and there. Air. Coffee. Gas."

"Boston, go get some rest. Alicia has been releasing a lot of evidence. She has a stack of results. There might be some good clues. You need to be ready to chase down those leads."

Boston laughed. "I'll see you bright and early. I'll bring the donuts."

Sarah smiled toward Shawn. "Good night, Boston. I'll bring my own breakfast." She disconnected the call.

"Was it important?" Shawn asked.

"Yes, but probably not urgent. I think he's just excited that he's finally getting some breaks. We may have a lead on the identity of our John Doe. Maybe even a lead on which direction his murderers went." Sarah walked to Shawn, took his face in her hands, and kissed him on the lips. "Now, didn't I hear something about being tucked in?" It was early, but she was ready for bed.

Shawn smiled and pulled her forward, causing her to topple into his lap. Sarah wrapped her arms around his neck and kissed him again.

Her body tensed, but the tension that swept over her was a welcome replacement for the aches of a day on the run without adequate sleep.

Sarah fully expected Shawn to at least try to lift himself and her up from the chair and carry her to the bedroom. Instead, he softly talked.

"I'd ask you to marry me if I wasn't afraid that I couldn't survive the rejection."

Sarah was momentarily caught off guard by the comment. She quickly regained her mental footing and replied, "You'll never know unless you ask." She pulled back to look deeply into his eyes.

Shawn's face twitched as uncertainty and remembered pain swept across it. "I lost a woman who I thought loved me. Lost her to a job."

Sarah felt a chill in her heart. She wasn't sure if the conversation was intended to go somewhere or if it was a cathartic moment for Shawn. A chance for him to expose his fears of commitment. A desperate attempt to rationalize an open-ended relationship that was destined to always be physical and never emotional. She fought to keep her voice from shaking and to sound compassionate. "Was it the job?"

Shawn's eyes averted for a moment. They moistened. His face was somber. "I love you with all my heart." His brown eyes fixed on her topaz eyes. "Yes, it was her job. Nothing mattered more than her job. I was an inconvenience. He was a fast track."

Sarah wanted to speak, but her experiences interviewing and interrogating told her to listen, to let him talk. Her words would influence whatever he said in response. Left alone, he would say what he meant to say.

"She wasn't faithful to him any more than she was to me. Still isn't, I imagine." Shawn looked away and sadly shook his head. "She would do anything to advance her career, to win a case. Not unlike that Assistant DA, Marcie Stapleton."

Sarah couldn't allow the comment to stand without rebuttal. "Marcie isn't like that at all."

Shawn's brow furrowed. "She certainly behaves like she is."

Sarah, still on Shawn's lap, leaned back slightly. "That's her courtroom persona. It's an act. Not one I would embrace, but it works for her."

Shawn's eyes hardened. "She comes across trashy."

"She does, I suppose, but it works for her. She uses her feminine guiles to influence the jury. She always appears to be overwhelmed to elicit sympathy as an overworked woman."

"And she flaunts herself."

Sarah scowled. "She dresses to keep the jurors' focus on her rather than the defense attorney's arguments. No different than some men lawyers in their fancy western wear. It's a costume."

"So, in her case, it's an act. I can accept that." Shawn's eyes softened somewhat. "Not in Jonelle's case. She did … probably still does … whatever will win a case or advance her career. It's not even about money. He has plenty. It's about status. Her status. No holds barred."

"Maybe she has self-esteem issues." Sarah didn't know why she suddenly found herself defending Shawn's ex-wife's behavior.

Shawn looked puzzled for a moment, then grinned. "Her behavior hasn't done her any favors. She's improved her status from that of a decent lawyer to an indecent lawyer. But it's what she wanted." He shrugged. "The past is the past. You're totally different. Your job is your obligation … and you don't use pheromones to enhance your status like most women."

Sarah's topaz eyes darkened. "Not all successful women use sex to succeed. As a matter of fact, very few do. I can name a lot of successful women in Devaney. Sharon Castleman. Taylor McCuskey. Maria Honeycutt. Cary Beecher. None of them used pheromones."

Shawn grinned apologetically. "Sorry. I didn't mean it that way."

"It sounded that way, like a man who can't accept successful women." Sarah caught herself before she said something she might regret. Something like *"Are you jealous of Jonelle's success and assuming she used sex to get it?"* She knew she had to learn more about Shawn. Was he as sexist as that particular conversation, or was he merely bringing his fears of being hurt again out into the open for discussion? It mattered.

Shawn pulled Sarah closer. She only slightly resisted. "At least I know you got where you are because of hard work."

Sarah knew his comment was his way of apologizing. It fell short of a complete apology, but it was a place to start. She replied, "I got this job because I was in the right place at the right time. Mayor Kamen wanted Chief Keck out and she believed she could control me, make me do what she wanted. I kept the job because she couldn't."

"I get that. I've heard only positive things about you. I also see that you work long hours and could use more downtime." Again, Shawn pulled her closer and leaned to kiss her.

Sarah considered where the kiss would lead. Without noticeably hesitation, she complied. "I'm ready to be tucked in. I'm exhausted." She smiled at the delight that filled Shawn's eyes. She led him toward her bedroom.

# CHAPTER 28

## 6:00 A.M. Thursday

Shawn was still sleeping at six o'clock when Sarah put her clothes for the day into a garment bag and drove to the gym. She focused on running the indoor track. That was her plan for the morning workout. She didn't intend to focus on time, only on distance. Her competitive nature prevailed. It wasn't her fastest run, but it was a rapid three miles.

After she showered, put on her panties and bra, and dried her hair, Sarah took a rose-colored blouse from the garment bag. She pulled the blouse over her head and settled it below her waist. Small neckline embroidery accented the garment with darker flourishes. She reached for her charcoal gray pants and bent to place her right foot into the leg.

"Good morning, Chief." A syrupy sweet voice called across the dressing room.

Sarah almost lost her balance when she looked up to see Bailey Stimpson, the gym manager. "Good morning, Bailey. I don't usually see you this early."

"Kevin took a vacation day. I'm covering for him. Have you finished your workout already?"

Sarah pulled her pants up and buckled the belt. "Yes. I have a full day ahead of me. I missed my workout yesterday, but I wasn't about to miss it today."

"Of course. That hostage thing. Is there anything I can help you with?"

Sarah was momentarily puzzled by the question until she realized Bailey was talking about the use of the gym. "No. Everyone here takes good care of me." The gym needed to be remodeled, but it was a well-maintained facility, aside from the odors associated with years of sweat within its walls. Newer, national franchise gyms were available, but the personal attention of her gym's staff kept her loyal. Almost ten years loyal. She realized her presence at the gym influenced several patrons to join … or remain, as the case may be. A successful female has a following, like it or not.

"Good to hear. If you need anything, please let me know."

Bailey left while Sarah was putting on her shoes, the bulky looking shoes she always wore. She wore them for comfort and stability, not fashion. Though she always dressed well, Sarah had no intentions of being a fashionista.

Buying an egg white sandwich and a plastic cup of orange juice from her favorite fast-food restaurant completed Sarah's pre-work routine. She parked near a charger in the garage then carried the paper bag with the sandwich and juice to her office. She set them on her desk and walked toward the coffee pot. The smell of fresh coffee wafted through the bullpen. Lieutenant McCuskey's blonde hair popped into view over a partition wall.

"Good morning, Chief. I thought I heard somebody. You look refreshed. Even radiant. Coffee is ready."

"Good morning, Taylor. Thank you … for the compliment and for the coffee. How was your night?" Sarah continued walking toward the coffee pot with Taylor at her side.

"Generally quiet. I slept like a log. How was yours? No late night calls?"

Sarah put a small amount of sugar in the bottom of her gray cup with pink lettering and filled it with coffee. No stirrer needed. "None. Thankfully. And I had a good run at the gym this morning. I see the Sit Room lights are on. Is Boston here?"

Without thinking, Taylor reacted by looking around the area. "I haven't seen him. He may be following up on some leads. I noticed a lot of pictures and notes on the table."

Sarah chuckled and replied, "Boston's filing system." With Taylor, she walked to the Situation Room and stepped inside. She studied the photographs and papers on the table. The items were generally sorted into jumbled piles Boston style. She looked at the corkboard that he used to tie different bits of evidence and clues together. She preferred a Pareto chart on the whiteboard, but Boston was the Senior Detective. It was his case to manage in his own way. The line drawing of Osage Road and the trailheads was the only thing on the whiteboard. On the corkboard, a picture of the Corolla was captioned with *Eugene Simpson*. It was attached to a fuzzy picture of the same Corolla followed by a white Ford pickup. A snapshot from the porch camera video that furthered the case. The picture appeared to be the last thing posted on the board.

"It looks like he might be focused on the car."

"Oh! When did it arrive?"

Sarah was surprised by the question. "Last evening, about six or six-thirty. I thought you were following up on something for Boston."

"I am. The Terrain. The one that the license plate was issued to."

"Were you able to contact the owner of the Terrain?"

"We were. I sent a unit to the address we got from Officer Wilson."

"Don't tell me. He wasn't even aware the license was stolen."

Taylor chuckled. "He wasn't."

"What time did you contact him?"

"It was after seven before the patrol could reach the owner. I told the Shift Commanders to let me know, so Sergeant Patterson called me." Taylor paused, waited for a sign to continue from Sarah. "The owner wasn't home until late." Taylor paused to think before continuing. "Lonnie Jameson. Goes by Bic. The investigating officers said he was suspicious of them. Kind of belligerent until he realized they weren't there to arrest him for something. His angry voice stirred up his dogs."

"Were his dogs aggressive?" The idea of a dog attacking a police officer was concerning to Sarah. Those incidents never ended well for the officer involved because sometimes the only recourse for the officer was self-preservation. Animal lovers hated that.

"No. Just loud. He had to shut the door to keep his house dog in check. He apparently has backyard dogs too. The investigating officer said the dogs were loud, but they were inside a wooden privacy fence and posed no danger. Jameson wanted to know why the officers were there. He didn't believe them until he walked out to look for himself. That's when they noticed that the license plate from his pickup was also missing."

"Sounds like it was a theft of convenience. That tells me the white Ford is running a fictitious tag also. We need to add that tag number to the BOLO."

"I should have thought of that," Taylor exclaimed. "I'll do it right away."

Lieutenant Glasgow came into the bullpen and stopped at the Situation Room doorway. "Good morning, Chief. Good morning, Taylor." He glanced toward the corkboard and the piles on the table. "Making any progress?"

"Good morning, Melvin. We got a break yesterday afternoon. Missouri Highway Patrol found the Corolla we think was involved in the murder. It's in Alicia's hands now."

"Boston called me and told me it was here. Do you need me to dust it or anything? I have another meeting with the school superintendent early this morning." Melvin grimaced as he made the last statement.

"Boston dusted it when it arrived. And took samples of blood from the fender."

"Blood?"

Sarah nodded. "It might be deer blood. Alicia will tell us. But it's likely Simpson's blood."

"Is Boston in yet?"

Taylor laughed. "We were wondering the same thing." She pointed toward the Situation Room ceiling lights. "The lights are on but nobody's home."

"Okay. Tell him that I'll be expanding the gas station search between here and where the car was found like he asked after I meet with the Superintendent. He thinks we may find video of the car getting air further than we already searched." Melvin shook his head. "In the meantime, the Superintendent is insistent on addressing driving rather than drugs. I think I've found a way to hit both forcefully."

Sarah suggested, "Maybe connect Mr. Glenn's death to both. Hopefully, the kids will see that their actions have consequences far beyond their own lives."

Sarah went to her office to eat her breakfast and review non-confidential folders Liz left on her desk. Her phone rang. Keith's ID. "Good morning, Keith."

"Good morning, Chief. Just a quick update. The Neighborhood Market manager said she had approval to release all the store videos including the parking lot."

"That's good. When do you get them?" Sarah thought the parking lot videos didn't require corporate approval, but she didn't comment.

"Maybe later today. So, if you see me sitting watching TV, it's security videos." Keith laughed.

"I'll try to remember that. Keep me posted."

Liz arrived a few minutes before eight o'clock. She brought Sarah two folders with confidential documents. "These personnel documents need your signature."

Sarah glanced at the first one. It was a request for promotion. Boston initiated the request to promote Keith Locke to Lieutenant. He hadn't mentioned it. Apparently, his distrust for Keith was tempered by his acceptance of Melvin Glasgow's worth. She knew signing it would be a final act for Keith, but it would improve his chances of securing a better position with the Omaha police department. She signed it and put it back in the folder. The other was a reprimand finalization from Paula Heston. A night shift jailer's attendance put him in disciplinary steps. She knew Lieutenant Jarrett had tried everything to improve the man's attendance. Some people simply aren't cut out for night shift. As junior man, there were no other options available. She signed the finalization, fully aware that she would likely have two openings very soon, Keith's and the jailer's.

Boston appeared at her door. "Good morning, Boss. Gotta minute?"

"Sure," Sarah said as she rose from her chair, "if you have time for me to refill my cup." She picked up her coffee cup.

"I need some myself. We can talk as we walk."

"What do you have?"

"I took advantage of Florida's time zone. They're an hour earlier than us."

"Did that pay off?" Sarah asked as they approached the coffee pot.

"Somewhat. I guess Florida DMV isn't accustomed to out-of-state cops calling for driver's license photos. And the approving supervisor was busy. Morning meeting." Boston shook his head. "They had several Eugene

Simpsons on record, a couple about the age of our victim. Like pulling teeth. I convinced them to cross-check VIN registrations with DL record." Boston held up a page with a photo. "I got them to e-mail the DL photo to me ... finally."

Sarah looked at the photo. "Looks familiar. What do you know about him?"

"Other than it looks like our victim, not a lot at this point. The vehicle registration has a different address than the DL. Fortunately, they are both in the same town. Panama City. I called Panama City PD. I couldn't get connected with anyone who could help, but I did get a call back promise." Boston shook his head, perturbed that his early arrival had not provided the answers he wanted.

"That's a start. Any idea when you'll get the call back?"

"None. When Detective Laborde is available, they said."

Sarah thought a moment. "Frustrating. I think I will contact the FBI. Let them know we may have an interstate crime on our hands."

"Do you think it started in Florida?"

"Maybe he was kidnapped in Florida and brought out here to kill. They stole license plates to cover their tracks, or at least to slow identification. It could be anything. I don't want to wait too long if the FBI needs to be involved." Sarah noticed Boston cringe when she mentioned the FBI. "But it's our case regardless."

"I suppose you're right. Maybe I'll learn something more when Laborde calls."

Sarah asked, "Have you talked to Alicia this morning?"

"No. I came in early. I didn't want to be disturbed. I went to Interrogation to make my calls. Quiet there. I need to check with Taylor. See if she has something on the stolen plate."

"Alright. I'll follow up later, after you've had time to process what you have." She already knew what Taylor had for him but telling Boston would indicate she was too deep into his business. There were boundaries even for the Police Chief. Sarah returned to her office.

FBI Agent Macon Caswell was a friend. Stationed at the FBI field office in Topeka, he was Senior Agent in charge. He had been promoted since he and Sarah last worked together on a case. Sarah was pleased that he had changed his mind about retiring early. He was someone she could trust to not overreact to the call she was about to make yet trust that he would do everything he could to help. He proved that when he stood toe-to-toe against Terrance Overton, Jr. and former Mayor Sebastian Clairmont. He skillfully defended her and Chief Keck from political interference in a murder case investigation that the Overton family wanted to control. She dialed his cell phone number.

"This is Agent Caswell," he answered.

"Agent Caswell, this is Chief Sarah James from Devaney. How are you doing?"

"Chief James? Sarah, I guess I've been out of touch. Congratulations! I'm glad to hear that. What came of the former Chief? Keck, wasn't it?"

"Thank you. Chief Keck retired and is now Mayor of Devaney."

"Good for him. I bet that makes the Police Chief's life easier, having a supporter in the Mayor's office."

Sarah laughed in return. "Somewhat, but I can't pull the wool over his eyes like I could if a civilian held the job."

Macon laughed loudly. "True. True. So, Sarah … Chief, I reckon this isn't a social call. How can the FBI assist you?"

"We have an ongoing murder investigation. A body was dumped near one of our walking trails. He died from a single gunshot to the head. That's preliminary. We don't have the full autopsy report yet. We aren't sure of the motive. We're leaning toward drugs, but there is nothing concrete on that. Nothing except we have a tentative identity on the victim. A resident of Panama City, Florida."

"We all know there is plenty of drug activity in and around that part of the country. How can I help?"

"This is mostly a heads-up call. We may find that the victim was kidnapped in Florida and brought here before being killed."

"Interstate crime. I got it. Do you need an agent on site? I can send someone."

"I'm not ready to call it out yet, but I didn't want to catch you flat-footed if it comes to that. Besides, it's good press to mention cooperation with the FBI. The public wants to believe we are doing everything possible to solve crimes. Right now, we're trying to gather information on our victim, see if he has a connection to drugs … or any other criminal activities."

"What's his name? I can have the office in Panama City do some leg work. They might have something related they are already working." Sarah paused. Agent Caswell was offering more than she was requesting. She decided it would be more helpful than not, especially if the FBI already had information about Eugene Simpson. "Tentatively, we believe his name is Eugene Lawrence Simpson. We don't have a fix on his address. His car and DL have different addresses."

"Odd but not rare. People move and don't update vehicle information until it's time to renew their license. Let me have my people down there take a look."

"Okay. I'm not sure how cooperative Panama City PD will be with my Senior Detective. Maybe the FBI can light a fire under them. Thank you, Macon. I owe you one."

Macon chuckled. "Not at all."

Sarah sat back after she disconnected the call. She hoped she hadn't stepped on Boston's toes. Surely, he would understand. Her experience with out-of-state police departments was that they had more work than they could handle with very little time to devote to someone else's investigation. The FBI, on the other hand, had something to prove … that they were the supreme investigative agency in the country. Boston would understand … as long as the FBI didn't take the lead from him.

Liz interrupted Sarah's thoughts. "Chief, the press is ready for an update. The stage is set up in the lobby."

Sarah exhaled. "Thank you, Liz. I almost forgot … or tried to forget," she said with a forced smile. She called for Taylor to join her.

On the way down the stairs, Sarah's phone rang. Alicia's ID. "Hello, Alicia. Do you have something?"

"More than I expected to find." Alicia's voice was excited.

Sarah paused her descent. "Alicia, I'm on my way to a press conference in the lobby. Can I come see you afterwards? Or do you have something I should share with the public right now?"

"You could share it, but I'm not sure it's ready for that. I'll wait until you get here. Waylon probably wants to add his input. You can see both of us."

"Thank you, Alicia." Sarah walked down the stairs and approached the dais that Sergeant Honeycutt had set up for her.

The presser went reasonably well, though Sarah cringed every time Tammy Nunn's voice challenged her. Mentioning the FBI fueled the novice reporter's fervor. The possibility of the network picking up a feed could be a boon to her career. Tammy lacked tact, but Sarah answered her sophomoric questions without obvious prejudice. The presser ended after everyone except Tammy was through asking questions. Sergeant Honeycutt took on the role of Sergeant-at-Arms from the fringe of the gathering and called the press conference to an end with a simple phrase, "Thank you, Chief."

Sarah couldn't hide her smile. She was going to miss Maria's strong presence. She hoped Devaney PD didn't suffer from the loss of the Sergeant's experiences. Maria was the Department historian. She not only knew the rules, but she also knew the reasons for the rules.

Sarah walked to the Forensics Lab. Alicia grinned at her when she entered the room. Deputy Steger stopped what he was doing and joined Alicia to meet with Sarah.

"Good morning, Chief," Alicia and Waylon said simultaneously.

"Good morning. I'm sorry I couldn't talk earlier. I assume you have something?"

"I do, or rather, Waylon does. You always talk about that single best clue. We may have found it." Alicia tapped on a keyboard and a DNA Paternity Report appeared.

Sarah's eyes quickly went to the bottom of the page. In a highlighted box entitled Probability of Paternity was the number 99.9999999%. "Interesting," she mused. "What is this telling us?"

Waylon answered, "On a lark ... not a good practice in a lab environment ..., I compared the baby poo DNA to our John Doe's DNA."

Sarah felt blood drain from her face. "He had a baby with him?"

"Not necessarily, but the baby's diapers were apparently in his car. He may have tossed them in the dumpster. Maybe he didn't realize they were there until they began to smell."

Sarah's brow furrowed with concern. "This is a big concern. It changes everything. If he had a baby with him, where's the baby?"

Waylon replied cautiously, "We're not saying he had a baby with him."

"But if he did have a baby with him, we need to find it. We could have a kidnapping on our hands."

"I suppose, but primarily, this tells us something about John Doe. Maybe help identify him."

"The car gave us an identity. Boston has confirmed him to be Eugene Simpson."

"Oh," Waylon responded, crestfallen.

Alicia perked up, "Waylon checked the car. He found two things." She held up an evidence bag with a smashed bullet slug. "It's not pretty and it may be hard to analyze, but he found a bullet. It was stuck in the fender well, above the tire. The shooter almost hit the tire. Even more important … I think … he found a dead cell phone between the passenger seat and the console. We have it on the charger so we can search it for the owner's identity. That will tell us more."

Sarah thought about the possibility of a child abduction. Her heart rate increased. She was distracted by dread. She needed more information before she could issue an Amber Alert, but she wanted it fast. "Focus on the phone. If it is Simpson's phone and he has a baby, surely it will have pictures of the child. We need something for an Amber Alert ASAP. The bullet will provide an answer after we catch the killers. It probably won't lead us to them."

Both Alicia and Deputy Steger were taken aback by Sarah's abruptness. In unison, they said, "Yes, Ma'am," and turned toward the phone.

Sarah watched impatiently. Her cell phone vibrated inside her jacket's breast pocket. She glanced at it. It was a text from Shawn. *Are you busy?* She responded. *"Very. Call you later."* She tucked the phone back in her jacket. She hoped her terse response wasn't misinterpreted.

The two forensics experts fiddled with the phone for an eternity in Sarah's mind before Waylon said, "Let me insert a new SIM card. That should default it."

Alicia pulled a SIM card from a drawer while explaining, "I keep some just in case I have to unlock a cell phone." She glanced at Sarah. "It works most of the time … and it's quick."

Sarah nodded her approval while she watched the two of them hovering over the phone. She was relieved when both of them grinned widely. "I take it you have something?"

"Yes. The phone belongs to Gene Simpson," Alicia replied. "I assume that is his nickname. Gene for Eugene." She held the phone up so Sarah could see the screensaver. "And he has a picture of a toddler as his screensaver." She tapped on the phone's screen. Her face erupted in an excited grin. "His Facebook page lists the little girl's name as Cassie. That may be short for Casandra."

"Find me a good photo and send it to my phone." Sarah turned to go, paused, and said, "Good job. Both of you. This could be our single best clue." She hurriedly left the lab. Her heart was pounding more than it probably should have, but she knew the statistics on kidnapping. Seventy-two hours was pushing the limit for hope of finding the kidnap victim alive, especially if that victim was a young child. If Cassie Simpson was kidnapped, the countdown clock had already expired. Child trafficking and drug trafficking were not dissimilar, and Simpson's murder fit the mold of both.

# CHAPTER 29

## 1:00 P.M. Thursday

Sarah contacted Senior Agent Macon Caswell while she anxiously ate a fast-food sandwich. Her mind was not on the food. If not for the salt, she probably wouldn't have tasted it. If she wasn't hungry, she wouldn't have finished it. Caswell updated her on his progress with the Florida field office. Not much yet. Operative word – yet. He said he would turn up the heat now that there was the possibility of a child kidnapping. Florida FBI might be able to confirm whether Eugene Simpson's child, Cassie, was missing or not.

Not knowing about Cassie was worse than knowing. Uncertainty clouded the investigation and intensified the need for answers. Any answers. A drug murder is not as heart-wrenching as a murder-kidnapping. It didn't rise to the same priority level. Not in Sarah's mind. A kidnapped child did nothing to put itself in danger. She reread notes she had made in her notebook after she talked to Agent Caswell. The notebook was like the ones she used when she was a detective. Unlike when she was a detective, her notebook was not complete. The case was not hers. She didn't know all the details. It frustrated her now that a kidnapping was possible. Cassie Simpson's life was in the hands of Devaney PD … maybe. Sarah didn't even know that for sure. Cassie could be in her mother's arms somewhere in Florida for all she knew.

Boston caught Sarah's attention when he stopped in her open doorway. "Do you have time to review?"

"Definitely." The look on Boston's face told her nothing. She wanted to know something. She had to know something. "Here or in the Sit Room?"

"Most of my notes are in the Sit Room," Boston replied and waited for Sarah.

In the Situation Room, Boston looked Sarah in the eyes and asked, "Is the FBI in on this?"

Sarah didn't hesitate to answer. She had already advised Boston of her contact and what the FBI was going to do. "Yes. There's a possibility the murder qualifies as an interstate crime. Also, if there's a kidnapping, this is bigger than Amber Alerts and BOLOs. We're already past the point of no return for a kidnapping."

"Who runs it?"

"Devaney PD. You run it, Boston. The FBI will be a resource to you until someone tells us something different." Sarah really didn't want to worry about Boston's ego ... but she had experienced the same feelings on the Overton Case. Her mentor, Carl Franken died and left her ... the Junior Detective ... to solve that case alone. Neither the Overtons nor the Mayor at the time were confident in her abilities to save a kidnapped child. "I'll stand behind you. What do you have?" She wanted to focus on the investigation, not the personalities.

Boston eyed Sarah suspiciously for a moment. He appeared ready to continue his quest for assurance. Instead, he pulled a page with scribbled notations from what an untrained observer would assume was a jumble of dissimilar papers. He knew where everything was on the table, where everything was within his organized chaos. "Not much. Not enough to find Simpson's killers. Definitely not enough to find a child." He scrawled *Walmart* on a piece of paper and pinned it and a blown-up picture of Eugene Simpson's driver's license on the corkboard. "Detective Laborde finally came back with something. The problem is, Simpson doesn't live at either of the addresses on his license or his vehicle registration."

"So, he doesn't live in Panama City? Did he move to Kansas?"

"Laborde thinks Eugene lives in or near Panama City. He just doesn't know where yet. The vehicle's address is his parent's house. His father co-signed the car because Eugene didn't have high enough credit score, so it was registered at that address. Simpson currently works at Walmart Supercenter in Panama City."

"The father?" Sarah asked.

"No. The son. Eugene. Here's the catch. The parents don't know where he lives. They only know he lives with a girlfriend … and his two-year old daughter."

"Has Detective Laborde talked to the girlfriend?"

"The parents don't know her last name. They only know her by Maggie."

Sarah shook her head despondently. "Probably short for something else. Maybe Margaret. So, I take it Eugene and the girlfriend aren't married?"

"That's what I'd assume. Laborde is checking records for marriage licenses. He had unies talk to the store manager. They were able to confirm Simpson's current employment." Boston checked his notes. "Store manager is Sean Caster."

Sarah perked at the name. It was a familiar sound. "Shawn?"

"Yes. S-E-A-N."

"Oh. Some people spell it differently."

Boston looked puzzled for a moment then continued. "The manager said Simpson was scheduled for work at midnight Tuesday night but was a no-show. The store tried to call him, but he didn't answer, and his voicemail was full. This Caster guy told them that was unusual because Simpson didn't miss. Worked anytime he was asked. Said he was thinking about calling the police."

"Walmart didn't have the girlfriend's contact information?" Sarah asked.

"Laborde didn't say." Boston studied his notes.

"That's something we need to know for sure. She might have Cassie. I assume she's the baby momma."

Boston scowled at his notes. "The grandparents didn't seem to indicate she was, but … who knows?"

Sarah stared at Boston for a moment. "*We* should know. We *need* to know. If the girlfriend is the mother, she probably has Cassie, and we aren't facing a kidnapping."

Lieutenant Glasgow softly rapped on the open doorway to announce his presence. "Sorry to interrupt. Is this private?"

Boston scowled in Glasgow's direction, then glanced at his watch. He responded, "No. Come on in, Melvin."

Sarah was glad to see the acceptance of the Lieutenant from Boston. "Hello, Melvin. How is the search of the gas stations going?"

Melvin entered the Situation Room and exhaled. "We've hit every possible place the car could have stopped for air or gas between here and where it was found." He glanced at Sarah. "Taylor volunteered a couple of off-duty unies. Nothing. I've looked at a lot of grainy videos in fast-forward. Cameras are everywhere." His tone reflected his exasperation for coming up empty.

Sarah replied, "A camera gave us our first good clue. Don't knock them."

"I'm not, but that's a lot of staring at tiny screens. I looked at every video taken between two o'clock Monday morning and noon Monday. Looking for the Corolla and a white Ford pickup. You know, those air pumps get a lot more use than I thought."

Boston explained, "Seasonal changes. Average temps are dropping. Tires pressures drop with the temps. People are having to add air."

Sarah looked at the whiteboard. Still nothing about the case than the line drawing of Osage Road. She looked at the corkboard. Boston had a lot of pictures and notes pinned to it, some with colored strings to show association. Nothing on the board showed her the answers they needed … unless they were overlooking something, overlooking that single best clue. "We need to know the girlfriend's name. How can we get that? Is Laborde still trying to help?"

Boston shrugged. "I've told him to find that information for me. Go back to the grandparents. They should know the baby's momma. He was complaining about his workload and how he's having to rely on unies."

Melvin interjected, "Is there something I can do to help? Give me the grandparents' names. I'll call them if you need me to."

Sarah heard Liz's voice approaching. "Agent Caswell, would you like a cup of coffee?"

Liz and Agent Caswell stopped at the doorway just as he answered, "Yes. Thank you." His face erupted in a wide smile when he saw Sarah. "Chief James, it's good to see you again." Macon Caswell's brown eyes glanced at both men. "I'm sorry to disturb you."

Sarah shook Macon's hand. The firm, black hand felt reassuring and confident. A feeling she needed at that moment. The case was moving at a snail's pace and a baby's life was depending on them. "You're not disturbing us. Agent Caswell, this is Detective Boston Mankowitz and Lieutenant Melvin Glasgow. Boston is the lead on the Simpson case."

Macon's smile was non-threatening as he extended his hand. "I've heard a lot about you, Detective. I understand you were an undercover agent back east before moving to Kansas. That's a big change."

Sarah had not given Macon that information. She reckoned he did his homework before arriving. Being a Senior Agent with a national investigative agency had its advantages.

Boston replied in his normal, suspicious manner. "I was undercover here until I had to blow my cover. The *big* change is being a regular detective."

"I imagine it is. I'm at your disposal, Detective Mankowitz. Call me Macon. I'm not here to interfere, if Chief James hasn't already told you that." Macon's eyes turned to Melvin as he extended his hand. "Lieutenant Glasgow. It's a pleasure to meet you."

Sarah quickly slid into updating Agent Caswell. "We are getting some background on our murder victim, Eugene Simpson. Panama City PD has assisted, but apparently, their hearts aren't in it."

Boston interjected defensively, "They probably have their hands full with their own cases. The detectives sent unies to ask specific questions." His disdain for non-detectives asking questions was undisguised.

Macon nodded agreement. "I imagine you are correct." He pulled an electronic notepad from his jacket. "What do you have thus far? I took the liberty of asking our Panama City office to do some digging before I came. Maybe they have something to add."

Boston scowled before answering, "Not a lot. He doesn't live at the address on his registration or the address on his driver's license. He works for Walmart. He was a no-show for work Tuesday night." He paused, then added, "Of course, we know why he didn't show. He lives with a girlfriend and his daughter. We don't know where he lives, and we don't know the girlfriend's last name or if she is the baby momma."

Macon listened intently. He didn't miss Boston's challenge about leadership on the case. "I think I can fill in some of the blanks. Our agents down there were assigned the task of gathering some information. They were dedicated to it without encumberments of other duties."

Boston stared at Macon. His eyes didn't waver. "And I'm sure the Feds have access to more information."

Macon grinned. "There is that, plus they knew what to look for. Trained investigators. They know which leads to follow."

"Whatcha got?" Boston asked impatiently. He glanced toward Sarah.

Sarah saw the break in Boston's intensity. He wanted answers more than he wanted turf.

"The girlfriend's name is Margaret Cantrell. Casandra Simpson lives with Eugene Simpson at Margaret's apartment. They have for about three months. Cassie's mother is Twyla Stoner-Simpson. She shares custody with Eugene on a three-month rotation. Margaret was reluctant to reveal the living arrangement because it is a violation of the no-cohabitation clauses in the custody agreement."

Sarah shook her head disbelievingly. "Don't they know the baby will eventually spill the beans?"

"Cassie's barely old enough to start talking. Beside, young people don't think far enough into the future to worry about what they do today," Boston replied.

Macon continued, "Twyla lives somewhere in Indiana, though Margaret … who goes by Maggie … doesn't know exactly where."

"Was Cassie with the girlfriend?" Boston asked.

"No. Apparently, Eugene was on his way to Indiana to hand Cassie over to Twyla as part of their custody agreement. She begged us not to tell anyone that Cassie has been living with her. She is apparently attached to the baby. Motherly instincts." Macon raised his eyebrows for emphasis of his final comment.

Boston thought about the added information. He grimaced when he looked toward Sarah. "Then we *do* have a kidnapping. Cassie went missing somewhere between Florida and here."

Melvin walked to a wall map of the United States and traced the logical route from Panama City, Florida to Indiana with his finger. "Nashville?"

Three sets of eyes looked at the map. Sarah asked, "What makes you think Nashville is the point of kidnapping?"

"Makes sense," Melvin replied uncomfortably. "The highways line-up from Nashville to here … sort of. He could have driven I-40 to I-49 to Joplin, then headed to Devaney."

Macon asked Boston, "Are you going to assign someone to check that?"

"You mean go to Nashville?" Boston looked toward Sarah. "We don't know the area, and we don't have the resources."

Sarah responded, "If we need it, I can provide resources. We aren't familiar with the area … plus it's out of our jurisdiction."

"It's not out of mine. If it will help, I can put agents on it within the hour. The FBI is at your disposal." Macon waited for an answer.

Boston replied without hesitation, "If you can. Sure. What about the baby momma? Can we find her? Can you send agents to talk with her?"

Sarah interjected before Macon could answer, "I haven't heard the one thing I expected to hear. We have a dead man. Has his family been notified?"

"No," Boston looked down at the pictures on the table. "I haven't authorized it yet."

"We need to do that ASAP. The parents need to know. The baby's mother … Twyla Stoner-Simpson … needs to know. The mother needs to know her baby is missing." Sarah's brow was furrowed with a mixture of concern and anger. Notification should have been a priority. They were so concerned with finding the kidnapper-killers that they were overlooking the human side of the case.

Boston replied, "I'll co-ordinate with Panama City PD to notify the parents."

"And the girlfriend, Maggie," Sarah insisted. "She's not exactly family, but she needs to know it officially. I don't want her to find out through the grapevine. She's emotionally invested if nothing else."

Macon said Boston, "I'll tell the Indiana agents to notify the baby's mother when they go to talk to her, if that's okay."

"It's okay with me, if it's okay with the Boss." Boston looked at Sarah.

Macon replied, "The Boss made it clear to me that you're the lead. I'll clear everything through you."

Boston noticeably relaxed. He smiled. "And I clear everything with the Boss. So, what will your people look for in Nashville? That's a big area."

Sarah said before Macon could answer, "I think the Corolla's EDR needs to be reviewed. The car is new enough to have a full event recording system. It might tell us where the trip to Indiana changed course. Look at the EDR. See whether it's Nashville or maybe it's somewhere else."

Melvin immediately volunteered. "I'll get with Taylor and see if I can pull Canton for that." He waited for Boston and Sarah to nod affirmation before he turned to leave the Situation Room.

"One thing," Sarah said to Melvin as he left, "I understand EDRs don't usually offer GPS tracking, but a careful analysis could tell us of a major direction change. Corporal Canton might have to backtrack the data from where we found the car, but it should be in there somewhere."

Macon cautioned, "That kind of analysis will be time consuming. I can provide an agent to help, but it won't be until tomorrow. I suggest we begin the leg work in Nashville, just in case."

"Okay," Sarah responded. "I just don't want to miss anything. Cassie can't afford for us to miss anything. Melvin," she said almost as an afterthought and without regard for Boston's leadership, "after you get Taylor on board, maybe we should check gas stations further north from where the car was found. Maybe the pickup stopped for gas."

Melvin almost groaned. "More videos."

Boston seemed unphased by Sarah's request, or interference. "It's a possibility. We might find something. Besides, Canton and Caswell's agent know what to look for in the car's black box."

# CHAPTER 30

## 4:00 P.M. Thursday

Keith knocked on Sarah's door frame. His face was beaming.

"Hello, Keith. From the look on your face, I'd say you have something."

Keith smiled broadly. "I do. This thing is about to be wrapped up in a neat little package."

Sarah was pleased that Keith was making progress on his case. Progress on a burglary didn't take away her wrenched-gut feeling about the Simpson child's abduction. "What do you have?"

"The videos from the Neighborhood Market showed who bought the water and the batteries."

"You have an ID for an arrest?"

Keith's face fell. "Not exactly, but I can issue a BOLO for the vehicle used."

Sarah hid her feeling of disappointment. Her hope of a cleared case fell flat. "What do you have?"

Keith settled into one of the office chairs. "The video showed the woman scanning the jug of water and the battery."

"So, you have a description?" Sarah asked, hope renewed.

"Not exactly. White female ... I'm pretty sure. Under five and a half feet tall, but she wasn't fully upright. Leaned forward to scan and bag the items. Paid cash."

Sarah knew Keith was reluctant to open up about what he had. He sensed her disappointment about his promised revelation. He didn't know how much the kidnapping case consumed her emotionally. "What did she look like?"

Keith squirmed and leaned back. "Hard to tell. She was wearing a covid mask and had a baseball cap pulled low. You can only see enough of her face to tell she's white ... or not very dark." He leaned forward abruptly, "But the parking lot video showed her getting into a white SUV. I can put out a BOLO on it."

Sarah scowled. "Do you know how many white SUVs there are in Devaney? In Kansas? White is the single most popular color for vehicles. Second only to gray in SUVs. Did you get a license number from the parking lot video? Or a vehicle model?"

"No. It didn't have a license plate. I reckon the vehicle was stolen." Keith smiled cautiously. "But ... it looked like a Terrain. I'll check for stolen Terrain's before I put out the BOLO."

Sarah leaned back. She worked her mouth as she thought about Keith's information. Keith watched her nervously. He knew her well enough to know she wasn't finished with the conversation. Finally, she said, "Go see Lieutenant McCuskey. Find out the address of the white Terrain her people checked. Its plate was stolen and used on Eugene Simpson's car. See if the Terrain matches your video."

"Do you think my copper thief has something to do with the murder?"

Sarah shook her head. "I don't think anything other than I'm not willing to waste a clue. We have a missing child. It doesn't make sense that he would use his own license plate to disguise a vehicle attached to a murder and kidnapping, but criminals don't always make sense. Plus, the murderers may be smart enough to know a fictitious plate will make the BOLO more difficult because the lookers will be focused on the license plate. Maybe Simpson inadvertently stumbled on the burglary and the thief had to get rid of the witness. If he did, there's no telling what the thief did with the baby. The fact that your lead seems to indicate a woman is involved, she may have Cassie with her. That's based on the assumption a woman would be less inclined to harm a child. Probably a bad assumption. Check it out. See where it leads."

Keith stood and turned toward the door. "I'll talk to McCuskey."

Sarah nodded, then added, "Ask her to send a unit with you." She rose from her chair. "As a matter of fact, I may tag along. This could be the best clue yet."

Before Sarah could leave her office, Agent Caswell appeared at her door. "Sarah, I have some information from Indiana." He watched Keith leave the office. "Unless you're busy right now."

Sarah felt blocked, hemmed in by her own duties. She smiled and motioned to the chair Keith had just vacated. "I was going to play tag along, but it's not necessary. Have a seat. Is this something Boston should hear?"

"I updated him in the Situation Room. He told me to bring you up to speed." Macon raised his eyebrows. "He's concerned about keeping you in the loop. He respects you a lot."

Sarah smiled. "And I respect him. More importantly, I trust him." She sat in her chair and leaned forward, elbows on her desk. "What have you learned? Did they locate Cassie's mother?"

"They did. It wasn't too difficult."

Sarah knew the FBI knew things, things about everyone in the country. Where they lived. Where they worked. Who they knew. If the FBI pulled out all the stops, they could get answers quickly.

Agent Caswell continued, reading from a printed sheet of paper, the e-mailed report from the Indiana FBI Agent. "Contacted Twyla Stoner-Simpson, aged 19, divorced wife of Eugene Simpson. Lives alone in Greenfield, a suburb of Indianapolis." He paused and continued relaying the information without reading the dry facts of the report. "I talked with Agent Piccolo. I'll recap what she sent. The mother is obviously upset. She wants to know what we are doing to find her daughter. She also wants to know what we are doing to find her ex's murderer. She wants to hear something that will make her feel confident that Casandra will be okay."

Sarah shuddered. Natural questions. Ones she would be asking as the mother of a kidnapped child. "Poor thing. What did Agent Piccolo tell her?"

"Nothing at the time. I didn't pass along anything. I just asked them to locate Mrs. Stoner-Simpson. To let her know what had happened and that we are doing everything possible."

Sarah winced. "Not enough. If I was the mother, everything possible isn't a very convincing answer. I would want details."

"Agreed. I shared some … but not all … of what you have done and are doing with Agent Piccolo. She can go back and share more if that's what you want."

"What did you share with her?"

"The BOLO for the white pickup with a stolen Kansas plate is about all you have that I could share. Everything else is up in the air."

Sarah looked down at her desk despondently. "Up in the air and out in the wind. When you put it like that, even the pickup is up in the air. We really don't have much to offer." She lifted her eyes and inhaled deeply, "But we are moving forward. We know a lot more today than we did Monday. Share everything that makes sense. Did she have anything to add? Something that might help us?"

"She's flustered and frustrated. Agent Piccolo told her the bad news first, so she vented a lot before she could get her to talk."

"I can only imagine. Does she have family close?"

"Her mother and father live on a farm about six miles away, she said. And a sister who lives in a trailer on the farm." Agent Caswell checked the report. "The sister is older. Divorced. Two children. I'm not sure why Piccolo added it, but apparently the sister, Cameron "Cammie" Jenkins' children are not her ex-husband's." He shook his head. "Information, for what it's worth."

"Free spirited woman. Probably a troubled teen," Sarah mused. "How did Twyla meet Eugene Simpson? Sounds like she was seventeen when she gave birth to Cassie."

"According to Agent Piccolo, she and Gene met while her family was on vacation in Florida. A summer fling on the beach. When she found out she was pregnant, she went back and married him. She didn't stay long. She was used to the rural life of Indiana." Agent Caswell looked up from the report. "I'm sure there is more to it than that, but Agent Piccolo didn't include it in the report."

"Maybe a female agent should have talked with her," Sarah suggested.

Macon laughed. "Piccolo is a female."

"Oh," Sarah replied embarrassedly. She had missed the pronouns used. "What else did she learn?"

"Agent Piccolo said Twyla was upset that Cassie wasn't already in Indiana. It was her turn to have custody, but Gene was late bringing her.

He should have arrived on Monday." Macon paused. "Piccolo said she became flustered during that part of her response. Apparently, Twyla tried to call Gene repeatedly, but he didn't answer. She said she couldn't leave a voicemail because his box was full."

"We found his phone in the car. It was dead … and there was no charger. He probably left his charger behind."

"Whatever the cause, Twyla was agitated about it. She said she thought about driving to Florida but was afraid she would miss Gene on the way. Piccolo asked her if Gene would have left Cassie with her parents if they missed connecting. Twyla told her that her dad would have beat the crap out of Gene. Apparently, getting his daughter pregnant didn't sit well with him. Gene would not have gone to the farm under any circumstance."

"Oh! Drama that Cassie will have to deal with …" Sarah paused, "provided we find her."

"I have faith in you, Sarah."

"We found out too late," Sarah said as she shook her head despondently. "I have faith in our abilities, in Boston's abilities, but I'm also a realist. We are in the disaster zone." She exhaled before she asked, "Did Agent Piccolo talk with the Stoner's?"

"She did. Twyla led her to the farm. Said she wanted to be there when her parents were told about Cassie. Mr. Stoner was ready to join the hunt."

"Volatile, I take it?"

"Piccolo said he seems to be a hot head." Macon looked at the report. "She even accented it by mentioning that he was a deer hunter with several impressive buck mounts on the walls."

"Sounds like a typical Kansas farmhouse. That's not a sign of a hot head."

Agent Caswell chuckled. "I agree, but I think Amy Piccolo is a Philadelphia native. Unexposed to the deer hunters of Pennsylvania and the nation."

"If you've not been exposed, it can appear brutal." Sarah knew the subject was immaterial. "Did she talk to the sister?"

"No. Her two children were with the Stoners. Cammie was at work in Indianapolis."

"She didn't work on the farm? That sounds like it would be a long drive."

"Mrs. Stoner seemed unhappy with the fact Cammie worked in town. She was left to babysit the two grandchildren, which interfered with her contributions to the farm. Piccolo said Mrs. Stoner was wringing her hands with worry."

"That's odd. Worried about Cassie or worried about the distraction?"

Macon held up the report. "Piccolo made a note wondering the same thing. I assume she was worried about Cassie's wellbeing … but I wasn't there to see Mrs. Stoner's body language."

"That's the problem with not doing the interrogation yourself," Sarah said.

Macon looked Sarah in the eyes. "That is the reality of leadership. We don't get to touch and smell the cases. Trust is tough."

Sarah nodded. "It is. Boston is doing everything I would do, just in a different order and at a different pace."

"He's probably moving at the only pace available with the existing evidence. An investigator can't get ahead of the evidence."

Sarah thought about Detective Daniel Sanders. His motto, taken from Davy Crockett, guided her every day. She glanced at her empty coffee cup and read the pink lettering. *Make sure you're right then go ahead.* A seemingly simple philosophy, but it required focus and commitment. "I have to remind myself of that sometimes. What else did Agent Piccolo give us?"

"Twyla wanted to know why Gene was in Kansas. She offered to come to Kansas if it would help. Agent Piccolo told her we don't know why Gene was in Kansas, though we suspect he was forced here by the murderers to cover their trail."

"How did she think she could help?"

"Piccolo chalked it up to frustration." Macon shrugged and paused before adding, "She said Twyla kept offering suggestions ranging from Gene being mixed up in drugs to gambling debts."

"Did Agent Piccolo ask why?"

Macon nodded. "Yes. Twyla rambled with reasons, interspersed with profanities about Gene not taking proper care of Cassie. She said the reason she left Gene was that he was into drugs and liked to gamble."

Sarah was puzzled. "Really? Did your people in Panama City turn up anything like that during their investigation?"

"Nothing. I called the Panama City office and asked if they missed something. Simpson's boss praised his work ethic, an hourly workaholic. His girlfriend praised his dedication to Cassie. Always home if not at work. There was nothing to lend credence to Twyla's assertions. Frustration. Twyla is the frustrated mother of a kidnapped child, trying to make sense of a senseless situation."

Sarah nodded understandingly. "I suppose that's true. I can't imagine what's going through her mind. If it was a missing person rather than a murder-kidnapping, I would think Gene ran away with Cassie so he wouldn't have to share custody."

"I wish we had that option to consider," Macon said sorrowfully.

# CHAPTER 31

5:30 P.M. Thursday

Sarah and Macon joined Boston in the Situation Room. They were tossing ideas back and forth when Taylor stepped into the room. Taylor's face looked strained. "What happened, Taylor?"

"We just got a call for back-up from the residence where the stolen plates were investigated. The Terrain."

"Back-up call? Keith was supposed to do some follow up on his case there. Did he place the call?" Sarah rose to her feet.

"Corporal Baldor made the call."

"Shots?" Boston asked.

"No. A disturbance with the homeowner. Sergeant Locke and Corporal Baldor's unit went there to check his lead. Honeycutt said the call was for a supervisor. Honeycutt was going to go, but her shift ended. I told her I'd go. It's not too far out of my way."

Sarah nodded. "I thought about going with Keith. Maybe I should have."

"You have bigger things to worry about," Taylor chided. "I'll go and let you know what's happening."

Sarah's phone rang. Shawn. She sent him to voice mail and followed Taylor into the bullpen. "Please do. It was a simple check ... unless the man is involved in something we don't suspect. Be ready for anything."

Taylor nodded. "Always."

Sarah watched Taylor as she left the bullpen to descend the front stairs. She wanted to know what caused the disturbance. The initial contact indicated the homeowner wasn't the trusting kind, especially with authority figures. Some people simply didn't like the police and weren't afraid to express their feelings. She wondered if the man had a rap sheet, if he had cause to be suspicious of the police.

Lieutenant Glasgow entered the bullpen from the back stairs. "Hello, Chief. Is Boston in the Sit Room?"

"Yes. Come on in." Sarah walked back inside the room but didn't sit. She heard her phone chime to indicate a voicemail. She knew it was Shawn. That would be the second of the day. Her text response earlier was abbreviated. Unemotional … like most texts.

Melvin looked tired. He greeted Agent Caswell, briefly suspicious of the FBI agent's presence.

Boston said, "Glad your back, Melvin. We were just recapping what we know. Hopefully, you have something to add."

Melvin relaxed and nodded. "I do. Do you want it now or do you want to wait?" He tried to not be obvious when he glanced toward Agent Caswell.

Boston noticed the look. Without expression, he replied, "I want to hear it now. I don't know about the others. Go ahead."

"Okay. I have some videos from a Love's Travel Stop in Harrisonville, south of Kansas City on I-49. About six or seven miles north of where the car was abandoned."

Sarah was puzzled. "They didn't stop for air?"

"I couldn't find anything to indicate they stopped. Did you?" Melvin asked Boston.

"Nothing. But I didn't put as much effort in as you."

Melvin put a thumb drive into a player built into a TV. The TV was used for reviewing video evidence in the Situation Room. "I sorted through several hours of fast forward video before I found this." He explained as he started the video. "It's from two different cameras." He stood silently while the video played.

The video showed a white Ford extended-cab pickup pull next to a gas pump and stop. A passenger and the driver exited the vehicle. The passenger hurried away from the pump islands toward the store.

"Stop it!" Sarah commanded; her voice filled with shock.

Melvin complied. He smiled wryly. "That's what I did when I first saw it. It caught me by surprise."

Boston said incredulously. "Women? Are you sure it's the right truck?"

Melvin paused the video to answer. "I am. I looked at several white Ford pickup trucks. You'll see in a minute. It has the same Kansas license plate as the one stolen from the Devaney pickup." He restarted the video. "Keep watching. This is important. Notice the dark streaks on the tailgate and the license plate. So you don't strain your eyes, I will tell you that there are no good face shots. I know because I looked at the video over and over. They're both wearing baseball caps."

Three sets of eyes watched intently while the fourth set watched the watchers. The driver began pumping gasoline then walked toward the back of the truck, as if stretching her legs. She stopped. Even though her face was obscured, she was obviously cognizant of the dark streaks. Her head swiveled side to side rapidly, checking to see if anyone else saw what she saw. She quickly grabbed a squeegee from a water bucket and scrubbed the streaks. After she returned the squeegee to the bucket, she saw but tried to ignore a vehicle that pulled behind her, waiting it's turn. She anxiously stood near the pump and returned the hose to its cradle when it finished. Without hesitation, she drove the truck away from the pump.

Melvin stopped the video. He zoomed in on the license plate. Kansas. "There. It's the same plate number as the one stolen. This is the same white Ford. I'm sure of it." He restarted the video.

The obviously edited video changed camera angle. Several men were standing near the corner of the building. They were smoking cigarettes and drinking from cups. They barely noticed the white pickup park in a parking spot near them. A short time later, the passenger emerged from the store, stopped, searched, and then hurried to climb inside the pickup. The pickup pulled away quickly and disappeared from camera view. The video ended.

"Women!" Boston said incredulously. "Was there video inside the store? Maybe a better look at the passenger's face?"

"No. Her ball cap was pulled too low, and the angle was from above. They must know how security cameras are angled," Melvin offered as insight.

Sarah watched and listened. The idea that the women were accustomed to criminal activities crossed her mind. Most people are oblivious to security cameras, unaware that they are routinely recorded as they go about their business.

Boston grimaced, perturbed by the lack of identity. "We now know it is women. We know they were headed north, but we don't know if their destination was east, north, or west. They could take 70 east or west. They could take 35 north, or they could take 29 north. Both of those would connect them to 80 which goes east and west."

"Was there any video that showed what was inside the truck?" Agent Caswell asked.

"The truck bed was empty … except for what appears to be blood stains." Melvin reversed the video and stopped it under the pump camera. He pointed to a dark spot inside the truck bed. "And a dark rectangle that could be the backside of a license plate."

"I mean inside the truck. Was there any video that showed the people inside the truck?"

"Oh, you mean with a better view of their faces? No. With the baseball caps, all I could see was their chins because of the camera angle."

"Actually, I meant could you see if there was a baby in the truck. If Simpson was a caring father and had the baby with him, he had a car seat."

"There wasn't one in his car," Boston interjected.

Macon nodded. "It follows that whoever took the baby took the car seat. Is there a view inside the truck that shows a car seat in the back seat?"

Melvin squirmed. "We know the truck. We can find out when we find it," he protested.

"If the baby isn't in the truck, we don't have a lead. We won't have a lead until we find the truck." Macon looked toward Sarah.

Sarah repeated his question, "Melvin, do you have more video?"

"I have some on another file." Melvin pressed the player control buttons. "These are longer. I'll search for front views. The back windows are too dark." All four sets of eyes stared at the TV as the video ran at eight times normal speed. Melvin returned the speed to normal when the truck came into view. He slowed the video when the pickup pulled into the pump island and stopped. The camera was behind the truck. "Nothing here." He opened another file. The camera angle was from the front of the store, on the opposite side of the building from where the truck parked.

"Not very promising," Sarah said. "Can you back it up and run it slowly when the truck comes into view?"

Melvin ran the video as Sarah suggested. Still nothing came into view while the truck was parked. When the truck backed out of its parking spot, the camera angle allowed a brief look inside the cab. He stopped the video and reran that portion in slow motion.

"There!" Sarah exclaimed. "Back up and do that part again."

All of them strained to see inside the cab. Melvin didn't need to be told to rerun that small portion repeatedly. After several viewings, Macon said, "There's definitely something in the back seat, behind the passenger. I can't make it out."

Boston said with unusual excitement, "Better than that, the passenger turned her head! We have a partial profile. Back it up, Melvin, so we can see it again."

Everyone focused on the passenger. The baseball cap didn't cover her face, but the camera angle didn't reveal as much as it could have. The rearview mirror blocked too much. Disappointment settled over the group.

"Not as much as I thought," Boston said dejectedly. "I guess I let my imagination take control."

Melvin slowly replayed the video, backward and forward. "The brain fills in the blanks sometimes. I think I can use FACES software to get something useful."

"How accurate will it be?" Sarah asked hopefully.

"Probably not enough for a BOLO, but it could be helpful if we need to sort potential suspects," Melvin replied. He then went on to explain, "If we get a lead on someone and they are a close match, we will know we could be on the right track. Nothing useful in court, though."

"Do it. It sounds worthwhile," Sarah looked at Boston. "Unless someone has a better idea."

Boston shrugged. "I'm game. At least, we have narrowed our search. The murderers are female and middle age or younger." He saw the puzzled looks on the others' faces. He pointed toward the screen where they had been watching the videos. "Walking. They didn't walk like they were elderly."

Sarah asked, "Are we getting anything on the pickup BOLO?"

Boston shook his head. "Too many white Fords out there. Taylor said she gets calls from other agencies, but so far this video is the only lead … and Melvin found it."

Macon nodded. "I doubt the description will yield much. I don't know the exact numbers, but you're probably looking at a million or more white Ford F-150s."

"In our area?" Sarah questioned.

"No. Nationwide, but there are a lot in this area."

Boston interjected, "And we don't know how big the dragnet needs to be. Kansas? Missouri? Iowa? All we know is north, east, or west from here. The best we could do is compile a list by state, but we'll need the state DMVs to help." He looked at his watch. "They're closed."

"Not the west coast," Sarah replied impatiently.

Boston nodded. "I can start there. Get the rest tomorrow."

"Sort by female owners," Sarah suggested. "That might help shorten the list." She inhaled deeply. "And it could be wrong."

"What about social media?" Macon asked. When everyone stared at him, he smiled, shrugged, and added. "Check social media for all the people we know who are connected to Mr. Simpson. Everyone has pictures. Some have pictures with their vehicles."

Melvin nodded enthusiastically. "You're right! If you have a list of names, I can help."

Macon replied as he looked at Boston, "I can provide the names the FBI has."

Boston nodded. "I'll write the names I have. I need to call the West Coast before they close."

Sarah's phone rattled in her jacket pocket. She checked it, expecting Shawn. It was Keith's ID.

# CHAPTER 32

## 7:00 P.M. Thursday

Sarah stepped away from the Situation Room to answer. "Hello, Keith. What have you found?"

"The Terrain owner barricaded himself inside his house."

Sarah wasn't sure why Keith was calling her. Taylor was on the way to the scene. He should have known that. "Why?"

"I'm not sure. He came to the door, I identified myself, and he instantly became belligerent. I think he might have been drinking. His house dog was intense. I was afraid he was going to turn it loose on us. His backyard dogs are going crazy."

"What did you say that set him off?" Sarah was concerned. She was afraid Keith had developed a short-timer's attitude, mentally prepared to move on to whatever his future held without concern for current duties.

"I didn't get a chance to say much of anything other than identify myself. He started angry and got worse. I showed him my badge and told him I needed to talk to him about his car."

"That's all?"

Keith paused before answering. "Pretty much. One of the officers was checking his pickup truck. I think Jameson saw him. That's when he started yelling. Told the officer to get away from his truck or he'd sic the dogs on us."

"He threatened you?"

"Pretty much. He slammed the door. His yelling set-off his backyard dogs."

"Is Lieutenant McCuskey there yet? She was going to meet you there."

"Not yet. I thought you ought to know." Keith's tone changed. He recognized Sarah's displeasure with his call to her, especially with the previous call for back-up. His action made it appear the situation had worsened.

Sarah contained her feelings. "Where are you now?"

"Beside our cars. On the street in front of his house. Did you know he has a white Ford F-150?"

Sarah couldn't keep her eyes from widening. She wondered why Taylor hadn't mentioned that important detail. "I knew he had a pickup. I didn't know it was a white Ford. That wasn't in the report. Wait for me before you do anything. Tell Taylor I'm on my way."

"That's why I called. Jameson doesn't act right."

"Set up a perimeter. Does he have a weapon? Are innocents at risk?"

"He hasn't said anything more since we left his yard. He peeks through the window every now and then. I suppose that's so he can see if we're still here. He's turned off all of his inside lights and turned on his outside lights. Curtains are drawn." Keith broke the sentences as if he was making observations as he spoke. "I'm thinking we may need a negotiator."

"I'll bring Melvin." Sarah hung up the phone only to have it ring. Shawn. "Hello, Shawn. I'm sorry I haven't answered. Things are piling up here."

Shawn's voice was calm and reassuring. "I suspected as much. I suppose there's no need for me to invite myself over this evening."

Sarah winced. "There's always a need, but I don't think I'll be home for a while. We have a developing situation."

"Understood." Shawn couldn't hide the disappointment in his voice.

Sarah struggled to suppress hers. "I'll talk to you tomorrow."

"If you need to talk to me later ... anytime. You know I'll answer."

Sarah gulped as the call ended. She wondered how normal people felt, how normal relationships worked. She had never had one. Melvin was exiting the Situation Room. "Lieutenant, we have a situation that might require a negotiator. Are you up for it?"

Melvin clutched two pieces of paper, the lists provided by Boston and Agent Caswell. His eyes danced between Boston and Sarah. He stammered. "Uh ... yes. What's happening?"

Sarah looked past Melvin toward Boston. "The man who owns the vehicles with the stolen plates has barricaded himself inside his house."

"Why?" Boston asked.

"I'm not sure. Keith went to investigate a white Terrain that may be affiliated with his copper theft case. The owner, Lonnie Jameson, became belligerent as soon as Keith showed his badge. Plus ..." Sarah paused, "he has a white Ford pickup. I'm on my way over there."

Boston sat up straight and asked, "Do you think he's involved in our kidnapping?"

"I really don't know, but it sounds like he's afraid of something. Keith did say he thinks the man was drinking. Could be nothing more than a cop-hating drunk. I'll let you know what I find."

"Maybe I should go."

"You have calls to make."

"Not if Keith's guy is the kidnapper."

Sarah couldn't argue against Boston's point. With the two Lieutenants following in their vehicles, she drove to the Jameson residence. She tried to recall the report from the original contact. Bic Jameson, wife Kelley, and brother-in-law Herb Falkenbury lived in the house. Only one female ... unless Herb had a girlfriend. She also wondered why the investigating officers didn't mention the white Ford. They only said Jameson's pickup's license plate was also missing. No description. She would talk with Taylor about that missed clue.

Sarah parked two houses away from Keith's car. She didn't want the scene to take on the appearance of a siege. Keith and a uniformed officer stood near his car, apparently explaining the situation to Taylor. The patrol unit was not in sight. She walked along the street with Melvin and Boston on either side, three abreast. "What's the situation, Taylor?" She directed her question to Taylor to send a message to Keith.

"It appears someone came out into the backyard. The dogs were stirred up for a while."

"Did he escape over the back fence?"

Taylor looked at Keith, obviously not completely caught up on the situation.

"I don't think so," Keith answered lamely.

"Have you set up a perimeter?" Sarah scowled at Keith. He ignored protocol and was disrespectful of a Lieutenant's authority. Short-timer or not, he needed to understand that.

Keith stammered. "Uh … Officer Payne drove the unit to the street behind. All these houses have wood privacy fences. It would be hard to see anything."

Boston was more interested in the pickup truck. He walked toward it.

"Get the Hell off my property!" an angry voice yelled from inside the privacy fence near the side gate.

Melvin immediately responded, "Mr. Jameson. I'm Lieutenant Melvin Glasgow. We are here to ask a few questions. Nothing more. We need some information to solve a crime …" he glanced at Sarah, then continued, "to locate a missing child. We were hoping you might help us figure out who stole your license plates."

"Stay away from my property. I saw that cop snooping around my truck. You don't have a warrant. Get out!" Bic's speech was thick, almost slurred. He ignored Melvin's reasoning for the police presence.

"I think you're right about him being drunk," Melvin said to Keith. "But something else is bothering him. The truck might be the key." Melvin spoke louder. "You're right, Mr. Jameson. We don't have a warrant, but we don't need one to look *at* your truck. We just can't open it without a warrant … or your permission. But we're not here to look in your truck. We are interested in your car. We want to know if someone borrowed your car Saturday."

"I don't loan my vehicles to anyone. You guys are trying to pin something on me. I'm going to call my lawyer."

Sarah said under her breath. "Everyone claims to have a lawyer." Louder, she said to Melvin, "He thinks we know something we don't. He's hiding something, for sure. I'll get a warrant. Taylor, see if you can get some more back-up while I call Judge Varadkar."

After Taylor stepped aside to make her call, Keith said, "Chief, I'm wondering if he's our copper thief. He probably figures we're on to him."

"That could be it, but the white Ford pickup is too convenient."

"Not all that convenient," Boston said.

"What do you mean?"

"It's a regular cab. Plus, it's older than our kidnapper's truck."

Sarah looked at the pickup. Boston was right. The missing license plate on the Corolla didn't make sense if Jameson was involved in the murder-kidnapping. Those plates pointed directly to him. The plates were stolen by the murderers to slow the investigation, not to help it. "I'm still going to get a warrant."

"I'm going to call California." Boston replied disgustedly as he turned to walk toward his car.

Judge Varadkar answered after several rings. Sarah had framed her request in her mind. Sarah knew she was reaching with the request. The Judge's reticence to issue the warrant made her doubt her justification for the request. A smart thief would have already sold his goods rather than keep them in his possession. There was very little chance that the copper was there. Large quantities of copper would have to be sold in a city larger than Devaney where the anonymity of construction copper scrap could hide the fact it was stolen. Even though Jameson was acting irrationally, that was not a solid reason to force a search. In essence, she had nothing beyond the Neighborhood Market video of a white Terrain without a license plate. After several minutes of intense questioning, Judge Varadkar relented and issued the warrant based upon reasonable suspicion of possession of stolen goods.

Officer Payne radioed his partner while Sarah was talking to Judge Varadkar. They got permission from Jameson's backyard neighbor to go into his backyard so they could look through Jameson's fence. That didn't require a warrant. Apparently, there was no love lost between the surrounding neighbors because of Jameson's aggressive dogs who barked anytime someone approached the fence. The backyard dogs were barking frantically at the officer when Sarah returned her attention to the scene.

"What's happening? Why are the dogs acting like that?" Sarah asked.

Taylor replied before Keith could say anything, "Officer Stevens got permission to approach from the back. Keith sent him in. The dogs are reacting to his presence on the other side of the fence."

"He went in there without backup?" Sarah was upset. "Jameson may see that as a threat and overreact."

Keith was taken aback by Sarah's reproach. He scrambled to make his decision seem right and cover his accumulating errors of judgement.

"Stevens only peeked through a crack. He got back when the dogs charged. He's not putting himself in danger."

"No," Sarah replied sternly, "but it sounds like we are putting the neighborhood in danger by creating an escalation. We have time to wait for the backup."

Keith was crestfallen. "I suppose you're right." He turned to Officer Payne. "Tell him to fall back." He then looked askance of Lieutenant McCuskey, who nodded affirmation.

Sarah realized she had been too harsh. Aside from the rashness of his move and seeming disregard for protocol, she allowed her disappointment that Keith was leaving to affect her reaction. It would be another position to fill in an environment where law enforcement was not viewed favorably, where law enforcement officers were almost pariah in their communities. The pay wasn't good enough to offset the disrespect. The department would lose a set of skills that only time and experience could replace. "Did he see anything?"

The question provided Keith with a small amount of validation. "He said there were two men in the back. They were standing near a cargo trailer. They were cussing the police, but he couldn't really hear anything other than that over the dogs. He couldn't see much more than that either. He said he had to retreat when one of the men investigated what created frenzy in the dogs."

Sarah mulled the information for a moment. She then asked Keith, "Do you know where Judge Varadkar lives?"

"Yes."

"He has a search warrant for us." Sarah turned to Lieutenant Glasgow. "Keep Jameson occupied. Let's keep some subtle pressure on him. Make him understand we're willing to talk. Taylor, if I step on your toes, tell me. Please."

Taylor's blonde hair bounced as she smiled and shook her head. "You're not bothering me, Chief. I'm not fully up to speed on the situation."

Melvin called out to Jameson, which elicited more barking from the dogs, but nothing from Jameson.

More units arrived. Sarah stepped back to allow Taylor to disperse her officers to cordon the area. Animal Control arrived as well. Their role would be to humanely control the guard dogs, if necessary.

Keith returned with the search warrant as the units were deployed in preparation for execution of the warrant.

After confirmation from Sarah, Melvin called out to Bic Jameson. "Mr. Jameson, we have a warrant to search your premises."

Melvin's words were met with silence for several minutes. Finally, a light came on in the living room. Jameson shouted, "Okay. You can search my truck. I've got nothing to hide. I'm coming out with the keys. I don't want you idiots to break the windows." After Melvin assured him that it was safe to do so, Jameson stepped onto the porch. He paused to shove his barking house dog away from the door as he closed it behind him.

Sarah saw two faces peering through the curtains. They were backlit by the living room lights, so their features weren't clear. One had longer hair than the other, possibly female. They appeared curious rather than aggressive. That didn't matter. To no one in particular, she said, "Keep an eye the other two for any signs of aggression."

Under Taylor's intense scrutiny, Keith and Melvin met Bic Jameson at the truck. Officer Payne followed them with his hand near the grip of his service weapon. They were taking no chances, even though Jameson seemed to be reluctantly cooperative.

Jameson unlocked the driver's side door and stepped away from the truck. He snarled, "There. Look. Nothing in there. This is bullcrap, and you know it. My lawyer will hear about this."

Jameson continued to grouse and curse while Keith used his LED investigation light to search inside the pickup. The tight beam illuminated a small area and enhanced scrutiny of everything within its light. He found a few assorted pieces of trash, mostly paper, all stomped and stained. Bic Jameson wasn't a neat freak with his vehicle. The floorboards were dirty and hadn't been vacuumed in a long time, if ever. In general, he found normal dirt for a vehicle. Candy bar wrappers and store receipts. Bits of detritus carried on the soles of shoes. Gravel. Dirt. Grass. Nothing out of the ordinary for an uncleaned vehicle.

Keith looked toward Sarah and grimly shook his head.

Jameson saw the gesture and laughed. He realized Sarah was in charge and snarled, "Now, get the hell off my property. I don't know what you were looking for, but apparently your woman's intuition ain't very good."

Sarah saw Jameson's neck bow defiantly. He was sure he had won. His head moved slightly toward the privacy fence and the continued barking of his yard dogs. She couldn't see his eyes in the poorly lighting, but she imagined they were looking in the direction of his backyard. She asked Taylor, "How do you recommend we contain the dogs?"

Jameson heard her question. He shouted angrily, "You better not try anything with my dogs, or I'll kill you!" The words barely left his mouth and he realized he had made a mistake.

Without warning, Officer Payne grabbed Bic's arm and twisted it until Bic dropped to his knees in pain. Before Bic could react, Officer Payne pushed him onto his belly and pulled both arms behind his back. The solid click of metal handcuffs ended the physical part of the confrontation. Officer Payne said, "Mr. Jameson, you have the right to remain silent. Anything you say can and will be used against you in a court of law. You are under arrest for threatening a police officer."

Taylor rushed to assist her officer. She and Officer Payne guided Jameson to a waiting squad car. Bic cursed and shouted indignantly every resistant step of the way.

Kelley Jameson rushed out of the house almost immediately after Bic was forced to the ground. She was shouting and adding more profanities to the ruckus. Herb Falkenbury followed her. His words were only directed toward his sister. He was attempting to stop her angry rush toward the police.

Sarah joined Keith and Melvin to block Kelley's attack.

Herb caught up with Kelley just as she reached Keith. He grabbed her arm and yanked her around to face him. "Kelley! Stop! You're only going to make matters worse." He didn't back away from his sister's withering glare. "Calm down."

"They can't arrest him. They didn't find anything in his truck." Kelley was adamant about the lack of evidence in the truck, even though she wasn't present for the search or the ensuing conversation.

Sarah spoke directly to Kelley. "Mrs. Jameson, we are going to search your house and property. We have a signed warrant to do so. Can you chain the dogs, or do I need to order Animal Control to subdue them?"

Bic screamed from the back seat of the squad car. "You better not hurt my dogs!"

Herb was the calmest of the three. "Kelley, I'll go chain the dogs."

"They're not going into my house. I have rights," Kelley screamed, her comment laced with profanities. "Call our lawyer."

Herb replied, "Sure. I'll call a lawyer. Who do you recommend?"

"Anyone. A lawyer will know what to do to stop this illegal search."

Sarah kept her eyes on Kelley. The woman was behaving irrationally, just like her husband. There was no doubt in her mind that Kelley was involved in anything her husband was. Herb might or might not be. He seemed resigned to the fact that the police were there. He was compliant. Too compliant. "Keith, search the cargo van first."

Even in the poor lighting of the streetlights, Kelley's red face reddened further. She yanked free from her brother's grasp and raced toward the fence gate.

Herb ran after her. "Kelley! Kelley! What do you think you're doing?"

Bic screamed from inside the squad car. His words were mixed with Herb's commands for Kelley to stop and Keith's commands for both of them to stop. Kelley's hand grabbed the gate handle. She tried to yank the gate open, but as with most privacy fence gates, it didn't open easily. The dogs snarled and barked frantically from the other side of the fence. Herb grabbed Kelley and spun her around. He pushed her against the gate, thereby ensuring she didn't open it further.

Keith arrived at that moment. Kelley tried to lunge toward him, but Herb held her in check. Keith quickly brought out his handcuffs. "Move aside, Sir," he said to Herb as he gripped Kelley's upper arm. "I'll cuff her, so she doesn't get herself into more trouble."

Kelley screamed and protested as she struggled against Keith's superior strength and training. Officer Payne arrived to assist and escort Kelley away from the gate toward Keith's police car. Herb stood helplessly near the gate.

Keith motioned to the gate. "Mr. Falkenbury, if you don't mind, go secure the dogs so we can search the cargo van and the storage shed."

"They're locked," Herb replied as he slowly opened the gate enough to step inside before latching it behind him. He spoke to the dog, commanding them to quieten. His voice trailed across the backyard as he encouraged the dogs to follow him. After several minutes of indecision by the dogs, he returned and opened the gate. "They're chained."

"Do you have a key for the cargo van lock?" Keith asked.

"I don't. Bic has it. He carries it in his pocket," Herb replied.

Keith glanced toward the car where Bic still ranted and, occasionally, kicked the back of the seat. "Do you think he will allow you to get it from his pocket?"

Herb hung his head. "I doubt it."

"Then I will cut the lock." Keith walked to his car and retrieved a pair of bolt cutters from the trunk. Back inside the privacy fence with Sarah, Taylor, and Melvin watching, he cut the lock and opened the back of the trailer. It was dark inside the cargo van but there was enough light spilling from the back porch light to recognize the contents. "Wow!" Keith exclaimed as he reached for his flashlight. "I think we just hit the jackpot." His flashlight illuminated stacks of heavy copper wire, cut into manageable lengths for stacking. Atop the stack were smaller wires, coiled into manageable bundles. There was little room for more.

Sarah leaned her head inside the back of the cargo van. "Jackpot indeed. Is this all of it?"

Keith surveyed the copper. "I doubt it." He looked at Herb who was standing dejectedly to the side, his head low. "Where's the rest of it?"

Herb was reluctant to answer. Softly and hesitantly, he replied, "In a friend's barn."

"How many of you were involved?"

Herb shook his head and responded. "I think I've helped enough. I'll not say anything else without a lawyer."

Sarah knew Herb had helped the police in the hopes of getting some leniency. He was probably a hesitant participant from the beginning. She wasn't sure she cared. She nodded to Taylor.

Taylor understood Sarah's nod. She motioned for another uniformed officer who followed them to the gate. He stepped forward, gently pulled Herb's arm behind his back, and said, "You have the right to remain silent. Anything you say can and will be used against you in a court of law. Do you understand?"

Meekly, Herb replied as he moved his other hand behind his back to be cuffed, "I do. I want a lawyer."

Keith walked with Sarah toward the street. "I guess that wraps that one up."

"Maybe. Maybe not. You still need to find out where the friend's barn is and if there were more people involved."

Keith's momentary elation ended. "I'll get all of this secured in evidence, then I'll see if Herb will talk after he sees a lawyer."

"Good idea. The friend could dispose of the rest of the evidence before you find him. Without it, your case may end here." Sarah paused near Keith's vehicle where Kelley sat dejectedly. "Not a bad end, but the loose ends need to be tied. Go book them ... and make sure Herb is separated from Bic." Sarah paused before adding, "Sergeant Locke, I know you were anxious about this case, but that's no excuse for going around Lieutenant McCuskey."

Keith hung his head. "I know. I ... have no excuse. It won't happen again."

"Here or Omaha," Sarah said. "You're better than that." She left for her apartment.

# CHAPTER 33

## 7:30 A.M. Friday

Sarah awakened tired. She had too much on her mind to sleep restfully. The encounter at the Jameson house kept her keyed even after she settled into her bed alone. She wondered about Keith, about his abilities as an investigator. She knew he was troubled by the decision he had had to make. Because of that, he relied on her too much to guide him through the investigation. She wondered if he was clinging to her because of their past, or if he was afraid to leave and lose her support. Or was she reading too much into his behaviors.

Blake House was independent. All he needed from Sarah was latitude. That was a good thing … and not. Sarah was a hands-on leader. She knew it. Too much so. The investigative side of her job consumed her. Even if she didn't do the groundwork, she wanted to know … emotionally needed to know … every step of every investigation. She wanted to be there to help. She wanted to be available to offer advice. Blake didn't need advice. She knew he was working on a lead to locate a new drug dealer. A female drug dealer who had a connection with the high school aged crowd. The danger to Devaney's young people was ramped up because of her. Sarah wanted her found quickly, before her fentanyl tainted drugs killed a kid.

Overshadowing everything was the kidnapping. Cassie was still missing without clues to her whereabouts. A toddler four days gone has little chance of being found, less chance of being found alive. With the help of Agent Caswell, Boston had moved the case forward but that single best clue to locate Cassie was yet to be found. That bothered her. Catching a copper thief meant very little when compared to the loss of a little girl.

At the gym, Sarah worked her way through her machine routine. Upper body conditioning was her least favorite. She only did it once a week. She preferred running the track or running the stairs. Those didn't seem as repetitive as lifting weights and resistance training. Running allowed her to think. Weights required focus. She knew most of the early morning gym users. They knew her. Everyone made it a point to greet her. Some addressed her as Chief or Chief James. Mostly the men. The women generally addressed her as Sarah. She liked both. She didn't like it when the very young patrons addressed her as Miss James. She simply cringed and smiled. They did so because they preferred to not acknowledge her as an authority figure in that setting, yet they wanted to be respectful. The salutation brought to mind her marital status.

The line at her favorite breakfast drive through was longer than usual. Sarah opted not to wait. Boston usually brought a box of donuts. It wouldn't hurt to indulge for a change. She arrived at the station as shift change was taking place. She parked near the side entrance and walked into the lobby. Sergeant Pete Blanchard was ending his rotation. Sergeant Jim Cron was relieving him. Both men were at the Shift Commander's desk. Sarah greeted them with a smile.

"Good morning, Chief," Sergeant Blanchard said as he handed her the daily summary. "You already know the highlights. It was routine after that."

Sarah nodded as she studied the summary sheet, held far enough from her eyes so she could see it clearly. "That's good. How did the booking go?"

"Bic kept up his tirade, demanding a lawyer and his rights all the way to his cell. Mrs. Jameson lost most of her fire. I guess the reality of handcuffs in the back seat of a squad car quenched the flames. We held the brother-in-law back until the other two were in their cells."

"Good. I'm sure he is hoping for some kind of leniency. Did he ever say where the rest of the copper is located?"

"Keith said he would interrogate him today. He asked for a lawyer, so we have to wait until he gets one."

Sarah nodded. "That makes sense. I'll talk with Keith when he arrives. How are the troops?"

"Ready for the day," Sergeant Cron replied.

Sergeant Blanchard answered, "Mine are ready for bed."

Sarah walked up the stairs into the bullpen. The lights were on, and the smell of fresh coffee greeted her as soon as she opened the door. She called out, "Good morning" to anyone listening.

Taylor chirped, "Good morning, Chief. Coffee's ready." After a moment's pause, she added, "Boston actually made coffee this morning." After a brief pause, she added, "Keith apologized."

Sarah smiled and nodded. Nothing more needed to be said. She saw that the Situation Room light was on. She made her way to the coffee pot where she knew her cup would be cleaned and ready. Liz never failed. One small spoonful of sugar in the bottom was roiled by coffee as it poured into the cup. Taylor stood near the Situation Room doorway, waiting for Sarah.

"You're in early, Boston," Sarah began. "Does this mean you have something?"

"Not exactly. "DMV is slow responding ... not that a list of a million suspects will help much." Boston sneered at a couple of printed lists he had added to the pile on the table. He then picked up his phone. "I decided to check social media. See what's out there."

"For ...?" Sarah questioned before taking a sip from her cup. The pink letters on her gray cup caught her eye. *Make sure your right then go ahead.* She needed to check herself, to make sure she was right. Checking social media was already on the table. She thought Melvin was assigned that task, but apparently Boston had a lead. She needed to allow him to follow it unquestioned.

"Social media is full of stupid stuff," Boston replied. "Especially pictures. People can't go a day without posting a picture of something. Selfies. Their kids. Their food. And everyone's favorite ... their cars."

"I take it you went fishing for cars?"

"Pickups. White pickups in particular." Boston tapped on his screen. "I focused on everyone we know with any connection to Eugene Simpson. I was able to determine he has a lot of friends with pickup trucks. A coworker named Kyle Wilson owns a white Ford." He held the phone so

Sarah could see the screen. Gene was in a selfie taken by another man. In the background was a white pickup.

"That's something. What next?" Sarah knew what she would do, but it was Boston's case.

"I'm going to call Agent Caswell. See if he can have his boys take a look for me."

Sarah thoughtfully sipped her coffee. "Do you need to go to Florida?" She offered the option. If the case was as close as she hoped, Boston might want to follow-up in Eugene's hometown.

Boston shook his head. "No. I think the FBI can take care of it. The real answer is somewhere else. That much, I'm sure."

"Where do you think it is?"

"I'm not sure. My gut, I guess. But it's not in Florida … even if this guy, Kyle Wilson, is involved. He and Simpson were in Kansas for a reason."

"What's your next step?" Sarah was deflated by Boston's uncertainty. Cassie needed one-hundred percent certainty.

"I'd like to go to Indiana. Talk to Cassie's mother myself."

"Has she done something that makes you suspicious?"

"Not especially. But I think she might be able to provide more than the FBI has been able to uncover. They're good but they're not as invested as we are. I think she knows something that she doesn't think is important. Maybe the FBI simply isn't asking the right questions. Either way, I'd like to talk to her personally."

Sarah thought about Boston's half-stated request. "I approve the travel. When do you plan to leave?"

Boston stood up and pulled a travel bag from beneath the table. "I'm ready to leave right now." He tapped on his cell phone a few times. "I'm booked on a flight out of Wichita that I can make if I run hot."

"Be safe. Let me know as soon as you learn something." Sarah and Taylor cleared the doorway so Boston could hurry. What Boston suggested - running hot - was not exactly legal … but if it would get them closer to Cassie, Sarah was okay with it.

Shawn called shortly after eight o'clock. Sarah was at her desk reviewing a proposal from Mayor Keck. Bill was sitting in a chair with a half-grin, watching her peruse his plan. She looked at her phone and reluctantly sent it to voicemail. She hoped Shawn wouldn't tire of being ignored.

271

"What do you think?" the Mayor asked. "Can we pull it off?"

Sarah bemusedly answered, "I think the better question is *can you pull this off?* I don't think I will have that much say on it."

Bill laughed. "You've never given yourself enough credit. The Council has a great deal of respect for you, for what you say. So do the citizens of Devaney. I can put the numbers out there, but you can put the soul into the proposal. Are you with me on this?"

"Of course!" Sarah grinned. "You've been promising more space as long as I can remember."

"It takes time to move a mountain. Now, it's time to turn that first shovelful of dirt. Can we meet with the architect tomorrow morning?" Bill saw Sarah's puzzled look. "I know it's Saturday, but I don't want a lot of interference such as we'd have with normal weekday interruptions. We need some time to process our thoughts, so we have a better idea of what we want."

Sarah looked through the envelope. There were no architectural drawings, only Bill's rough rendering of a building with inner walls for offices. "Will the architect have something to show us? I'm not sure this is complete."

"I promise you it's not. You and I will lay out our ideas and he will draw up a preliminary plan. This will be *your* police station."

"Mine?"

"Built to suit the needs of Devaney PD for the next forty years or more, just like the old station has done."

"Not a remodel?"

"Nope. The old building has been remodeled to death. It can't keep up with technological changes. Tomorrow? My office?"

Sarah was excited. "Of course. I'll be there at eight, if that's early enough."

"Make it nine. Architects don't do early," Bill laughed as he rose to leave.

Sarah smiled to herself after Mayor Keck left. She knew a new police station was a long-time goal of Bill Keck's when he was Police Chief. Between the two of them, she knew they could make it happen. The project was at least five years from completion. She already knew what she wanted to name the building. The Keck-Honeycutt Building. The new police station would be Bill's legacy and a tribute to Maria.

Sarah phoned Shawn. Unlike her, he answered. She immediately apologized, "I'm sorry. I was in a meeting with the Mayor."

Shawn chuckled. "Did he need advice on how to run the city?"

Sarah didn't blanche at the good-natured jab that was rife with meaning. Shawn loved her and wanted to remind her that she had another part to her life. "I'll cover that with him tomorrow. We have a meeting scheduled for long range planning."

"Oh." Shawn sounded crestfallen. "Does that mean you won't be available for dinner tonight?"

Sarah's heart quickened. "The meeting is tomorrow. I'm available," she paused, then added, "all night." She looked around to see if anyone was listening.

"Then I'll pick you up at seven."

Sarah knew her schedule could change without notice. She also knew that if she didn't try to commit, the opportunity would evaporate. "I'll be ready. Someplace nice, or can I wear my sweats?" she asked with a light-hearted laugh.

"Nicer than sweats … but you do look sharp even in sweats."

Sarah sighed and stared at her phone after the call ended. For better or worse, she wanted to make it work. She had not visited the departments that opened at eight o'clock. The Mayor's unannounced arrival disrupted her routine. It was almost nine. She stuck her cell phone in her jacket's breast pocket and told Liz she was doing her walk-around.

Sarah's first stop was in Human Resources.

Paula Heston saw her enter the area. "Good morning, Chief. I have some good news."

"I could certainly use some. What have you got, Paula?"

"Our sexual harassment complaint has been rescinded. The complainant dismissed it when I asked her to come in and talk to me." Paula paused to grin. "Maybe because I mentioned the officer was a female. Our attorney recommended that I file our response with the EEOC, just in case they become aware of it. Officer Caudle will only have a note in her file … with disposition."

"Good … not the note, the disposition. What about the jailer?"

"Terminated himself before we could get to it. Said being a jailer is too stressful. I suppose that's a reasonable conclusion." Paula sighed heavily. "Now, I have to hire someone to replace him."

"Police work is draining," Sarah commented. "Don't let it get you down."

"Is it getting you down, Sarah?" The HR Manager asked with undisguised concern.

Sarah smiled dismissively. "I enjoy it too much. I may get tired, but I don't get down."

Sarah stopped and talked with several PD employees as she made her way through the small building. She seldom thought about how crowded, even cramped, the building was. It was what it was. Suddenly, Mayor Keck's plan heightened her awareness of the problems and of the possibilities. Room to work without constant distractions. She knew the conditions presented by the bullpen with its cubicles. She worked there for several years. That was no worse than the placement of office workers in and around filing cabinets and equipment. She made the Lab her last stop.

Alicia was expecting Sarah. As soon as Sarah entered the Forensics Lab, Alicia met her. "Chief, we have a problem." Her face reflected sadness mixed with concern.

"What's wrong?" Sarah quickly glanced around the lab, fully expecting to see a piece of test equipment broken and smoking.

"I know I promised the jacket epithelials for yesterday ... late, but we ... I made an error with the test."

Deputy Steger joined them and countered Alicia's comment. "It was my error."

Sarah acknowledged his comment. "What does that mean? There were no epithelials?"

"No," Alicia replied. "There are epithelials. We apparently didn't have a clean enough sample for the test."

"That happens sometimes," Waylon said. "I've already started pulling more samples to rerun the test. We'll get it, but it will be at least tomorrow before we have something. Sorry."

Sarah felt relieved. Better late than never. Besides, the epithelials, as conclusive as they could be, might not have a DNA match in CODIS. The results could be nothing more than a tantalizing piece of data that would only be useful after they caught the killer. "Have you told Boston?"

"No. I called him, but it went to voicemail," Alicia replied.

"He's flying to Indiana," Sarah said.

"Oh," Alicia said excitedly, "does he have a suspect? Make sure he gets a DNA swab to compare to the jacket."

"Not yet. He wants to talk to Cassie's mother. He hopes the mother knows more than she thinks she knows."

"He thinks she's hiding something?" Waylon asked.

"No. He thinks she hasn't been asked the right questions yet. She may know something that she doesn't think is important, but it could be a key clue."

"That single best clue could come from anywhere," Alicia said musingly.

"It could. Call us when you have something. Anything else showing up?"

"Not really. We've processed most of the evidence from the murder scene and the car. We do know more about Eugene Simpson's cell phone."

"What have you learned?"

"We got the GPS data from his phone. It went dead somewhere near Memphis, Tennessee. Highway 22."

Sarah's brow furrowed. "Memphis? Have you told anyone that?"

"Not yet. Is it important?"

"I think so. Corporal Canton and an FBI agent are trying to determine from the car's EDR where the car deviated from traveling to Indiana. We figured Nashville. Memphis was not on the list." Sarah left the Lab.

Sarah called Corporal Canton, "Hello, Corporal. How is your search of the EDR going?"

"Hello, Chief. Funny you should ask. Not very well. There is a lot of data there but none of it clearly depicts a major change in direction from north to west."

"Maybe the car didn't deviate from its original course. Alicia checked the GPS coordinates on our victim's cell phone. He went through Memphis by way of Interstate 22."

"22?" Corporal Canton asked a question of someone in the room with him. "Does Interstate 22 go through Nashville?"

Sarah heard the FBI agent assisting Corporal Canton respond in the negative. She also answered, "It does not. It goes to Memphis from

Birmingham, Alabama. If Simpson was highjacked, it occurred in Birmingham, not Nashville."

After a few minutes of discussion on his end of the call, Corporal Canton said, "Agent Watts will call Agent Caswell to apprise him of the information so the FBI can shift their search to Birmingham. We didn't know Alicia had the victim's phone."

Sarah responded. "It was lost inside the car. The battery was dead. Alicia was able to get past the phone's security." She paused, then added. "Tell the Agent to have Agent Caswell call me so we can compare notes." She needed to tell Macon that Boston was headed to Indiana. The FBI in Indiana would need to know he would be there.

Liz called within minutes of Sarah's call to Corporal Canton. "Agent Caswell has arrived. Do you want him to wait in your office?"

"Good. I need to see him. I just asked Agent Watts to have him call me. Have him wait in the Situation Room."

Sarah stopped to get her coffee cup from her office before she met with Agent Caswell. "Good morning, Macon. Coffee?" She held her cup for him to see.

"Sure," Macon said with a grin. "I hear your Lab Tech tracked the victim's GPS near Memphis." He walked to the coffee pot with Sarah. "I would like to help with the phone."

Sarah was amazed that Agent Watts had reached out to Macon that quickly. The Feds didn't waste any time. "What can the FBI do that we can't?" Sarah was hesitant to step on Alicia's toes.

"Resources. Agent Watts is pretty keen on all electronic devices. He's here. Use him."

Sarah filled her cup while she was thinking. "Let me call Alicia. I want to make sure they haven't finished with it." She dialed Alicia's number and explained the FBI offer. After a brief discussion with Deputy Steger, Alicia agreed that it would be helpful because they were doing some rush work for undercover detective Blake House. She nodded to Macon as they returned to the Situation Room. "Alicia's on board. What will your guy look for?"

"Everything he can find. He will geofence the phone. Check phone calls. Text messages. Detailed GPS information."

"What about voicemail?"

"That too. He can get everything the phone company has in its data records."

"Sounds like a lot of data."

"It is, but he knows where to focus. It may take him a couple of hours to get a warrant, but he'll get it. Maybe something will turn up."

"We need something. By the way," Sarah sat in a chair at the Situation Room table and motioned for Macon to do the same, "Boston is on his way to Indiana. He wants to get a face to face with Cassie's mother."

Agent Caswell sipped his coffee and nodded. "That's what I would do if it was my case. Let me Slack Agent Piccolo in Indiana. She can introduce him to the players. Save some time. She can meet Boston at the airport and provide transportation if you want." He waited for a response.

"Sure. I'll Slack Boston." Sarah laughed. "That'll save a few dollars on his expense report … if he sees it before he rents a car."

# CHAPTER 34

## 3:00 P.M. Friday

Agent Caswell stayed at the station, close to Sarah, close to the case. He managed to convince Sarah to go out for lunch, something she would not have done otherwise. He wasn't underfoot. Instead, he was on the phone with the FBI in Tennessee, Alabama, and Florida. Every bit of new information he received from those three states, he shared with Sarah and forwarded to Agent Amy Piccolo, who would immediately share with Boston when she met him at the Indianapolis airport.

Boston called shortly after 3:00 o'clock. He had made his initial contact with Twyla Stoner-Simpson. She was at work when he arrived. Agent Piccolo met him at the airport and took him to Twyla's workplace. Boston was concerned about Twyla's reaction to his presence there. "For a mother whose baby is missing, she was more upset that I *jeopardized* her job by coming there unannounced than she was about finding Cassie." Boston said.

"I would think she would be happy to know everyone is trying to find her daughter. Besides, I'm sure her employee understands the situation."

"You'd think that. She's a bitter woman. Angry toward the daddy. Thinks he is responsible for the kidnapping."

"How so?"

"She said it's not a shock that his body was dumped in the woods. She said he hangs with dangerous people. People who would do anything for money, even sell a child … or kill a child."

Sarah's blood cooled at the images the accusation conjured. A knot formed in the pit of her stomach. "Exactly what is she implying?"

"She said he was into drugs and drug trafficking. He should have never had shared custody of Cassie. She said she's going to sue the Judge that let a drug dealer have custody."

"I thought the Florida FBI determined that was not the case."

"They did. Agent Piccolo Slacked them to double check while Twyla was saying it. We're on our way to check-in at my hotel, then we'll go to the family farm. It's late, but I want to make contact ASAP. I'll talk to the grandparents. Let them know I'm dedicated to finding their granddaughter. Maybe I can get the sister to open up. Piccolo says the sister has been hesitant to talk."

"That makes no sense. You would think everyone in the family would be trying to help."

"Makes no sense at all. I suppose that's why I'm here. Someone to put a personal touch on the case." Boston chuckled at his self-deprecating comment.

"Just be personable," Sarah encouraged. "How is your DMV search going? Any results?"

"More long lists. My e-mail may get full," Boston replied. "I think my social media DMV search will yield more. Agent Piccolo said the Florida agents checked on Simpson's friend, the one with the white Ford. He was at work last Sunday night, covering for Simpson. He has a solid alibi. Parking lot video shows his truck there."

"Dead end?"

"Not really. I'm still checking Facebook accounts of everyone on Simpson's friend list. So far, nothing, but I haven't given up." Boston paused to listen to Agent Piccolo. "Agent Piccolo suggested I look at the mother's friend list too. That'll widen the net."

"That makes sense. Do you want me to have someone start on that for you?"

"I can do it. It'll give me something to do while we're driving. It's nice to have a chauffeur," Boston replied. "I'll keep you posted."

Sarah let Boston end the call. He initiated it. Her curiosity got the better of her. She opened Facebook on her phone. She couldn't remember the last time she opened the app. She had to think to remember her password. When it opened to her page, she was shocked to see the 20+ notice that indicated she had more notifications than she cared to read. She didn't open them. She had no desire to see what someone might have posted years earlier. She searched for the name Twyla Stoner-Simpson and found one. She opened the page.

Twyla's account was public. Easy to access. She had hundreds of pictures. Many were of Cassie. They dated back to her birth. There were no pictures of Eugene. That was understandable. If the FBI agents who had interviewed her were correct, the split was less than amicable. She undoubtedly purged his pictures and all references to him. Boston's interaction with her confirmed the animosity still existed. Aside from some selfies at work, at home, and at play, most of the photos were too old to be germane to the kidnapping. Family get-togethers for Thanksgiving, Christmas, and summer cookouts offered some insight into the family structure. Pictures of a woman near Twyla's age and similar appearance were probably of her sister, Cammie. One picture of Cammie was of her proudly showing off her newly purchased pickup truck. At first, Sarah's heartrate accelerated. That quickly abated when she focused on the color. It wasn't white. It was a silver-colored Ford. Even if the doorbell camera might have confused the color of the pickup under poor streetlighting, the Love's cameras in daylight did not. The suspect's pickup was definitely white.

Sarah checked a few more of Twyla's family member's accounts. Her mother had one, but she had very few pictures. She searched for several variations of Cammie's name. Cameron Stoner. Cameron Jenkins. Cameron Stoner-Jenkins. Cammie as a variable. Nothing showed her having a Facebook account. That wasn't unheard of, but it was rare for someone her age.

Agent Caswell knocked on Sarah's door. She beckoned him in and offered him a chair. "Have you heard from Boston?" he asked without ceremony. He knew Sarah was always focused on the situation at hand.

"I have. A few minutes ago. He seems to be getting along well with Agent Piccolo. They're on their way to the Stoner farm. Have you heard anything from your agents in Birmingham or Memphis?"

"I have. I'm really focusing on Memphis. The Senor Agent there has engaged Memphis PD as well as PDs in Northeast Arkansas. They're looking for gas station videos north and west of Memphis. Simpson could have driven west on Interstate 40, or it's possible the car went north on Interstate 55 then took Highway 60 across Missouri. If we can find where he stopped for gas, maybe there's video of a passenger … or someone who followed him. Someone driving a white pickup."

A thought struck Sarah. She dwelled momentarily on the fact that she should have already considered the thought. "What about credit card or debit card transactions? If he bought gas, he had to use a card. The FBI can access financial data easier than Devaney PD."

"We have already done that. We can't find that he used his debit card. His girlfriend said he seldom used his credit card, and he was careful with his debit card. He doesn't trust using them at gas stations except Walmart, where he can use his Walmart app. Too many skimmers at gas pumps. He took cash for gas."

"The app is on a cell phone, isn't it?"

"Yes."

"Did you check Walmart stations up until his phone died?"

"We did. He used it twice in the timeframe we checked. He gassed up at his Walmart before he left Panama City and then refilled in Birmingham. Since his phone died, it's a good thing he took cash … good for him, at least. Otherwise, we might have had a trail."

"Videos it is," Sarah lamented. "That's a large area."

"It will take a while."

Sarah had another thought. "I'll have Lieutenant Glasgow check south on 49 as far as the Arkansas border and east on 60 as far as Springfield, in case Simpson came that direction. The car wasn't on any videos between here and north on 49. The car still had gas when it was found. Simpson gassed up somewhere within a couple hundred miles."

"Makes sense. Do you want some assistance?"

"I think Melvin can do it. He knows the time frame for the video search. He'll make quick work of it." Without hesitation, she called Melvin and explained what she needed him to do. Even though it was late Friday afternoon, he didn't argue about the assignment. He also knew the stakes involved. Besides, after three years, he was still trying to prove himself worthy of her trust. Sarah used that.

"You've got good people here, Chief," Agent Caswell said. "I was impressed with Devaney PD back when Keck was Chief. It's even better now. You're doing a good job here. What are your plans for the future?"

The question caught Sarah off guard. She stammered and blushed. "This is my future. Like you said, good people. Family. I've already achieved more than I thought I could."

Macon glanced around the room for personal effects. "I don't see photos of family. What grounds you?"

Sarah blushed more. "The job grounds me. These people are my family. It started with Carl Franken. He made me feel important. Wanted. Significant. So did Chief Keck. Mayor Keck still does."

Macon nodded but didn't say anything more on the subject. "What do you need from the FBI at this time?"

"We need to know if there is evidence of the car between here and Memphis. If someone was with Simpson and the baby, or following them, we need to know who they are. We know they didn't steal the license plates until they arrived in Devaney. Maybe it was a spur of the moment decision."

"Or planned ahead of time and executed when they arrived."

Sarah contemplated Macon's words. "Possibly. I can't imagine the killers would have stopped after murdering Simpson to steal plates."

"No. I have to believe that part was already conceived before they arrived here. The question after that is, *why here*? Devaney, Kansas is a long way from Panama City, Florida."

"And Indiana," Sarah added. "The answer to that question will probably fill in a lot of blanks." She checked the wall clock. It was almost four o'clock. Only three hours until Shawn would arrive at her apartment. "It's a waiting game now. Wait for a hit on our white Ford with a Kansas license plate BOLO. Wait for a video to indicate whether someone was traveling with or following Simpson. And hope. Hope that the Stoner family can offer something concrete, a lead to explain why Simpson would be in Kansas."

Macon nodded agreement. "Who knows? Maybe Simpson has friends in Kansas and detoured for a visit."

"With the baby?"

"Maybe the friend had never seen Cassie," Macon offered as a possibility.

"Possible, but from what your people told us from Florida, Simpson was a solid citizen, not prone to spur of the moment actions. If he was going to make a detour, he would have planned it and told his girlfriend."

"Don't take anything off the table until it needs to be removed," the Senior Agent cautioned. "The answers could come from anywhere." He stood, "I'm going to drive back to Topeka tonight. I'm just a phone call away." He shook Sarah's hand when she stood and offered it.

"Wait!" Sarah exclaimed. "We've narrowed our BOLO to white Fords with Kansas tags. We hurt ourselves! If they were smart enough to steal the tag, they're smart enough to toss it."

Macon thought for a moment. "I agree. They might have put the correct license plate back on it. The BOLO needs to be amended so agencies aren't focused on Kansas tags."

Sarah shook her head. She was disappointed in herself for not considering the damage the limited focus might create. She allowed doubt to creep into her mind. She may have increased the danger to Cassie by giving the kidnappers a way to avoid detection. She hid her feelings of dejection as she escorted Macon to the exit. To disguise her internal conflict, she asked him about his weekend plans. He was going home to his wife. The two of them had plans to visit their grandchildren over the weekend. Macon had a family life outside of work. She updated the BOLO knowing that it was probably too late for the change. Afterward, she decided to leave early. Boston could call her. So could Agent Caswell. She wanted to dress for a romantic evening. She needed it. Moreover, she deserved it.

Boston didn't call until after six-thirty. Sarah was putting the finishing touches on her face, a minor addition of make-up, something she normally eschewed. She anxiously answered. She knew the call would come, but she didn't want it to detract from her time with Shawn. "Hello, Boston. Are you still interviewing the Stoner family?"

"Hello, Boss. Agent Piccolo is taking me back to Indianapolis for the night. I'm going back tomorrow. I have some follow ups."

"Did they share anything that might be helpful?"

Boston paused. "I can't say I heard anything helpful. I was surprised that Twyla, who was so concerned about me affecting her job, arrived at the farm before we did."

"Really?" Sarah paused what she was doing. "Why did she do that?"

"Beats me. Apparently, she left work as soon as we left for the hotel. She met me at the door and wanted to know why I was there bothering them when I should be in Kansas looking for the kidnappers."

"I suppose that makes sense, more sense than complaining about you visiting her at work. Were you able to get anything substantive from her?"

"Not really. She wanted to know if her baby was kidnapped at the church. She was concerned that the baby might have seen Gene get shot."

"She knew about the church?"

"Piccolo said Agent Caswell told her to tell the mother all we knew that made sense."

"That makes sense. I told him to do that." Sarah thought a moment before returning to Twyla's concern. "That would be traumatic if Cassie witnessed the murder, but so is being kidnapped. I'm sure Twyla is irrationally distraught. You probably won't get much from her. What about the grandparents and the sister? Did they add anything the FBI didn't get?"

"The Stoners, especially the old man, were angry that I was there wasting time rather than tracking the killer in Kansas. Same theme as Twyla. Maybe it's an Indiana thing, or a farmer thing, but they were suspicious of everything I said or asked."

"I imagine it's an *upset* thing. People handle traumatic events in different ways. If you don't provide answers, you are providing doubt."

"Probably true. Aside from their anger, their house tells a lot about the family. It's a nice, two-story farmhouse. Old style but well maintained. Good furniture. Used but clean. The grandkids seemed well behaved … for little tykes. Apparently, there are a lot of big deer in Indiana. Or used to be. They have a lot of trophy deer heads on the walls."

Sarah was impatient. The details of the Stoner family house were interesting, but she had Shawn on her mind. "Were the grandkids with you during the interview?"

"Most of the time. Grandma took them out of the room when Twyla and Mr. Stoner got loud. I guess she didn't want them to hear the cussing."

"If they were cussing, I imagine the kids hear it often anyway."

"I agree with that. Also, I wasn't able to talk to the sister, Cammie. Her two children were with the grandparents, but she was *away on business.* Whatever that means."

Sarah thought a moment before she mentioned her foray into social media. "I went ahead and did a little research into the family's Facebook activity. Cammie doesn't have a page, which seems odd. Twyla's page has a lot of pictures. A lot of pictures of Cassie. There were pictures of Cammie, one with her silver pickup. Other than that, just normal stuff."

Boston talked aside to Agent Piccolo, too garbled for Sarah to hear. He finally said, "Agent Piccolo is going to ask Indianapolis PD for Cammie's truck registration information. If she won't come to us, we'll go to her. She'll put out a BOLO as soon as we get the tag number."

"What do you think she can offer?"

"Nothing, but I don't like it when people avoid me," Boston replied emphatically. "If Agent Piccolo can meet me early, we'll show up at the Stoner farm at daylight."

"Careful, Boston. We don't want to harass them."

Boston chuckled. "I'll be nice." He disconnected the call.

Sarah worried. Boston could be abrasive with witnesses. He was accustomed to confronting suspects and was able to pull information out of the most reticent of them. Confronting victims required finesse. The information they had was sometimes suppressed by the trauma of the event. He could be gentle, but it was not his normal style. Her doorbell rang.

Shawn's eyes lit when Sarah opened the door. "Wow! You look … well … beautiful. Not that you don't always look beautiful, but you look beautiful."

Sarah blushed lightly and leaned to receive a kiss before she said, "Come in. Do you want a drink before we go? I think you're a few minutes early."

The comment caused Shawn to check his watch. He laughed. "One minute. But, yes, I'll take that drink. I need something to steady my nerves if I'm going to be seen in public with you."

"What does that mean?"

"I won't even be noticed, and my ego might not be able to handle being relegated to background clutter. By the way, should I expect phone calls to interrupt us?"

Sarah wasn't sure which comment to embrace. The supreme compliment or the snide remark. She addressed both, "I don't expect calls, but I do expect you to show me a good time ... ego non-withstanding."

Shawn laughed the laugh that made Sarah want to know him better.

There were no calls while at dinner. There were no calls during the night. There was time for Sarah to embrace normalcy ... and Shawn.

# CHAPTER 35

## Saturday

Shawn awakened before Sarah. Unusual to say the least. His sounds in the kitchen startled her awake. She gained her bearings and went into the bathroom to shower. It was after 6:30. She had a meeting with the Mayor at 9:00. Plenty of time, though she wanted to stop by the station for her normal early morning updates. Dressed in a robe, she smiled at Shawn who was busily preparing breakfast using the few items she kept in her apartment.

"French toast?" Shawn said as he leaned to kiss her. "Mmmm. You smell good."

Sarah laughed. Eating sweets for breakfast wasn't her first choice, but she was determined to enjoy it. Besides, Shawn was doing the best he could with the available ingredients. "It's my shampoo but thank you for the thought." She looked at the steaming coffee maker. "Coffee. I need coffee." She took a steaming cup that Shawn handed her. She sat at the small dining table and waited for him to prepare a plate for her. "I'm surprised you found the ingredients."

"I improvised, but as long as I have bread, butter, and cinnamon, I can make it work." Shawn laughed as he set a plate in front of her. "Your syrup is questionable ... if the best used by date means anything."

"I'll risk it," Sarah laughed. "I hope that doesn't come back to haunt me while meeting with the Mayor."

"What was that about again?"

"Confidential. I told you that."

"You can trust me."

"I'm sure I can, but who's to say you aren't being nice to me just to gain insider information."

Shawn bent to kiss Sarah's forehead before taking a seat at the table. "I was nice to you long before you planned the meeting."

"See how devious you are? Who's to say you didn't have this planned for months?"

"How long will you be?"

"I have no idea. I need to drop by the station before I go."

Sarah entered the station through the garage entrance. She stopped in Booking to check the entry logs. Blake House made an arrest and booked the suspect. She asked the Sergeant at the desk, "What can you tell me about Blake's arrest?"

"A drug dealer. Female, believe it or not. He brought her in before midnight. I wasn't here then." The Sergeant shuffled in a desk drawer. "He left this for you."

Blake didn't normally make arrests. He used patrol officers for the formality while he remained in the shadows. Sarah knew this case was special to him. More than likely, he was able to make the arrest without being conspicuous, without blowing his cover. She read the report he left for her.

*"Female suspect apprehended on suspicion of dealing tainted methamphetamines. Subject gave her name as Arlene Lawton. Confirmation of identity should come from prints. She is the mother of three. Single. She lives in the county. Bought the drugs over the Dark Net. Says she didn't know they were laced with fentanyl. Child Protective Service notified and took the children, ages 8, 10, 11."*

Sarah looked at the mug shot. Thin. Gaunt face. Too much pale make-up with dark lipstick. Black, apparently dyed hair. Goth styled clothing. Frightened eyes. Otherwise, she could be considered pretty. "What do you know about her?"

"She's in a pod. She woke up to eat breakfast. She's asking about her kids. She started crying when we told her CPS had them. She didn't want her kids in the system. She said she was only trying to make a living for them. But it's probably just an excuse."

"Probably." Sarah wasn't sure. A desperate mother protecting her children would go to any extreme to provide for them. Prostitution. Theft. Selling drugs. The woman had a family. Questioning her motives wasn't something the police should do. Excusing her reasons wasn't either. Family was an important motivator.

Sarah walked through the lower offices, generally empty for the weekend, to the Shift Commander's desk. Sergeant Cron saw her approach. He handed her the daily summary. "All quiet, Chief."

"That's good. Nothing to report on potential leads to find Cassie Simpson?"

"Sorry, Chief. Nothing. We've been drawing a blank. Pretty much every white Ford pickup in eastern Kansas has been stopped at least once. I wish we had more to go on."

Sarah's phone rang. It was Melvin Glasgow's ID. "Good morning, Melvin."

"Good morning, Chief. I found a video of Simpson's car." Melvin paused to allow Sarah to respond.

"Good! Where? Was there someone with him?"

"That's why I didn't bother you last night. He was alone, except for the baby. He took the baby out and let her walk into the station with him. The little tyke was probably exhausted from riding in the car seat."

"Where?"

"At a Kum and Go on Highway 60 near the I-49 intersection."

"Did anyone go near the car while he was in the station?"

"No. He went inside with the little girl. Apparently, paid for the gas and came back out. He put the girl back in the car seat, pumped his gas, drove to the air pump, and aired up the driver's side tire before he drove away."

"Did any other vehicle follow him?"

"I can't swear to it, but I don't think so. The cameras don't cover the parking lot entrance or exit points. They only cover the pumps and the doorway from the inside. You know, with the height markers on the doorway. If another vehicle did follow, it came from somewhere not covered by cameras."

Sarah thought. Gene Simpson knew about the leaky tire. The murderers probably did not. Know or not know, they drove until the tire went flat. They were either planning to steal the car after they murdered him, or they planned to dispose of it far from the murder site. The flat tire spoiled their plan. A thought crossed her mind. She sent a Slack message to Boston. *"Call me when you can."*

Boston called within five minutes. "What's up, Boss?"

"How is it going in Indiana?"

"Slow. We caught up with Cammie. Actually, she was in her trailer on the property when we arrived."

"Has she offered anything?"

"Nervous. Afraid every question is a trick question. The whole family acts like cops are their enemies. Do you have something for me?"

"Melvin found a video of Simpson's car. Simpson stopped for gas and aired his tire before he got to Kansas. Stopped at the intersection of Highway 60 and Interstate 49 in Missouri. He and Cassie went inside the store to pay cash for gas. No one else was there at the time. He was alone, and no one was following him as far as the cameras show."

"He knew the tire was bad," Boston said slowly, thoughtfully. "The killers probably didn't know, at least not before they killed him. Why did he pay cash? Most people pay with a card."

"His girlfriend said he didn't trust gas pumps. He was afraid of card skimmers. He last used his Walmart app to gas up at a Walmart supercenter in Birmingham." Sarah heard a rooster crow in Boston's background. "You're outside, I take it."

"I stepped out to make the call. Amy … Agent Piccolo … is still inside. Those little tykes are wired this morning. I think they stay with Grandma more than with their momma. Of course, it's not very far from the trailer." Almost as an afterthought, Boston stated, "It makes me wonder where Simpson's wallet went. Most thieves take the valuables and toss the rest."

"We know they cleaned out the car, except for the phone, and tossed everything in the church dumpster. No wallet was found. Apparently, they still have it … or tossed it in a trash can somewhere."

"They didn't toss it at the Love's station. We would have seen it on the videos." Boston paused. His breathing changed.

"What are you doing?"

"If I stole someone's wallet, I would want to dispose of it so it could never be found. I wouldn't toss it in a public trashcan. I'm going to check something. I'll call you back."

Mayor Keck was all smiles when Sarah arrived at his office. The building was locked for the weekend, but she had the passcode for the cipher lock on the back entrance. The architect, Grayson Paulsen, Jr., didn't arrive until after nine. That gave the two of them time to organize their thoughts. The meeting was a brainstorming session. Grayson expertly guided Sarah and Bill through the process of clarifying their wants, needs, and expectations of the new police station. Both Sarah and Bill cautioned Grayson about "grand edifices." They wanted a practical building that would last for decades, not a showplace for Grayson's architectural talents.

The meeting culminated in lunch at a downtown café, the bistro Bill preferred. The simple menu was a final statement to Grayson that the city wasn't prepared to spend more than necessary.

Grayson excused himself as soon as the meal was finished. Sarah and Bill lingered to savor a final cup of coffee. It was after one o'clock.

"We were so focused on this project, I forgot to ask if there has been any progress finding the kidnapped girl," Bill said. "I suppose not, since you didn't lead with that this morning."

"Nothing significant. Our focus has been on trying to understand Eugene Simpson. We know he left Florida to give Cassie to his ex-wife, part of an alternating custody agreement. He should have gone to Indiana, but he changed directions in Birmingham. We thought someone coerced him at that point, but we have video evidence of him traveling alone with Cassie near Neosho, Missouri. Boston is in Indiana talking with the ex-wife and her family. He's looking for clues regarding Eugene's behavior." Sarah made the download as short as possible. She left a lot out, but it was enough update so Bill would not seem out of touch if asked.

"How is the baby's mother taking it? That's got to be rough."

"Boston's confused by her behaviors. The whole family seems to have a dislike for the police. To make matters worse, the FBI has been there longer than Boston. He's faced with overcoming the family's suspicions of another useless lawman brought into the mix."

"When is Boston due back?"

"No real time limit, though I expect late tonight or tomorrow. He wasn't very optimistic about what he was finding in Indiana. We're up against the clock, as far as Cassie is concerned, and we have no good clues."

Bill sipped his coffee and studied Sarah. "I think Carl would tell you different," he said with a knowing smile.

Sarah averted her topaz eyes for a moment. She felt moisture well in them. Carl Franken was a good detective. A great detective. Better yet, he was a good man, a family man who cared about people. "You're right. He would tell me I have the clues. I just need to identify the single best clue." She paused, then added, "I haven't identified it yet."

Bill set his empty coffee cup on the table. "Well, you are the Police Chief. It's not yours to identify. Detective Mankowitz can do that for you. I have faith in Devaney PD to find Cassie and bring her home safe."

Returning to her apartment, Sarah's phone rang through her car's Bluetooth. The ID was Boston's. "Tell me you found something, Boston." Her voice was pleading.

Boston laughed. His voice was light and unstrained. "Good news first. Cassie is alive and well."

Sarah felt a lump in her throat. She pulled her car to the side of the street without signaling, oblivious to the angry horn honk of the car behind her. "What? Where? When? How?"

Boston continued, elation in his voice. "One of Cammie's kids, the youngest one, blurted out to Amy while I was on the phone with you that Cousin Cassie came to visit."

Sarah was anxious to hear the details. First, she had to calm her emotions. For the first time in her career, she wanted to cry. Tears of joy. She felt guilty. She had given Cassie up for dead, or at least as lost to the decent world. She sniffed and swallowed the throat lump. "Okay. That doesn't tell me much. Give me the details."

"While I was on the phone with you, talking about Simpson's wallet, I noticed they have a burn barrel. I guess lots of farm folks burn their trash."

"Is that legal in Indiana?"

"Not at all. That and the little girl's comment was enough for Agent Piccolo and me to decide to get a search warrant for the Stoner property. It wasn't easy to do, but Amy was able to pull it off. She knows her stuff." Boston chuckled. "Reminds me of you."

Sarah blushed. Boston was effusive. She understood the reasons for his excitement. She simply wasn't familiar with that side of the Detective. "Apparently, you found something big," she posed querulously.

"We found remnants of Simpson's wallet in the burn barrel. The idiots should have pulled out his license and cards to expose everything to the flames evenly. They only partially burned. Enough left to identify without going to the lab. But we bagged and tagged them for analysis. More than enough to get a conviction."

"They had his wallet?" Sarah asked incredulously.

"Part of their plan. They didn't want anyone to identify the body too quickly. Give them time to get back to Indiana and destroy the evidence. They weren't very good at destroying evidence. The Florida plate from his car was in the burn barrel along with the Kansas plate stolen from the pickup. Paint was burned, but they were still legible. We found Cammie's white Ford pickup behind some haybales in a barn."

"White? A different one than was on Twyla's Facebook page?"

"Same one. She painted it white but didn't change the registration. Lots of people don't realize they are supposed to update the registration. I used phenolphthalein on the truck bed and the tailgate. You can't wash away evidence of human blood with windshield wash water at a truck stop. Or a garden hose." Boston chuckled again. "The FBI also retrieved the data from her closed Facebook page. If it's been closed for less than thirty days, that stuff is still available. She had all kinds of pictures of her repainted truck. She was farm girl proud of it."

"So, Cassie was in the Stoner house all along?"

"Pretty much. Apparently, when I stopped at Twyla's workplace, she was desperate to tell her parents to hide Cassie and for Cammie to hide her truck. That explains all the suspicion and anger from her and her family. They were all accessories and thought we were getting too close."

"Who did it? I think the FBI said the dad was an avid deer hunter. Probably pretty good with a deer rifle." Sarah's hands were shaking with excitement … and relief.

"Twyla and Cammie. Apparently, they are also handy with a deer rifle. A lot of the trophy mounts in the Stoner house were theirs. Daddy's little girls."

"Who pulled the trigger?"

Boston hesitated. "Nobody confessed, but my money is on Twyla. The dad may try to take the fall, but we know there wasn't a man involved. The FBI has all the weapons they could find on the property. They'll check which gun matches the bullet found in the car fender well. It'll be there. Deer hunters don't toss their favorite rifles."

"It sounds like your trip to Indiana paid big dividends."

"The FBI made it happen. I've gotta give them credit. They can get things that we struggle to get. They were able to get Twyla and Cammie's cell phone records. Aside from the fact Twyla lied about calling Eugene Sunday evening, their cell tower connection records show they were in Devaney Sunday night. Twyla was in Devaney a week before the murder. Her phone movement indicates she scouted the church and the bike trail, among other things. She stole the license plates they used to disguise the vehicles. Definitely premeditated."

Exhaustion hit Sarah. A lot had transpired since Monday morning. Robberies. Murder. Kidnapping. Drug overdoses. Traffic accidents. Her shoulders slumped. "When are you coming back?"

"That's up to you, I suppose. It felt good to click those cuffs. The FBI took the whole family into custody. I took the liberty of telling them we wanted Twyla and Cammie extradited."

"Of course! I'll call Marcie and get it started." Sarah straightened her shoulders. There was still work to be done. Update the Mayor. Update Devaney PD personnel. Hold a press conference to inform the city. An incoming call clicked. Alicia's ID. "Is there anything else you need from me?"

"No. Just keeping the Boss informed," Boston said. "Twyla was pissed-off and singing like a canary. Apparently, Eugene was trying to change the custody agreement, declare her an unfit mother."

"Seems like he was right," Sarah said. "Alicia's calling. I'm not sure why."

"Okay. Amy ... Agent Piccolo and I are going out to celebrate. See you tomorrow."

"Hello, Alicia. Are you working?" Sarah's voice was still shaking with excitement and relief.

"The epithelials, remember? I have the results. You're not going to believe it."

"They are a familial match to the baby poo. Probably mitochondrial DNA," Sarah said with a chuckle.

Alicia paused before responding. "Yes. Good guess. Or did Waylon call you?"

Sarah laughed. "No. I just got off the phone with Boston. He arrested Cassie's mother and aunt for the murder and kidnapping. The mother was the kidnapper. Cassie's safe."

"Alive and well. That is good."

"Alive, yes. Well? I'm not sure. Indiana CPS has her and the sister's two children. The whole family was involved as accessories. But at least she is alive."

"I guess my epithelials weren't needed after all." Alicia sounded disheartened.

"They are definitely needed. They are the hard evidence that links Twyla to Gene's murder. Everything else is circumstantial. The jacket was our single best clue."

Sergeant Jim Cron knew the routine well. He prepped the lobby for a formal press conference while Sarah contacted the people who needed to be present. Mayor Keck attended. Lieutenant McCuskey and Lieutenant Glasgow were there in their dress uniforms. Marcie Stapleton was there with her errant strand of blonde hair pestering her eye. The reporters' questions came rapid fire, but the pace didn't bother Sarah. The fact that the murderers were in custody and Cassie was safe made them easy to bear. The only question that aggravated her was from Tammy Nunn.

"Chief James, would the case have been solved sooner if we had a larger, more responsive regional forensics lab?"

Sarah knew Sheriff Berringer had gotten to the eager and gullible young reporter. He had not given up on his attempts to create a laboratory under his control. She responded graciously, "No one can say what might have been. We can say that the murderers planned the kidnapping very well. I can say that without the assistance of all the agencies that I credited at the beginning, the FBI in five states, the Missouri State Police, and the Sheriff's Department, this case would not yet be solved. Cooperative effort, not big laboratories, is the answer to crime solving."

After the press conference ended, Sarah and Taylor decompressed in the Situation Room. For no reason other than mutual respect, they expunged the emotions of the week from their minds by talking about them, exposing the guttural pain of every agonizing moment they endured.

Sarah talked the most. She didn't get moments like that often. The normal stressor outlets weren't available to her. No dinner table conversation. No pillow talk to process the events of the day. Her talk with Taylor helped more than she could have imagined it would. She felt the weight of the job lift, adjusted slightly to better balance the load.

"Shouldn't you be home with family?" Sarah asked when it seemed everything that could be recapped was covered. "It is Saturday ..." she glanced at the wall clock, "almost evening."

Taylor smiled. "I am with part of my family. It's been a rough week ... but it ended as well as it could for a police officer. We all get to go home safe. Go do something fun tonight, Sarah."

Sarah smiled, stood, and exchanged a hug with Taylor. Taylor turned off the bullpen lights as she exited down the stairs. After a final look at Boston's pictures, notes, and documents, Sarah turned off the Situation Room light. The building hummed with sounds from the HVAC system and from the weekend staff downstairs in the jail and the lobby. The bullpen cubicle partitions dampened most of the sound in the room, but they couldn't stop the sounds of a living building. A note of melancholy passed through her mind. A new, modern police station would be nice, but it would not embody the memories of five decades of police officers. The lobby memorials to officers who died in the line of duty would be moved to the new building, but it would not be familiar to the deceased officers' memories. She didn't know if she believed in ghosts or not, but she wondered.

Shawn called while Sarah was absorbing the memories of the building, of the family she chose. "Congratulations," he said as soon as she answered.

"Thank you. It wasn't me. It was Boston and the team behind him."

"Well, I think a good leader made it possible." Shawn chuckled his good-natured laugh. "I was wondering, do you have a clue what you're going to do the rest of the weekend without a crisis to handle?"

Sarah, alone in the darkened bullpen, smiled. She had a single best clue about Shawn.

Printed in the United States
by Baker & Taylor Publisher Services